"I WANT TO MAKE LOVE TO YOU, VICTORIA...."

Jason's voice was husky as he caressed her, awakening a frenzy of response.

Vicki didn't answer—couldn't answer. She was drowning in the intoxicating wonder of his touch. Of their own accord, her lips were sliding softly over the smooth masculine warmth of his shoulder, tasting the faint saltiness of his skin.

"When I kissed you the first time, I felt like taking you then and there," he whispered, burying his face in her hair. "I want you so much. More than I remember wanting any woman...."

Through the languorous magic his words slowly registered. He had loved so many others....

Instinctively Vicki recoiled. What was she doing here with a man incapable of committing himself to love?

ROSALIND CARSON

Is also the author of

SUPERROMANCE #16

THIS DARK ENCHANTMENT

A fantastic job offer lured Karin into the enchantment of Quebec, a city long known for its exciting but dangerous traditions of conflict and romance. Right now she didn't need either!

Karin's heart was vulnerable, and unfortunately it was Dr. Paul Dufresne who captured it. Charming, definitely; but under the smooth seductiveness that tempted Karin she knew he was quite corrupt. It seemed he'd manipulated others, too—sometimes illegally, and always immorally.

But Karin couldn't extricate herself from his power. She thirsted for his magic, however black, as though it were life itself....

Rosalind Carson

SONG OF DESIRE

A SUPERROMANCE FROM
WORLDWIDE

TORONTO · NEW YORK · LOS ANGELES · LONDON

For my sister June, with love

Published November 1982

First printing September 1982

ISBN 0-373-70040-7

CHAPTER ONE

THE LONG GLEAMING CAR seemed to appear out of nowhere. Until that moment Vicki had enjoyed the drive from London, feeling totally relaxed once she got used to driving on the wrong side of the road. Occasionally she recited to herself: "Oh, to be in England, now that April's there." The only other sound she'd heard since she left the main highway and entered this maze of winding country lanes was the cheerful chugging of the car's engine. She'd rented the green Mini the previous day, partly because its shape reminded her irresistibly of a lunch pail.

Although the air was cool, the sky was clear and blue, the scenery enchanting. Trees arched over the lanes, their leafy branches meeting and tangling above her head, letting through just enough sunlight to create a chiaroscuro of sun and shadow on the surface of the narrow road. Fields stretched out on either side, neat rectangles of green and brown occupied by a few drowsy-looking cows.

Vicki's spirits were rising steadily. She felt suddenly confident that the hoped-for healing of her recently damaged spirit was already beginning. She was... content, she decided.

In blue jeans and a white cotton shirt she was comfortably dressed for her journey to Derringham. Her long blond hair lifted in the breeze that blew in through the car's open windows, and her guitar, which she had carefully guarded all the way from Los Angeles, lay on the seat next to her making her feel she was not completely alone. "God's in his heaven— All's right with the world!" she chanted: then laughed at her new habit of quoting Robert Browning. England was definitely having a beneficial effect on her.

It was then that the other car appeared behind her, its silver body reflecting sunlight in a blinding flash from her rearview mirror. The sound of its impatient horn ricocheted from the tree trunks, startling her out of her tranquil mood.

For a split second Vicki panicked, unable to remember which side of the road was which. The Mini swerved erratically until she finally recovered her senses enough to pull to the left, and the silver monster roared past her with another blare of its horn.

She was left with a palpitating heart, a rising surge of anger that threatened to choke her, and an after-image of a man at the wheel of the silver car—a big man wearing an Irish tweed hat, dark sunglasses and a bad-tempered expression.

She braked the Mini to a stop, then leaned forward over the steering wheel, breathing deeply until her heartbeat slowed. What kind of idiot would drive so fast on these meandering lanes? True, she *had* been driving in the center of the narrow road, but still. . . .

After a moment she started the car again and drove on, but her cheerful mood had been shattered. She didn't recover it until the lane ended abruptly, and she found herself turning onto a wide thoroughfare. A sign proclaimed Derringham, Buckinghamshire, and there before her stretched the most charming town she had ever seen. Vicki gazed with delight at the half-timbered shops with their latticed windows. On her right was an enchanting old pub with a hanging wooden sign The Black Swan. Next to it, beyond a small graveyard, an ancient gray stone church attracted her attention, and she marveled for a moment at the beauty of its stained-glass windows.

After stopping briefly at a traffic light, she drove on down the street past more timber-framed shops, craning her neck as she went. A tall brick building seemed to be a bank; there was another pub, a quaint-looking supermarket and a café whose picture window offered afternoon cream teas. Pedestrians were few, mostly mothers pushing babies in high-wheeled carriages, and occasional couples.

Just past the next intersection the road widened, and on her left, in the middle of a grassy oval, she saw the signboard she was looking for. On it were painted some large leafy trees and the words The Singing Tree Inn.

The building beyond, in typical black-and-white Tudor style, was elaborately timbered and featured jutting walls, pointed gables, bay windows and steep roofs with numerous chimneys. Including its grounds, the inn obviously occupied an entire block, Vicki noted.

Enchanted by its picturesque beauty, she almost missed the entranceway, but just in time she saw the discreet sign Car Park, with an arrow pointing toward an archway in the building. She drove on through into a large cobbled courtyard that, except for the modern automobiles parked there, looked as though it had been untouched for centuries.

Beyond the courtyard a wide river gleamed in the

afternoon sunlight, with willows dipping tasseled branches in the quiet water. Across the stream stood a grove of trees—exactly the same as those on the inn's signboard, Vicki realized. In the distance a handsome Georgian manor house stood against a rich back cloth of woods. Whoever owned *that* house, Vicki thought, had to be very affluent indeed.

She parked the Mini between an M.G. and a Mercedes-Benz in an arched section that once must have stabled horses. Then she climbed out and stretched, looking around her with pleasure. She'd had no idea her Aunt Abigail's hotel would be so big or so prosperous looking. The U-shaped building, as picturesque at the back as at the front, was four stories high. Many of the rooms had bay windows, and Vicki secretly hoped her room would have one. Abby had said she would give Vicki a room in her own self-contained apartment on the top floor of the hotel. How lovely it would be to sit in a window like that in the evening and play her guitar. Since she'd lost her job, she'd had little heart for guitar practice—or for anything else. But she was determined to make a fresh start here. . . .

Brought back to earth by the memory of her aborted career, Vicki forced herself to stop daydreaming. It was time she made her presence known. She hoped once again that Abby wouldn't be too taken aback by her arrival. After all, she wasn't expected for another week, she thought as she lifted her precious guitar from the car and slung it over her shoulder by its wide woven band. Maybe she should have called from London yesterday. But the temptation to surprise her aunt had been too strong. And besides, Abby would have insisted on coming into the city to pick her up.

She had always had a tendency to mother her niece, and one doting mother was enough. Vicki was determined to be independent right from the start.

As she went through the back door of the hotel, she was struck by the peace of the place. Rather too peaceful, even for a Sunday afternoon, she thought as she walked down a wainscoted hall, her footsteps echoing on the burnished oak floor. Surely there ought to be some bustle going on in such a big hotel. Even the large open area with its high beamed ceiling, obviously the main lobby, was deserted. That was strange.

Ahead of her stood the registration desk, of dark highly polished wood. Behind it a tall bank of pigeon-holes contained keys and several pieces of mail. There was also a complicated-looking switchboard, unmanned.

One one side of the lobby, between a florist's and a jeweler's, was a small gift shop. All three stores seemed locked up tight, even though the attractive display windows begged to be admired. Why wasn't a host of chattering guests coming and going through the wide front doors or taking advantage of the high-backed chairs and sofas that formed conversation groupings here and there?

Catching a glimpse of her own reflection in one of the display cases gave Vicki a start. For a moment there, she wouldn't have been surprised to see a ghost; the place seemed so unnaturally quiet. All she could hear was a faint buzzing sound that might be an air conditioner, and distant strains of music—violins.

Frowning, she approached the registration desk and tentatively jabbed one finger at a button set into its gleaming surface. The immediate *ping* sounded loud in the stillness, making her jump again, but it did bring results. A door opened in the back wall, and a round-faced young woman, her mop of frizzy hair an improbable shade of red, poked her head out. "Hello, love," she said cheerfully. "Were you wantin' a room? We're full up, actually."

"I have a room," Vicki told her. "At least, I think I have."

"That's all right, then, isn't it?" Smiling brightly, the girl came out from around the door and studied Vicki across the counter. She was attractively plump—*voluptuous* was the word that came to Vicki's mind—and her ample curves were putting a severe strain on the seams of her black skirt and the buttons of her white satin blouse.

"American, are you, miss?" the girl asked, arching penciled eyebrows.

"Yes. I'm Vicki Dennison. Abby—Mrs. Carstairs—is my aunt. She's expecting me next week, but I got here early. I hope she's here?"

"Oh, yes, dear, Mrs. Carstairs is always here. 'Er 'ole world, this 'otel is." She frowned. "She's up in one of the conference rooms with most of the staff, 'aving a meeting. We've 'ad a bit of a carfuffle. I'm sure I don't know when she'll be down."

"A carfuffle?"

"Right kettle of fish, that's what it is. But not to worry, dear. Would you like to wait in Mrs. Carstairs's office? It's over there." She pointed to a door at the other end of the room.

Vicki nodded. "Are all the guests at the meeting, too?" she asked. "The place seems deserted."

"Teatime, love," the girl said. "Every day from three till five, this 'otel serves the best afternoon tea you ever tasted. Sandwiches and little cakes—crumpets if you want 'em—and there's an orchestra and everything. Very popular with the guests, it is. You could 'ave tea there while you're waiting if you'd rather. It's in the Blue Room.''

Vicki looked down at her shirt and blue jeans. "I'm hardly dressed for afternoon tea. I probably shouldn't even be seen in the lobby looking like this.''

The girl grinned. "You look smashing, love. Mrs. Carstairs said you were pretty, but she didn't say 'ow pretty. Gawd, you've got super teeth. And that tan. . . .'' She rolled her eyes, then gave Vicki a confiding smile. "Mrs. Carstairs told us all you'd be coming, and that we were to be nice to you because you're family. My name's Kimberly. My friends at the disco call me Kim.''

Vicki smiled. "You like to dance, Kim?''

"Oh, yes, love. 'Ow about you? Can you play that?'' She nodded toward the guitar.

"Fairly well, but it's a classical guitar. I do enjoy disco music, though,'' she added.

The girl's eyes lighted up. She had prominent blue eyes and a friendly, slightly bucktoothed smile. A cockney, Vicki decided as she started toward the door the girl had indicated. There was no mistaking those dropped "aitches'' and odd vowel sounds.

"Perhaps we can go to this disco I know in London sometime,'' Kim called after her. "There's nowhere decent to dance around 'ere.'' She seemed suddenly to feel she'd overstepped herself. "If you would like to go with me, that is,'' she added shyly.

"If I have time, I'd love to,'' Vicki told her sincerely. She liked this friendly young woman. Then she smiled again and pushed open the door, which was marked simply A. Carstairs.

She was still smiling as she entered the rather dim room, but it faded quickly when she saw the man sitting behind the desk in front of her. He was smoking a cigarette, his chair tilted back. She certainly hadn't expected to see the driver of the silver car again. But here he was, looking completely at home in Abby's office. He was still wearing his shapeless tweed hat and his dark glasses, both of which seemed very affected to Vicki. Who did he think he was—some movie star traveling incognito?

The man made no move to alter his precarious position, but his shoulders stiffened, and she was immediately sure that he recognized her. She felt irritation rising as she closed the door behind her. "What are *you* doing here?" she demanded.

The cigarette paused halfway to his mouth. "My dear young lady, I have a perfect right to be here."

His voice surprised her, setting her off balance. It was a beautiful voice, well modulated, very English and cultured sounding, with a deep yet clear timbre to it. For some reason it sounded familiar—which was impossible, of course.

"And you?" he drawled. "You are a wandering minstrel, perhaps, traveling from town to town and terrorizing the natives with your reckless driving?"

"How can you call *me* reckless?" she demanded indignantly. "You were the one who forced me off the road, driving that great monster of a car at such a speed on those little roads."

"Now, now, don't be so irascible, my dear. No one should refer to a Jaguar as a monster. It's a very aristocratic car."

"I have a right to be...irascible." To her chagrin, she stumbled a little over the word. It was not one she normally used.

"Irascible means hot tempered," he said mildly.

"I know what it means." She was furious now; she couldn't stand men who treated her like a dumb blonde. "I am *irascible*," she said coldly, biting off each word, "because I object to drivers who are a menace on the highway."

"I might point out that *you* were driving all over the middle of the road," he said, totally unruffled. "And I was *not* exceeding the speed limit. *You* were driving too slowly."

Vicki swallowed. His carefully controlled voice was diffusing her anger, making her feel foolish. And there was some truth in his statement. She took a deep breath. She really didn't want to begin her visit to England with bad feelings, especially not when the man must either be a guest in the hotel or one of Abby's employees.

Approaching the desk, she forced herself to smile, even though her face felt stiff. "Perhaps we should start over," she suggested. "I'm Vicki Dennison, and I'm sorry I blew up at you. I'm not usually so...belligerent, but you really scared me back there. I just arrived in this country yesterday, and I'm not used to driving on the left."

"Vicki?" he repeated, with a querulous note in his voice.

"It's short for Victoria." Now why had she told him that? She didn't usually tell anyone her full name.

"Victoria," he echoed. "Yes. I like that much better. I accept your gracious apology, Victoria, and extend one of my own."

He hadn't told her his name, she noted with a frown. Suddenly she felt irritated all over again.

The eyes hidden behind the sunglasses seemed to be examining her closely, taking in her rumpled shirt and jeans and her long tangled hair. He still had made no attempt to remove his hat or glasses. Obviously, in spite of his cultured accent, hand-tailored tweed jacket, impeccable white shirt and dark silk tie, he was no gentleman.

This opinion was confirmed a moment later when he gestured lazily with his cigarette toward her guitar, still slung over her shoulder. "*Are* you a wandering minstrel?" he asked.

Vicki gave an exasperated sigh. "Hardly. Mrs. Carstairs, the owner of this hotel, is my aunt. I'm here to assist her in some remodeling."

"My dear girl, why didn't you say so?" He let his chair down with an abrupt thump, stubbed out his cigarette in an ashtray and stood up, holding out his hand across the desk. "I have the greatest respect and affection for Abigail Carstairs. Our association has been a long and happy one, and I'm delighted to meet her niece."

Taken aback by his sudden change of manner, she stared up at him as she reluctantly gave him her hand. He was a tall man, powerfully built, with broad shoulders and a rugged physique. There was something formidable about him, and those concealed eyes gave an impression of secretiveness and unknown perils. Yet his handshake was surprisingly gentle—and warm. Unexpectedly the touch of his hand on hers sent a tremor of nervousness up her spine. Against her will she felt drawn to him in some way she couldn't define. Before she could withdraw her hand, her fingers quivered, and in immediate response his grip tightened.

"I was asked to wait in here for Abby," she said, pulling her hand free and dismayed to find that she sounded breathless.

He nodded as he sat down again, indicating a chair at the side of the desk. "Please have a seat."

A dazzling smile accompanied the invitation, and a little alarm bell sounded in Vicki's brain, telling her to beware. She had been misled by dazzling smiles before. All the same, she was glad to prop her guitar against the desk and sit down, for her knees were feeling quite weak. Fatigue, she decided.

"Are you one of Abby's assistants?" she asked hesitantly.

The eyes behind the dark glasses studied her for a second, then he smiled again, ruefully this time. "I should be making myself useful, shouldn't I?" he said lightly. "I could at least jot down some details for the records." He leaned forward to switch on a small desk light, picked up a pen and took a form of some kind from a pile in a metal tray. "Where are you from, Victoria?"

Vicki frowned. Why didn't he know where she was from? Kim had said the whole staff had been told to expect her. Surely, if he was Abby's assistant, he should have recognized her name when she first gave it?

There was something peculiar about the man, she realized. Why did he persist in wearing that awful hat and those sunglasses? Was he bald, perhaps, and vain about it? Did he have weak eyes? He didn't seem to have any other noticeable flaws. What she could see of his face in the lamplight seemed fairly attractive: strong features; a tanned complexion with just a hint of dark shadow around the firm jawline; a beautifully shaped mouth that curved sensually at the corners. Lines bracketed his mouth, making it look almost stern in repose. No, not stern—grim—and perhaps a little bitter. He was probably about thirty-five or so, she decided.

She wished she could resolve the feeling of familiarity she had about him. That smile, and the voice. Especially the voice.... The memory was there on the threshold of her subconscious mind, but she couldn't quite grasp it.

She felt herself flushing as she realized he'd noticed her appraisal. He had cleared his throat and was tapping his pen lightly on the desk, as though to remind her she hadn't answered his question.

"I'm from Los Angeles," she said hastily and watched him write down her answer.

"Not one of my favorite cities," he commented.

"Oh? You've been there?"

"I have." He paused. "Your age?"

"Twenty-five. Is this some kind of employment application?"

"Something of the sort." His tone was brisk. "Let me see now. Physical description. Height? Five-feet-five?"

"Six."

"Mmm. Weight? Eight-stone-three or thereabouts? That would be about a hundred and fifteen pounds."

"Close enough."

"Green eyes." He glanced up at her. "Sea green. Did you know they glow when you're angry? Like a ferocious kitten's. Quite stunning, actually."

Vicki glared at him. Was it his intention to deliberately goad her?

He was still staring at her. "How would you describe the color of your hair?" he asked.

"The color? I . . . blond, I suppose."

"Mmm. It's a striking color, rather like ripe wheat. Do you put those lighter streaks in yourself?"

"I do not," Vicki said curtly. Whatever his intentions were, his remarks were becoming far too personal. And it was a mistake to allow any kind of intimacy on the job. She'd learned that lesson thoroughly and didn't ever intend to forget it.

"Are you single or married?" he asked, apparently not a bit disturbed by her terse answers.

"Single."

He looked up. "You said that very forcefully. You aren't divorced or widowed, are you?"

"No."

"No children, then."

"Of course no children! What kind of form *is* this?"

He ignored her question, writing busily. "Previous employment?" he asked, not looking up.

"Interior design. With the firm of Hendrickson and Marriott in Los Angeles."

"You left of your own accord?"

She hesitated a fraction of a second too long. His head came up. "You were sacked?" he asked matter-of-factly.

"Not exactly. That is—" She took a deep breath. "Is all of this necessary? The work I'm going to do is for Mrs. Carstairs herself. Surely I don't have to answer—"

"Paperwork is of the utmost importance in England, Victoria," he said pompously. "There are rules and regulations to be obeyed."

"Oh." She hesitated. "Then I guess you'll have to put down that I was fired—sacked."

"For what reason?"

"Really, Mr.—what did you say your name was?"

"I didn't."

"Oh." She paused, trying to collect her thoughts, which were getting more and more scattered. "I don't think I want to answer any more questions," she said firmly. "I'll wait for Abby and—"

"Vicki?" a voice exclaimed behind her.

Vicki stood up and turned around, relieved to see her aunt. Dressed in a navy blue suit and a crisp white blouse, Abby looked more elegant than ever. She had changed her hairstyle since her last visit to California, Vicki noticed at once. Her dark brown hair was drawn back into a heavy chignon, an old-fashioned style that suited her perfectly and emphasized her high cheekbones. Her makeup was light but effective—a trace of brown eyeshadow to accent her hazel eyes, a touch of pale coral lipstick. Abby wasn't tall, perhaps five-foot-four, but she had superb posture and such great presence that she gave the impression of tallness. And she invariably wore very high-heeled shoes.

Vicki had always envied her aunt's businesslike and tailored appearance. "People look at me and say, 'Ah, a California girl,'" she'd often complained. "They assume I run around all the time with a surfboard under my arm. It never occurs to them that I might have a brain or two in my head."

Abby had sympathized, but had scolded her niece lightly. "There's nothing wrong with looking like an ad for sunshine and vitamins," she'd said with an affectionate smile. "You know who you are and what you're capable of; that's all that matters."

Her smile was just as loving now as she hugged Vicki enthusiastically and kissed her on the cheek. "It's so great to see you," she exclaimed. She held Vicki at arms' length, smiling as she studied her face. "You look marvelous, darling! I'd forgotten what a California tan could do for a woman. We don't get a whole lot of sunshine here, as you may have heard." She grinned. "I do believe you've grown another inch. Goodness, how time flies. It seems only yesterday you were toddling around in diapers, building sand castles on the beach. What a darling baby you were."

"Abby!" Vicki warned, conscious of the man behind her.

Abby laughed. "Can I help it if I adore my sister's only daughter?" A small frown puckered her forehead. "But what are you doing here *this* week, darling? I was amazed when Kimberly told me you'd arrived. You said in your letter you'd be here on June 28. There's nothing wrong at home, is there?"

"No. Daddy's happily grubbing around with his beloved animals, and mom's still selling every bit of L.A. real estate she can get her hands on. They both send you their love. There was going to be an airline strike, you see, and no one knew how long it might go on. I thought I'd better come while I could. I didn't want to mess up your weekend schedule, so I spent last night in London. I rented a car, something called a Mini."

"Of a rather poisonous shade of green," the man behind her said, standing up.

Startled, Abby looked at him. She seemed suddenly anxious, biting her lower lip in an uncharacteristically nervous manner as she looked from him to Vicki and back again. "I didn't even see you there," she said hastily. "Have you been waiting long? Nobody told me you'd arrived."

"Nobody knew," he said flatly. "I came in the back way. I thought I should see you before going upstairs."

Abby's expression was apologetic. "I'm so sorry I had to drag you away from London, but I thought you'd want to know about your sister."

"What exactly has she done this time?" he asked. "The message I received was a little muddled."

Abby started to speak, then shook her head and looked at Vicki. "I'm afraid you've caught me in the middle of a...situation, darling," she said. "Everything's 'iggledy-piggledy, as Kimberley would say. We've just had the third in a series of thefts—this time Mrs. Wilson's diamond pendant, of all things. It's frightfully valuable."

The man gave a muffled exclamation. "Look here, Abby, surely that has nothing to do with—"

Abby shook her head. "No, probably not," she said. "I called you for something that happened yesterday—a prank, nothing more. The theft occurred sometime today. I've just had a meeting of the staff, in fact. We've got to get to the bottom of this, or people won't want to stay here." She looked at Vicki again and smiled ruefully. "Would you mind if I have Kimberly show you to your room, darling? Perhaps you could unpack and get settled, and then we can have dinner together?"

"Of course," Vicki agreed promptly, though by now she was filled with curiosity about the man in the tweed hat. Abby hadn't introduced him to her, and she'd spoken to him in a voice that held a note of... deference. Evidently he *wasn't* one of the hotel employees. In which case, why had he pretended he was? All those questions! Abby had dragged him away from London because of some prank to do with his sister, whoever *she* was. Mystery upon mystery.

The man was looking at her again, amusement hovering around the corners of his mouth. She felt distinctly uncomfortable. For some reason of his own he'd played a trick on her, and she had fallen for it. About to demand an explanation for his deceitfulness, she glanced again at Abby's unusually anxious face, then shrugged and moved toward the door. She didn't want to make a scene, and it was probably wiser to just ignore the man. Let him enjoy his little joke, whoever he was.

Abby followed her out to the now bustling lobby. "I'm sorry I have to pack you off like this," she apologized. "But Kimberly will take you up to your room." Her face brightened. "What do you think of our Kim?"

"I like her," Vicki said promptly.

Abby smiled warmly. "So do I. Sometimes she's a bit of a shock to our customers, but they all end up loving her. She has such a kind heart, and she's always cheerful. Plus, she's extremely competent and trustworthy, and marvelous at arranging tours."

Delivering Vicki to Kim, she patted her niece on the arm, promised to join her as soon as possible, then returned to her office and closed the door.

Several people were now working behind the registration desk. They watched with interest as Vicki followed Kim into a small elevator that was enclosed by iron grillwork. Apparently the receptionist had spread word of her identity.

About to ask Kim about the "mystery man," Vicki

restrained herself. It would probably be indiscreet to question one of Abby's employees, and she certainly didn't want to admit she'd been duped into telling him things he evidently had no right to ask.

The lift, as Kim called it, ascended in rather bumpy fashion to the fourth floor. Vicki was relieved when it stopped. She would in future avoid the elevator as much as possible, she decided. It might be as safe as Kim had assured her it was, but she'd never cared much for any elevators, and this one might be as old as the rest of the building....

But she was delighted by her room, which was beautifully decorated with antique furniture. Many of her ex-clients in Los Angeles would have given a fortune for just one of these pieces. There was a lovely old bed, large and comfortable looking, with a bright bedspread patterned in stylized flowers. A nineteenth-century design, Vicki decided. The headboard was draped with sunny yellow chintz, a fabric that was repeated at the windows and on cushions scattered across the elegant chaise longue. A triple-mirrored dressing table and stool, two Chippendale armchairs drawn up to a pedestal table, gilt-framed paintings of English country scenes and lots of bookshelves completed the decor. The window was diamond paned and bowed, and the cushioned window seat just right for curling up with a book—or a guitar. As she had hoped, it overlooked the courtyard and offered a view of the river, the trees and the imposing Georgian house in the distance. "Fantastic," Vicki murmured.

For a while she stood in contemplative silence, enjoying the view. But when a shy young man arrived with her luggage, which he'd removed at Kim's direction from her car, she set about unpacking and making the room her own. Then for a long and relaxing time she soaked in the beautiful claw-footed tub in the adjoining bathroom.

Feeling refreshed, she wrapped herself in her old white terry robe and sat down at the dressing table to apply the small amount of makeup she usually wore.

She found herself taking unusual pains with her stubbornly straight hair, first coiling it up on top of her head, then brushing it smooth again, trying to decide which style showed off the sun-streaked strands to best advantage.

She was *not* hoping to see the "mystery man" again, she told herself firmly, though she couldn't deny she'd like a chance to get even with him for the way he'd tricked her. But if she did see him, she had no desire to make an impression on him. He was far too inquisitive, too presumptuous and deceitful. In any case, without his awful hat and glasses, he might very well turn out to be bald and cross-eyed. Those muscular shoulders could be the result of Savile Row tailoring. No doubt the real "mystery man" was a scrawny pigeon-chested character with a paunch, and lifts in his shoes.

She laughed at the image she'd conjured up, though she didn't believe in it for a minute. She wished she could; it would be a good way to put him in his place so that he no longer intrigued her.

He *did* intrigue her, she admitted—and she didn't want to be intrigued. She had made up her mind that she was going to remain uninvolved with men for some time to come, no matter how firm the chin or how dazzling the smile. Vicki Dennison was finally going to develop an independent spirit and take charge of her own life. To protect herself she would build up a wall of emotional detachment, and she wouldn't allow any cracks in it.

Glancing at her wristwatch, she noted that a couple of hours had passed. Would Abby be ready for her now? She should have asked what time dinner would be served. Well, there was nothing preventing her from going down to the lobby to find out.

Firmly pinning her hair at the nape of her neck with a flat gold barrette, she let her robe fall from her shoulders as she considered what to wear. She had no idea where she and Abby would be dining.

Finally she decided on an apple green crepe de chine dress with long sleeves, one that she'd bought at her mother's urging. "It intensifies the color of your eyes," Ellen had proclaimed.

Satisfied after one final glance at the mirror that she would do Abby credit, Vicki slipped her feet into low-heeled sandals and went out to the little foyer of the apartment. Hesitantly she opened another door and looked into what was evidently Abby's sitting room, another stunningly lovely room decorated in warm shades of pinkish red and gold. "Abby," she called tentatively, but there was no answer.

She found the staircase around the corner, a wide curving staircase that any child with an ounce of adventure would have loved to slide down.

Smiling at the thought, she sedately descended to the next landing, admiring the multihued Axminster carpeting that covered the stairs and hallway.

About to go down the next flight, she stopped to look at a faded notice board that hung on the corridor wall.

"Rules of This Tavern," she read. "Four pence a

night for bed. No more than five to sleep in one bed. No boots to be worn in bed. Organ-grinders to sleep in the washhouse.''

She chuckled. The notice must date back a long time! Still smiling, she turned away, but was startled by the sound of a familiar and very loud male voice coming from the room right next to the notice board. The door was ajar, she noticed.

''I've told you a thousand times I will not put up with your behavior,'' the man was shouting.

''You're such a damnable prude,'' a young female voice said mockingly.

''And you are a whore, madam,'' he yelled. ''A vain whoring slut without an ounce of conscience. I'd be within my rights to kill you here and now.''

''You don't have the intestinal fortitude to kill me,'' the girl taunted. ''You're a coward, for all your brave talk.''

''A coward, am I?'' the man said in a quieter tone, and Vicki felt a thrill of fear at the menace in his voice. Still frozen in place on the landing, not breathing, she waited for the girl's reply. But instead she heard the sickening sound of flesh hitting something solid—wood furniture? Then, to her absolute horror, the girl screamed loudly and agonizingly.

Immediately after the scream there was a deathly throbbing silence.

CHAPTER TWO

VICKI REACTED INSTINCTIVELY. Not pausing to think, she pushed open the door and stepped into a small hallway. There was an arched entranceway on her right, and she rushed through it into a large b⁻'ghtly lighted room.

Beyond an expanse of cream-colored carpeting was the man she had last seen in Abby's office. He was standing with his back to a wood-framed fireplace and was looking directly at her with a startled expression.

Vicki's breath caught in her throat. The "mystery man" was no longer a mystery. Without his tweed hat and dark glasses he was instantly recognizable.

"You're Jason Meredith," she said accusingly.

She could say nothing more. Her wits had temporarily deserted her. For several long moments she could only stand and stare. She'd even forgotten the reason why she'd burst in on him. All she could think was, *my God, Jason Meredith*. No wonder his voice had sounded familiar. She'd seen the highly successful movie he'd made recently in the States, had watched him on television several times playing roles created by Ibsen, O'Neill, Shaw. Only last month she'd sat entranced every Thursday evening from nine until eleven while he performed the role of Lothario in a modern revival of Nicholas Rowe's play *The Fair Penitent*.

Jason Meredith, one of the leading lights of England's classical and Shakespearean theaters; an actor acclaimed by critics on both sides of the Atlantic. His name was often mentioned in the same reverent breath as Lord Laurence Olivier, Sir John Gielgud, Richard Burton and other giants of the stage, including his own father, Sir Giles Meredith, long since deceased.

In person he was even more striking than he was on the screen. Since she'd seen him last he'd taken off his jacket and tie and had opened his shirt collar. Her facetious imaginings had been totally mistaken; no Savile Row tailoring was responsible for those muscular shoulders and that rugged physique. In his white cotton shirt and tight-fitting dark pants he looked... magnificent. The original swashbuckling buccaneer. All he needed was a sword in one hand and a balcony to leap over. Thick dark brown hair tumbled across his forehead in an unruly fashion, almost begging to be smoothed back by a female hand. His features were strongly carved. His eyes, capable of showing a wide range of emotions on camera—from love to hatred, from rage to indifference—were the pewter gray of mist over a stormy sea.

And right now, she realized, finally becoming aware that she was still staring at him—*gawking* at him—those luminous eyes were regarding her with the patient inquiry of a well-mannered king, into whose presence one of the peasantry has inadvertently blundered.

At the same moment she realized that another man had entered the room by a side door, a tall and stately man with silver hair. He was formally dressed in a black jacket, striped trousers and a white shirt with a high starched collar. His back ramrod straight, this intimidating figure was approaching her in a very menacing manner, with the obvious intention of throwing her out—bodily if necessary. Alarmed, she backed up a step.

"It's all right, Royce," Jason Meredith said in an amused voice. "I don't think Miss Dennison poses much of a threat. She's more of a kitten than a tiger."

The man stopped in his tracks. He continued to watch her, however, his head tipped slightly back, his glacial eyes narrowed on her face.

Vicki swallowed. "The door was open, and I heard...I thought I heard a scream," she stammered, at last remembering what had so abruptly propelled her into the room. "I thought—naturally I thought...." Her voice trailed away as she became aware that yet another person was in the room.

A young girl was looking at her over the back of a crimson sofa, her light-colored eyes glinting wickedly with mischief. A pretty girl with an elfin face and pixie-like brown curls, she looked no more than fifteen years old. "She actually thought you were doing me in, brother Jason," she said gaily, still looking mockingly at Vicki.

"Not a bad idea," her brother remarked. "You had no business screaming so loudly. It's a wonder you didn't rouse the entire hotel. It was probably you who left the door open in the first place, too. When are you ever going to learn to be more careful?"

The girl made a face at him. "Were you coming to my rescue?" she asked Vicki in her clear young voice. "How terribly brave of you. But we were only acting, actually."

Vicki felt heat flooding her face. So stunned had she been by the sight of Jason Meredith that she hadn't even noticed the bound manuscript he held open in his hands. Now she saw that the girl was also holding a notebook with a similar blue cover. "You were reading a script," she said flatly, wishing that the cream-colored rug would open under her feet and allow her to sink mercifully out of sight.

"Not a very *good* script," he said, his voice taking on an irritated edge. "How any author can expect an actor to shout such long lines, I can't imagine. And as for phrases like 'intestinal fortitude...!'" He dropped the manuscript on the sofa beside his sister and looked at Vicki with a glimmer of amusement in his eyes. "I suppose, however, that if you were convinced the damsel was in distress, the dialogue can't be as banal as I thought. There may be hope for the playwright, after all."

Vicki's face felt hotter than ever. There must be some way, she thought helplessly, to extricate herself from this humiliating situation with some semblance of dignity.

"I'm sorry," she said hesitantly. "I didn't recognize...I didn't know you were Jason Meredith, and I didn't think...it didn't occur to me that you were just, well, reading something. I thought—" She stopped abruptly before she sounded even more inane.

"My dear Victoria, no apology is necessary. You mustn't take this so much to heart." His voice was suddenly gentle. "Let me give you a drink to help you recover from your shock. That's the least I can do to make amends."

She wasn't sure if he was making fun of her or not.

He didn't seem to be. His face was quite serious now, and he really had sounded apologetic.

"A sherry, perhaps?" he suggested.

When she hesitated, he added, "Please, Victoria," in that resonant voice of his. Her pulse began racing at twice its normal speed. *Jason Meredith,* she thought again.

She let out a small helpless sigh. "Sherry would be nice," she said faintly.

He smiled. She had thought earlier that his smile was dazzling. This smile was more than dazzling; it was breathtaking. No woman on earth could have resisted it.

Afterward she realized that she must have walked across the carpet to take the seat he indicated, a very soft upholstered armchair that seemed to enfold her as she sat down in it. At some time, too, the hostile-looking butler—she supposed he was the butler—must have left the room. But she didn't see him go, nor did she notice when the girl stood up and went to pour the sherry. She didn't really come to her senses until the girl cleared her throat in an exaggerated manner. She was standing in front of her holding out a delicate stemmed wineglass filled with amber liquid while she waited with eyebrows raised for Vicki to take it from her.

Vicki tried to sit up straight, a difficult feat in the soft chiar. "I'm sorry," she said. "I didn't notice. . . I mean, I didn't see. . . ."

"That's quite all right," the girl said sardonically. "Jason has that effect on most women."

Vicki bit her lip as she accepted the glass. She'd behaved like a groupie. The girl probably thought she was an absolute idiot. She took a calming sip of sherry and sat up even straighter, trying to look reasonably alert and intelligent.

"I should introduce my sister, Portia," Jason said dryly. He was still standing, still smiling at her. The smile was a little on the crooked side now, as though he knew full well the effect that his earlier blinding smile had had on her. He'd probably felled hundreds of women with that smile, Vicki thought, and he was obviously amused by her stunned condition. She could hardly blame him for that, but he didn't have to look so smug about it.

"This is Miss Dennison, Portia," he said in the polite voice of an adult making a concession to a child. "She's Abigail Carstairs's niece from Los Angeles."

"How do you do," Portia said perfunctorily, almost rudely. She flashed a petulant glance at her brother. "You aren't going to make me read any more of that awful stuff, are you?"

He sighed. "I think we've done enough damage for one day. Run along and change for dinner. But don't leave your room," he added as Portia started away. "The rules still stand. You are not to go anywhere without Royce or David or me."

She stuck her tongue out at him, but didn't comment. With another slightly mocking glance at Vicki, she performed an exaggerated curtsy toward her brother, then hurried out through the archway.

Watching her go, Vicki realized that this room was part of a suite of rooms, a self-contained apartment like Abby's, judging by the kitchen sounds she could hear close by. She vaguely remembered seeing several doors leading from the hallway as she hurtled across it.

The memory of her melodramatic entrance caused her to squirm mentally, and she took another sip of sherry, grateful for having something to do. Her host had poured himself a drink and was seating himself on the sofa at right angles to her chair. He lighted a cigarette and leaned back, his head dark against the crimson cushions. He looked relaxed, Vicki thought, though even when seated, he seemed to radiate energy.

"I hope you'll forgive Portia's rudeness," he said with a sigh. "She was angry with me because I wouldn't let her go to a film she wanted to see, and then I compounded my villainy by enlisting her aid with the reading. I'm afraid Portia is a blot on the family escutcheon," he added dryly. "She looks upon reading a script as punishment."

"Punishment?" Vicki echoed, still trying to collect her senses.

"My young sister is inclined to get into mischief, I'm afraid. She caused Abby considerable embarrassment yesterday, and I've confined her to quarters for a while. Rather than waste my time here, I insisted she help me read that script. It's one a young playwright blessed me with recently." He sighed. "The boy has a talent for plotting, but he needs to improve his dialogue considerably. He has a tendency to use far too many clichés."

From the corner of her eye she saw him turn his head in her direction, probably to check if she'd recovered her sanity yet.

Hastily she fixed her own gaze on the glass of sherry in her hand.

"You may have gathered, Victoria," he continued, "that Abby called me in from London because of my sister's ill-advised behavior. Normally I don't stay in town during a play's run. I find it more relaxing to come back here. But I had some...business this weekend that was very important to me, and I was not pleased at being called away to attend to Portia. That's why I was so bloody-minded about the car incident. I *am* sorry if my behavior offended you."

There'd been a marked hesitation in his voice before he said "business." Vicki was suddenly sure that his "business" had involved a woman. Hadn't she heard or read stories about Jason Meredith and women?

She shouldn't think about that now, she admonished herself hastily. The great man was expending a considerable amount of charm on her. He'd even apologized, and she should at least make a contribution to the conversation. If she could just think of something to say....

"Why on earth did you pretend to be working here?" she blurted out. "All that stuff about details for the records."

His face was innocently bland as he put out his cigarette, but there was a glint in his gray eyes that reminded her of Portia's sly expression. "I didn't say *whose* records," he pointed out. "Actually the form had something to do with supplies for the hotel." He glanced at her sideways. "You seemed to think I might be a hotel employee, so I thought I'd oblige. I realized, of course, that you hadn't recognized me. I thought it would be rather...bombastic to announce my identity, and in spite of reports to the contrary, I really am not bombastic. So rather than appear so, I played the role you had assigned me." He hesitated, then unleashed that blazing smile again. "It seemed a fairly harmless way to learn something about you."

The implication was that he'd been interested in her, but she couldn't quite let herself believe that. She still wasn't sure if he was mocking her or not. He seemed sincere, but.... "Your sister's a very pretty girl," she said neutrally.

"Pretty, yes." The lines bracketing the corners of his mouth deepened as his lips tightened. "I seem to be making a hash of things where Portia is concerned, Victoria."

His marvelously vibrant voice lingered on her name, making it sound far more attractive than she'd ever thought it. She felt uncomfortably self-conscious. Just being in the same room with this larger-than-life man was totally destroying her usual equilibrium. She could hear her pulse pounding in her ears and could almost believe he heard it, too. She was relieved when a telephone rang somewhere in the suite, and Royce came in to tell him someone wanted to speak to him.

She watched him stride across the room, moving with the kind of athletic vitality that had impressed her when she saw him in *The Fair Penitent. Jason Meredith,* she thought dazedly. *I've actually been sitting in the same room as Jason Meredith.*

She must pull herself together and get out of here. Abby would be looking for her by now, and Jason Meredith's patience must be wearing thin. But she could hardly walk out while he was gone.

She could hear him talking in the next room, heard that distinctive voice of his say, "But Sabrina, darling...."

Deliberately Vicki turned her attention away, not

wanting to eavesdrop. It was a beautiful room, she observed, consciously trying to distract herself. So far she hadn't seen any area of the inn that needed redecorating. She was beginning to realize that Abby's invitation might have been more than the casual one it seemed. Vicki's mother had certainly agreed it would be best for her own daughter to leave Los Angeles for a while. It was rather too much of a coincidence that this godsend had come right on the heels of her problems with Hendrickson and Marriott. . . .

This particular room was more formal than her own, but just as attractive. The rich primary tones of the draperies and upholstery provided an effective contrast to the pale color of the ceiling, walls and carpeting. The pieces of Queen Anne furniture, polished to a smooth luster, were no more reproductions than were those in Abby's apartment. And the large oil paintings on the walls looked like originals. Vicki was pretty sure two of them were Gainsboroughs, and one was a Vandyke, and she definitely recognized a painting of a church as a Canaletto. Surely the whole hotel wasn't furnished like this?

When Jason came back into the room, she stood up, still clutching her sherry glass. "I must be going," she said. "Abby will be wondering—"

"I telephoned Abby after my other call was completed," he informed her, seating himself comfortably. "She is about to go upstairs to prepare for dinner, and she was delighted to know you were being entertained. Dinner will be served in her apartment. She'll expect you there in forty-five minutes."

Vicki stared at him. She had always resented people who tried to arrange her time or her activities for her. But somehow she didn't seem to have a mind of her own right now. The force of this man's personality was such that, without even thinking about what she was doing, she found herself automatically sitting down again.

He retrieved his glass from the lovely little table next to the sofa. "What were we talking about?" he asked.

Why was he prolonging the conversation? Was he playing games with her again? "Portia," she said hesitantly.

"Oh, yes. I'm afraid she has become very difficult recently. When she was small, my housekeeper, Mrs. Powell, and I were able to manage her very well. An enchanting little thing, she was. But now...." His voice trailed away, and he took a thoughtful sip of his drink.

Vicki remembered abruptly that Sir Giles Meredith had died in a riding accident shortly before Jason's mother, Elizabeth, gave birth to a baby girl. That must have been Portia. She'd read the details in a movie magazine quite recently while she was waiting at the beauty parlor to have her hair trimmed.

According to the article, Portia's birth had been difficult. Lady Meredith had been over forty. Already devastated by her husband's death, she herself had died a year or so after the child's birth.

The writer had gone on to say that Sir Giles and Lady Meredith, both of them wealthy in their own rights from inherited money, had also been very well known Shakespearean actors. In fact, Sir Giles had received his knighthood *because* of his acting. Supposedly the famous couple had been so devoted to each other that they had refused to work in any play that didn't have roles for both of them.

Jason must have been about twenty when his mother died, Vicki realized. Evidently he had taken on the responsibility of his orphaned sister. That couldn't have been easy for such a young man, she thought with a flash of sympathy.

He had married Claire Bellamy, the opera singer, soon after his mother's death, she remembered. If the gossip columnists could be believed, the marriage had been fraught with public quarrels and just as public and tumultuous reconciliations. Since Claire's death in an airplane crash—what was it, three years ago—he had supposedly been involved in wild affairs with almost every famous beauty in the world.

"You are very quiet, Victoria," he said, and she came back to herself with a start.

"I was wondering what play you were in, Mr. Meredith—just now, I mean," she stammered. She could hardly confess she'd been mulling over the lurid stories she'd read about him.

"Shakespearean at the moment. The company is performing *Othello* this week, then *As You Like It*, and *Hamlet* after that." He raised his eyebrows. "Do call me Jason, please. Our meetings haven't been too terribly formal so far, have they? I quite feel we're old friends."

She wasn't sure how to respond. "That's a fascinating story," she said, then realized she wasn't making sense. "I mean *Hamlet*. I haven't seen it performed on the stage, but I studied it in school, and I saw the Olivier movie on television. I always felt sorry for Hamlet—the duty of vengeance was such a burden to him. It would have destroyed even a less sensitive man."

Was she actually telling Jason Meredith what

Hamlet was about? Had she lost her mind completely? She took a deep breath and changed the subject. "Do you live in this hotel? I seem to remember reading that you'd inherited your parents' house. There were pictures of it in a movie magazine." Now she'd revealed that she read gossip columns. If she kept on like this, he'd be inviting her to start a fan club.

She was suddenly struck by the memory of the Georgian house she'd seen on her way into the inn. "Is that your house across the river?" she exclaimed.

The muscles in his face tightened. "It is," he said shortly. Then he glanced at her apologetically. "Sorry, I didn't mean to snap your head off. You just happened to touch on a nerve. We had a fire there eleven weeks ago. Actually the fire itself didn't do a lot of harm—more smoke damage than anything else—but the fire department was rather too efficient. The water damage was incredible, and some helpful chap hacked holes in the roof. That's why we're living here. Abby has taken us in for the duration. Mrs. Powell and my secretary, David Brent, are with us, and Royce, of course. The rest of the staff are billeted around the town, helping with the work on the house when necessary. It will take another two or three months to make the place habitable, I'm afraid."

"Was it arson?" Vicki asked, automatically so sympathetic that she forgot her nervousness.

His expression was suddenly bleak. "It seems so. The resulting smoke was black, which I'm told would indicate the presence of petrol." After a perceptible pause he smiled briefly. "Luckily no one was hurt."

"Why would anyone want to burn down your house?"

His mouth twisted. "I'm afraid those of us who dwell in the public eye often become the targets of unbalanced people. The fire followed on the heels of a rather threatening letter. Incidentally the letter is the reason Royce tends to be overprotective." He stared gloomily into his glass for a moment, then shrugged and smiled, seeming deliberately to throw off his suddenly somber mood. "Royce has been with us for years and is totally devoted. He really looks the part of a butler, wouldn't you say? I'm rather in awe of him, actually."

"I thought he was going to pick me up and put me out like a stray cat," Vicki admitted.

"Yes, I must say you looked a bit frightened. I'm sorry about that. Royce is really a very gentle person."

With a decided click he placed his glass down on the table again and leaned back, fixing his intense gaze on her face. "Enough about the Meredith household, Victoria. Tell me about you—an interior designer, you said?"

"Yes," she answered curtly, afraid he was going to ask again about the reasons for her unemployment. But it seemed, incredibly, that he really wanted to draw her out, to know about her life. He made her feel he was genuinely interested in her, as though he would rather be sitting here listening to her than doing anything else at all.

Vicki was surprised to find herself opening up to him, telling him about her zoologist father and her mother's success with real estate. She even told him what she loved about her own work—not just the sensuous pleasure of working with beautiful fabrics, furnishings, houses that she couldn't afford herself, but also of the creative joy she felt in putting together an environment that fitted the person who had hired her, the sense of triumph when she heard that person say, "This is exactly what I wanted! How did you know that when I didn't know it myself?"

After a while she felt embarrassed by her own enthusiasm and deliberately tried to tone it down. "I guess you could say I love my work," she ended with a consciously self-deprecating smile.

He nodded appreciatively. "I can certainly identify." He sipped thoughtfully at his drink. "Have you ever done any acting?"

"A little. In high school and college. But I wasn't very good."

"No? You surprise me. You move very well. That was a marvelous entrance you made just now, I thought. There ought to have been trumpets. And you certainly register emotion clearly."

Unexpectedly he stood up. In one fluid motion he knelt beside her chair and reached out to cup her chin in his hand, forcing her to look at him. While she sat there, paralyzed, his brilliant gray eyes searched her face intently, as though he were trying to look below the surface of her skin.

"Let me see now," he said thoughtfully. "So far I have seen you register anger, startled recognition, fear and, yes, I think perhaps a little reluctant admiration. At the moment you are again afraid, I think, but not unpleasantly so."

Something very odd was happening to Vicki while he spoke. The combination of his strong fingers touching her face, the close regard of those shining gray eyes and the sound of his vibrant voice had awakened a whole set of responses that she hadn't ex-

perienced before, at least not all at once. A warmth
had begun deep inside her, a warmth that was spread-
ing through all her veins. It was a languorous
warmth; she felt unable to move or look away from
his compelling gaze. "You have remarkably beautiful eyes," he said softly.

Hardly an original line, one part of her mind commented. Yet she knew he could have gone on to say
that her eyes were like deep pools, and coming from
his lips the words would have sounded fresh and new.
"Eyes colored like a water-flower," he said instead.
"And deeper than the green sea's glass."

"Swinburne," she said automatically.

He released her chin and sat back on his heels,
smiling delightedly at her. Her temperature went up
several more degrees.

"Shakespeare *and* Swinburne," he said approvingly. "I do appreciate a woman who reads."

Before she could comment on that, he got to his
feet and picked up the script Portia had abandoned.

"Perhaps you'd like to help me get on with this,"
he said in a matter-of-fact tone of voice. "Now that
I've lost Portia, I really think it's the least you can
do."

"Oh, I don't think. . . ." Nervously Vicki eased
herself to the edge of her chair and set down her
glass. "I should be going. . . ."

"Nonsense, you have fifteen minutes still." He
settled himself comfortably on the arm of her chair
and opened the script in front of her. She was suddenly acutely conscious of the way the tightened
fabric of his pants molded the contours of his well-
muscled thighs. Good God, what was wrong with
her? She was behaving like a star-struck teenager.

"Here we are," he said, apparently unaware of the effect he was having on her. "The woman—what's her name, Theresa—has just screamed after Bradley knocked her to the floor. She's looking up at him in terror. He reaches down, sorry now that he's gone so far."

He glanced down at her, gray eyes brimming with amusement. "I didn't hit Portia, by the way. I slapped my hand on the mantelpiece there. Hurt like the devil, too. I do tend to get carried away when I'm acting."

Vicki smiled nervously and edged another inch forward.

"Now, Victoria, don't desert me," he protested. "I promised the boy I'd read his play, and I *always* keep my promises."

Awkwardly Vicki took the folder he was thrusting into her hands. "Well, I don't know..." she said tentatively.

"Here it is, you see," he said, pointing. "Bradley helps her up and into a chair and then sits on the arm of the chair beside her."

Vicki looked helplessly at the next line on the script. "Why do you treat me so when you know how much I love you?" she read aloud in a voice that had a tendency to stumble.

"Because I love you, my darling," he responded promptly. "I love you so much that I can't bear it when you even look at another man."

The words were trite, but his deep voice imbued them with meaning, thrilling her with his intensity. He had entered immediately into the role.

"I look at others only to make you jealous," she read.

"I know that," he said softly.

About to turn the page, she was stopped by his hand on hers. Startled, she glanced at him. Her glance was held. His expression was utterly tender, his mouth parted to show the edges of his teeth. His breathing had quickened, and hers quickened in immediate response. He was looking at her as though she were the most beautiful, the most desirable woman in the world, and there was no way she could withstand the tidal wave of responding emotion that was rushing through her. As his head bent slowly toward hers, she let go of the manuscript, one hand touching his arm and moving slowly upward to the back of his head. Somehow his arms were around her, pulling her toward him, closer and closer.

All of it seemed to happen in slow motion, until she was pressed against him so tightly that she could feel the soft roundness of her breasts against the tensed muscles of his chest as acutely and sensuously as though the fabric of her dress and the fine cotton of his shirt were not between them. His hair was coarse beneath her hands, and alive, so alive! His powerful hands held her firmly, the heat of them seeming to burn through her clothing into her skin. And then his mouth—his beautiful mouth—was on hers, touching delicately, brushing against her suddenly dry lips in a way that was terribly soft and gentle and careful and deliberate all at the same time.

Vicki was melting, quite literally. She felt as though all of her bones were softening and becoming fluid. There was nothing real in the world except herself and Jason Meredith, locked in an embrace she hoped would never end.

After an incalculable time he lifted his head, and

she found herself looking directly into his luminous eyes, inches from hers. For a brief second he looked as bemused as she felt, and then abruptly he released her. "I *am* sorry," he said with a slightly sardonic note in his voice. "As I told you, I do tend to get carried away." He smiled briefly. "Actually I was merely following instructions."

Dazed, she looked down at the manuscript, unable to focus on it at first. Her whole body was trembling. And then she saw that he was pointing to the stage directions at the bottom of the page. They were written in italics, and she hadn't noticed them before. *He looks at her tenderly, slowly takes her in his arms. They kiss lingeringly.*

She swallowed hard, glad he wasn't looking at her for the moment. Of course he'd been acting! What had she thought? That Jason Meredith—*the* Jason Meredith—had fallen madly in love at first sight with Vicki Dennison? After all the famous beauties he had known?

She *hadn't* thought, that was the trouble. For a few seconds of absolute madness she had been incapable of thought.

Somehow she managed to laugh—a little breathlessly, but fairly convincingly. "You're right," she said, and to her relief her voice gave away none of her inner turmoil. "The writing *is* trite."

He made a sound that she took to be agreement, then stood up and held out a hand to assist her to her feet. "I mustn't keep you any longer," he said lightly. "I don't want Abigail to be cross with me. She must be wondering what the devil happened to you."

What *had* happened to her, Vicki wondered as she tried to arrange her face into as unreadable an expression as his. Why did she feel as though someone had just dealt a tremendous blow to some key point in her body, so that if she didn't hold onto herself very tightly, she would shatter into a thousand little pieces on the beautiful cream-colored rug?

She took a deep breath and called on her pride to come to her rescue. "Thanks for the acting lesson," she said, and by some miracle her voice was steady.

"My pleasure," he replied, but he didn't smile. A mask had come down over his face, erasing all expression. If anything, he seemed merely bored by her continued presence.

At least, she thought as she walked slowly back up the stairs to Abby's apartment, still feeling as fragile as a piece of cracked sculpture, she had managed to make her exit with some measure of dignity. At least, Jason Meredith would never know that Victoria Dennison—she of the independent nature and supposedly controlled emotions—had, during the course of one kiss, quite suddenly and completely lost her heart.

CHAPTER THREE

"THIS IS INCREDIBLY DELICIOUS," Vicki said to Abby half an hour later. "I always thought I didn't care for fish, but now I know I've never really eaten it. This sauce is fantastic."

She was feeling whole again, though still a little weak in spots, like a convalescent slowly recovering from an acute illness. To her relief Abby hadn't questioned her about Jason Meredith, had just hugged her and apologized for not welcoming her properly before. There hadn't been time for anything more. A moment after Vicki had walked into the apartment, a maid had wheeled a trolley laden with silver-covered dishes of bouillabaisse, stuffed fillets of fish, creamed spinach, buttered carrots, salads for each of them, and a basket full of the best-tasting garlic bread Vicki had ever eaten.

So far she had managed to eat with surprisingly good appetite, determined not to allow embarrassing thoughts of Jason Meredith to interfere with her enjoyment of her first evening with Abby. And gradually, now that she was away from the actor's charismatic presence, it had become possible for her to be more objective about her recent experience. Of course she hadn't lost her heart to Jason Meredith; it wasn't possible for any heart to be lost so easily. She didn't even know the man. He was a stranger to her, an apparently insensitive stranger who hadn't been able to resist playing with a silly woman's emotions. All she really knew about him she had gleaned from magazine articles, which might or might not be true. If the stories *were* true, then she wasn't sure she *wanted* to get to know him.

Probably their paths wouldn't cross again, anyway. Three chance meetings, more like near collisions, were surely more than enough to satisfy the laws of fate. He certainly wasn't likely to come searching for her. She had nothing to worry about, nothing at all.

"What are you looking so worried about?" Abby asked.

Startled, Vicki almost dropped her fork, but she managed to recover quickly and smile at Abby. "If you feed me this well all the time, I'm going to become as fat as an elephant," she said evasively.

Abby laughed. "This is a special occasion, darling. Usually I nibble on a steak and salad or something like that—when I manage to eat at all. We'll take it easy after tonight."

Vicki looked at her aunt fondly, grateful to her for not pursuing her question. The glass of wine Abby had drunk with dinner had brought a pink flush to her cheeks, and the color was heightened by the pale pink of the silk shirt she wore with her tailored black skirt. She looked unusually pretty and feminine, especially as a few strands of her brown hair had escaped from her chignon and were feathering around her cheeks. She looked a little tired, though. Hardly surprising, Vicki thought, considering the enormous responsibilities she had on her hands.

How well did Abby know Jason Meredith, she

wondered abruptly. And exactly what kind of mischief had Portia Meredith been involved in? Should she ask?

No. She wasn't going to mention either of them. Abby was talking again, anyway, saying something about the problems inherent in running a hotel, particularly the recent rash of thefts. She must pay attention. . . .

"There are always thefts from hotels," Abby was saying. "Ashtrays, towels, even sheets and light fixtures. Unfortunately one has to accept the fact that many people think anything that isn't nailed down is theirs for the taking. But these items have been personal things, stolen from guests. Someone's gold watch, a few small but very valuable pieces of jewelry—always things that can be slipped into a pocket." She sighed. "We have a safe, but guests often refuse to leave their valuables in it. Especially wealthy guests. It's very worrying."

Jason must be wealthy, Vicki thought, then forced him out of her mind again. She was getting angry with herself for her obvious obsession with the man.

Abby was explaining that the hotel had a security department, employing a man and a woman, but the staff couldn't be everywhere at once. "What we're trying to discover," she told Vicki, "is how the thief is getting into the rooms. There's never any sign of a break-in, yet Kim keeps an eagle eye on the extra keys, and the night manager is just as reliable."

No one had been watching the keys today when she arrived, Vicki remembered. But that was possibly an isolated occasion because of the staff meeting. She didn't say anything, not wanting to get Kim into trouble.

"Guests are sometimes careless with their keys, of course," Abby continued. "And professional thieves watch for such carelessness. I'm hoping it's a professional," she added. "I'd hate to think one of my own staff could be involved. We're a pretty close-knit unit." She sighed deeply. "I've notified the local police, of course. An officer has come each time and questioned the staff. I just hope whoever it is has moved on, but I have a feeling he hasn't. So far he's escaped discovery, a fact that must surely persuade him it's safe to try again."

"This place must keep you going all the time," Vicki said.

"That it does, especially since I've been handling it alone." For an instant a shadow darkened Abby's hazel eyes, and she began busily piling dishes onto the trolley. Vicki helped her, thinking how tragic it was that Simon Carstairs, the quiet courtly man Abby had married so unexpectedly five years ago, had died at such an early age, the victim of a heart attack.

"We had four good years," Abby said softly, apparently reading her thoughts. "Many people don't even have that. I certainly didn't expect to marry again after Dan was killed in Vietnam. I thought I'd be managing that poky little hotel in Encino for the rest of my days." She smiled reminiscently. "How odd life is! If I hadn't gone to that hoteliers' convention in Denver, I wouldn't have met Simon, wouldn't have come to England and certainly wouldn't have inherited a four-hundred-year-old inn." She reached across the table and patted Vicki's hand. "Don't look so sad, darling. I'm grateful that I had Simon even for so short a time. I've been lucky. Two marvelous husbands in one lifetime. And I love it here. I always was an anglophile, and this hotel pretty well runs itself, really. I have good people around me, and I learned how to delegate authority long ago. I must admit, though, it does occasionally get lonely."

"Perhaps you should marry again."

Abby smiled. "To be truthful, I have thought about it. Independent as I am, I *like* being married. However, at the great age of fifty, I find there aren't too many offers pouring in—none that I've wanted to consider seriously, at least." She grinned at Vicki. "What about you? According to Ellen's letters, you don't lack male admirers."

"Marriage is a big step," Vicki murmured, feeling uncomfortable as she always did when the subject came up. She'd heard enough about it from her mother. *Time to settle down, Vicki. You're twenty-five years old, Vicki. In my day you'd have been considered an old maid.* And most recently, *Aren't you ever going to make me a grandmother?*

"I just haven't met anyone I want to spend the rest of my life with," she said awkwardly. "I want to be very sure. So many of my friends' marriages have... disintegrated. I don't want that to happen to me. I still believe in 'till death do us part.'"

That was hardly a tactful thing to say to Abby, she realized, horrified.

But her aunt smiled, apparently not offended.

"Men always *say* they don't mind having a wife who combines a career with marriage," Vicki continued pensively, "but after the fact, they start getting old-fashioned again. One of my friends' husbands actually said, 'A woman's place is in the home.' And she was a stockbroker! It was all right as long as she earned less than he did, but when her salary passed his, he started having inferiority pangs.''

She shook her head. "I do want to marry, Abby. I have all the normal impulses, but I'm afraid the sexual revolution passed me by. I can't bring myself to sleep around—too much pride, I guess. What I'm looking for is an equal partner, who will respect my need for a life of my own and still love me to distraction. Is that too much to ask?''

"Not at all," Abby said warmly. "You hold onto your values, Vicki." She raised her eyebrows. "What about this recent trouble?" she asked. "Ellen was almost hysterical on the phone.''

"So mother did call you! I thought so. This trip was cooked up between the two of you, wasn't it? A conspiracy.''

"A loving conspiracy," Abby corrected gently. "And I really do need your advice. The public rooms are in dire need of redoing, especially the Blue Room and the Wine Cellar—that's our main lounge. Some of the guest rooms seem a bit disorganized to me, too. They look...cluttered, somehow. I'm hoping you might have some suggestions there. But there's plenty of time for us to discuss what might be done. You'll need to take a look around first. I've told the entire staff to help you in any way they can. But I don't want you working all the time. Ellen tells me you're inclined to be a bit of a workaholic. I want you to take some time off, see the country, get to know England.''

She tilted her head to one side, raised her dark eyebrows and looked at Vicki, her hazel eyes level and challenging. "You almost got me off the track there. Come on now, give me the facts. Ellen made it sound as though you'd been raped on the job.''

Vicki sighed. "I suppose I'd better straighten out the story for you," she said reluctantly. "It's simple enough, I guess. One of my bosses, Ken Marriott, suddenly decided he wanted to go to bed with me. I was astonished. For one thing, he was much older than I, and we'd become pretty good friends, I thought. We worked well together, and he seemed to think I was an asset to the firm. He started giving me little gifts when I'd done a job that pleased him. I didn't think anything of it. I was just glad that he was satisfied with my work. Then he began wanting me to have a drink with him after office hours, to 'discuss things.' I didn't see anything wrong with that, either. I'd met his wife, had often had dinner at their house.

"Then last January he came up with a job in Santa Barbara and asked me to go with him. I'd gone on similar jaunts with Josh Hendrickson, the other partner. We did a penthouse in New York together, and a couple of old Victorian mansions in San Francisco. It didn't seem at all unusual to go with Ken."

"He made a pass?"

"Nothing so subtle. He walked into my hotel bedroom in the middle of the night, stark naked, and literally jumped on me. He'd booked a two-bedroom suite, you see—which again seemed okay. We were going to use the living-room portion to lay out swatches and sketches and so on. Anyway, I thought he'd lost his mind. But evidently he'd been leading up to it for all that time and fully expected me to fall into his arms. He said I'd been leading him on."

"What on earth did you do?"

"I threw him out of my bed. He wasn't terribly strong—a bit on the frail side—and I'm afraid I hurt him quite a bit. He hit his head on the dresser, you see. He accused me of trying to kill him.''

She shuddered, remembering how horrified, how humiliated, she'd felt. And how ugly Ken had turned.

"Surely he didn't fire you!" Abby exclaimed. "The last I heard, the Equal Employment Opportunity Commission had rules that made sexual harassment a violation of the Civil Rights Act.''

"Oh, he was aware of those rules," Vicki said tiredly. "He didn't make any threats about me losing my job. He just started a campaign to make me look inefficient. Drawings disappeared; stock didn't get delivered on time because the orders had 'gone astray'; appointments I'd made with clients were changed without my knowledge. I'd be waiting for them in my office while they were expecting me at their homes—that sort of thing. It was Josh who finally asked for my 'resignation.' I didn't blame him. Ken had made me look like an absolute idiot.''

"You could have told Josh the truth.''

Vicki managed a smile. "Yes, I could have. But he and Ken had been together for thirty years. They built the business from scratch after they graduated from university. Josh is a good man, a gentle man. He would have suffered a lot if I'd told him about Ken.''

"So *you* suffered instead.''

"I'm young enough to take it." Vicki smiled wryly. "At least, I *thought* I could take it. I didn't guess at the time that Ken's campaign to discredit me would continue. He led the other designers in town to believe that I was unreliable and incompetent. He even hinted that I had a habit of propositioning male

clients, and that I'd tried on many occasions to
seduce *him*. He was a respected man. People believed
him. I didn't know he'd spread rumors about me,
and for a while I couldn't understand why prospective employers kept leering at me. One of them even
offered me a job as his mistress.

"I'm good at my work, Abby. I had expected to
get another job immediately. When I finally figured
out what was going on, I faced Ken with his lies. He
admitted to them quite triumphantly." She sighed.
"I had no idea any man could be so vindictive. Pretty
naive of me." She made a face and tried to speak
more lightly. "So here I am and grateful to you for
offering me a job, conspiracy or not. Maybe by the
time I go home again, things will have improved."

"Well, I sure hope so!" During her niece's account
Abby's face had tightened with indignation. But now
she smiled sympathetically and patted Vicki's arm as
she stood up to ring for a maid to clear away the
dishes. "'It's an ill wind,' as they say," she remarked. "I can certainly use your help, and this will
be a great chance for us to get acquainted all over
again."

"I'm looking forward to that, too," Vicki said.
She felt suddenly drained by their discussion. The
wounds were still raw, but she was glad that she'd
managed to talk about it. Now she wouldn't have to
think about it again.

A few minutes later she and Abby descended the
stairs to the lobby to begin what Abby called a
"minitour." They started with the kitchen, a surprisingly modern affair of gleaming chrome and glass
that had all the latest appliances.

"Simon remodeled the kitchen before I came

along," Abby remarked. "It was one of Jean-Paul's stipulations—that the kitchens be brought up-to-date before he would consent to work here."

Jean-Paul, it transpired, was the head chef. Abby introduced him with great ceremony, announcing, to his evident satisfaction, that he was the most important person in the hotel, one on whom they all depended.

He was a surprisingly diminutive middle-aged man with black curly hair and a mustache, and snapping black eyes that gave him a youthful expression.

"You're the head chef?" Vicki exclaimed unthinkingly.

"You are surprised, *mademoiselle*," he said at once. "You think all chefs are fat, no, like this?" His hands described a circle around his slight body, and Vicki laughingly admitted that she had indeed thought so.

"It is often so that chefs are fat," he said blithely. "We must taste a little here, a little there, *n'est-ce pas?* But as you see, we have here a very long room, and Jean-Paul must run all day, back and fore, fore and back, making sure everything is just so. The English, you see—" he gestured disparagingly toward the long table where the kitchen staff were now eating their own dinner "—the English do not know how to cook. They make everything taste like mutton and cabbage. Unless it happens to *be* mutton and cabbage. That they make taste like suet pudding. Tell me, *mademoiselle*, have you ever eaten suet pudding?"

"No," Vicki admitted.

"That is very wise of you. The suet pudding lies in the stomach like a cannonball." He pointed to a tall red-haired man Abby had already introduced as the sous chef, Hugh Lester. "My underling there," he went on in a scornful voice that carried across the room, "*he* is in charge of meals for the saloon bar and for those guests who do not appreciate the delights of French cuisine. *He* makes the plowman's lunch and the shepherd's pie and the Yorkshire puddings. And, yes, the suet pudding."

Hugh Lester made a face at the chef, then cast his eyes toward the ceiling in a droll grimace for Vicki's benefit.

"On the other hand," Jean-Paul continued, dramatically pressing both hands to the breast of his starched white apron, "*my* taste buds were educated to finer things. You enjoyed my bouillabaisse and my *paupiettes* of flounder, no?"

"I certainly did," Vicki said truthfully.

She was rewarded with a beaming smile. "I sent the same dishes to Monsieur Jason Meredith," the chief confided to Abby. "He has sent down many compliments."

He put his hand over his mouth abruptly, as though afraid he had spoken out of turn.

Abby reassured him. "It's all right, Jean-Paul. My niece has already met Mr. Meredith. She know he's living here."

Does she ever, Vicki thought wryly.

Her facial expression must have betrayed her thoughts. Jean-Paul cocked his head and grinned impudently at her, but he didn't question her. "You, beautiful *mademoiselle*, will be welcome in my kitchen at any time. We must fatten you up, no?"

"No!" Vicki exclaimed in mock horror, at which

he threw both hands in the air and went back to join his colleagues.

"Jean-Paul must have fallen for you," Abby teased her as they headed down the hall, Abby's high heels clicking on the parquet floor. "Normally he doesn't invite anyone to his domain. I'm only allowed in on sufferance myself. Which I don't mind. Jean-Paul is a treasure. People even come from London to eat here. Jean-Paul is one of the main reasons we're usually filled to capacity, though the good fishing in our river and our historical associations have something to do with it, too."

She paused outside the open doors to the Blue Room. "We'll just glance in here, and then go down to the Wine Cellar for a liqueur," she said. "I often do that before I go to bed. It relaxes me and also gives me a chance to see if everything is going smoothly."

As far as Vicki could tell, everything seemed to be going smoothly tonight. There were only a few diners left in the Blue Room, lingering over demitasses of coffee, talking softly.

The room itself was of regal proportions, with heavy blue curtains, now closed, covering one long wall. Slightly worn light blue carpeting covered the floor up to a raised platform that held chairs and music stands, and which was framed by more blue draperies. The tables were covered with fringed blue cloths on which glass and cutlery gleamed in the light from several huge and remarkably ugly chandeliers. What a housekeeping chore to clean all those pieces of glass, Vicki thought, and what a shame to obscure that magnificent oak-beamed ceiling.

"This section of the hotel was last redesigned during the Victorian era," Abby was saying.

"Are you...*committed* to calling it the Blue Room?" Vicki asked in a hesitant voice.

Her aunt laughed. "Don't worry about hurting my feelings, dear. I told you I need your help. You'll find that in daylight this room is pretty shabby, so we might as well have a clean sweep. I'm looking forward to any suggestions you make. My Simon was a darling, but he resisted changes of any kind, even if they were obviously necessary."

She slipped a hand under Vicki's arm and turned her around. "Come along. I can see your mind working, and as I said before, there's no hurry. Let's have that drink."

Reluctantly Vicki allowed herself to be led downstairs to the Wine Cellar in the basement. As Abby had suspected, her mind was already visualizing ideas. The beamed ceiling must be preserved, of course, and she might even replace the carpeting in the same hue. But some other color must definitely be introduced, and those awful chandeliers would have to go. Individual candles on each table, perhaps. Candles in some kind of lanterns. Elizabethan lanterns? She'd need to do some research. Bookstores, there must be bookstores, or perhaps Abby had some books she could use.

She welcomed the influx of ideas. She was doing very well, she thought; she hadn't allowed Jason Meredith to enter her mind for at least ten minutes.

While she was still musing, she and Abby entered the Wine Cellar, and Abby introduced her to the head barman, a thin young man with a rather supercilious expression. Abby gave him as flattering a buildup as she'd given Jean-Paul, using almost the same words. "We couldn't get along without

George," she added. "There isn't a drink known to man or woman that he can't mix perfectly."

George smiled deferentially. He was obviously as pleased as the chef had been at Abby's praise, but more reserved about showing it. "Your usual, madam?" he asked.

"Drambuie," Abby agreed with relish. "Vicki?"

"Yes, please."

A fresh-complexioned girl in the costume of a Tudor serving wench led them to a table. The dimly lighted room wasn't very crowded, though it was fairly large and contained a number of round tables and comb-back chairs with cushioned seats. The bar was central, an oval shape open in the middle. Only George was on duty and one other waitress. A plump dark-haired woman was playing a piano and singing in a far corner of the room, beyond a small dance floor. The few people present were mostly ignoring her as they conversed in muted voices.

Sunday evening must not be one of the big nights in town, Vicki decided. But at least the atmosphere was restful. She was beginning to feel tired after her long and eventful day. Gratefully she accepted the drink the waitress brought and lifted it to her lips.

"What did you think of Jason Meredith?" Abby asked unexpectedly.

Vicki was just taking a sip of her liqueur, and the question startled her. A few drops of liquid splashed over the side of the small glass onto the table. She mopped them up with her cocktail napkin, aware that telltale color had immediately suffused her face.

"He seems very—well, he's all right, I guess," she managed, trying hard to recover her composure. Only seconds ago she'd congratulated herself on how well she was doing. Yet as soon as Abby mentioned Jason's name, she'd had a sudden vivid recollection of his mouth touching hers, his powerful hands burning against her spine. Desperately she searched her mind for something else to say. Abby had noticed her embarrassed reaction and was waiting with eyebrows raised for an explanation.

"I'm afraid I didn't recognize him when I saw him in your office," she said lamely at last.

"Hardly surprising," Abby said, still studying Vicki's face with alert hazel eyes. "He goes out of his way to avoid recognition. We don't advertise the fact that he's staying here, by the way," she added casually. "That's why I didn't introduce him to you. Some of the staff know he's in residence, of course, but we don't want word to get out, or we'll be swamped. He has quite a following."

She sipped her Drambuie pensively, then went on, "Jason is a very special person to me. He and Simon were great friends. They used to go fishing together when Jason was a boy. He was very kind to me when Simon died, so I'm glad to have a chance to return some favors. He tends to be reclusive when he's home, so I was amazed that you found your way into his rooms so quickly. How did that come about?"

Vicki felt her color deepening even more. She was glad of the dim lighting in the room. Obviously Jason hadn't told Abby about her bursting in on him, for which she was grateful. "We just happened to run into each other," she said evasively. "He invited me to have a drink."

"Uh-huh." Abby's eyes were twinkling now, but to Vicki's relief she didn't insist on more details. "An extraordinarily attractive man, isn't he? I've always thought that most stars are probably not what they seem to be—I imagine their magnetism disappears once they're away from the footlights—but Jason Meredith stays full-size. All that rugged masculinity is tremendously appealing, isn't it? And his voice ought to be classified as a deadly weapon. Did you notice his mouth? Positively sinful. Ah, to be ten years younger." She laughed. "Or even five." She tilted her head. "I'd be wary of his reputation if I were you, though, darling. Bit of a heartbreaker is our Jason. Not that I wonder at that; women flock to him like bees to the proverbial honey."

Vicki grimaced, remembering how she'd "flocked" herself. "It's true, then, his reputation? I've read stories...."

"Well, you can't believe everything you read in the columns, of course, but he does have a lusty appetite for women, there's no doubt about that." Abby sighed. "I've noticed throughout my long and observant life that if a man has a reputation as a womanizer, he usually cares little for women as people, but is more likely to treat them as objects or decorative conveniences. However, it's my own personal opinion that Jason has never quite recovered from Claire's death. And perhaps he never will. He was married to Claire Bellamy, you know—the opera singer. God, what an impossible woman she was. A miniature volcano, a magnificent singer, but an exasperating person. Simon never liked her, though he didn't let her know that, of course."

She laughed shortly. "Just listen to me. Gossiping about guests is something I never do. Very bad practice." Frowning, she pushed a few errant strands of hair away from her forehead, then shrugged. "Oh,

well, you're family, so it can't be called gossip.'' Her
gaze sharpened suddenly on Vicki's face. ''Do be
careful, honey. He *is* an awfully attractive man. If
he's decided to pay attention to you, you might find
him difficult to resist. And I'm quite sure he doesn't
ever intend to marry again. In fact, he's told me so—
emphatically. And platonic friendship isn't quite his
forte, not with a gorgeous young thing like you, anyway.''

''I can resist any man,'' Vicki said with forced
lightness.

''I'm sure you can, darling, if he's a *normal* man,
but Jason Meredith is—''

''Abnormal?''

''Above normal,'' Abby corrected. ''That's a lot
more man than most. Just be careful, okay? You've
a good head on your shoulders, but I have an idea
you are pretty vulnerable. I wouldn't want to see you
get hurt.''

''Good grief, Abby, all I did was have a drink with
the man.''

Abby grinned at her. ''All I did was say good-
morning to Simon, and the next thing I knew I was
being carried across the threshold of this hotel.'' She
laughed. ''Quit scowling at me, Vicki, I'm through
lecturing.''

She took another sip of Drambuie and set her glass
down. Her expression had suddenly grown worried
again. Abby had aged a little in the past few years,
Vicki saw. There were lines in her forehead that
hadn't been there before, and threads of gray in her
glossy brown hair. ''Is something wrong?'' Vicki
asked.

''Not really. I was just thinking about Portia. I

really don't know what Jason's going to do about that girl.''

Vicki sighed. She had hoped for a change of subject. But she *was* curious. "You said something about a prank," she prompted. "What did Portia do?"

Abby looked worried for a moment longer, then her face cleared, and she chuckled. "It really was quite creative." She paused. "In order for you to understand what she was up to, I'll have to explain our local legend. Have I ever written you about it?"

Vicki shook her head. "Tell me," she said, glad that she could relax her guard a little. This topic ought to be safe. "I want to learn all I can about the area, anyway," she continued. "I might be able to use the background to promote some ideas for the task you've set me."

Abby nodded. "You might at that. You're sure you're not too tired? All right, then. We have to go back to the eighteenth century. This inn was here, of course. The original was built in the late 1500s and was called The Gray Horse. It was quite small at the time, but later on, the houses on either side were incorporated into the inn. It must have been quite a sight—stabling for fifty horses, mail coaches rattling in and out. Traveling apothecaries used to set up shop here, offering to cure anything from gout to the pox. Whole armies were quartered here from time to time. Traveling troupes of players performed in the courtyard. Simon loved to speculate about the inn's history. And of course, there were the singing trees, from which we get our name. You must have seen them on the way in."

"Across the river? What kind are they?"

"Plane trees. Relatives of the American sycamore. They're actually on the grounds of Meredith Manor now, but our inn lays claim to the legend. Some say the trees are well over two hundred years old. Supposedly they were here during the Battle of Culloden in 1746, for that's when the legend dates back to. A young man of the town, it seems, went off to Scotland to fight, leaving behind his pregnant bride, Amanda. When rumors came that the battle was over, Amanda waited and waited for her young husband to come home. Instead, his groom galloped into town with the news that his master was dead.

"Amanda was brokenhearted. In her distraught state she decided she didn't want to live in a world that was suddenly so empty. One evening, just at twilight, she ran down to the river, fully prepared to throw herself in. But as she neared the water, so the story goes, she heard a strange sound. It seemed to her that the trees were singing. She stopped to marvel at the sound. If the trees could sing, she decided, then her husband could not be dead. She returned home, and sure enough, within a matter of hours her husband was brought in, wounded but very much alive. Since that day, whenever the trees sing, happiness is in store for those who are in love. And also since that day, this hotel has been known as The Singing Tree Inn."

"What a lovely story!" Vicki said. "It's unusual to have a legend with a happy ending. Do the trees really sing?"

Abby smiled. "Not exactly. When the breeze blows in the right direction, they make a kind of humming sound, something like the sound you sometimes hear on telephone wires out in the country. I've only heard them once myself. Strangely enough, it was the night Simon brought me here for the first time. So who knows? Maybe the legend is true. People hereabouts staunchly defend it, anyway.''

."What does the legend have to do with Portia?'' Vicki asked.

Abby laughed. "Like all good legends, this one has become embellished over the years. There are those in the town who swear they have seen the ghost of the pregnant Amanda under the trees by the river, dressed in a long white gown. So dear little Portia tied a pillow around her middle last night, put on a long white nightgown and went drifting and wailing under the trees. There was a full moon, so I guess the effect was pretty eerie. I didn't see her myself, but unfortunately one of the hotel guests did. He immediately had some kind of fit.''

"He thought she was a ghost?''

"So he said. According to George, he'd imbibed quite a bit—he's a whiskey-and-soda man, apparently. He was stumbling a little when he left the bar, so George offered to have someone show him to his room. But he said he wanted to get some air. He went out into the courtyard and down to the river, and there she was. Unfortunately he's quite an elderly man, and he went into shock. I thought he'd had a heart attack.''

"It's lucky he didn't fall into the river,'' Vicki commented.

"Don't think that didn't occur to me,'' Abby said with a shudder. "As it was, he collapsed in the courtyard. Another guest drove in and almost ran over him.''

"Good God, is he all right?''

"Apart from a mammoth hangover, he's in great shape. He was threatening to sue everyone in sight, but I charmed him out of that idea." She looked smug. "There *are* advantages to being a woman."

"Especially a good-looking woman," Vicki agreed in a teasing voice.

Abby wrinkled her nose. "Yes, well, it all ended okay, but I thought it best to call Jason down here, mainly to impress Portia with the potential gravity of the situation. It's not the first time she's made her presence known. Last week she got interested in magic and decided to whip one of the tablecloths off a table in the Blue Room without first removing the china and cutlery."

"Ouch!" Vicki exclaimed.

"Yes. Jason made good the breakage, naturally. He's such a dear, and so concerned about the girl . . . as he should be." She hesitated, her brow furrowing. "To be perfectly honest, Vicki, I'm not too sure that Portia didn't have something to do with the thefts we've had here."

"Oh, surely not. She's mischievous, perhaps, but—"

"The fact is, we didn't have any problems until she moved in, and she does have a way of roaming around the hotel and popping up in the most unexpected places." Abby shrugged. "She's bored, of course. Right now she's in school part of the time, thank God. What will happen after school vacation starts, I don't know."

"Her brother has confined her to the suite," Vicki said, not trusting herself to say Jason's name with any degree of indifference.

Abby sniffed disdainfully. "That will work only as

long as he himself is in residence. Mrs. Powell lets her have her own way in all things, and Portia can even twist Royce around her little finger." She sighed. "I hope I'm wrong about her. I want to be wrong. I like the girl. But I do know that Jason has had his hands full for the past few years. There were several instances of her playing with matches some years ago, and she got picked up for shoplifting a couple of times right here in the High Street when she was about ten years old, about the time I came here. Naturally the shopkeepers kept it quiet for Jason's sake."

"Many children shoplift at some time in their lives," Vicki protested, feeling a sudden need to defend the girl. "Just as almost every child has experimented with matches."

"Meredith Manor caught on fire," Abby reminded her.

"Surely you don't think...."

"I don't know, Vicki. Nobody knows. Portia denied all involvement, of course; what else would she do? And Jason accepted her word. But the fact remains that she was, very conveniently, the one who discovered the fire. Mrs. Powell was in the kitchen; David Brent, Jason's secretary, was in the study, working on some papers; Jason himself was napping in his bedroom. But instead of calling for help or alerting anyone, Portia tried to put the fire out herself—at least that's what she said. She panicked, she said; all she could think of was that she should try to smother the flames. By the time she did alert someone, half the top story was engulfed."

"People do panic," Vicki pointed out.

Abby smiled suddenly. "I guess Portia made a good impression on you."

"Not particularly. In fact, she seemed a little rude. But it can't be easy for her. No parents, and her brother such a celebrity. Kids closely related to celebrities often have major problems, you know. Look how many have committed suicide or turned to alcohol or drugs."

"Or crime," Abby interposed dryly.

Vicki sighed. "I suppose you may be right. And I'm not so sure Jason doesn't agree with you. He looked very bleak when I asked him if the fire was due to arson."

"You had quite a chat, didn't you?"

"Mostly about Portia," Vicki said defensively, but she felt color rising in her cheeks as Abby's eyebrows raised once again.

"Uh-huh," Abby said with a slight note of derision. Then she laughed. "I'm sorry, Vicki, I shouldn't tease you. As for Portia, for goodness' sake, don't go getting yourself involved. She's Jason's problem, not yours, and his secretary tries to keep an eye on her. Have you met David Brent yet?"

Vicki shook her head.

"I expect you will. A nice young man. About your own age." Her eyes narrowed as though a sudden thought had occurred to her, and she studied Vicki's face in a way that was familiar to the younger woman. Her own mother looked exactly like that when she was planning some matchmaking and didn't want her daughter to know about it in advance.

"No, you don't, Abigail Carstairs!" Vicki said firmly.

Her aunt's face immediately assumed an injured expression. "I was just making an observation," she said. "He *is* a nice young man. Quite handsome. And single," she added as an afterthought.

"I'm not in the market," Vicki reminded her.

"Uh-huh. Yes, dear, I know that. Of course. I'll say no more about it."

And for the rest of the evening she made no more references to David Brent or to Jason Meredith. Mostly she talked about "the old days" in Los Angeles.

But Vicki knew her well. Abby wouldn't rest until she brought Vicki and this David Brent together. Sooner or later, she thought grimly, she would have to take a firm stand with her aunt. She had come to England to do a job and to try to gather together the pieces of her shattered career.

It was going to take her a long time to get over those last few weeks in Los Angeles. She had felt so...so soiled, so ashamed, almost as though she had been guilty of the awful things Ken Marriott had said about her. No, she wasn't about to get involved in any kind of romantic entanglements. Not now, possibly not ever. Certainly not with a man who was Jason's secretary. And definitely not, she added to herself with what she hoped was firm conviction, definitely not with Jason Meredith himself. She laughed inwardly, suddenly realizing she was being presumptuous to say the least. There wasn't a ghost of a chance that a superstar like Jason Meredith was going to want to get entangled with *her*.

CHAPTER FOUR

DURING THE NEXT TWO WEEKS Vicki explored the hotel, dressed in her working "uniform" of dark linen pants, cotton shirt knotted at the waist and rolled-up sleeves. Her blond hair plaited into a single neat braid and tied with a narrow ribbon, she wandered in and out of the public rooms, carrying a large sketchbook in which she jotted down ideas and sketches. Most of the time she didn't notice other people around, she was so thoroughly engrossed, and the staff, with typical English courtesy, respected her concentration. If she did happen to glance up, though, when one of Abby's employees was passing, the man or woman would always smile in a friendly way and make some amicable remark, usually about the weather, which was wet most of the time.

She didn't see Jason Meredith at all, though one day at noon she saw his car pull out through the hotel archway. She was standing at the window of an empty guest room directly above, looking out at the steady drizzle of rain.

For a few minutes she had been gazing dreamily beyond the grassy oval toward a charming cottage across the street, thinking how much she would like to live in a little house like that. The building was now a boutique, but according to Abby, it had once housed a chair factory, of all things.

Vicki was well aware that she shouldn't be day-dreaming, that she had come in to study the room for possible improvements. But to her annoyance, when she saw the silver car, she couldn't resist opening the casement window and leaning out to watch Jason drive down the wide street. Her heartbeat had increased, and heat had invaded her whole body the moment she recognized the car.

Ridiculous behavior, she scolded herself, pulling the window closed with a snap. Deliberately she turned away from the street, leaned back against the windowsill and bent her head over her sketchbook. But within a few minutes she found herself sketching a profile view of Jason Meredith's face, trying to capture the arrogant angle of his head, the amused, sometimes bitter, twist to his full sensual mouth.

It was Portia's fault that her mind kept focusing on the actor, she decided. Portia had made up her mind that Vicki's work was fascinating. Every day after school, therefore, she hunted her out and dogged her footsteps, asking innumerable questions and chatting blithely about Jason. It had quickly become obvious to Vicki that the girl adored her much older brother, even though she resented the strict rules he laid down for her behavior.

"Jason had eight curtain calls last night," she would say proudly, or, "Jason is going to play Hamlet all next week. He's been playing Othello, you know. Of course, he's played both roles several times, so they are familiar to him, but he still feels he hasn't quite managed Hamlet the way he wants to. He's always reaching for perfection. He's terribly hard on himself."

Without being asked, she had also told Vicki all

about Jason's marriage to Claire Bellamy, describing in great detail Claire's penchant for throwing china at walls—and people, if they got in the way. "She finished off all the Belleek," she'd said with relish one day, "and she'd made a pretty good start on the Crown Derby before she was killed. She didn't care much for me," she had added laconically. "Luckily I had Mrs. Powell, so I wasn't neglected maternally."

On the subject of Claire's death she was fairly reticent, saying only that Jason had been devastated. "Which surprised me," she admitted. "I didn't think he was all that besotted with her. But of course, I was only a child then, and I didn't know anything about sex, so I didn't see why he put up with her. She *was* very sexy, I can see that now."

After this much too private glimpse into Jason Meredith's life, Vicki had tried to discourage Portia from discussing her brother. But the girl was incorrigible and insisted on telling Vicki about all the women her brother had been involved with since his wife's death. "Sabrina Lindstrom seems to be the latest," she had said scornfully the previous day. "I suppose she's pretty sexy, too, in her brittle way, but I wouldn't turn my back on her. She's not the type to be trusted. And anyway, she's married—though she doesn't seem to remember that when Jason's around."

Sabrina, Vicki remembered, was the woman Jason had been talking to on the telephone that first day. She'd heard his voice saying, "But Sabrina, darling...."

Why on earth did she feel that she disliked the woman, she wondered. She had only Portia's description to go by. It was ridiculous to feel animosity toward someone she hadn't even met.

Work, she ordered herself. In a couple of hours Portia would be searching her out again, and she wouldn't be able to concentrate. Not that she objected to the girl's company. Portia had long since apologized for her behavior the day of their meeting. She'd been feeling "grotty" she'd said, whatever that meant, and besides, she'd thought Vicki was going to be another one of Jason's silly women. Now that she realized her error, she hoped Vicki would be her friend. She'd always wanted to go to Los Angeles, she had added, but Jason wouldn't take her last year when he went to make a film there. He thought she shouldn't ever miss even a day of school.

Vicki felt sorry for the girl now that she knew her better. She was so obviously bored and lonely, especially as she was still confined to the hotel because of the ghost incident. That had only been a lark, she'd explained to Vicki; she thought it "grotty" that nobody else but her had a sense of humor. Although, she'd confided, Jason had had a hard time holding back a smile when he was scolding her about it. After all, it hadn't been *her* fault that the guest had drunk too much.

Jason was rarely home. "He's always slogging away at something, even when he's 'resting' between plays," Portia had complained. "Jason can't stand to sit around doing nothing. He's got a board meeting, or he's rehearsing for a television production, or reading scripts, or performing in benefits for charity. He takes fencing lessons all the time, too, and he rows with a team. Has to stay fit, you see. Some of those Shakespeare things are pretty grueling. When he does take time off, he starts messing around with Sabrina on that project of theirs.''

She hadn't spelled out exactly what the project was, and Vicki, though tempted, hadn't asked.

Jason couldn't really be counted as company for Portia, anyway, she thought. Twenty years her senior, he was more of a father figure to the girl than a companion. And Portia didn't seem to have friends her own age. ''They don't really see me as a person,'' she'd explained when Vicki questioned her about the girls at school. ''The teachers aren't any better. They're always trying to get me to take part in their plays and pageants so they can say they've got a Meredith in the cast. And of course, my name is Portia—my mother called me that because she was playing Portia in *The Merchant of Venice* when she found out she was pregnant. My teachers think anyone with a name like Portia *ought* to be an actress. So they get miffed when I won't have anything to do with their silly dramatics.''

She sighed. ''As for the girls, either they fawn all over me, hoping I'll bring them home to meet Jason, or they ignore me because they are quite sure I must be toffee nosed and think I'm better than anyone else. Actually I quite often *do* think I'm better than *them*,'' she'd added with what Vicki had come to recognize as characteristic honesty. ''I'm a bit of a snob, I suppose.''

Vicki had chosen not to comment, merely remarking that it was too bad people couldn't accept Portia for herself alone.

To which Portia had replied, astonished, ''But why should they? I'm not anybody. I don't even act. And I'm not going to.'' She shuddered melodramatically. "Acting would be a fate worse than death for me. Imagine having to pretend to be somebody else all the time. I have enough trouble being me. But the girls at school don't care what I want to be. All they can say is, 'Whoever heard of a Meredith who doesn't act?' Can't blame them, really. After all, I don't actually do anything. Don't know how to."

Remembering this conversation, Vicki decided that Portia's self-image needed refurbishing. It must be even more difficult to be a member of a famous family if you felt you had no particular skills of your own. And if Portia's account of Jason's rules for her behavior could be believed, she couldn't really blame the girl for feeling rebellious sometimes. In bed by nine on school nights, ten on weekends. No makeup. Extremely limited pocket money. No friends of the opposite sex. Portia might not yet be sixteen, but such an attitude was positively archaic.

At the same time, now that she knew Jason's sister quite well, she couldn't agree with Abby's suspicions about her. Portia might be something of a loner and inclined toward mischief, but she was an intelligent attractive girl, who was obviously just looking for attention—and affection. Vicki was quite sure she would never do anything to harm Jason or his public image. And her own account of her behavior at the fire had convinced Vicki that she was innocent of causing it. She'd been terrified, she'd said, and still felt guilty because she'd done all the wrong things. One of the firemen had assured her that many people's first instincts were to try to handle a blaze themselves, but that hadn't made her feel better. "I acted like a stupid child," she'd said bitterly.

Vicki sighed. She had to stop her obsession with the Merediths and get some work done.

She sat down on a chair and stared at the room plan she'd drawn up. Abby was right, some of the guest rooms weren't too well organized. Now, if she were to move that chest of drawers, put the bed so. . . .

By the middle of the afternoon she had accomplished quite a lot of work, after all, moving from room to room, making notes and drawing up ideas. She had just left the Blue Room, where the first few patrons were arriving for afternoon tea, when she ran into Portia in the hall.

It was the first time she'd seen the girl in her school uniform, for she usually went up to the Meredith suite and changed into blue jeans before seeking Vicki out. She looked younger than ever in her white blouse and her navy blue skirt and blazer. Her cream straw hat was jammed down over her forehead, and a bulging school satchel dragged down one shoulder. In her other hand she was swinging a tennis racket. "Any chance you'd like to play tennis?" she asked as Vicki paused to say hello. "There's a pretty good court in the park. It's not far, and the rain is easing off. I think Mrs. Powell would let me out if I was with you."

"Another time I'd love to," Vicki said. "I could certainly use the fresh air, for I've hardly been outside since I got here. I'll have to buy a racket, I guess."

Portia looked disappointed. "I suppose Jason's racket would be too heavy for you," she said slowly. "Can I watch you work, then?" she asked in a hopeful tone of voice.

"I'm through for the day," Vicki said apologetically. "My head is spinning with ideas, and I feel a need to sit down with a cup of tea somewhere and let my brain have a rest."

"We could give you tea," Portia said at once. "Mrs. Powell loves to have company."

Vicki searched her mind for an excuse. There was no logical reason for refusal. Abby was never available until dinnertime, hours away. And she'd already told the girl she was free. Portia looked so hopeful, so lonely, how could she disappoint her? Jason didn't get home until very late at night, she remembered suddenly. Portia had told her that several times.

"Okay," she said finally. "Tea would be nice."

Portia's elfin face lighted up. "Would you bring your guitar?" she asked shyly. "I'd love to hear you play. I've always wanted to play a guitar. I've had loads of piano lessons, but piano is dreadfully boring—all those scales and finger exercises. I should think a guitar would be much more fun."

"How did you know I played a guitar?" Vicki asked.

Portia's forehead puckered. "I suppose Jason must have told me."

Perhaps not unnaturally, Vicki felt flattered to think he'd spoken about her. But what else had he said, she wondered anxiously. Surely he hadn't told Portia about the scene they had enacted together that day? No, Portia wasn't the type to hold anything back. She'd have questioned Vicki about the incident if she'd known about it. She had already asked her several times if she didn't think Jason was the most divine-looking man in the world. All the girls at school thought so, she'd said. Vicki had grunted non-committally.

"I guess I could bring my guitar," she said reluctantly. Then, without thinking over the idea that had popped into her head, she added, "Perhaps I could give you a few lessons."

"Would you? Would you really?" Portia exclaimed.

Vicki had to smother a groan as she realized she had committed herself to spending even more time with the girl. But she couldn't back out now, not in the face of Portia's immediate excitement. "I'd be happy to," she said.

A FEW MINUTES LATER she was already regretting her promise. For when the Merediths' housekeeper opened the door to her, she found not only Royce, but Jason's secretary, David Brent, ensconced in the living room of the suite, invited by a still-excited Portia to hear Vicki's performance.

Royce stood up and inclined his head toward her in a very formal manner, giving her what she supposed was meant to be a friendly smile, though he still managed to look dignified. "How do you do, miss," he said in a voice like a BBC announcer. He looked exactly like the Hollywood stereotype of a British butler, she thought. Portia had told her he had other duties, though. While she was in school, he supervised the work at Meredith Manor. And he always escorted her to and from the bus she took to school. "He's acting as my bodyguard, you see," she'd explained dramatically.

David Brent was much younger than Royce, but no less formally dressed in a plain navy blue suit, pale blue shirt and striped tie. He also had that "look" about him, that air of an English gentleman, at once reserved and stiff and unapproachable. He was of average height and very slim, perhaps even a little too thin. He was resting one arm on the mantelpiece above the empty fireplace, his other hand in his trouser pocket. His fine hair was light brown and smoothly brushed from a side parting, his face thin and intelligent looking with prominent cheekbones. His eyes were an unremarkable pale blue.

Vicki felt uncomfortable as he came forward to shake her hand, probably because of Abby's comments about the young man's eligibility. Awkwardly she transferred her guitar to her left hand and shook hands with him. His grip was hesitant, his hand cool and rather bony.

"Portia has talked a good deal about you, Miss Dennison," he said. His English accent was precise and elegant, similar to Jason's. But his smile was shy, and she warmed to him because of it.

"Please call me Vicki," she suggested, and he agreed in his stilted way that he would indeed, and that she must call him David.

Mrs. Powell, a plump motherly looking woman in a severe black dress with a white lace collar, brought in a tea service on a silver tray. In her warm country-flavored voice she urged Portia to be "mum," which evidently meant she was to pour the tea.

Portia did so with great aplomb, looking perfectly at ease and very ladylike in spite of the fact that she was now dressed in her usual blue jeans and T-shirt.

Besides the rather strong tea, there was a platter of cucumber sandwiches cut into dainty triangles, a large toasted currant bun, which Portia called a tea cake, and some excellent sponge cake spread with strawberry jam. Portia did most of the talking during the short meal, explaining to Vicki that some of the furnishings and all of the paintings had been brought from Meredith Manor to make them feel more at home.

"I thought they looked...well, extravagant for a hotel," Vicki said.

"You should see the rest," Portia said gloomily. "We could furnish a museum if we wanted to. I would, if it were up to me. I'd throw the whole lot out. I rather fancy the modern look—you know, glass-cube tables, steel-framed furniture and bean bags, that sort of thing."

Vicki suppressed a shudder over Portia's idea of modern decor and changed the subject to the artworks on the walls, a conversation in which David and Royce joined knowledgeably. They both seemed to be thawing considerably.

As soon as the teapot was empty, Mrs. Powell cleared away the dishes, then sat down and beamed at Vicki. "You *are* going to play for us, love, aren't you?" she asked. "Miss Portia said you would. It will be a rare treat."

"I didn't really expect an audience," Vicki said, feeling a shade self-conscious.

"We aren't a critical audience," David said, smiling shyly. "And I'm afraid we fully expect you to sing for your supper, so to speak." He flushed a little as though abashed by his daring.

"Okay, then." Vicki reached for her guitar, settled herself on a large hassock near the fireplace and started to play. She began with her own arrangement of "Somewhere Over the Rainbow," which was fair-

ly intricate. Then she worked her way into some classical selections—one of Bach's church cantatas, a little Beethoven, and then the rousing "Ritual Fire
Dance."

When her rather oddly mixed audience demanded
more, she played "Greensleeves" to an Elizabethan
score she had adapted. The old tune seemed to fit her
surroundings, and now that she had lost her self-
consciousness, as she always did after she'd played
for a while, Vicki sang the ancient words. She wasn't
a great singer by any means, but she could carry a
tune, and she'd been told often that her husky voice
was a pleasure to listen to.

She had just begun the last verse when the outer
door to the suite was flung wide, and Jason Meredith
strode in, his tweed jacket flying open and his dark
hair untidy. Energy seemed to spark ahead of him
into the room, and he was complaining loudly about
the hellish traffic on the motorway.

Vicki broke off at once, and Royce and Mrs. Powell got nervously to their feet. But Jason, apparently
taking in the scene in one swift glance, waved them
down and told them all to carry on; he hadn't known
he was interrupting a concert.

"I was through, anyway," Vicki stammered, but
Portia wouldn't let her get away with the lie.

"She wasn't finished at all," she said to her
brother. "You must hear her, Jason. She's really
good; she plays as well as Julian Bream."

"I'd like very much to hear you," Jason said,
looking directly at Vicki. He had stopped just inside
the entranceway several yards away from her, and yet
when he looked at her, she felt as though he had
touched her. There was such intensity in those bril-

liant gray eyes. He was looking at her as though no one else in the room existed for him at that moment. It was very flattering, but disturbing. She was afraid his penetrating gaze could see right into her, see the turmoil his sudden appearance had caused inside her. For a long moment she was unable to look away. There seemed to be a stillness in the room, or perhaps it was just that her pulse was beating so loudly in her ears that she couldn't hear anything else.

Someone must have moved, because when Jason seated himself in the chair she had occupied on her last visit to this room, Mrs. Powell handed him a full teacup. She must have gone out to the kitchen to make more tea. When had she done that, Vicki wondered. And why did she, Vicki, have these lapses of consciousness when Jason Meredith was around?

He was still looking at her, one eyebrow raised now, as if to remind her he was waiting to be entertained. His mouth was curving as though he were about to smile.

Vicki made an effort and averted her gaze. If he smiled at her, she wouldn't be able to sing a note.

She didn't look at him at all while she finished the song and was relieved when she reached the end. To her surprise, however, her voice had sounded quite strong and confident, though perhaps a little huskier than usual.

Portia applauded vigorously at the end, then immediately demanded that Vicki begin giving her the lesson she'd promised.

"Not now," her brother said sternly. "You must have homework to do."

"Only some Latin and a composition," Portia protested.

"Is that all?" His voice was loaded with sarcasm.

"But Jason," Portia pleaded to no avail. Jason kept his stern gaze directed at her until at last she flounced out, muttering under her breath about tyrants.

Vicki started to rise to her feet. Royce and Mrs. Powell had melted away into the kitchen, and David Brent was standing hesitantly in front of the fireplace, as though he wanted to speak to his employer.

"Please don't go yet, Victoria," Jason said, surprising her. As was becoming her habit in his presence, she subsided obediently. "Did you have letters for me to sign?" he asked David.

The young man nodded. "Yes, sir. There's some correspondence about the Derringham theater that should go out in the evening post."

"You did the letter for Sabrina?" At David's nod, he grunted and stood up. "I might as well see to it," he said impatiently. "Victoria won't mind waiting." With that he strode from the room without a backward glance.

Vicki looked at David, who was gazing at her rather ruefully. "Does he always expect instant obedience?" she asked indignantly.

He smiled noncommittally. Of course, Vicki thought, feeling suddenly embarrassed, she could hardly expect him to agree with criticism of his employer.

"Mr. Meredith is a busy man," he said carefully. "He's very...punctilious. If something needs to be attended to, he believes in taking care of it at once so that he can put it out of his mind. He doesn't intend any rudeness, I'm sure."

"David," Jason called in an impatient voice from

beyond the hall, and the young man gave her an apologetic smile. "Excuse me, please, Vicki."

At the archway he turned and looked at her gravely. "Thank you for the music. It was, as Mrs. Powell said, a rare treat." He hesitated. "I hope I'll see you again soon."

"I expect so," Vicki said. "Portia's not going to forget those guitar lessons."

"No, indeed." He seemed about to say more, but then with a final shy smile he turned and left the room.

A nice young man, Vicki thought—and as Abby had said, quite a handsome one, if a bit on the stiff side. She was fully aware that he'd thought her attractive. He'd kept his gaze on her during her entire performance, and there had been no mistaking the shy approval in his eyes. Rather a gentle person, she thought, sensitive and well-bred. But not the kind of man she'd want to encourage, not her type at all.

What *was* her type, she wondered as she continued to sit there, obediently waiting for the lord and master of the Meredith household to return. In college she'd gone steady with the captain of the varsity baseball team, and later she'd dated, among others, a race-car driver, an Olympic skier and a young man who jogged eight miles every day and ate only raw vegetables and fruit. All these men had ever seemed to want from her was meaningless sex, which she'd refused them, and not too much conversation. And while she enjoyed sports and outdoor activities, she hadn't ever wanted to dedicate her *life* to them.

She had dated other types of men, of course—men who shared her interests in reading, music, museum browsing and anything to do with the arts. Many of

them had become her very good friends. But so far
she hadn't met anyone she wanted to marry. She
especially didn't want to spend her life with a chau-
vinistic man, one who thought he could order her
around. And yet she wasn't usually attracted to more
malleable men who were too easily awed by her—
men like David Brent.

Probably Jason Meredith came closer than anyone
she'd ever met to combining all the traits she liked.
He was obviously a physical man, and yet he was also
dedicated to the arts. Portia had told her he was a
voracious reader, and that he enjoyed symphony
concerts and the opera and showings at the Tate
Gallery.

Unfortunately he was also a high-handed type. The
mere fact that she had some things in common with
him didn't mean she should go about thinking of him
all the time or letting herself be affected by his
magnetism, or whatever it was that kept striking her
into paralytic subservience. Why on earth was she sitting here waiting for him now? She sighed. Because
she wanted to, obviously.

Apparently she was suffering from a case of arrest-
ed development. During her teens she had never worshiped at the shrines of rock or movie stars as many
of her contemporaries had. She had never belonged
to a fan club or gone searching Los Angeles for the
current sex symbols who might be out and about. In
fact, when her girl friends had done so, she had often
wondered why they were making such a fuss. Now
she knew. Jason Meredith was a superstar, and she'd
evidently developed a king-size crush on him. She
could only hope that it would pass soon, for it was a
very disquieting state to be in.

Still waiting, she began to finger the strings of the guitar. Soon she was engrossed in picking out "Lara's Theme" from *Doctor Zhivago*, not consciously remembering it as a love song. It was some time before she realized Jason had come back into the room and was standing there, both hands resting on the back of the crimson couch, studying her intently while she played.

With a slightly self-conscious laugh she laid the guitar aside and attempted a smile. "I'm sorry, I didn't know you were back," she said.

He didn't seem to have heard her. He was still gazing at her with those penetrating gray eyes, as though he were trying to make up his mind about something. At last he shrugged and came around the sofa to sit down. "It's rather an odd thing," he said slowly. "When you...burst in here that day in your lovely green dress, my first thought was that here was Lady Greensleeves come to call. And now today you were playing that song. It's one of my favorites, actually. Did you know that the words are attributed to Henry VIII?"

Without waiting for an answer, he leaned his dark head back against the sofa and closed his eyes, intoning softly:

"Alas, my love, you do me wrong,
To cast me off discourteously,
And I have loved you so long,
Delighting in your company.
Greensleeves was all my joy,
Greensleeves was my delight,
Greensleeves was my heart of gold,
And who but Lady Greensleeves?"

His rich voice made its own music for the words and gave them a new and deeper meaning. She waited, hoping he would continue, but instead, he suddenly opened his eyes and caught her gazing raptly at him. "Quite a coincidence, isn't it?" he asked, holding her glance while his own eyes seemed to darken.

"I guess so," she stammered.

He was looking very thoughtful again, as though searching for the right words before saying whatever was on his mind. "What do you think of Derringham?" he asked at last.

"It's a pretty town, what I've seen of it. I haven't explored it yet. I've been too busy. I didn't even realize it had a theater."

"It doesn't."

"But David said. . . ."

His eyebrows lifted at her use of his secretary's first name, but he didn't comment. "Actually I'm in the process of getting together a repertory theater for Derringham, but we don't have a building yet. All we have is a plot of land, a foundation stone and a lot of good people. Christopher Hammond is in it with me—you've heard of him? He's one of the best young actors in the country, a tremendous talent. And his wife, Susan Carmody, is also on the board, and many others."

Including Sabrina, Vicki wondered. Was this the project Portia had mentioned?

"It will be a workshop, as well as a theater," Jason continued. "It's intended to encourage some of the younger actors and playwrights." He hesitated, then darted an amused glance at her. "Like our friend of the other day."

She was not going to blush, Vicki told herself, no

matter how many allusions he made to their last meeting.

She was relieved all the same when he returned to their earlier topic. "Derringham is a pleasant town," he said. "You should see some of it as soon as you have the opportunity."

"I intend to."

"How about this evening?"

The question had come so abruptly that she wasn't sure she'd heard him correctly. "This evening?" she repeated stupidly.

"With me." His smile was disarming. "In my clumsy way, Victoria, I'm asking you to have dinner with me. Not here at the hotel, but at The Black Swan Inn—you've seen it, perhaps?"

Stunned, she nodded. "I saw it on the way here, but—"

"The Black Swan serves traditional English food, which often comes in for a lot of criticism. I assure you it's quite palatable, though perhaps high in calories. Dennis Fotheringham, the proprietor, prides himself on his porkpies and sausage rolls and steak-and-kidney pudding. I'm sure you would enjoy the meal. I like to go there because it's not much frequented by tourists, and the local people leave me in peace. They've known me since I was born, after all, so they aren't terribly impressed by me. I thought perhaps we could stroll down to Derringham church. The rain has stopped, and it looks as though we'll have a pleasant evening. Parts of the church date back to the thirteenth century, and it's well worth a visit. There's a particularly fine east window. After that we could have a pint or two in Dennis's pub before dinner." He hesitated. "There's something I'd like to discuss with you, away from here." He looked around the room, then back at her. "What do you say?"

How could she refuse Jason Meredith? "I'd like to see the church," she said slowly. "And dinner would be nice, but—"

"Fine," he said, standing up, not giving her a chance to ask what he could possibly want to discuss with her.

Awkwardly she stood up also, clutching her guitar. "When. . . what time should I be ready?"

He looked surprised. "Now?"

"I—right now?"

"Why not?"

Now that she was committed, there were a dozen reasons that she could think of, not the least of which was the fact that, standing so close to him, she was aware of him in a way she had never been aware of a man before, aware of his strength, his solidness, his magnetism. It was as though the air around him were charged with electricity. He was so totally masculine, so absolutely sure of himself, so. . . dictatorial. Probably it had never occurred to him that she might refuse him. Well, she could hardly expect him not to be conceited. He had a lot to be conceited about.

"Don't you have a performance tonight?" she asked abruptly.

He shook his head. "The company is performing *As You Like It* this week. I won't be on until Monday, when *Hamlet* begins. I have a board meeting coming up tomorrow, and then some rehearsals, but I'm at loose ends tonight."

At loose ends. She could hear Portia's voice in her

mind saying, *Jason can't stand to sit around doing nothing.*

Was he asking her out because he was bored?

"What did you want to talk to me about?" she asked.

The question brought her an enigmatic smile. "I'll tell you later. You ought to have dinner in you first, make you more amenable."

"That sounds...ominous," she said hesitantly.

He shrugged, but didn't elucidate. "Shall we go?" he asked, smiling his devastating smile.

"I...I'll need to change. And Abby...I have to let Abby know...."

"You look exactly right for The Black Swan," he said promptly, after a swift all-encompassing glance at her knotted white shirt and tight dark pants. "You might need a jacket, perhaps, to keep the evening chill out. We can pick one up for you and tell Abby you're dining out at the same time."

Was she really going to let him take over her evening just because he had nothing else to do, Vicki wondered as he went out to inform Mrs. Powell of his plans. It seemed that she was. She couldn't think of any objections to offer. It was too late to remind herself that she had firmly and sensibly decided not to get involved with any man while she was here, especially not with one who could so easily demolish her emotional well-being.

She was reminded suddenly of a time in her college days when one of those athletic boyfriends of hers had persuaded her to try skydiving. She was suffering now from the same kind of terrified exhilaration she'd experienced when the time came to separate herself from the airplane.

She was courting disaster, she thought helplessly as he returned, putting his arm casually around her shoulders to steer her toward the door and incidentally starting up a whole new sequence of fiery sensations in her nervous system. But it was too late now to have second thoughts. She had agreed to go out with him, and her whole traitorous body was alive with anticipation. She was poised in the doorway of the airplane, about to jump into the unknown, and there was no way she could retreat now.

CHAPTER FIVE

IT WAS A WHILE before Jason told her what had prompted his invitation. Obviously, Vicki decided later, he had felt it was necessary to charm her before dropping his bombshell.

And charm her he did. First, with a kind of self-deprecating humor he demonstrated his method of getting out of the hotel undetected. There was a narrow back staircase at the other end of the hall from the Merediths' suite that Vicki hadn't noticed in her explorations. From there, he told her, with an absurdly furtive portrayal of the way he looked at such times, he usually ducked out a side door to the car park. But today, he said, straightening up, they would first use the staircase to go up to Abby's apartment so that she could drop off her guitar and pick up a jacket. She was smiling as she preceded him up the stairs. She had exaggerated the threat to her emotional safety, she thought with relief. Jason Meredith promised to be good company—amusing company—nothing more.

While she repaired her makeup and brushed out her hair, she could hear him talking to Abby in the next room, explaining very precisely that he'd invited Victoria out to dinner on the spur of the moment, and that he wouldn't keep her out too late.

Yes, she'd definitely exaggerated the danger,

though she did wonder why he felt it so necessary to set Abby's mind at rest. The older woman had looked a little surprised to see them together, but she hadn't commented, though from the thoughtful look in her wide hazel eyes Vicki had received the impression that she was going to be in for some motherly advice later on.

But when she emerged from her bedroom, Abby was talking easily, telling Jason that she planned to work this evening with her accountant. "You wouldn't believe how much paperwork a hotel generates," she was saying with an expression of mock despair on her face.

"I can imagine," Jason said with a sidelong glance at Vicki, obviously thinking of the fake form he'd filled out with her statistics.

Abby intercepted the glance and immediately looked anxious, but when they left, she merely said, "Enjoy yourselves, you two."

Vicki knew her aunt well. She was fairly certain that Abby was adding two and two together and coming up with six. She would have to set her straight later, explain that there was nothing between Jason Meredith and herself. Which there wasn't, of course.

As they descended the narrow stairs, Jason produced his tweed hat and sunglasses from a jacket pocket, apologizing for the fact that it was best for him to wear them out in the street. She had an idea he rather enjoyed assuming his disguise and was sure of it when he tilted his head and smiled at her in a boyishly appealing way, as though inviting her approval.

"You look like Rex Harrison playing Henry Higgins in *My Fair Lady*," she told him, relieved that she was feeling relaxed enough to tease *him* for a change.

He looked absurdly pleased. "I carry a tune as well as Rex does, too," he said and proceeded to prove it by singing "The Rain in Spain" under his breath as they crossed the street.

He was certainly in good spirits, she thought, and her own spirits felt unaccountably high. Probably because she was outside for the first time in days. The air smelled marvelously fresh after all the recent rain, and the sky was a pristine blue with only a few slashes of white cloud. The sun was low in the sky, adding a few pink streaks of its own. There was a chill breeze, however, and she was glad she'd worn a jacket.

Beside her, Jason took a deep breath and exhaled it, evidently enjoying the fresh air, too. As they walked along the wide sidewalk toward the churchyard, and she tried to ignore the fluttering sensations his hand on her elbow was generating throughout her body, she noticed that none of the people they passed gave him a second glance.

"I guess your disguise fools everybody," she said as he opened a small wrought-iron gate and stood back for her to enter the churchyard.

"Not the people who really know me," he admitted. "But it has been known to dupe an American tourist or two." His smile flashed at her, taking the sting out of the teasing comment.

"I was hardly expecting to see Jason Meredith sitting in my Aunt Abby's office," she retorted defensively.

"No one expects to see an actor walking around in public," he said with a crooked smile. "That's why it takes very little in the way of disguise. Unless he's blatantly obvious about himself, he can get away with it. And of course, in public, I turn myself off."

"You do what?"

He smiled wickedly. "I'll show you."

They had been walking up a narrow path between some ancient-looking headstones. Just ahead, an elderly couple wearing plastic raincoats were taking photographs of the church's squat square tower, exclaiming about the way the stark gray stone showed up against the pink-and-white-streaked sky. "Try to get that lovely window in there," the woman was advising her partner in a pronounced cockney accent. As Jason and Vicki approached, she glanced at them, then glanced away disinterestedly.

But as they stepped off the path to go around the couple, Jason, walking ahead of Vicki, made some indefinable change in his posture, adopting a walk that was not exactly swaggering, but somehow more commanding. Until that moment she hadn't realized he'd been walking along in a rather slouched manner. Now his shoulders were erect, his head at that arrogant angle she'd tried to capture in her sketchbook.

Both the man and his wife glanced at him casually as he passed. Then they exchanged startled glances, did a decidedly humorous double take and gasped in unison. "It's 'im," the woman said in an awed whisper. "It's Jason Meredith. From the telly."

The man nodded, staring. Jason touched his hat brim and kept walking, Vicki behind him. The woman recovered faster than her husband. Grabbing the camera from his hand, she called after Jason, "Ooh, Mr. Meredith, could I take a picture?"

"Why not?" he said graciously, turning to smile at her. "Where would you like me to pose?"

"Ooh, right there's fine," she said breathlessly. "If you wouldn't mind taking off your glasses and maybe your 'at, or the girls at bingo won't believe it's really you.''

"Of course," Jason said, obliging at once.

"Q.E.D.," he said to Vicki after the picture was taken. He had also graciously consented to sign his autograph "for the grandchildren in Shepherd's Bush." They were entering the church now, leaving behind a very delighted pair of old people. "I used to put Q.E.D. on all my mathematics papers at school," he explained. "It stands for *quod erat demonstrandum*, which means, loosely translated, 'which has been proven.' "

"It has, indeed," Vicki said laughing. "I'm impressed."

"Don't misunderstand me," he said, suddenly serious again. "I'm not belittling the people who get excited when they see me. Without fans I'd be like the tree that falls in the forest when nobody is there—I wouldn't make any sound at all. An actor must have an audience, or he's just a demented person standing in a corner talking to himself and making grandiose gestures. All the same, one can't stay on stage all the time. Hence the disguise." He hesitated. "I wouldn't want you to think it's a matter of conceit. I want you to like me."

She glanced at him, startled. He was looking at her with a solemnly questioning expression on his face, his gray gaze penetrating. "I did think for a while that you were conceited," she admitted.

His laughter rang out, echoing against the ancient stone walls. "Do you always tell the truth, Victoria?"

"I try to, yes."

"I admire your candor. It's a refreshing change.

You're the first person who's ever told me to my face that I have too high an opinion of myself.''

"Well, I don't believe it now," she said firmly. That was also the truth. With those few words about his attitude toward his fans, he'd made himself much more human and definitely likable. "And of course, I like you," she added awkwardly.

"I like you, too, Victoria," he said warmly. "You are a genuine person, I think." He paused. "I know few really genuine people. Abby is one of them, and Simon was...." Those disconcertingly piercing gray eyes were studying her face again. It seemed as though he were about to say something even more personal. Tension filled her in immediate response, but then he apparently changed his mind and made some mild comment about continuing their tour. She was able to turn away then and make some equally casual comment in return.

But now she began wondering in earnest about his reason for inviting her out. She was still pondering possibilities when she realized they had stopped again, and that Jason was attempting to draw her attention to some medieval brass figures, a man and a woman, which were inlaid in the floor. They represented an earl and his lady who had lived hereabouts, he told her. Their identity had been lost in antiquity, though his father had been sure they must be Merediths. "My father had a bit of a nobility complex," he told her. "He always wanted to believe there was a belted earl or a baron in the family tree somewhere. He regretted the fact that his own knighthood could not be passed on to me. He rather fancied himself as the founder of a dynasty."

"Perhaps you'll be the founder of a dynasty yourself," she suggested, beginning to relax again.

"Not I," he said with a mock shudder. "I'm no believer in marriage and family life."

His voice had sounded more emphatic than seemed called for, Vicki thought. Was he warning her not to get romantic ideas?

Before she could reply, he cocked an eyebrow at her. "Are you unencumbered, also, Victoria? Or is a fiancé waiting in the wings, ready to drag you back to America?"

"No fiancé," she said firmly and added to straighten him out, "I'm a career woman, too independent for marriage."

"How intelligent of you." He was smiling at her as though she'd just passed a difficult test of some kind. What was he up to, she wondered. She couldn't get away from the feeling that he was up to *something*.

Feeling suddenly uneasy, she looked back at the floor, concentrating her gaze on the stiffly posed figures. The man was in armor, the woman in full court dress, but both lay on their backs, hands folded in prayerful attitudes on their respective breasts. Their facial expressions were devoutly pious. "They look terribly formal," she said.

"Don't you believe it," he said cheerfully. "A lot of frolicking went on in those days." He glanced at her sideways, raising his marvelously mobile eyebrows. Once again she had the feeling he was about to say something personal. This time she was right. "Does that shock you?" he asked. "The idea of frolicking, I mean."

How could she possibly answer that?

He seemed to realize he'd disconcerted her again,

and he shrugged and changed the subject. "Portia tells me you're very artistic," he said briskly. "You might ask the vicar if he'll let you do some rubbings of the brasses, if that sort of thing appeals to you. Most churches don't allow it anymore. Too many tourists have rubbed the surfaces off too many brasses all over the country. Most of them supply replicas now. But if you tell the vicar you're a friend of mine, he'll give permission, I'm sure. Portia would probably like to show you how it's done." His head lifted. "Speaking of the vicar," he said softly. He was looking toward the rear of the church, and now Vicki could hear footsteps approaching from what seemed to be some distance away.

"Let's go," Jason said. Before she could react, he took hold of her hand and pulled her out of the building. Once outside, he kept her moving, hurrying her along the path to the gate, not allowing her to slow down until they were back on the sidewalk. "Whew, that was close," he muttered.

"What have you got against the vicar?" she asked curiously. "Are you afraid he'll take you to task for your sins?"

He grinned at her, a mischievous little-boy grin that brought a smile to her own lips. "You've been listening to gossip," he accused. "As a matter of fact, Bram Seaton and I are the best of friends. But the annual Derringham country fair is coming up soon, and he wants me to take part in the opening ceremonies—cut a ribbon or some such foolishness. I've done it before, but I've no intention of making such an exhibition of myself again. However, Bram can be terribly persuasive, so I've been avoiding him."

He grinned again. "It's about time we had that beer, isn't it? I'm sure you must be curious about the proposition I have for you."

Before Vicki could respond, she found herself being escorted firmly through a door and up a short flight of stairs into the saloon bar of The Black Swan Inn.

But still she was kept in ignorance of Jason's plans for her. As soon as they sat down at a table in the barroom, the proprietor came over to be introduced, carrying a huge foaming tankard of beer that he'd drawn the instant he saw Jason. In his other hand he carried a smaller version, which he set down in front of Vicki before holding out a slightly damp hand. "One of your lasses from London?" he asked Jason with a wink of one bright blue eye. He was a rather stout man with tufts of bushy ginger hair over his ears, but no hair at all on top. His cheery smile widened approvingly as he shook hands with Vicki.

"America," Jason said through a mouthful of foam. "She's Abigail's niece from Los Angeles. This is Dennis Fotheringham," he told Vicki. "He's one of the original stouthearted yeomen of England."

Dennis laughed, showing very large white teeth, then immediately launched into what was evidently a long-standing argument with Jason about the relative merits of various cricket teams. After a few minutes he brought himself a tankard of beer and sat down opposite them. There was no chance for her to question Jason. Resigned to more waiting, Vicki sipped her slightly warm beer and looked around the pub's interior, idly admiring the profusion of brass objects, the pewter tankards and toby jugs that hung from the rafters and the paneled walls. *Proposition,* she thought. What kind of proposition could Jason have in mind?

She found out after they'd eaten their meal. She'd opted for a steak-and-kidney pie, which was served in an oval dish complete with a china blackbird poking through the crust. She found the pie deliciously savory, though far too filling. Jason had dined just as well on a huge veal pie. She couldn't fault his table manners, which were superb, but he had obviously enjoyed every bite. A man with a lusty appetite, she thought, and immediately remembered Abby's warning that his appetite extended to women.

She looked at him nervously as he ordered coffee for them both. He seemed completely at home here, she thought. The superstar had given way to the country squire. What an unpredictable man he was! Sometimes he was like a mischievous small boy, sometimes the arrogant star, sometimes the charming gallant. Which was the real Jason Meredith? *You have remarkably beautiful eyes,* her memory repeated.

She'd noticed that he hadn't put his hat and sunglasses back on since the woman in the churchyard took his photograph, not even since they came into the pub. Evidently he felt it wasn't necessary to hide his identity here. She had noticed, too, that as the local people wandered in, they glanced at Jason and looked pleased to see him there, but they didn't intrude on his privacy. For a short time two young women had hovered in his vicinity after they entered, looking as though they hoped he would glance up and speak to them. But Jason, happily drinking beer and talking, was too involved in his argument with Dennis to notice. After a while a young man perched on a stool at the bar had yelled at the women to stop acting like a pair of loons and come and sit down.

Jason had remained oblivious to them all, and to Vicki, too, until he suddenly decided it was time to eat. But since they'd moved to this corner banquette in one of the bowed-and-mullioned windows that hung out over the High Street, he'd set himself to be a charming and attentive host, regaling her with stories of the mishaps that befell every stage production he'd ever been involved in.

Now, as coffee was served to them by a buxom young waitress in a short cotton dress, he smiled at Vicki in a very friendly manner and lighted a cigarette.

"Dinner all right?" he asked.

"Fine," she said tersely, frowning, feeling that the moment of truth had arrived. He had turned on the upholstered bench and was looking at her rather uncertainly. She was pretty sure Jason Meredith was not often uncertain of himself. Here it comes, she thought nervously.

"Does my smoking bother you?" he asked. Evidently he'd mistaken her frown for disapproval.

"No, not at all. You don't seem to smoke much, anyway."

"I can't. The breath, you see. Some of the Shakespearean speeches are pretty long, and I can't take a chance on getting winded."

She nodded, still tensely waiting, but when he did speak again, he spoke of Portia. For an awful moment she was afraid the proposition was going to turn out to be a request for her to befriend his sister. As though she needed to be asked....

"I understand Portia has been following you

around," he said. "I hope she's not making a nuisance of herself?"

"Not at all," she replied warily.

"I'm relieved." He laughed. "She's been giving me daily reports of your progress through the hotel. No doubt she entertains you with similar stories about me?"

"She admires you very much," Vicki said evasively.

"Mmm, yes. If she had as much respect for me as a guardian as she does for my acting ability, we'd all be much better off, but I suppose one can't ask for everything. I'm grateful to you for being patient with her. She also admires *you*, by the way. She thinks you are sexy. That's her favorite accolade at the moment."

Vicki grimaced.

"You don't like to be called sexy?"

She gave an embarrassed laugh. "I guess nobody really minds being thought...sexy," she said slowly. "But—"

"But there's a lot more to you than the way you look, and you want people to know it?"

"Something like that, yes."

He smiled. "I know what you mean. I suffer from a little of that myself."

She felt embarrassed again. In a way, *she* had put him into that category. She managed a smile. "Abby always says it's only important to recognize your own capabilities," she told him.

"Abby's a wise woman."

"Yes."

He looked at her over the rim of his cup as he sipped his coffee. "I wanted to ask you...."

He paused and Vicki braced herself.

"You mentioned that you hadn't seen *Hamlet* on the stage. I wondered how you'd feel about coming to a performance as my guest."

"Me?" she asked stupidly.

"You."

"Oh. With Portia you mean?"

"No, not with Portia. Alone." He hesitated. "Actually not alone. We'd have lunch first with another couple, then perhaps do a few sights in London and go on to the theater. On Monday, I thought. That's the first performance of the new run. It's a shortened version of *Hamlet*, of course. No one has the patience to sit still for four and a quarter hours nowadays."

The *first* performance. She would see him in person, on the stage, as Hamlet. At the old and highly venerated English Theatre. She'd heard about it, read about it. "I'd love to go," she said warmly.

He looked relieved. "That's marvelous," he said with a winning smile.

There was something about that smile that bothered her. It didn't seem quite genuine. And why should he look relieved? Why had he referred to an invitation to see him perform—an invitation any woman would give her eyeteeth for—as a *proposition*? And why on earth had he made such a mystery of it? Why couldn't he have asked her at the hotel in front of Portia and David, and anyone else who was around?

"What's the catch?" she blurted out.

He looked taken aback and thoroughly guilty.

"I'd forgotten how direct you are," he murmured, pushing his fingers through his hair.

"Then there is a catch?" To cover her sudden feeling of disappointment she picked up her cup and took a sip of coffee.

"A slight one, I'm afraid. You see, I want you to... well, perform a role for me, act a part."

"As what?"

"My fiancée."

She almost choked on the coffee. "Why on earth—"

"I've got myself in a bit of a pickle, I'm afraid." He was looking at her very earnestly, his gray eyes clear and candid.

"I think you'd better explain," Vicki said faintly, setting down her cup.

He proceeded to do so, and as she realized what he was asking of her and the reason for it, she felt more and more indignant. She also felt extremely stupid for having thought for one moment that he had asked her to the theater because he wanted her, Vicki Dennison, to see him perform. How foolish she had been, worrying about damage to her emotions. The only damage here was to her pride!

The other couple he'd referred to, he told her hesitantly, were Sig and Sabrina Lindstrom, who had been friends of his for years. Unfortunately—his word—Sabrina Lindstrom was a strikingly attractive woman. And Sig was a jealous man. Somehow Sig had come up with the idea that Jason and Sabrina were having an affair, a suggestion Jason ridiculed as completely unfounded. Vicki wondered about that, remembering again his voice saying, "But Sabrina, darling..." on the telephone.

"What does all of this have to do with me?" she asked when he paused for a moment.

He gave her his boyishly appealing smile, and she decided suspiciously that he was again deliberately playing a role, trying to make her feel sympathetic toward him for the way he'd been misunderstood. This whole evening, the visit to the church, the charming conversation through dinner, the dinner itself, had obviously been intended to disarm her, to make her fall in with his plans.

"I'm afraid I told Sig I was engaged to you," he admitted.

She sat up very straight on the bench, suddenly seeing the whole sordid picture quite clearly. "Let me see if I've got this straight," she said flatly. "You figured that if this man, Sig, thought you were engaged to me, he'd be less suspicious of your relationship with his wife?"

"Exactly." He was beaming at her again as though she'd been particularly bright. "The idea came to me in a flash when Sig was making wounded-husband noises. I didn't really mean to involve you. All I said was that I'd hardly be making love to his wife when I was engaged to marry someone else. He immediately demanded to know who I was engaged *to*, and yours was the first name that came to mind. I'd met you so recently, you see, and been absolutely charmed by you. It was easy enough to convince Sig that we'd fallen in love when I was in Hollywood last year. I told him you were rather shy and didn't want a lot of publicity, so we'd kept our engagement a secret."

Had he really been charmed by her, she wondered. Or had he thrown that in as an added inducement? "Very inventive," she managed.

He didn't seem to notice her sarcasm. "Unfortunately," he continued, "Sig then suggested I bring you to meet him and Sabrina on Monday. They'd already arranged to go to the theater. It would be nice, he said, if we could all lunch together and introduce you to some of London's attractions. That way he and Sabrina could get to know you.''

"It sounds as though he wasn't as convinced as you say.''

He smiled at her ruefully. "Sig *is* a bit of a cynic. But you do see the spot I'm in?''

"I do indeed.'' She took a deep breath. "Tell me, what exactly *is* your relationship with Sabrina?'' When he hesitated, she added tartly, "Don't you think that as your fiancée, I have a right to know?''

"You'll do it, then? Oh, bless you, Victoria. I'll be eternally grateful.''

"Wait a minute. I haven't said I'll do it. I asked a question.''

His disappointment might have seemed comic if she hadn't still felt so indignant over the way he'd used her and still intended to use her. After a moment he nodded, as though he agreed with her right to know the truth. "Sabrina and I met five or six years ago. We were both involved in a campaign to save London's theaters, many of which were being threatened by redevelopment schemes,'' he explained. "Sabrina is a drama critic. She's quite influential, and she's been very kind to me. She will be my literary adviser when the Derringham theater gets off the ground—advising on the commissioning of new works. She's planning in advance so that we'll have a balance of comedy, tragedy, classical and modern and so on. Sabrina also has a lot of ideas on the actual theater building. Because of this, we've been spending a lot of time together...consulting.''

"You're saying your relationship is all business."

"Absolutely." Again his gaze was candid. Too candid?

"And Sig?" she asked. "Why is it so important that he believe in your innocence? Surely he wouldn't shoot you?"

"No, but he probably would decide to withdraw. . . ." He hesitated, then continued very rapidly. "Sig's a merchant banker, you see. In America you'd call him an investment banker. He has offices here and in New York. He's very wealthy. And he also happens to be executive director of a private foundation that provides grants for worthy projects. He's promised a sizable contribution to our theater."

"So it comes down to money?"

"In a way."

She might almost have felt better if he'd confessed that he really was madly in love with Sabrina. To ask her to deceive someone for the sake of money. . . .

"It's not for myself, you understand," he went on hastily. "The theater is a very good cause, Victoria, and will also be a sound business proposition. And I do assure you that Sig's suspicions are totally unfounded."

Again his gray eyes were clear and candid. He was an actor, Vicki reminded herself, a very *good* actor.

"Will you do it?" he urged. "It's only for one day, and no one else will know. I've told them both our engagement's to remain a secret right up to the actual wedding day, a year or so away. And I would very much enjoy your company—apart from any other considerations."

Without her noticing it, he had picked up her hand in his and was idly stroking the back of it with one finger. He was looking at her with an appealing expression in those fine gray eyes of his, that endearingly crooked smile hovering around the corners of his full sensual mouth.

Vicki's indignation faded as abruptly as it had come. "I imagine," she said, to give herself time to think—an impossibility while he was holding her hand so gently between his "—I imagine Sabrina must have been rather surprised by your announcement of our engagement."

His smile turned rueful. "That she was."

His answer gave her immense satisfaction. It might be rather pleasing at that, she thought suddenly, to appear in front of Sabrina as Jason's official fiancée. *Sexy in her brittle way,* Portia had characterized the woman, and Vicki's mind had formed a picture of a prototypical femme fatale.

But of course, she couldn't lend herself to such a deception. And she had every right to feel furious with Jason for the underhanded way he'd gone about this whole affair. As soon as she'd realized exactly what he wanted her to do, she had started mentally rehearsing all the most cutting ways she could say no. And yet. . . .

How marvelous it would be to spend a day in London with Jason Meredith! How exciting to see him perform. No doubt, she would be invited to go backstage afterward. She'd meet the other actors—Christopher Hammond was playing Laertes, Portia had told her, and his wife, Susan Carmody, was Ophelia. She'd catch a glimpse of life behind the scenes at a great theater. All she had to do was pretend for one day. . . .

But no, she couldn't possibly. She looked directly

at Jason, hardening her heart against that boyishly appealing smile, still determined to say no. But instead, she found herself recklessly throwing caution to the winds. She *had* jumped, after all, from that airplane—and once committed, she had thoroughly enjoyed the adventurous experience.

"I'll do it," she said and immediately found herself being enthusiastically hugged.

CHAPTER SIX

THE RESTAURANT the Lindstroms had chosen was in the Knightsbridge district of London, not far from the world-famous Harrods store. It was a disconcertingly elegant establishment, featuring a procession of tall gilded mirrors on the pastel walls, a forest of marble pillars and ceilings that were elaborately embellished with stucco rosettes and garlands. Vicki imagined the decor might rival that of Louis XIV's palace in Versailles. The atmosphere was as formal and hushed as the interior of a cathedral.

Vicki and Jason were "received" with due ceremony by a tail-coated waiter, who could have been a twin for Royce. After a courtly bow he led them in stately progression past dozens of dazzlingly white-draped tables and carved and gilded chairs. Most of these were occupied by business-suited men or expensively attired women conversing in low cultured voices. Obviously none of them would dream of looking up to see what dignitary might be passing.

The carpeting seemed to be several inches thick. Vicki felt her spirits sinking with every step. For once she was glad of Jason's hand at her elbow and unaware of any emotional response to his touch. She was suddenly feeling extremely nervous.

She had dressed carefully for this meeting. Jason had suggested a suit, and she'd picked out her most

attractive one, a slim-skirted cream-colored linen
that emphasized her California suntan. With it she
wore an apricot silk shirt, black high-heeled pumps
and her favorite purse, an Anne Klein black leather
shoulder bag. Her hair was coiled around her head in
a style she'd found in *Vogue*, and her makeup was as
flawless as she could make it.

But in spite of all her preparations, she felt insig-
nificant when faced with the sophisticated-looking
couple who awaited them at a small table in a private
alcove at the far end of the room.

Sig Lindstrom stood up to greet them in a pleasant
but reserved voice that held just a trace of his Scandinavian origins. He was an extremely tall slender
man with thinning fair hair brushed carefully over his
scalp. As he and Jason shook hands, Vicki was
struck by the contrast between the two men. Both
were wearing well-cut expensive-looking suits,
though Sig's was of a lighter gray and pin-striped.
But Sig's jacket was buttoned, where Jason's was flying open as usual. Sig's tie was tightly knotted;
Jason's was beginning to work loose. Jason was always well dressed, but he never quite looked put
together. He had started out this morning with neatly
brushed brown hair, but already it was tumbling in
an unruly fashion over his wide forehead, thanks to
his habit of raking one hand through it while he was
talking, as though to emphasize his words. Sig was a
more meticulous type. Of the two styles, she thought,
she preferred Jason's.

"You really do exist," Sig said dryly as he bowed
formally to Vicki. His smile was on the wintry side,
she thought, and his blue eyes held rather a hard
light. His face was lined, but he was a good-looking
man, elegant and enigmatic.

Sabrina, who appeared to be several years younger than her husband, remained seated, smoking a cigarette in an ebony holder. She looked up at Vicki through narrowed eyes with the calculating expression some women get when they sense competition. Vicki had the feeling that she had immediately totaled up the cost of her outfit and had dismissed it as negligible, then had gone on to guess the modest size of the split-level house Vicki had grown up in, the background of her parents and grandparents, and their probable income to within five or ten percent.

Sabrina herself was about thirty. She was not conventionally beautiful, but she was the most dramatically stylish woman Vicki had seen outside the pages of *Harper's Bazaar*. She obviously had a strong sense of her own unique style, as well. She used little makeup on her alabaster pale skin, only a slash of dusky blusher under cheekbones that would have done justice to a fashion model. A trace of plum eyeshadow created effective hollows at the corners of her dark eyes, and a glistening lip gloss defined her thin but well-shaped mouth. Her strongly marked eyebrows and long thick eyelashes required no artificial enhancement, and her black hair was glossy smooth, beautifully cut, drawn back from a center parting to curve like commas around her ears. She was wearing a simple black raw-silk suit that said haute couture in every superbly cut line. No blouse interfered with the view of her formidable cleavage. She was immaculate, well-groomed, sensational. Vicki disliked her on sight.

Probably, she thought later, she'd already been conditioned by Portia to dislike the woman. But even so, after suffering through that one raking glance that had eliminated her as competition, she would have reacted negatively, anyway.

The woman was polite enough. After darting a seductive glance at Jason, one that ought to have sent his blood pressure soaring, she drawled, "How do you do," in a light unmistakably British voice. She patted the seat of the ornately carved chair beside her, insisting Vicki should sit with her so that they could talk. "I've always found Americans to be *fascinating*," she said. "They are always so *outspoken*, so *forthright*, a refreshing contrast to our British reserve."

After which, of course, Vicki could think of nothing at all to say. She cast a helpless glance at Jason, but he was busily supervising the pouring of wine into crystal glasses and gave her no help at all.

"It's *astonishing* that you and Jason have been engaged all this time without telling a soul," Sabrina continued with an enthusiasm that didn't sound at all genuine. "It's terribly naughty of Jason to deceive us, but we've quite forgiven him now that he's consented to present you to us."

She paused for a dainty sip of wine. Vicki followed suit, feeling a distinct need for some Dutch courage.

Sabrina had turned toward her again, her beautifully shaped eyebrows arching over eyes that were so dark it was impossible to tell where the pupil ended and the iris began. "You *are* going to show me your ring, aren't you, my dear?" she asked.

Vicki set down her glass and swallowed. "My ring," she echoed flatly.

Luckily Jason had overheard Sabrina's question. "There isn't a ring yet," he said easily while Vicki was still racking her brains for an answer. "I'm having one designed at Cartier's. An emerald, of course, to match Victoria's marvelous eyes.''

He reached across the table to cover Vicki's hand with his own, gazing at her with the same utterly tender expression that had so overwhelmed her during their last acting performance. His grip was reassuring, comforting, and she automatically turned her hand over to clasp his. The pressure of his fingers increased at once, and he smiled warmly. She felt suddenly distanced from the others, as though they had faded into the background, leaving her and Jason alone in their own private world. His eyes held hers.

''Such a charming name, Victoria,'' Sabrina mused beside her. ''Reminiscent of strings of jet beads and long frocks with bustles.''

Vicki came back to herself and her surroundings, but couldn't quite manage to tear her gaze from Jason's. He was still holding her hand, his fingers exerting a subtle pressure that was quickening her senses to an alarming degree. Yet why should she feel alarmed, she thought suddenly. She was *supposed* to be a dewy-eyed girl madly in love with the man of her dreams. She didn't have to hide her reactions at all; she had to exaggerate them. Accordingly she let her eyes warm with affection, and she curled her fingers even more tightly around his.

His gaze continued to hold hers, his gray eyes luminous, his mouth still curved in that so genuine-looking tender smile. ''Victoria's not at all old-fashioned,'' he said in a fond tone. ''She's very much a contemporary woman, bright and independent, and excruciatingly honest. Those are the qualities I love most about her.''

Sig favored him with a laconic smile. ''She's also

damn good to look at, Jason," he said dryly. "Haven't you noticed?"

"I've noticed," Jason said emphatically,

> ". . . her beauty makes
> This vault a feasting presence full of light."

With another melting smile he lifted Vicki's hand to his lips and kissed it lingeringly.

Sabrina stubbed out her cigarette in a crystal ash-tray and exhaled sharply. "If you're going to quote *Romeo and Juliet*, Jason, I shall have to leave." Her voice was light, but there was an undercurrent of irritation in her tone. "You know it's not one of my favorite plays. Nor yours, either—you've always refused to play Romeo because you considered him such a ninny."

Jason was apparently unconcerned by Sabrina's remarks. "That's not the case at all," he protested mildly. "I've merely felt that *I* should look like a ninny trying to play a sixteen-year-old in the grip of adolescent love. Though the role has become more appealing since I met Victoria," he added with yet another adoring smile.

Vicki drew her hand reluctantly from his and immediately clasped both hands in her lap to hide their trembling. If Jason continued to act like this, she would have trouble remembering this was all a charade.

She had expected, of course, that he would behave lovingly in front of the other couple. In the car, driving up to London, he had explained to her that they must put on a good show in order to still any lingering doubts Sig might have. What she hadn't expected was that she would find it difficult not to be taken in herself. Her body was responding to his words and touch and loving glances in a way that was totally at odds with logic. For a moment there, when he kissed her hand, her blood had literally sung in her ears, and a wave of heat was still traveling from her scalp down through her body to her toes.

"Where exactly did you young lovers meet?" Sig asked, looking directly at Vicki.

She exchanged a startled glance with Jason. This was a question neither of them had anticipated.

Luckily a waiter arrived at that moment with their hors d'oeuvres. To give herself time, Vicki spread pâté on a dainty square of toast and sampled it thoughtfully. "This is delicious," she said, managing to smile at Sig. "I guess I haven't thanked you and Sabrina for inviting me to join you. It was kind of you. This is a beautiful restaurant."

Sig produced a thin smile. "Your meeting place is a secret?"

"Not at all," Jason said easily. His eyes met Vicki's in a conspiratorial way. "We'll have to tell them, darling, no matter how silly it sounds."

While she was still looking at him blankly, he began telling an authentic-sounding tale of their meeting—in Disneyland, of all places. They had been "queuing up" to get into the haunted mansion, he explained airily. Vicki's escort, it seemed, had somehow got lost in the crowd, and she and Jason had ended up in the same carriage or whatever the thing was called, without any connivance on their part.

While the four of them ate their way through smoked salmon, fillets of lamb in Madeira sauce, a mixed vegetable that resembled ratatouille and two kinds of green salad, he went on to describe their ensuing ride in great and colorful detail, so vividly that Vicki found herself reliving the whole imaginary experience. Jason was obviously totally caught up in the absurd fairy tale he'd created, his mobile features reflecting in turn expressions of nostalgia, amusement and enthusiasm.

They had had to part after the ride, he explained, because Vicki's escort had, quite understandably, taken charge of her as soon as they emerged from the hall of mirrors. But they had managed to exchange telephone numbers. "The rest is history," he concluded.

Sig was nodding and smiling quite warmly now, obviously completely deceived. "How enchanting," he exclaimed with a chuckle. "Only to you, Jason, could such a romantic thing happen."

Sabrina also appeared to believe the story, though she wasn't smiling at all.

How inventive Jason was, Vicki thought. He had created a whole believable background for their supposed romance. Who could be suspected of making up an encounter in Disneyland?

His inventiveness made her realize that she ought to be very much on guard with this man. The line between fantasy and reality seemed to be very thin in his mind, and he could step easily from one side to the other. Not a surprising trait for an actor to possess, of course, but one that made it necessary to pause before trusting in anything he might say. However, it was very difficult for her to bear this in mind as long as he was flashing her those amorous glances and pressing her knee with his under the table.

She was relieved when the conversation changed

with dessert—a fabulous *gâteau* with pieces of man-
darin orange in it—especially when the discussion
turned away from her and gave her time to recover her
composure. She was feeling very peculiar, she decided, a little light-headed, as though her brain's oxygen
supply had diminished. It was not an unpleasant sensation. Probably her slight case of vertigo was due to
the wine she'd drunk and the unusually large lunch.
Jason had explained earlier that when he was working,
he ate a bigger midday meal and a light snack later so
that he wouldn't feel lethargic during a performance.

Yes, that was it. Too much food in the middle of
the day. Her bemusement had nothing to do with the
irresistible attractiveness of the ruggedly handsome
and charmingly devious man sitting opposite her.

And yet, what an endearing rogue he was, to be
sure. It was impossible to keep from smiling back at
him as he continued to gaze so tenderly at her, his
gray eyes guileless. This playacting was turning out to
be fun, after all; she had become quite absorbed in
her role. It was hard for her to concentrate on the
conversation, but she really must try....

Sabrina was describing to Jason a recent garden
party at Buckingham Palace. "Once you've seen one,
you've seen them all," she observed in an aside to
Vicki. "Quite a bore, actually, with everyone standing around in circles staring at the queen. But there's
nothing else to do."

Impressed by this evidence of sophistication, Vicki
managed at last to tear her gaze from Jason's face.
She listened attentively as Sabrina went on to talk
about the London theatrical scene in a way that
showed she knew the luminaries involved.

Evidently dear Glenda Jackson was giving a sublime performance as Rose at the Duke of York's Theatre. Yul Brynner was drawing raves for the revival of *The King and I* at the Palladium, and Joan Collins had just opened in *The Last of Mrs. Cheyney*. The 1920s decor used for this play included original posters provided by Cinzano, who had also supplied two bottles of champagne for every box taken during the run.

Somehow these inside glimpses of Sabrina's glamorous world added to Vicki's feeling of unreality, so much so that when Sig abruptly asked her how she was spending her time in England, she answered without thinking that she was advising her Aunt Abigail on the remodeling of her hotel, The Singing Tree Inn.

"But that's in Derringham!" Sig exclaimed.

"Yes," Vicki replied blankly, wondering why he seemed so surprised.

"What an unbelievable coincidence that you should have a relative living so near to Jason's home."

For a second, Vicki thought the whole charade was at an end, but once again Jason covered the situation smoothly. "Isn't it?" he agreed. "But, of course, that's what drew Vicki and me together. When we met, she recognized my English accent and told me about her Aunt Abigail who lived in Derringham. I've known Abigail for years, so we immediately had something in common. And that's why I moved into Abby's hotel after the fire. It's a very small world, isn't it?"

Once again Vicki had to admire his aplomb. But then she noticed with a sinking sensation that although Sig looked satisfied, Sabrina was regarding

Jason suspiciously, her eyes narrowed so that only a dark gleam showed through her thick lashes.

Yet there was no reason for her to worry, Vicki reminded herself. This was Jason's masquerade more than hers. All the same, she was relieved when Sabrina shrugged carelessly and fished another cigarette out of a slim gold case. It would be very embarrassing if the deception was discovered right then and there.

But she had to stop believing in this hoax herself, she cautioned herself a moment later. She'd felt quite disturbed when Jason produced a lighter and leaned over to light Sabrina's cigarette, especially when the other woman's red-lacquered fingernails rested lightly on the back of his hand, ostensibly to steady the flame. She couldn't help noticing the caressing movement of Sabrina's long slim fingers over his, but she had no business feeling so annoyed and so...proprietary. Nor had she any right to feel smug when they all stood up to leave, and Jason slipped his hand under *her* arm. She was letting the success of their joint performance go to her head.

To avoid the problem of struggling through London's traffic, Jason suggested they call a taxi for their sight-seeing trip. Over coffee Sig and Jason had decided that they should concentrate on the Tower of London, to prepare Vicki for tonight's play. Not that there was much similarity between England's Tower and the castle at Elsinore, Sig explained. But after mulling on the fates of Anne Boleyn, Thomas More and others who had been executed there, she would be in the proper melancholy frame of mind for a performance of *Hamlet*.

Evidently Sig had decided to be friendly. Perhaps

now that his mind was at rest, he felt he could afford to be less suspicious, more outgoing and genial. He continued to be pleasant as they took a quick look at Buckingham Palace, then rode past St. James's Park, Big Ben and the Houses of Parliament. After a brief but impressive glimpse of St. Paul's Cathedral, they drove directly to the Tower, a medieval complex of castellated and domed buildings that comprised a fortress of massive proportions.

Helping Vicki from the cab, Jason put on his sunglasses, probably more for their protection as a disguise than to guard his eyes from the sunlight, she thought. As they waited while Sig paid the driver, he placed an arm around her shoulders, his fingers brushing lightly against her upper arm in a movement she felt all the way through her linen jacket sleeve and the thin fabric of her blouse. She couldn't suppress an involuntary shiver. His grip tightened, and she glanced up at his face, feeling suddenly breathless and confused again by the turmoil his merest touch could stir in her.

He was smiling approvingly at her. "You're doing well," he said, bending to kiss her cheek—for Sig's benefit, she supposed. "I told you you were meant to be an actress."

What would his reaction be, Vicki wondered, if he knew that her response to him was not part of this elaborate pretense? Right this minute, for example, she had to restrain herself from reaching up to touch the place on her cheek his lips had caressed.

Sabrina was walking on Vicki's other side. Her slim hand was thrust possessively under Sig's arm, but her attention was focused coldly on Jason and Vicki. She had evidently noticed their byplay. "Such tours as this usually bore me to tears," she said to Jason. "Sight-seeing is so terribly plebeian, isn't it? But I expect Vicki will enjoy it immensely."

Vicki didn't even try to figure out the implications inherent in that remark. She could barely cope with her reactions to Jason without worrying about possible insults from Sabrina. And anyway, she decided, plebeian or not, English history had always fascinated her. She would concentrate on that aspect of this visit and not on anything else.

After the guards at the gate had searched their belongings, a custom that had become necessary at all public buildings because of terrorist activities, they began their tour.

They started with the White Tower, which housed the chapel of St. John, a wonderful example of pure Norman architecture. This tower also contained a huge collection of arms and armor, and instruments of torture. As Vicki might have expected, Jason knew a great deal about English history, and he entertained her with all kinds of fascinating stories as they moved on to the Traitors' Gate, an enormous arch below the outer walls. "A multitude of prisoners passed through this portcullis on their final journey," he told her with apparent relish, still holding her close to his side. He informed her cheerfully that the delightful Tower Green, where happy tourists were posing for photographs with some of the colorfully dressed yeoman warders, popularly known as "beefeaters," had once been the site of the scaffold where the most distinguished prisoners had met their end.

From there it seemed a natural progression to go to the Bloody Tower, where King Richard III allegedly murdered his two young nephews, the "little princes," in 1483. "I've played Richard," Jason said lightly. "Not a sterling character at all. But villains are much more intriguing than heroes, don't you think?"

She felt it safer not to answer that. With Sig and Sabrina trailing behind, they strolled on to view the gruesome-looking block where Anne Boleyn had lost her head. An ax and sword were positioned nearby.

"There was so much cruelty in those days," Vicki observed.

"There still is," Jason said. "That's why we have to love one another whenever we can."

She glanced at him, surprised by the sudden solemnity of his tone. "Is that your general philosophy of life?" she asked lightly.

"It is." His smile was breezy, but there was a questioning look in his gray eyes that she didn't quite understand—and wasn't sure she wanted to.

There was probably a lesson to be learned here, she thought as she caught herself watching Jason's face. She was enjoying the dramatic cadences of his vibrant voice as he described Anne Boleyn's last days. Something was happening to the wall of emotional detachment she'd thought was so firmly in place. There was no doubt in her mind now that Jason Meredith was the most dynamically attractive man she had ever known. And since he'd set himself to prove to all onlookers that Vicki Dennison was the only woman in the world for him, the likelihood of losing her own head was increasing by the hour. It was difficult under any circumstances to withstand Jason's charm. When he was holding her this close, lavishing upon her the full force of his personality, he was impossible to resist.

With a total disregard for possible consequences, she impulsively decided not to worry about her emotions for the rest of the tour. This was a glorious summer day, in spite of the cool breeze coming from the River Thames. She was in London, a city that was itself casting a spell on her. And she had as her sight-seeing guide the most attractive, most exciting escort any woman could hope to have. Why should she keep on reminding herself that Jason's attentions were all part of an act? Why shouldn't she just enjoy him while she had the chance?

"Are you enjoying yourself, Victoria?" he asked as they recrossed the Tower Green. He could even read her mind, it seemed.

"I am," she said, smiling up at him, abandoning all caution and letting her growing attraction to him show in her eyes.

"So am I," he said softly, taking off his sunglasses. "I've never felt so relaxed before a performance. Usually I'm a mass of nerves, growling at everyone, ricocheting from the walls. I'll probably be a disaster tonight."

He didn't really seem to be thinking about what he was saying, however. She wondered what he *was* thinking. He was looking at her steadily, his pewter gray eyes brilliant with some powerful emotion. Desire? Surely not. Sig and Sabrina weren't even watching; they were walking ahead. Vicki was suddenly convinced that Jason wasn't acting any more than she was. The idea was a new one, and quite terrifying.

Eventually he replaced his glasses, smiled and pointed out some huge black ravens that were strutting across the green. His hand had slipped down to the small of her back and was absentmindedly mas-saging her spine, causing chaos in her nervous system. "There is a prophecy that should the ravens ever leave the Tower, England will fall to a foreign power," he told her, apparently unaware of his hand's stroking motion.

Sig added in an amused voice, "However, Vicki, the ravens' wings have been clipped so they cannot fly away. And if one dies, it is immediately re-placed." He smiled briefly. "The Britons believe in insuring their traditions."

Jason inclined his head, smiling, but his hand had stilled against Vicki's spine, and she felt he wasn't really amused. He was proud of his heritage, she thought, as he had a right to be. Portia had told her that their ancestors had lived in Meredith Manor for two hundred years, and they could trace their lineage back to the time of William the Conqueror, the king who had founded this stronghold.

She wished she knew her own background beyond her great grandparents. They had gone to the United States as immigrants, one pair from France, another from Finland, the rest from—yes, of course—from England. So this was all part of her own heritage, too. The thought caused her to take a proprietary in-terest in the remainder of the tour.

The afternoon was over all too soon. Crowds of tourists had descended upon the place, forming long patient lines at the entranceways of every building. Vicki would have gladly waited with them as long as Jason was beside her, but he was due at the theater, he said regretfully at last.

Vicki was abruptly conscious of time running out. In a few hours this day would be over, never to be repeated. It was a disturbingly depressing thought.

But there was still the play to come, she reminded herself as Jason hailed a cab outside the Tower gates. She would have to spend some time alone with Sig and Sabrina—over the tea that had been arranged for them at the theater. It was a prospect she wasn't looking forward to, but after that there would be the play and then the drive home alone with Jason.

A whisper of caution flickered through her mind. She was behaving like a child, rationing out treats. She was anticipating too much, enjoying too much. Tomorrow—no, she was not going to think about it. Tomorrow could take care of itself.

CHAPTER SEVEN

SHE NEEDN'T HAVE WORRIED about being alone with the Lindstroms, after all. Perhaps conscious of Sig's watchful presence, Sabrina set herself to be charming. She told Vicki quite a lot about her background—the schools she'd attended in Switzerland, the glamorous aspects of her job as a drama critic, the marvelous people she came in contact with from day to day. All of this was a little intimidating, especially because she spoke of her experiences casually, as though they were not at all unusual.

Sig opened up a little, too, and tried to explain his business interests to Vicki. She hadn't ever really thought of a bank as anything except a building with tellers doling out money to customers, and she was fascinated by the finer points of international corporations making complicated deals involving millions of dollars or pounds or francs. Sig seemed happy to answer her questions, and he didn't talk down to her.

The time passed quickly and fairly pleasantly, and she was pleased to find herself liking Sig more. She still couldn't relax completely with Sabrina, however, any more than Sabrina could apparently relax with her.

There was only one awkward moment. It came when Sig mentioned Claire, Jason's former wife, wanting to know if Vicki had ever heard her sing.

"No," she told him. "I've read about her, though. She must have been very talented."

"She was indeed. She made her debut in Giuseppe Verdi's *La Forza del Destino* at Covent Garden. I was there. Such a huge voice from that tiny little girl. She couldn't have been more than seventeen."

"She was twenty," Sabrina said flatly. "She lied about her age early so that she wouldn't have to amend it later."

Husband and wife exchanged a glance that made Vicki shiver; there was so much hostility in it. "You never did like Claire," he said with an edge to his voice.

"But, darling, why on earth shouldn't I have liked her? You've told me so many times how wonderful and beautiful and marvelous she was; what an angel she was to put up with Jason. Of course I liked Claire! I revere her sainted memory."

Sig's eyes narrowed. But then he seemed to remember Vicki's presence, and the moment passed without further discord.

After tea and a chance to freshen up for the evening in the theater-manager's private bathroom, Vicki was astonished and delighted to find that the Lindstroms had engaged a box for the performance. "I feel like royalty," she declared after entering, looking happily around at the throngs of people in the auditorium.

"I'm afraid not, Vicki," Sig said, smiling indulgently at her. "The royal box is traditionally on the right-hand side of the theater—there, you see. But you can still be noticed. Everyone will be asking who is the beautiful blond young lady with the glorious

suntan and brilliant green eyes. You will be the sensation of the evening.''

Sabrina didn't seem to approve of Sig's gentle
teasing. Her mouth had set in a hard straight line.
Probably, Vicki thought, she'd had enough of male
attention going to someone other than herself. No,
that was catty; Sig was her husband, after all, and
he had sounded definitely flirtatious.

"Have you seen Jason perform in *Hamlet* before?" she asked Sabrina as she seated herself, trying
to ease the atmosphere.

Sabrina didn't bother to reply, but merely smiled
thinly, leaving Vicki feeling that she'd been guilty of
the most ingenuous behavior. She *was* ingenuous, she
supposed, but there was nothing wrong with that. Being in this marvelous old theater, with its great dome
and its fine Victorian auditorium, eminently regal in
red, gold and cream, was very exciting to her. She
wasn't going to pretend to be sophisticated and blasé.

A moment later the houselights dimmed and went
out, and she stopped concerning herself with
Sabrina's opinion of her. The vast auditorium had
hushed, and she sensed an electric excitement in the
air. *Hamlet* was about to begin.

Vicki had loved the theater since she was a small
child and was taken to see a performance of Tchai-
kovsky's *Nutcracker Suite*. At home in Los Angeles
she went to see as many plays as she could manage in
a year, and had never understood how some people
could be content with television or movies. There was
no comparison, she felt. A piece of film projected on
a screen might tell the same story, but the magic was
missing—that almost tangible sense of being drawn
into the action.

The performance was superb. From the moment the first actors appeared on stage, two sentinels coming from opposite directions to meet on a platform outside the castle at Elsinore, Vicki was not a spectator, but a participant in the wonderful drama. When the second scene began, Jason walked onto the stage and set it alight with his presence. He looked different, unfamiliar in his funereal black doublet and hose. But she soon forgot the transformation in his appearance, forgot that he was Jason Meredith. He was Hamlet, sensitive and bitter and introspective, reeling from the shock of his father's murder and his mother's marriage to his Uncle Claudius. Having already succumbed to melancholy, he had then been repulsed by Ophelia, and all of life had grown dark to his vision.

It was a rare and marvelous performance. He didn't rant and rave, but created his effects with discipline and control, every line rhythmically articulated with clarity and resonance. Even when he whispered, Vicki could feel the passion, the fervor, coming from him in waves across the footlights, and she could sense that the audience had given itself over to him completely.

When he came to the famous soliloquy, "To be, or not to be...," the pathos he achieved was almost unbearable. His perfectly timed silences, combined with small touching gestures and a masterly delivery of the lines, overwhelmingly conveyed the agony of a tormented soul. The audience agonized with him all the way, enthralled, dominated. His handling of the blank verse was beautiful—pure and eloquent.

In the climactic scene, as Laertes lay dying, and Claudius was revealed for the villain that he was, the wounded Hamlet's cry of "Then, venom to thy

work," rang out like a trumpet call, carrying so
much realism that it raised the hair on the back of
Vicki's neck.

The suspense was incredible, even though the end of
the play was surely known to everyone in the theater.
No one moved, or coughed, or even breathed. All attention was riveted on the stage, where Hamlet was
dying.

It was a long moment after his body was borne off
the stage, and a final salute of gunfire was heard,
before the first tentative applause commenced. The
sound gradually built and built to a deafening roar.
Vicki was on her feet without knowing she'd stood
up, clapping so hard she could feel her whole body
reverberating. Tears were running unchecked down
her cheeks.

The company took twelve curtain calls that night.
Unsmiling at first, Jason was still Hamlet, looking
mysteriously lean in his tight black clothing. Princely
and grim, he barely acknowledged the almost hysterical applause. Vicki's eyes, like those of everyone
else, fixed only on him, observed the moment when
he changed and became Jason Meredith again. He
was suddenly bowing, smiling that dazzling smile of
his. Gesturing to his fellow players, who had stepped
back a few paces, he was urging them forward to
share in the plaudits. But they wouldn't come forward; they were applauding *him*. And at last he stood
alone in center stage, his head bowed, his hands
turned palm upward toward the audience, accepting
their acclaim with dignified humility.

At the end, before he strode off the stage for the
last time, there was a moment when he straightened.
His head turned toward the box where Vicki was

standing, still applauding, still caught up in the magic
of the play. He didn't bow or acknowledge her presence in any way, but their eyes met, and something
passed between them—something almost tangible, as
though he had touched her in the most intimate way.

It was at that moment that she knew she was totally, irrevocably, in love with Jason Meredith. At the
same time she accepted the fact that he was unattain-
able. It was unthinkable that this man, this superstar,
this fantasy figure, could ever feel for her a tenth of
what she felt for him. There was grief in the knowledge, yet joy over all. She was changed forever.
There could be no going back, even if whatever happened to her was going to break her heart.

JASON'S DRESSING ROOM was crowded with well-
wishers, colleagues and members of the press. In
order to get to his side, Vicki would literally have had
to shoulder her way through the throng. She didn't
feel she had the right to do that, so she hung back,
staying close to the wall, watching and listening in
amazement at the pandemonium. All around her she
heard cries of "genius," "superb," "marvelous."
Jason stood in the center of it all, smiling, sometimes
laughing. Wearing a blue velour robe over his black
costume, he accepted handshakes and claps on his
shoulder from the men, kisses from the women.
There was a lot of embracing going on, Vicki noticed. Everyone who came in was greeted by everyone
else with great enthusiasm and apparent affection,
though many of the kisses between women were of
the   mouth-pursed-kiss-the-air-in-the-area-of-the-
cheek variety.

Sabrina had made it through to Jason and was

standing by his side, talking to the people around him, her dark eyes glowing like rare jewels. Sig was there, too, looking around the room, presumably for Vicki herself. Yes, he *was* looking for her. As he caught her glance, he signaled to her to join them. She smiled helplessly, trying to indicate with her eyes that the crush was too great. She saw him lean toward Jason and say something.

At once the actor looked in her direction and started moving toward her. Then he was in front of her. For a second, no one's attention was fixed on him.

Under the velour robe, his clothing was soaking wet, she saw. His hair was curling damply over his forehead. In repose, his face was drawn with fatigue. No wonder. A performance like that would take a lot out of anyone.

He smiled at her tiredly. "You enjoyed it, didn't you?" he said quietly. "I could see your eyes shining in the darkness."

"You were magnificent," she said and was at once afraid the word was too fulsome. To her horror, she realized that again there were tears in her eyes.

Jason noticed them, too. He reached up and caught one on a gentle fingertip, his face solemn now, his gray eyes eloquent with some emotion she couldn't name. "Thank you, Victoria," he murmured, then smiled briefly. "You brought me luck. I've never felt so in command. You must promise to be with me before every performance."

Vicki swallowed, totally unable to tear her gaze from his.

And then the crowd surged around them again. Christopher Hammond, who had already changed into street clothes, pushed his way through, and he and Jason slapped each other on the shoulders in the way men do when they want to show affection. "You were awfully ferocious, old chap," Christopher scolded. "At one point there, I was afraid you were really going to run me through with your sword."

"You wrung the neck of your own part," Jason countered. "What was that business with the trembling pointed finger that you introduced along with 'The king, the king's to blame'?"

"Sheer inspiration, old boy; you know how it is." The younger actor's eyes had suddenly discovered Vicki. "And who is this rare and radiant maiden?" he asked, raising slanted eyebrows so that they almost met in a point above his nose. He was a good-looking man, Vicki noted. Tall and lean, with a Mephistophelian beard and dancing brown eyes.

"Forgive me," Jason said. "Vicki Dennison, Christopher Hammond. Vicki's visiting from the United States—Los Angeles. She's staying with her aunt, an old friend of mine." His voice was without inflection, almost dismissing.

"From Filmland?" Christopher queried. "Mention my name, old dear, when you go home again, will you? I've been waiting for the call—my turn to make some of those lovely dollars, don't you know?"

Vicki managed a smile. She was feeling—what— hurt? The introduction had made her feel like a child trotted out for adult approval. And why had Jason suddenly decided to call her Vicki? He hadn't done that before. "I'll do what I can," she said in as light a tone as she could manage. "I'm afraid I don't have much pull, but I could direct you to the drugstore where Lana Turner was supposedly discovered."

"God bless us all, a woman with a sense of humor! What a rare find." Christopher grinned at her with an absurdly melodramatic leer. "Tarry awhile, love, and I'll murder my wife and fly off to Los Angeles with you."

"I heard that!" a female voice exclaimed behind him. Susan Carmody, who had made a wonderfully ethereal Ophelia, was smiling at Vicki in a very friendly way. After Jason again performed introductions, Susan winked at her. "Sit with me at supper, my dear, and I'll tell you all about friends Christopher and Jason. Their wild and wicked ways, their deviousness, their womanizing—"

"Enough!" Christopher roared, turning several heads toward him. "It's time to eat, people," he shouted with a magnanimous gesture that included everyone in the room. On cue people started to leave, Sabrina and Sig lingering at the rear. "We'll catch up with you," Jason said, and Sabrina nodded, giving him one of her smoky glances before she followed the others out.

Sig smiled at Vicki. "Mad, isn't it?"

Vicki smiled noncommittally, and he chuckled. "Such a tactful girl." He turned to Jason. "Congratulations, my friend. I was watching your fiancée throughout your performance. If ever a woman was in love...." He patted Jason's shoulder, touched Vicki's cheek. "I'll see you at supper." Then he was gone.

There was a moment's silence that seemed intense in contrast to the recent pandemonium. Vicki didn't know where to look. She couldn't look at Jason after Sig's comment. "Supper?" she queried finally.

Jason had moved away to his dressing table and

was wiping makeup from his face. His gaze seemed to avoid hers in the mirror. "Usually we all gather together for a meal," he said evenly. "I'm never hungry at such times, but it's a tradition of a sort." He straightened up, excused himself and went into the adjoining bathroom to wash and change his clothes.

Vicki stood where she was, feeling awkward and suddenly very tired. In the past several hours she had run through a whole gamut of emotions. Uppermost at the moment was a feeling of melancholy, but beneath that was annoyance at herself. Why had she felt so hurt by Jason's attitude toward her in those last few minutes before everyone had left?

She became abruptly aware that he'd come out from the bathroom and was looking at her. He was wearing the suit he'd worn earlier, and his hair was freshly washed. "I'm sorry I had to make light of our acquaintance to the Hammonds," he said as though he'd read her mind again. "Any hint in public of a romance between us would have brought the paparazzi buzzing around. I'm sure you wouldn't want that any more than I would."

"Of course not," she agreed, feeling slightly better. "It was only playacting, anyway," she added with what felt like a stiff smile.

"Yes."

He was still looking at her. There was a razor edge of tension about him, perhaps left over from the play. He seemed. . . not tired exactly, but withdrawn, unrelaxed, strained. "Are you very hungry, Victoria?" he asked.

She was amazed at her elated response to his use of her full name. It *was* strange, considering that she'd never liked it, and no one else had ever called her that. She smiled at him more naturally. "I couldn't eat a bite. I've already eaten more today than I usually do."

"How would you feel about going straight home? Would it disappoint you to miss the party?"

"Not at all. But won't everyone miss you? Won't they wonder?"

"I'm not noted for being predictable. No one will be surprised."

"Then I . . . yes, I would prefer to go home."

He nodded almost absently. "William Hazlitt, the English essayist, once said that an actor, having performed his part well, instead of courting further distinction, should affect obscurity and steal most guiltylike away."

He was smiling, but in a perfunctory way. Vicki couldn't quite read his mood. Probably, she thought, it was difficult for any actor to become oriented to everyday living after the altered state of consciousness required for his role.

WHEN THEY WERE in the Jaguar, traveling toward Derringham, she said as much to him, hoping to break the rather tense silence that seemed to have built up between them.

He agreed thoughtfully, quoting again from another historical figure, this time a great actor. "Sir Henry Irving said that there was only two ways of portraying a character on the stage. Either you can turn yourself into that person, or you can take that person and turn him into yourself. That's the way I try to do it. In other words, rather than becoming the character, I try to make the character become me.

It's a subtle distinction. It's rather like being possessed, I suppose.''

He paused a moment before going on. ''Most of
acting is technique, of course, but one's emotions inevitably get involved. It's not possible to counterfeit
great passion of any kind. It has to come from...
well, the soul, if you will. So, yes, it is extremely difficult to become plain old Meredith again, free of
that other person inside me. Sometimes it's weeks
after a run before I'm wholly myself again—whoever
that is.''

There was another silence, not quite as tense now
that they'd spoken, but still filled with some kind of
special atmosphere. Jason was sitting erectly in the
driver's seat, not relaxed as he had been when they
drove to London earlier in the day. His hands were
gripping the wheel, his foot pressing down on the ac-
celerator. It seemed to Vicki that he was driving
much too fast, although she had to admit he wasn't
passing any other cars and was just keeping up with
the stream.

The traffic was fairly heavy. Most of the other cars
were small. She wasn't really nervous about Jason's
driving; he handled the wheel with confidence and
skill. The only times she was a little afraid were when
they came to what the man who'd rented her the Mini
had called roundabouts—large traffic islands into
which half a dozen roads converged. The driver coming from the right had the right-of-way, the rental
agent had told her; those entering from subsequent
roads were supposed to yield. But as far as Vicki
could tell, no one had told *them* that. Seated on the
left side of the car, she was quite often alarmed by
the sudden proximity of another automobile. But

somehow the other driver always managed to squeeze through. Jason paid no attention to any of them. Apparently he counted on his right-of-way and expected everyone else to stay out of his path.

Once they were on the winding roads that led to Derringham, she was able to relax a little, though still not completely. Theirs was the only car on the road now. Even so, the lanes seemed narrower in the dark, and the headlights swung and swerved in front of them, lighting up trees and hedgerows. She prayed fervently that no one would come in the opposite direction. She could almost hear the grinding squeal of metal on metal in the head-on crash that would be sure to result.

"Are you tired, Victoria?" Jason asked.

"Not really." It was true, she realized. Once she'd left the theater, her exhaustion had disappeared. Mostly she felt strangely saddened. "I feel like Cinderella returning from the ball," she admitted.

"Does that mean I'm liable to turn into a frog?" There was amusement in his voice. For a moment the tension had retreated, though she felt strangely that it was hovering somewhere outside the car's windows, waiting to descend on them again if they stopped talking.

"I think you've got your fairy tales mixed up," she said lightly.."Cinderella's driver was a rat."

"Thank you very much," he said.

She laughed. "Anyway, in the story you're thinking of, the prince didn't turn into a frog, the frog turned into a prince."

"Only when he was kissed by the princess," he said.

Vicki swallowed. The tension was back again with

a vengeance, and now she recognized it for what it was. Sexual tension, pure and simple. And she didn't think it was emanating solely from her. She was suddenly aware, even more than before, of the muscular size and shape of the man beside her. Aware, too, of her own body, stiff with nervous strain. Her fingers were curled tightly into the palms of her hands, she realized, and she was feeling light-headed again, as though she'd forgotten how to breathe.

"Did I offend you, Victoria?" he asked.

Startled, she glanced at him. They had driven under the hotel's archway into the courtyard without her noticing. Even as she hesitated, he brought the big car to a smooth stop and turned off the ignition. "Offend me?" she echoed.

He turned to look at her, leaning back in his seat. "Only when he was kissed by the princess," he repeated gravely.

She couldn't make out his expression in the diffused light coming from the hotel, but she didn't think he was smiling. And his voice had sounded solemn—ominously so.

"How could that offend me?" she asked hesitantly. "It's just a fairy tale, after all."

"It has been something of a fairy-tale day, hasn't it?"

"Yes." She swallowed hard, desperately afraid she was on the verge of tears again. Why did she feel like crying? "I had a wonderful time," she said, forcing her voice to sound level.

"I'm glad."

He wasn't making any move to go. Should she open the door on her side, she wondered. Abby was possibly waiting up for her. Her aunt hadn't said

much about the day's excursion, and of course, she
didn't know anything about the deceptive aspects of
it. God, how horrified she would be if she did know!
All the same, she had looked at Vicki long and hard
when she'd heard about Jason's invitation to see him
perform. "You'll enjoy the play, I'm sure, dear,"
she'd said. "But do remember my warning, okay?
You're playing with fire. Try not to get burned."

"There'll be other people there," Vicki had pointed out.

"Uh-huh." Abby had said no more, but Vicki had
the feeling she would be studying her very carefully
when she came in, watching for signs of singe marks
around the edges. They were there, she felt sure.
Would they show?

"Would you like to join me for a drink?" Jason
asked.

"Oh, I—yes, I guess so. In the bar, you mean?"

"Nothing in England stays open this late. I meant
in my suite."

"Oh." Should she? No, of course she shouldn't.
"Yes," she said. After all, she rationalized, what
harm could there be in extending this magical day a
few minutes longer?

A lot of harm, she realized as she accompanied
him up the dimly lighted back stairs. Their footsteps
seemed to echo along the walls, their shadows now
preceding them, now streaming back between them
as they climbed, not speaking, not touching. On the
third-floor landing he opened the door for her and
stood back, his hand lightly brushing her sleeve as
she passed him. The effect was electric. She hurried
ahead of him to his suite and stood well aside as he
unlocked it. Her throat seemed to be packed with

cotton. Her body was a tingling mass of sensation. If
he touched her again, she feared she would explode.

But he kept his distance, to her relief and possibly,
if she was honest, to her disappointment. There was
no one in the living room of the suite. None of the
staff appeared to be around, although a couple of
lamps had been left burning. It was very late, she
supposed. Yes, there was a square wood-framed
clock on the mantel. Two o'clock in the morning.
The witching hour was well past, and Cinderella had
not yet broken through the spell of her enchantment.
She could hear the clock ticking rhythmically, counterpoint to the rapid thudding of her heart.

"Brandy?" Jason murmured, heading for the bar.
He was taking off his suit jacket and loosening his tie
as he went.

"Fine," she managed.

She took a deep breath, trying to fill her painful
lungs, gratefully accepting the pear-shaped glass
when he held it out to her. He didn't suggest they sit
down. "To a successful day," he proposed, raising
his glass. "You did a marvelous job, Victoria."

A *job*?

There didn't seem to be anything to say. She took a
sip of brandy, wishing he would turn away. He was
standing very close, gazing at her. "You looked very
lovely today," he said gently. "I don't believe I told
you that."

Another sip of brandy. "Thank you," she said.

"I like your hairstyle. Very sophisticated. But I
think I prefer your hair down."

Before she could guess his intentions, he had set his
glass down and was removing the pins from her hair.
His fingers were skillful, and so quick that she was

still standing there, stunned, her glass half-raised to
her lips, when it all tumbled down around her neck
and shoulders.

Pensively he studied the effect he'd created, his
face only inches from hers, his eyes luminous. There
was a smooth look to his strong features that she'd
never seen before, as if all lines had disappeared. He
looked much younger suddenly—and dangerously attractive. Vicki's pulse was hammering in her ears,
and she felt sure that if he looked down, he would see
her heart moving rhythmically against the thin fabric
of her blouse.

But he didn't look down. He kept his gaze fixed on
her face as he took the brandy glass from her nerve-
less fingers and set it aside. Then his hand lifted slowly and touched her. "You have the softest hair," he
said.

A heartbeat later he was drawing her face up to his
and kissing her, his lips firm yet gentle. She felt her
senses awaken in a frenzy of response, astounding
her with the violence of her emotions. This couldn't
be happening, she thought vaguely. It just wasn't
possible that this was happening. She seemed to have
moved into another dimension—a magical place, a
fairy-tale place that was a continuation of the
magical day. A dream, only a dream. . . .

Slowly her hands crept over his shoulders, discov-
ering and caressing the resilient strength of muscles
beneath the cotton of his shirt. Then they were pulling him closer to her as her own body strained toward
his. His mouth had eased its pressure now, and one
of his hands cupped her chin as his tongue moved
over her lips. The tip of it was very slowly tracing the
sensitive areas within, a marvelously erotic stimula-

tion she had never experienced like this before. At the same time his other hand slipped under her open jacket and curved around her breast. The nipple stiffened immediately in response, and she felt his mouth tense against hers.

"Victoria?" he said against her lips, and there was a question in his voice.

"Yes," her dream self answered.

He lifted her chin, forcing her to meet his direct gaze. His eyes were dark gray now, no longer luminous, but opaque from the light of one of the lamps. "Yes?" he repeated.

She nodded, gazing directly back at him, not trusting herself to speak in case she woke up. Don't let him ask me again, she pleaded inwardly.

As though from far away, she saw him swallow, felt a tremor in his fingers. When he spoke, there was a hoarseness in his voice. "What I want to do," he said softly, "is make love to you all night."

She didn't answer, couldn't answer. She wanted to stand like this in the circle of his arms forever, close to him, held by him, cherished by him.

But after a moment he released her, took hold of her hand and led her across the hall to his bedroom. There he let go of her hand to switch on a light in what was evidently the bathroom, adjusting the door so that the indirect glow fell across the room and the large four-poster bed against the opposite wall. Some still functioning part of Vicki's mind noted that the covers had been turned down for him. He was well cared for, this man.

He returned to her before she could recover from the suspended feeling that had overcome her. With infinite care he slipped her linen jacket from her shoulders, draping it on a wooden-armed chair. Then his fingers reached for the buttons of her blouse. Still bemused with wonder, she stood quietly while he unfastened them, and then her bra. She heard his breath catch in his throat and saw that he was staring at the white strip across her breasts where her bikini top had protected her skin from the sun. The whiteness seemed almost phosphorescent in the half-light. "You're so lovely," he said huskily.

"I want to be for you," she whispered, meeting his gaze with her own.

With trembling fingers she reached behind her to unzip her skirt. "Let me," he commanded, and obediently she remained motionless while he finished the task. When she stood naked before him, he gazed down at her, his fingers tracing tenderly the curve of her hips, caressing lightly the patch of pale hair between her legs.

"So lovely," he murmured again, and then his arms were around her, carrying her to the bed.

With an economy of movement Jason removed his own clothing, then lay down beside her, gathering her close against his beautifully proportioned body. He seemed content for a while to simply hold her close, his mouth pressed against her hair, one hand gently stroking her back. Then he raised his head and rested his cheek against hers. "I've wanted you since the first moment you walked into Abby's office," he murmured. "There was such a shining quality about you. When I kissed you the first time, I wanted to take you then and there. But it was too soon. You were so lovely, so startled. I want you so much, Victoria, more than I ever remember wanting a woman."

She could feel his heart beating against her own as he buried his face in her neck. Her lips were sliding softly of their own accord over the hard smooth masculine texture of his skin, her mouth opening to taste the faint intoxicating saltiness of his shoulder. She marveled at the firmness of him, the wonderful smell of him, the feel of his hard strength against her own slender softness. It seemed a time out of mind, a sensuous languorous time in which they touched each other, hesitantly at first, then more knowingly. There was every sensation in the world as his hands moved over her lovingly, his mouth moving after them, touching delicately her lips, her shoulders, her breasts.

And then quite suddenly the languorousness was gone, replaced by an urgency in his body that finally started to pierce through her rapturous state. This was not a fairy tale, she realized dazedly. This was life, real life, and she was about to let a man—a comparative stranger—take possession of her. Her memory was abruptly flooded with an image of Ken Marriott's face looming over her. Instinctively she recoiled. She had been so irreparably soiled by him! And afterward those other men had leered at her....

Struggling to free herself, she tried to ignore the waves of heat that were flashing through her, threatening to lift her onto a plane of feeling where nothing existed but the sound of her own jagged breathing and the delight of Jason's body against hers. All her muscles tightened, drawn in as she fought to free herself from the passionate urgings of her traitorous other self. "No, Jason!" she cried out in panic. "We can't do this!"

He released her at once and stared at her. Whatever he saw in her face shocked him into a silence that seemed to last an eternity. And then he was rolling away from her, standing, reaching for a robe that hung on the back of a chair.

Miserably she watched him as he struggled into it, the air straining through her lungs as she tried desperately to control her breathing. The brief glimpse she'd had of his face before he turned from her would be engraved forever on her memory, she felt sure. Dear God, he had looked so... so grim. In a moment he would turn to face her. What would she see on his face then? Contempt?

Unable to bear the prospect, she rolled over and buried her face in the pillow, hiding like a child. She felt so humiliated that she wanted only to disappear.

CHAPTER EIGHT

WHEN SHE MANAGED to turn over again long minutes later, she saw that Jason had turned out the bathroom light. Faint shadows cast by the street lamps outside had penetrated the darkness of the room. There was a slight odor of smoke. Jason was standing by the window, smoking a cigarette, his dressing gown belted tightly around his lean waist. He was looking out at the street, his strong profile etched sharply against the pale rectangular outline of the window.

For a few seconds she gazed at him, trying to decide what to say. "I'm sorry, Jason," she murmured at last.

His head turned. With the faint light behind him, she couldn't see his expression. "It's all right, Victoria," he said. His voice was extremely polite.

"It was just that I—"

"You don't have to explain," he interrupted. He hesitated. "It would probably be best if you left before the others. . . ." He let the rest of the sentence trail away.

She felt a terrible chill. He had spoken softly, out of caution, of course, but his voice had sounded too. . .too even. Too cold. Surely he didn't expect her simply to leave without explaining how she felt?

Probably he just meant that they should leave the

bedroom. Yes, that was it. They could talk in the living room. She certainly didn't want to be discovered in his bed by the stately Royce or by any of the others. He was right, she must get out of here at once.

She sat up, dragging the sheet with her to cover her breasts, and looked around vaguely. "My clothes?"

"They're on the chair." He gestured with his cigarette, then put it out in an ashtray on the table next to the bed. "I'll leave you to dress," he said in that same level tone. Then he turned and left the room.

She freshened up briefly in his bathroom, dressed hastily, then wondered what to do next. He'd gone through the door that led to the little hall of the suite. Was he waiting for her in the living room? Or did he expect her just to go?

Abby! Had she waited up for her? What would she think? Foolish question. It was obvious what she would think. But if her aunt *had* gone to sleep, and Vicki could get back to her own room without waking her, then perhaps. . . .

Quietly she opened the bedroom door. No one seemed to be stirring anywhere. She glanced through the archway into the shadowed living room. No one was there. Frowning irresolutely, she hesitated for a second or two, then reluctantly let herself out of the suite.

Creeping up the back stairs to Abby's apartment, she felt clouds of dismay wash over her. The way Jason had more or less ejected her, without one word of understanding, without allowing her to explain, made her feel like a useless object that had been cast aside. Was that how he thought of her now? Surely not. She couldn't bear it if he thought so little of her. She couldn't bear. . . .

She cut off her thoughts as tears pricked behind her eyelids. She must hold herself together, at least until she gained the privacy of her own bedroom.

She used the key Abby had given her, feeling furtive and soiled again as she tried not to make a sound. Luckily Abby didn't awaken.

In the safety of her own room, Vicki let out the breath she hadn't realized she was holding. Quickly, trying not to think about anything, she stripped off her clothes, pulled on her white terry robe and climbed into bed. There she stretched out and tried consciously to relax. Her heart was thudding. From her fear of being seen by some early riser? Or because she was afraid Jason's reaction to her abrupt about-face might be a total rejection of her?

She stared at the ceiling, remembering. Jason had been so considerate toward her when he began to make love to her. He hadn't forced himself upon her at any time. There was no comparison between him and Ken Marriott. So why had she remembered her old boss at that particular moment?

She had said yes to Jason without hesitation, and she couldn't really blame him if he was furious with her. No wonder he had let her go so coldly. Probably he wouldn't want to see her again. He must think she was a silly, naive tease.... Her mind skittered away from the thought.

Vicki was not a virgin; she hadn't been since her college days. But neither was she promiscuous in any way. She'd had only one lover, the race-car driver, who had pursued her with such dogged obstinacy that she had at last given in to his pleas, more to prove to herself that she was not abnormal than for any other reason. The experience had been a disaster.

He had hurt her quite badly and then expressed surprise and amusement that she was a virgin. She had always regretted giving in to the man's demands and had not repeated the experience. Not until tonight, with Jason Meredith.

She began to make excuses for his coldness. He must be very tired. He hadn't slept at all. After that fabulous performance at the theater, he must have been exhausted. Perhaps, when he thought over the events of the night, he would realize that she couldn't let him complete his lovemaking, not yet—not when she didn't really know him well enough to trust him. Perhaps when he thought it over, he *would* want to see her again.

This last was a little difficult to believe, even for someone who wanted desperately to hope, but she clung to it and at last drifted into an uneasy sleep.

ABBY WOKE HER AT NINE, looking fresh and efficient in a brown suit and cream-colored blouse. Every glossy brown hair was in place, neatly tucked into her S-shaped chignon, and she was carrying a small round tray with two cups of coffee on it. "You must have come home pretty late, sleepyhead," she chided gently with a smile. "I went to bed about eleven. Very virtuous of me, don't you think?" She chuckled, plunking herself down on the side of Vicki's bed. "I guess I must have been pretty tired. A convention arrived yesterday, and everything went wrong—par for the course. I slept like a log and didn't even hear you come in. Did you have a good time? How was the play?"

Vicki sat up and accepted a cup of coffee gratefully, taking a scalding sip before trusting herself to reply. She was feeling a mixture of relief and shame. Abby obviously suspected nothing, and somehow that made last night's experience seem even more sordid. "The play was great. Jason was tremendous as Hamlet." She'd managed to say his name quite casually.

For a second, Abby looked as if she were about to say something, but she evidently changed her mind.

"Afterward a lot of people wanted to go on somewhere," Vicki went on vaguely, not wanting to deceive Abby, but supposing some excuse was in order.

Her aunt cut her off. "You don't owe me any explanations, dear," she said hastily. "I'm just glad you had a nice day. What did you think of London?"

Glad to have a safe subject to pursue, Vicki told her about the restaurant and the trip to the Tower. (How long ago that seemed—another world!) Then she went on to tell her a little about Sabrina and Sig, whom Abby hadn't met.

At last, Abby stood up, smoothing her skirt. "I'd better get to work," she said. "I've already had breakfast. Want me to order some for you?"

"I guess so—something light. I have to get started, too."

"No, you don't. Just because I'm an old workhorse doesn't mean you have to be one."

"I'd rather work, really. The designs are coming along. I'll probably have something to show you in the next few days."

"Well, you take it easy, dear. You look a little shadowy around the eyes." Abby paused, chewing on her lower lip for a moment, a puzzled frown creasing her forehead. "There's something I have to tell you. Jason called."

"This morning?" Her heart soared, then as quick-ly plummeted. There was an odd look in Abby's eyes—was it sympathy?

"He asked me to tell you he was going to London right away," she said. "He'll be gone for some time, probably until the end of the run. He's going to stay with the Hammonds—something about a lot of board meetings and rehearsals. He was pretty terse." She paused. "He gets that way sometimes when he's in a hurry, but—" she looked at Vicki directly "—you two didn't have a fight, did you?"

Vicki made herself smile. "Heavens, no. Why? Did he say something that gave you that impres-sion?"

"Well, no, not exactly. But I asked him if he want-ed me to wake you—I was sure you'd like to speak to him yourself—and he said very curtly that the last thing he wanted was to bother you. It struck me as strange, but I guess he just didn't want to disturb your sleep." She smiled. "I'm glad to hear nothing's wrong. I'm not sure you should get too involved with our Jason Meredith, but he *is* a good friend, and I'd be upset if he hurt your feelings. You're sure every-thing's okay?"

"Everything's fine," Vicki lied. Her smile felt as if it was cracking her face. "Thanks for giving me the message."

When Abby had gone, Vicki sank back against her pillows, feeling as though she'd just sustained a severe blow. The message was very clear, she thought. She had rejected him, he had rejected her, and he didn't want to hear any explanations. If she wasn't willing to give herself to him, he wanted no part of her.

You are not going to cry, she ordered herself. She stared blankly at the ceiling, willing the tears away, willing cynicism in their place. In cynicism lay strength. Probably someday she would look upon last night as a learning experience. There was no reason for her to feel so totally at fault. After all, Jason wasn't in love with her. He had simply wanted to use her to satisfy his own temporary needs. Maybe he, too, had been affected by the make-believe aspects of the day. All those loving glances. . . . What had he said? "I try to make the character become me." For Sig's benefit, his character yesterday had been the leading man in a tale of love, and she had been the leading lady. Vicki had often read of movie stars who fell in love during the filming of a romance. They always seemed to fall out of love when the movie was over, too.

Harsh but true, she thought bleakly. It was only in fairy tales that the prince came along afterward, searching for the woman whose foot fitted into the glass slipper. And this particular Cinderella was no more.

Determinedly she pulled back the bedclothes, stood up and headed for the shower. She had to forget Jason Meredith, forget she had ever met him and thought she loved him. Work—that was the answer. Lots of work with no time for thought, and no time to indulge such an imaginary thing as a broken heart.

It was a good thing she had plenty of work to do. She had completed the plans for the improvements, but she still had to make drawings of how the finished projects would look. After Abby approved the ideas, if she did, Vicki could start scouting out carpeting and accessories and then supervise the work.

She worked steadily on sketches in Abby's living room until shortly after three, when Portia sought her out and again invited her to play tennis. The girl had Mrs. Powell's permission to go out, she said, as long as Royce came along.

Vicki had thought about Portia during the morning and had decided that under the circumstances it would probably be best to ease out of her friendship with the girl. But when she was confronted with Portia's pixielike face, so earnestly pleading, her light gray eyes so hopeful, she couldn't send her away. The girl so obviously needed her—needed someone.

Finally she accepted Portia's invitation. The physical exercise would be good for her after her sedentary day, she reasoned, and anyway, it would be wrong to let last night's debacle influence her growing fondness for the troubled young girl.

Fortunately Vicki had brought her tennis whites and shoes with her. All she had to do was buy a tennis racket.

It was a beautiful day, the warmest since she had arrived. For once the wind wasn't blowing. The park turned out to be a small one on the far edge of town. After Vicki had made her purchase, they walked to it. Royce followed them at a discreet distance, looking like a British diplomat in his formal clothing, complete with bowler hat. Vicki was rather daunted by his presence and felt suddenly nervous when she remembered the reason for it. Jason had said something about a threatening letter, and even Portia had referred to the butler as her bodyguard. . . . The idea that Royce was there to protect Portia from harm seemed incongruous against the background of this enchantingly picturesque town. Jason Meredith's world was very different to hers, Vicki realized. Perhaps there were advantages to being unknown and not too well-off, after all.

The park was very pretty, its flower beds bright with roses and mixed annuals. To Vicki's surprise it was being enjoyed by a number of people, too. Besides the two tennis courts, there was a playground for small children that was fairly crowded, and on a large stretch of manicured lawn some older men and women were bowling with wooden balls, encouraged by a small knot of onlookers.

In a fenced-off field a cricket match was in progress, and beyond that was a small wood. Royce explained that the huge open area visible at the edge of the park was the site of the annual country fair.

"The fair starts next Saturday," Portia said as Royce turned away to watch the bowlers. "It's really a lot of fun in an old-fashioned way. People come from all over to see it." She smiled shyly up at Vicki. "Will you go with me?"

Vicki kept her gaze fixed on her tennis racket as she unfastened its press. Jason had mentioned the fair; the vicar wanted him to open it. But he'd said he had no intention of doing so. No doubt, he wouldn't be there.

She smiled at Portia. "I'd love to go," she said.

"Would you mind if I asked David, too? He doesn't get out much."

"Why should I mind?"

Portia grinned. "He likes you."

Vicki managed another smile. "I suppose you think he's sexy?"

"Well, he's not bad. Kim thinks he's sexy. She has a crush on him. Actually he spends quite a bit of time with her."

"Kim? On the front desk?" Vicki wasn't sure why she was so surprised. Somehow Kim hadn't struck her as the type of girl someone like David would be interested in. Then she scolded herself mildly for being a snob. Despite Kim's flamboyant looks, she was a very nice girl.

Portia turned out to be a competent tennis player—not too strong, but fast and accurate. She gave Vicki a good workout. Afterward the two of them went up to Vicki's room for the promised guitar lesson. Vicki got her new pupil started on some chords and even loaned her the guitar so she could practice.

Portia's delight knew no bounds. "I knew I was going to like you a lot," she exclaimed as she was finally learning. "I told Jason so." Then she hesitated. "I almost forgot to ask you. What did you think of his performance yesterday?"

Vicki swallowed, but managed to keep her face under control. "I thought he was superb as Hamlet," she said truthfully. She forced herself to smile. "You'd better get back to your suite. Mrs. Powell will be expecting you for dinner."

Portia lingered in the doorway, her tennis racket under her arm, and the guitar cradled carefully in her hands. There was a puzzled expression on her face. "I don't understand why Jason suddenly shot off to London. He's not coming back till the play's over, and he's never done that before. He was in a really grotty mood, too; I don't know why—the notices were terrific. So it's not that he was upset with his performance."

"I expect he's just extra busy," Vicki said carefully.

"I suppose so." Portia sighed. "I miss him when he's gone. He's sometimes a cross old bear, but most of the time he's pretty nice to have around. I'm going to be awfully lonely."

Her need was clear. *Damn Jason Meredith,* Vicki said vehemently to herself. "Perhaps we could do something together again tomorrow," she suggested.

She was rewarded with a beaming smile. "I could take you to see Meredith Manor," Portia suggested.

"No." Vicki took a deep breath. She hadn't meant to sound so abrupt, but the very thought of seeing Jason's house now.... "I'd rather wait until the repairs are finished, okay?" she excused herself. "What do you say we walk along the river if it's a nice day? Maybe you can show me a few of the local sights."

"Lovely," Portia said promptly.

WEDNESDAY WAS ANOTHER WARM DAY. Followed by the ubiquitous Royce, Vicki enjoyed her stroll with Portia along the river's edge. She'd slept badly the night before, dreaming as she did of Jason Meredith pursuing her while she ran naked through the halls of the hotel. He hadn't caught her, and she'd awakened with a feeling of regret, one that she quickly suppressed.

The tree-lined river was fairly wide, with little wooden footbridges at intervals along its length. Portia pointed out the singing trees and recounted the legend about them, which Vicki pretended she hadn't heard before. They fed crumbs to some ducks from the small picnic Portia had brought along in lieu of afternoon tea. Royce joined them, looking very out of place sitting on the grassy bank. But he was a good sport about it.

All in all, it was a very pleasant couple of hours except for the fact that Vicki was bothered by a constant feeling of anticipation, almost as though she expected something to happen. She couldn't quite place the feeling until Portia started talking about Jason. Then she realized that subconsciously she'd been hoping he would walk back into her life as suddenly as he'd walked out of it. Hoping they could start over, more slowly, more conventionally. . . .

Angry with herself, she cut the outing shorter than Portia had obviously hoped.

By Thursday afternoon Vicki's drawings were complete. She spread them out on the desk in Abby's office, which had been cleared off in preparation for the show.

Her aunt's approval was immediate and enthusiastic. "I love the way you've rearranged the furniture in those guest rooms!" she exclaimed. "Why didn't I think of that? They're so long and narrow they always look like waiting rooms. All you've done is move the drawer chests, the writing desks and chairs, and presto—the room is divided into sections. We don't even have to spend much money, except on new draperies and carpeting."

"I'm afraid you'll need a hefty amount of cash to redo the Blue Room," Vicki said, pulling out the relevant plans and sketches.

She'd thought long and hard about the dining room, knowing instinctively that it had great potential. In her drawings she'd removed the chandeliers and had left the tall diamond-paned windows undraped. "I thought perhaps you could put more lighting into the courtyard and along the river," she told Abby. "Without draperies, the diners would be able to enjoy the view."

On the opposite wall she'd suggested a mural depicting the legend of the singing trees. "You'd have to commission an artist, of course," she said.

"I'm sure we could find one," Abby replied promptly. "As a matter of fact, the sous chef's nephew is an accomplished artist. I bought a couple of his watercolors for one of the conference rooms. They're huge pieces, so I know he's used to working on a large scale. What a marvelous idea!" she went on. "But what are these squiggles between the windows?"

"I'm insulted!" Vicki retorted with a teasing grin. Her smiles still felt strained, but she kept working on them. "Squiggles indeed! Those details are intended to represent heraldic designs. I've researched a few, which I'll show to you later, by the way. But I thought they'd go with the beamed ceiling and the windows.

"We can still have a blue carpet if you like, though green might be more in keeping. I think the tablecloths should be white. They look more...more appetizing somehow, and they'll brighten up the whole room. And green and white were the Tudor colors, you know. As you see here, I've added a small candle lantern to each table—for decoration, mostly, as the main lighting could be recessed at the top of the walls. I'm not sure whether we'll be able to find lanterns like these, but perhaps we could have them specially made. I found them in a book I bought in town; they're a genuine Tudor design."

"We could call it the Tudor Room," Abby suggested, looking pleased with herself.

"Good idea," Vicki said, rescuing the piece of paper on which she'd written the same suggestion. "What do you think?"

Beaming in approval, Abby looked up at her. "I think you are a very talented young lady, and I like everything you've done. What a treasure you are!"

"Like Jean-Paul and George?"

The older woman laughed. "Even more so. I'm terribly impressed, Vicki." She thumbed through the loose sketches. "What's this? There's more?"

"The Wine Cellar. Not much to do there. I thought maybe some banquettes along the walls to close in the room a bit and give a feeling of intimacy." She hesitated. "I did have a couple of other ideas. Not for decorating, but. . . ."

"Go on," Abby ordered. "I'm open to anything."

"Well, I did wonder if you couldn't do something about the entertainment. Maybe you could get a small group in on weekends, at least. Kim says there isn't a decent place to go dancing this side of London."

"You mean disco?" Abby looked alarmed.

"No, not disco necessarily. Something for general dancing. Maybe a little light rock wouldn't hurt."

Abby pursed her mouth thoughtfully. "Hmm. I'll have to think about all of this." She stood up and hugged Vicki warmly. "Thank you so much, darling. I knew you'd do a good job." She held her niece at arms' length for a moment, studying her face. "Is anything wrong? You've seemed. . . well, not like yourself the past few days."

"I'm fine," Vicki replied steadily.

"You're sure? You've always been such a shining girl, and you seem a bit subdued lately. Maybe you've been working too hard. You need to get out and about more. I think I'll speak to David Brent and—"

"Don't do anything of the sort!" Vicki broke in hastily. "I'm fine, honestly. Anyway, Portia and I are going to the fair this weekend, and David might come along. Portia's going to ask him."

Abby seemed satisfied with that and went back to looking at the sketches. She made a few minor suggestions of her own, and ruminated aloud on where Vicki might find the things she needed.

Vicki barely heard her. Her mind had stuck on the words Abby had used to describe her: "such a shining girl." Jason had said there was a "shining quality" about her....

No matter how she tried, she couldn't forget Jason's arms around her, his mouth on hers. He kept flashing across her inward vision, smiling his dazzling smile or grinning wickedly, his gray eyes guileless. Often during her sleepless nights his vibrant voice would echo in her ears. How could she have thought she didn't really love him? Of course, she loved him! But somehow she must *stop* loving him. Every day must be a minute-by-minute hour-by-hour struggle to keep him out of her mind. Foolishly she had let him into her own private center. But it followed that there must be a way to pry him out. She *had* to get over him. She couldn't go on loving a man who didn't love her.

CHAPTER NINE

VICKI WAS JUST LEAVING Abby's office after a budget consultation on Friday afternoon when she saw Sig and Sabrina Lindstrom enter the hotel. She froze in horror. What if Abby were to follow her out, and she'd have to introduce them? What if they mentioned Vicki's supposed engagement? Abby had enough on her mind. There were still no clues about the disappearance of Mrs. Wilson's diamond pendant, nor about any of the prior thefts. She certainly didn't need anything else to worry about.

Numbly Vicki stood there in indecision. Should she duck behind one of the display cases and hope they hadn't seen her? Or would it be better to meet them and steer them away from Abby's vicinity? Before she could react physically, however, they had spotted her and were coming over.

Sig was smiling broadly, but Sabrina's own smile didn't seem to affect the rest of her face. Even so, she looked striking in a superbly cut suit of cherry red, its skirt slit to the thigh. Her lipstick matched her outfit exactly, accentuating the marble whiteness of her skin and the ebony of her hair. She looked like an exotic flower, Vicki decided, at once conscious of her own working clothes and her braided hair. Self-consciously she moved toward them, shaking hands with Sig and nodding at Sabrina.

"What on earth are you doing here?" she blurted out.

"We've come to see Jason, of course," Sabrina said in a somewhat patronizing tone.

"But he's in London! He decided—"

"My dear Vicki, didn't you know?" Sig interrupted her. "Jason returned to Derringham this morning. Surely you've see him?"

"I...no—" Vicki's mind was racing as she tried to come up with some excuse. She shouldn't have spoken so impulsively, but should have waited until they spoke. Then she'd have been warned. She couldn't let them find out now that the "engagement" was a hoax. The explanations alone were impossible to imagine. "I've been pretty busy," she said at last. "I expect he couldn't find me."

Sabrina's perfect eyebrows arched. "Then you must come up with us. He must have missed you dreadfully all week."

There was a spiteful note in her voice. Vicki was suddenly sure that the other woman knew the whole engagement business was a sham. But Sig didn't....

"I have to see the chef," she improvised. "My aunt asked me to check something...." Her voice trailed away as her imagination faltered. "I'm sure you and Jason have business to discuss," she went on hastily. "I'd only be in the way." She was already retreating. "You can get the elevator over there." She pointed across the lobby, then fled.

Vicki did visit Jean-Paul in the kitchens, so at least her excuse wasn't quite so much a lie. Then she went up to Abby's apartment, trying to ignore the feeling of expectancy that had assailed her as soon as she'd learned Jason was at home.

HE TELEPHONED within the hour. "Victoria, darling," he exclaimed as soon as she answered, and
Vicki guessed at once that Sig must be listening nearby. "Sig and Sabrina insist that you join us for tea.
I'm sure you've been working long enough. What do
you say?"

His voice was light and loving. In spite of herself,
she felt her bones softening. She swallowed hard.
"No, thank you," she replied in a low voice.

"But, darling...." He paused, and she heard him
say in a jocular aside, "Sig, old man, how can I
speak to my fiancée if you keep hovering like that?
Give a man some privacy, there's a good chap." She
could imagine him talking over his shoulder, smiling
his crooked smile.

Indignation filled her. She welcomed the feeling,
welcomed the strength it gave her. "You said originally that our charade would only last for one day,"
she reminded him. "Then you—we—extended it into
the night. That was obviously a mistake, *my* mistake.
The masquerade is over, Jason."

There was a moment's silence, then he said softly,
"I made a mess of everything, didn't I?"

She didn't answer, and after a second or two he
spoke again calmly and reasonably. "I didn't expect
Sig and Sabrina to come out here, for they never have
before. But Sabrina wanted to consult with me about
the theater. It's just damn bad luck. I'm returning to
London almost immediately because *Hamlet* has
been extended for two more weeks. Another hour
and they'd have missed me." He paused. "Victoria, I
know it's a lot to ask under the circumstances, but if
you come for tea, we could talk after Sig and Sabrina
leave." He hesitated again. "Actually I came back so

that I *could* talk to you. Kim said you were closeted with Abby, and I didn't want to disturb you. I was about to check on you again when the Lindstroms arrived.''

So her excuse to the couple hadn't been such a lie, after all. She waited.

"I can't delay my departure, I'm afraid," he continued. "But we would possibly have a few minutes...."

"No, Jason. I can't face them. I can't pretend. And we have nothing to talk about."

"But what on earth shall I tell them?"

"How about the truth? That there never was an engagement, and there never will be."

There was another silence. To Vicki's dismay, her heart was beating like a drum. Probably because of anger, she decided. What gall the man had to expect her to go on with the hoax as though nothing had happened between them. As though he hadn't stayed away from her all week.

And yet way down deep she knew that anger wasn't her chief emotion. Instead she was hurt, hurt that her rejection of him had been enough to turn him away from her altogether—except when it suited his own convenience.

At the same time she longed to do as he asked. She longed to go to his suite and have tea with him, to talk with him, to explain....

"I have to go now," she said before she could weaken. Deliberately she made her voice cold. "I'm sure you'll think of something to tell the Lindstroms. You're very good at storytelling." She hung up quickly before he had a chance to reply.

For a long moment Vicki leaned her head against

the wall next to the telephone, then she straightened determinedly. At least, she'd found out he was going back to London, and she wouldn't have to worry about bumping into him in the hotel. And she could still go to the fair; obviously he wasn't going to be there. Perhaps the event would distract her from her misery; there must be something that would!

WHEN THEY ARRIVED at the fair the next day, Vicki was amazed at the number of cars parked in the field next to the fairgrounds. More cars were arriving from all directions, sending clouds of dust into the air as she, Portia and David Brent walked toward the field, Royce as usual bringing up the rear. Portia was still under guard, it seemed, but whether Royce's presence was meant to discourage the girl from getting into mischief or to protect her from some unknown peril, Vicki had no idea.

Portia and Vicki were dressed almost alike in tight-fitting blue jeans, cotton shirts and sneakers. David was wearing one of his correct dark suits, an opennecked shirt his only concession to the casual nature of the outing. He was being very attentive, Vicki noticed, taking her elbow whenever they came to a rough patch of ground, or when a car crept alongside. She was beginning to feel like somebody's maiden aunt. So far he had said very little except to remark on the weather, which was sunny and warm, with only a few puffy white clouds in a cornflower blue sky.

Stalls had been set up all over the field, and as they came closer, they could hear the cries of peddlers selling their wares. In the distance a Ferris wheel was turning slowly, as yet unoccupied. Crowds of people strolled everywhere, looking happy and relaxed. Many of the couples were wheeling plump pink-cheeked babies in strollers—"pushchairs" as they were called here.

Several of the townspeople wore old-fashioned country clothing, the women in long flowered cotton dresses, and the men in waistcoats, breeches and shirts with full sleeves. At one side of the field a calliope blared its own unique music.

Vicki felt the heaviness that had hung over her like a dark cloud begin to lift a little. Though this fair was different from any she had attended, the air of excitement was common to fairs everywhere. Portia was positively dancing along, and Vicki conceded that it was impossible to be dejected on such a day in such an atmosphere. With that decision made, she gave David a deliberately dazzling smile, which brought a flush to his cheeks.

"This is fun, isn't it?" she said determinedly.

"I suppose it is."

His voice sounded doubtful, and she laughed. "Not quite your cup of tea, as Mrs. Powell would say?"

He smiled deprecatingly, but made no comment.

David was something of a snob, she decided as they strolled toward a stall selling cider. Probably he'd feel more at home on the cricket field, clapping politely and saying, "Oh, jolly well played." She remembered a conversation she'd had with Portia about public schools, which, Portia had said, were really very private and "terribly hoity-toity." No doubt, David was a product of such a school.

"What's the history of the fair?" Vicki asked conversationally as they stood in a group sipping cider out of paper cups. Behind them was a large wooden platform on which a group of people were settling themselves on folding chairs.

David looked blank, but Portia answered eagerly. "It used to be a hiring fair, a kind of unofficial employment exchange for farmers looking for workers and farmhands wanting new jobs," she explained, smiling smugly at David, as though pleased to know something he didn't. "Sometime in history it got combined with the cattle-and-produce market that was chartered by King Henry III. Now it's just for fun, but it draws a big crowd because of the old-fashioned games, the antique sales and so on." She looked beyond Vicki, her pale gray eyes darkening into a frown. "And because of Jason, of course," she added gloomily.

Vicki forced herself to turn around. Sure enough, there was Jason, climbing up onto the platform ahead of a bald-headed man in clerical dress. Portia let out a melodramatic groan. "He said on the phone this morning that he'd agreed at the last minute to be here, but I was hoping he wouldn't make it," she said disconsolately. "He's been in a rotten mood lately. He probably won't want me to have any fun."

Vicki barely heard her. Her whole attention was taken up with the sight of Jason Meredith. Standing up there, he looked every inch the superstar in a lightweight tan suit of European cut and a white ribbed-cotton turtleneck.

Some of the ladies on the makeshift stage were simpering up at him as he bent over their hands. She really couldn't blame them; he was favoring all and sundry with his thousand-watt smile. He exuded such an air of confidence and charm that even at this distance she was affected by it. She wanted to turn around, to move away before he could see her—at first sight of him her body had tensed for flight—but she seemed paralyzed. So she just stood there gazing at him, probably with her heart in her eyes.

As the vicar motioned to a man at the side of the stage, and the man raised a horn and blew a long blast on it, Jason turned and looked directly at her, as though he'd known all along right where she was. Across the heads of the people between them their eyes met and held for a long moment. The corners of Jason's mouth twitched as if he were about to smile, but then the vicar touched his arm. He turned his head, leaning down a little to help the vicar with his fussy manipulations of the microphone.

At the same moment Vicki was jostled forward by the crush of the crowd that was gathering in response to the horn. Her heart was hammering, the palms of her hands felt damp. She had never realized that emotion could have so many physical effects, and she was almost deafened by the sound of her own heart-beats, so much so that she missed entirely the vicar's opening remarks. The crowd roared when Jason was introduced, pressing forward as if wanting to get closer to him. Evidently everyone, too, felt the magnetism he projected just standing there, smiling his crooked smile. Virility personified.

When the crowd quieted, he spread his arms wide in a theatrical gesture, and his distinctive voice rang out through the loudspeakers. "Friends, Romans, countrymen, lend me your ears." He was hamming it up, and the crowd loved it. There was another wave of applause.

"I have to get out of here," Vicki murmured to

David, grasping his arm. He looked startled, but he responded at once, very politely clearing a path for her, heading obliquely out to one side.

"Are you unwell?" he asked solicitously when they finally emerged into a clear space.

"I'm...just a little claustrophobic, I guess." She could hardly tell David Brent that at the first sound of Jason's voice she had yearned so much to touch him that she could barely stand.

His voice was still booming out across the fairgrounds, but they were far enough away from the loudspeakers that it was distorted now. "You go on back," she suggested to the young man. "There's no need for you to miss the speech."

He smiled thinly. "I've heard many of Mr. Meredith's speeches. I don't need to hear them all. One does have some rights."

It was the first near criticism he'd ever given of his employer, and she looked at him, startled. "Don't you like Jason?" she asked curiously.

His expression didn't change, but one light brown eyebrow flickered for an instant. "Of course, I do," he said promptly. "Mr. Meredith is an extremely considerate fellow to work for. I consider it a rare privilege to work for such a great man."

Vicki frowned. The words in themselves were favorable, but his voice had sounded almost parrotlike, as though he were repeating a well-rehearsed speech.

And what if it were rehearsed, she thought, chiding herself for reading something into David's words that wasn't there. Probably he was often asked his opinion of Jason Meredith. All he'd said was that he'd heard a lot of Jason's speeches; that didn't mean he had anything against Jason himself.

"So what shall we do with ourselves?" she asked with an attempt at her earlier gaiety.

"I thought we'd go to the antique stalls later," he said vaguely. "They probably aren't open yet, though." He looked around, then pointed to a large roped-off area. "The games are going to be held over there. We could get a good view if we go now. Shall I tell Royce to bring Portia over there when the speeches are finished?"

Vicki nodded, and he plunged back into the crowd. A minute later he reappeared, straightening his jacket fussily and smoothing his hair in a way that irritated her. No, David was not the irritation—it was the sight of Jason that had upset her. She wished she could suggest that they go back to the hotel, but she could hardly do that. She'd just have to hope that Jason, having done his duty, would zoom back to London in his silver car without attempting to talk to her.

Which he probably would do, her mind added in glum contradiction. What a mixture of emotions that man inspired in her.

She forced herself to pay attention as David described the various games they were about to see. But her mind kept losing track of his words, and she realized her ears were straining to hear Jason's voice. She was relieved when the speeches ended, and the crowds surged toward the games area. Trying to keep her mind blank, determined not to turn around to see where Jason might have gone, Vicki kept her gaze fixed on the contestants in front of her.

The games were unusual and very rowdy. Portia got very much into the spirit of them, cheering on the participants and nearly having to be restrained by Royce from joining in.

One of the rowdiest was something called "dwylie flunking," which involved a ring of men holding sticks with beer-soaked cloths fastened to the ends of them. Whenever the one who was "it" was hit with a cloth, he had to drink a chamberpot full of beer. Or at least, as far as Vicki could see, those were the rules.

As soon as the men allowed a few young women into their midst, Portia wanted to try it, but David dissuaded her. "Your brother wouldn't approve," he said sternly.

That seemed to be enough to subdue the girl. "May I go on the rides, then?" she asked demurely. "Royce will go with me, won't you, Royce?"

Royce's answer was an audible sigh and a pained expression, but then he looked at Portia's pleading face and relented. "I'd be happy to escort you, Miss Portia," he said gallantly.

A moment later the tall elegant old man and the sprite of a girl were walking off together across the fields. Vicki watched them go, smiling at the incongruous couple they made.

When she turned back, Kim had materialized next to David. The receptionist grinned cheerfully at Vicki. "Are you 'aving a good time, love?" she asked.

Vicki nodded, making an effort to return the smile. Kim looked even more curvaceous than usual today in a bright yellow halter and brief white shorts. She was standing very close to David, Vicki observed, and David was looking embarrassed, even though his attention was apparently fixed on the boisterous goings-on in front of him.

"I didn't mean to steal your date," Vicki whispered apologetically to Kim.

"Oh, 'e wasn't my date, love. 'E never takes me

out. We're just friends-like, at the 'otel. 'E's a bit of a toff, see. 'E can't be seen with the likes of me.''

"I don't see why not," Vicki answered indignantly.

Kim shrugged, smiling wistfully. "I don't mind. 'E's a bit of all right, anyhow. I'm real flattered that 'e talks to me at all."

About to protest again, Vicki stopped herself. This was Kim's business, not hers. And she was hardly an expert on male-female relationships; she'd pretty well proved that.

After the dwylie flunking came falconry. Vicki felt sorry for the birds, hooded and jessed to their owners' wrists. But her sympathy gave way to admiration when the birds were released and flew, soaring and swooping high above the crowd.

"Impressive, aren't they?" said a familiar voice behind her.

She didn't turn. "Very," she managed through a suddenly dry throat.

Jason's hand touched her elbow, and she stiffened. He dropped his hand at once. "I want to talk to you, Victoria," he said, making no attempt to lower his voice. "Shall we find a quieter spot?"

She hesitated. Kim was obviously all ears, glancing from Jason to Vicki with an alert and knowing grin on her round face.

"I came with David," Vicki said finally.

Jason raised one eyebrow at David as he leaned back behind Kim. "Do you mind?" he asked.

David shook his head. "Of course not, sir."

How could he say anything else?

"I rather like the falcons," he added quietly to Vicki. "I'll watch them for a while and look for you later, if you like."

Kim's expression had changed to a pleased one. She'd probably hoped for a chance to be alone with David. And anyway, Vicki told herself, she could hardly refuse to go with Jason now. He had really left her no choice.

Still not looking at him, she allowed him to lead her away. A crowd was still in place around the platform, she saw. They were watching some men in costume dancing to the jingle of bells strapped around their knees. "Morris dancers," Jason told her.

She stole a glance at him. He'd discarded his jacket somewhere. The short sleeves of his turtleneck were pressing against the muscles of his tanned arms. She could remember the way those muscles had felt under her hands. No. She was not going to think of that.

"It took me several minutes to find you," he said. "Portia and Royce told me where you were. It was kind of you to come with her. Thank you."

Vicki sighed in exasperation. "It wasn't meant to be a kindness. I enjoy Portia's company." Without meaning to, she had accented Portia's name, probably giving the impression that she preferred Portia's company to his. He glanced at her sideways, but didn't say anything.

"What did you tell Sig and Sabrina, after all?" she asked stiffly.

"I said we'd had a minor disagreement, and that you were cross with me."

"Oh."

Again he looked at her sideways. "Sig gave me some good advice on making up."

"I'm sure," she said neutrally.

He'd put on his sunglasses and was walking beside her in his "trying-not-to-be-noticed" slouch. It didn't work for long here. They hadn't gone far when he was spotted and surrounded by a group of teenage girls waving autograph books. Evidently they'd come prepared.

Once trapped, Jason was gracious, talking and smiling as he signed his name over and over. The girls were giggling and squealing with delight, pressing as close to him as they could, gazing at him with awestruck wonder. One or two of the most daring stretched out hesitant fingers to touch his arm, his hand. The hubbub around him attracted others, and Vicki began to wonder if he would ever manage to break free. She was reminded of an experiment in a high-school physics class, scattering iron filings on a sheet of paper. When she'd held the page over a magnet, all the tiny flakes of iron had hurtled toward the magnetized center, so that she could see the lines of force. This "star-quality" was a strange phenomenon, she thought. Like magnets, certain individuals seemed to possess the power to draw people's attention to them, to make the atmosphere around them crackle with electricity. Jason had it in abundance. He was an almost mythical personality, a superstar who not only possessed that mysterious but unmistakable quality, but was a skilled professional actor, as well.

Vicki noticed several of the girls looking at her enviously when Jason finally managed to extricate himself from the circle of fans and came toward her. It was impossible not to feel flattered that he chose to be with her.

She swallowed. Flattered indeed! Her heart was hammering in her breast like a wild thing. She loved him so. Dear God, how she loved him! But it was foolish to go off with him like this; she had determined to forget him, hadn't she? She must make some excuse, get away from him, leave the fair.

Once again her plans for flight came to nothing. As soon as Jason reached her, he grabbed her hand and ran with her toward the woods, not allowing her to stop or draw breath until they reached the safety of the first group of trees.

He was smiling as he drew her down beside him on the grass, but his face became solemn as he looked at her. "It's been a rotten week, hasn't it?" he asked.

"Yes." The word was out before she could stop it.

"What happened, Victoria? What went wrong?" He laughed shortly. "No woman ever looked at me like that before. Shook me to my very foundation. Was I so repugnant to you?"

"Of course not." She swallowed hard. "I. . . remembered something that had happened to me. . . a while ago."

He waited, watching her face. And at last she forced herself to tell him about Ken Marriott's attack, and the humiliating time that had followed.

He frowned. "Surely that wasn't your only experience of sex?" he asked.

"No." Taking a deep breath, she went on to explain about the race-car driver.

His intense gaze didn't leave her face. "I suppose men like that would tend to put you off the whole idea," he said slowly.

"It wasn't just that, Jason," she admitted. The time had come for complete honesty, so she told him of the doubts that had accumulated in her mind. "I guess I just can't force myself to. . . sleep around," she concluded.

He winced. "I hardly thought of it as 'sleeping around,' " he said hastily. "I'm not—"

He broke off. "I've got to admit to some doubts myself," he said at last. "When you stopped me... the look on your face.... I realized you aren't like most of the women I know. You don't treat sex casually, do you?"

She shook her head.

He took off his sunglasses and pushed them into a trouser pocket. For a long moment his gray eyes studied her face. "I suppose you know that I was married for several years," he finally said, surprising her.

"I read about it, yes."

"My marriage was well documented, wasn't it? Every fight Claire and I ever had found its way into print." He sighed. "There was some truth in those stories, Victoria; there usually is, though it's often exaggerated. But Claire was a fine woman. I was the one at fault."

This was not something she particularly wanted to hear, but in spite of herself she was distressed by the jagged note in his voice. He was sitting up, his hands clasped around one knee, tension in every line of his body. The bitterness she'd noticed around his mouth when she first met him was more pronounced now. He was looking straight ahead, his eyes dark with memories.

"You don't have to talk about your marriage, Jason," she said awkwardly. "We don't have to talk about this at all. I made a mistake. I thought...I wanted...."

His gaze shifted to her face, and she was appalled at the pain that showed in his eyes. "Please let me finish, Victoria," he said. "I have to explain why I'm the way I am. After Claire died, I swore I would never commit myself to a woman again. I'm flawed in some area, I'm afraid." He laughed shortly. "It's funny in a way—typecasting. All of Shakespeare's heroes had fatal flaws: Macbeth's was overambition; Lear's was pride; Hamlet's, indecisiveness. And mine is insensitivity. Claire told me that often enough, and she was right. I'm just not good romantic material.

"The other night I acted impulsively," he went on. "I wanted you, and I suppose I'm used to getting what I want. Anyway, I didn't stop to think about the consequences to you. Even though I didn't know about your former experiences, I should have had sense enough to recognize that you're the type of woman who expects sex to lead inevitably to marriage." He held up one hand as she started to speak. "There's nothing wrong with that. Way things ought to be. It's just out where I'm concerned."

There didn't seem to be anything she could say. In any case, he didn't give her time to respond. "You see, Victoria," he said. "I have only one priority—my work. It means everything to me. I can't live with a woman or put her interests ahead of my own. And I realized that night that what I have to offer is not enough for a woman like you." He glanced at her sideways. "At the time my ego was badly bruised, also," he admitted. "The way you looked at me made me feel I was a monster who'd tried to rape you."

"It wasn't you, Jason."

"I realize that now. But I also realize I did the right thing by leaving. I'm not sure I could have trusted myself not to. . .touch you again. I'm not sure I can trust myself now."

She glanced at him in alarm, and he laughed softly. "Don't worry, Victoria, I'm not a glutton for rejection."

She really had hurt his pride, Vicki thought. Her mother had always said that a man's ego was a fragile thing, easily bruised. And Jason Meredith, of course, had had no experience with rejection.

But she didn't want to reject him, not totally. She loved him. If only there was some middle ground where she could meet him. . . .

But no, he had made himself quite clear. He had told her that he hadn't recovered from his wife's death. He had implied that there was room in his life only for quick and casual couplings. And as she wasn't interested in casual couplings, there was no room in his life for her. Had it really been necessary for him to be quite so honest, Vicki wondered bitterly. She must not let him see how desperately wounded she felt. She must at least hang onto whatever shred of pride was left to her. She must shut all her grief inside her and pretend not to mind.

"Victoria?" he said softly, reaching out with one hand to touch her face.

She held her breath, willing herself not to respond to the tenderness of his touch. "You look so sad," he said wonderingly.

His hand slid down to cup her chin, turning her face toward him. "I'm so sorry it didn't work out," he murmured. "But we can be friends, can't we? I do enjoy your company so much." He dropped his hand. "Do you understand what I mean. . . about my career having to come first? About Claire?"

A hard tight knot was gathering inside her. To protect herself, she withdrew behind her coolest façade. "Oh, yes," she said levelly. "I've got it perfectly straight now, thank you."

"Victoria—" He had turned on the grass to face

her, his eyes darkening. One hand was again reaching out to touch her, but if he touched her again, she would fall apart....

She scrambled to her feet, almost stumbling in her haste. He stood up, too, and grasped her arms under the elbows, forcing her to look up at him. His formerly grim expression had softened; she couldn't bear it if he pitied her! But she couldn't move away; his grip was too powerful.

"I've hurt you, haven't I?" he asked. "The one thing I didn't want to do!" His expression changed again, to a tenderness that was even more unbearable. "Is it absolutely impossible for us to—" he began, but before he could say anything more, they were interrupted by a shout, and they both swung around.

Royce was hurrying across the grass, obviously out of breath, his dignity cast aside. "I can't find Miss Portia," he panted.

Jason let go of Vicki's arms abruptly. "Where did you see her last?" he demanded.

The butler took a deep breath, his face quite red from his exertions. "She wanted to ride the merry-go-round, sir. And I didn't think she could come to harm as long as I was watching her. But she dismounted on the other side, and by the time I'd found out, she was running off so fast I couldn't catch her." He looked apologetic. "I just can't run as well as I used to, sir."

Jason shook his head impatiently. "But there wasn't anyone with her? No one *took* her away?"

"Oh, no, sir. I saw her running all alone toward the games arena. I followed, but David hadn't seen her."

Jason was beginning to look relieved. Evidently he still worried that someone might harm the girl, given the opportunity. He shook his head. "She knows she's not supposed to go anywhere alone," he said mildly. "What do you suppose she's up to?"

Royce shrugged, still trying to catch his breath. "Possibly she just wanted some time alone, sir," he suggested.

Jason frowned. "That may be so, but *why* would she want to be alone, that's the question."

"Everyone needs to be alone sometimes," Vicki pointed out. "She's hardly a child, Jason."

Jason looked at her impatiently. "That's no reason to go running away from poor old Royce here. She must have had some other purpose. And I want to know what it is."

Apparently dismissing Vicki altogether, he started across the field at a pace she could barely keep up with. Whatever he'd been about to say to her earlier had been cut off very neatly, she thought as she followed him. Which was probably just as well. He'd made his position clear; there was no need for him to add anything more. She could not have borne more, anyway.

It was Vicki who spotted Portia. The morris dancers on the platform had given way to a small rock group dressed in what looked like Daniel Boone outfits. Their music was loud but good, and a crowd of young people were on stage dancing, cheered on by the onlookers. Portia was dancing alone, quite expertly, Vicki noted. As a matter of fact, several girls were dancing alone, but Portia had positioned herself in front of the lead-guitar player, a nice-looking boy with long curly black hair. He didn't look more than sixteen himself. As Vicki watched, not at all surprised to see that the girl was safe, the boy set his electric guitar aside and joined Portia, moving his body in perfect unison with hers. Portia started talking animatedly to him, and he responded with obvious interest.

Vicki pushed through the crowd until she found Jason and David, who were standing together looking helplessly around them. "I've found her," she said as she reached them, glad that Portia's disappearance had at least given her time to recover her composure. The knot of bitterness was still there inside her, but she'd managed to keep its influence out of her voice. She had sounded quite calm, she thought.

Jason followed the direction of her pointing hand, and anger immediately darkened his strong features. "Get her down from there," he ordered David.

"Yes, sir," David replied promptly, but Vicki grabbed the young man's arm before he could obediently move away.

"She's not doing any harm," she said furiously to Jason, glad to have a chance to vent some emotion. "You've got to stop treating her like a child. She's almost sixteen. All she wants is a chance to have a little fun and an opportunity to make friends. Look at her—I've never seen her so happy."

"I don't want her associating with that sort of person," he said flatly.

"*That* sort of person?" she echoed. "That sort of person is no different from you. He's an entertainer, just like you are."

An expression of startled astonishment crossed Jason's face. For a moment she thought she'd insulted him unforgivably, but then his sense of humor surfaced, and he tipped his head back and roared with laughter. "Lord, Victoria," he said when he'd recovered his breath. "You do have a way of taking the wind out of my sails."

"Sir?" David queried, evidently not sure what he was supposed to do now.

"Leave her there," Jason said, still smiling. "Keep an eye on her, though. Victoria, we haven't finished our talk."

"Yes, we have," Vicki said abruptly. "And David can't keep an eye on Portia right now. He promised to show me where the antiques are being sold. I want to look for something for Abby." She glanced at David, who was looking absolutely aghast. Probably he'd never heard anyone argue with his autocratic employer before. "Royce can watch Portia," she continued to Jason before her courage could fail her. "That's his job, isn't it? Tell him we'll meet them by the tea tent at four o'clock."

And with that she dragged David away, noting with satisfaction that Jason was looking even more astonished than before. Conscious that he was watching them, she smiled at David as brightly as she could and slipped her hand further under his arm. He looked almost as amazed as Jason did, but his arm squeezed her hand convulsively, letting her know that he was not unaffected by her flirtatious behavior. The knowledge gave her a feeling of power, which she intended to cling to for as long as possible. Once it passed, she knew she was going to have to face the pain of those minutes with Jason under the trees, the pain of losing him.

No, not that, she amended in her mind. She could hardly lose what she'd never really had.

CHAPTER TEN

HIS NAME WAS COLLY WINTERS, Portia said, and he was nineteen years old. His group was called the Explorers, and they'd been working together for four years, traveling from town to town and hoping someday to make it big. He was supernice, she added emphatically, and had liked her without knowing who she was related to. He thought she'd been named after the Porsche car.

She, Vicki and Abby were in the Blue Room having lunch together two days after the fair. Portia had a half holiday and, still wearing her school uniform, was looking about twelve years old.

Vicki smiled at her. "I was amazed at how well you dance," she said.

Portia's elfin face showed pleasure. "I've never had lessons, except for the silly reels and things we learn at school. I've watched people on television, though, and practiced in my room. Colly said I was a fab dancer," she added dreamily. "I gave him my telephone number. Don't tell Jason."

"Where is the group staying?" Abby asked.

"At the George," she said, naming a pub on the outskirts of town.

"The group is really good?" Abby asked Vicki.

"Very. Are you thinking of hiring them?"

"Well, I've thought about your suggestion, and

it's certainly worth trying. I suppose I could talk to their manager and—''

"Colly's the manager," Portia interrupted, her face lighting up with excitement. "Would you really have them here, Mrs. Carstairs? That would be absolutely fab."

Evidently she'd picked up a new word—from Colly, Vicki surmised.

"You wouldn't be able to dance in the Wine Cellar," Abby warned. "You aren't old enough."

"I know, but he'd be staying in the area longer. I could see him when he's not working."

"You really like him, don't you?" Vicki asked.

Portia nodded eagerly, her gray eyes shining so that they looked as luminous as Jason's. "He's so sophisticated," she said. "He has his own flat in London. I wish I lived in London," she added wistfully.

Vicki couldn't quite accept "sophisticated" in connection with the curly-haired oddly clad youth she remembered, but she certainly wasn't going to argue the point. "What do you think, Abby?" she asked.

Abby rose, crumpling her damask napkin and dropping it on the table. "We'll see," she said. "I suppose I'll have to audition them first and see if we can reach an agreement." She gave a mock shudder. "Rock music in these hallowed halls—Simon would be horrified!" She laughed, reaching down to hug Portia's shoulders. "Don't get carried away now, dear. Nothing's definite, but I promise you I'll set aside my basic old-fogy attitude and give them a fair trial. I'll take Kimberly along; she's an expert on such matters."

"Kim loved them," Portia cried triumphantly.

"They're as good as in." Her brow clouded. "You won't tell Colly who I am, will you, Mrs. Carstairs? It makes things so... grotty when people know about Jason."

"I won't breathe a word," she promised, smiling. "And now I have to leave you young things and get to work. I've got an appointment with some insurance people."

"Mrs. Wilson's pendant?" Vicki queried.

"We're still trying to reach a settlement. There are still no clues." She sighed. "At least, there haven't been any more thefts."

"Colly's bound to find out sooner or later who you are," Vicki said to Portia after Abby had gone. "If he's worth having as a friend, it shouldn't make any difference to him."

Portia sighed. "I know. But I'd like him to see *me* first before he finds out. Do you know what I mean?"

"Of course I do."

"I am proud of Jason," the girl continued. "It's not that I want to disown him or anything. But this is the first time anyone's met me without knowing about him. And Colly really did like me. He said so." She seemed amazed at the fact.

Vicki found herself worrying like a mother hen, afraid this Colly Winters might not be the sterling character Portia thought him. She didn't want the girl to get hurt.

"Do you really think Mrs. Carstairs will engage the Explorers?" Portia asked.

Vicki hesitated. "Maybe," she said evasively, but privately she didn't hold out much hope. It would be quite an innovation for The Singing Tree Inn, and her aunt was basically conservative. Then she smiled inwardly, thinking of Abby sitting in on a rock session. She probably would be horrified.

BUT TO HER AMAZEMENT, Abby wasn't horrified at all. The Explorers were given a limited engagement in the Wine Cellar "to test the waters," Abby told Vicki as they sat in her office a couple of days later.

She grinned when Vicki expressed her surprise. "I haven't always been fifty years old," she pointed out. "I was quite a fan of Elvis Presley's in my salad days. The Explorers' music isn't the same, of course, but the beat is there. My toes were tapping while I listened. I think they have a good future if Colly makes the right moves."

Vicki stared at her. "Colly?"

Abby grinned, obviously enjoying Vicki's amazement. "We got along great. He's a smart young man, if a bit rough around the edges." She looked a little self-conscious. "He reminded me a little of Dan."

Vicki remembered Abby's first husband quite well. She'd liked him a lot. He was very shy, she remembered, but easygoing and good-natured most of the time, slow to anger and quick to make up. Evidently Abby was remembering him, too, for her face had become quite wistful.

"Don't tell me you're going to dance in the Wine Cellar?" Vicki teased her, deliberately changing the subject.

Abby's hazel eyes sparkled. "You know, I'd really love to, but I guess it wouldn't suit my position as chatelaine, would it? I wouldn't want to shock my more staid guests. No reason why you can't dance, though," she added. "Do you good. You need some cheering up."

Vicki darted a glance at her. Abby was looking at her with an expression of sympathy on her face. "You want to talk about it?" she asked softly.

Vicki shook her head.

"Okay. But whatever the problem is—and I think I have a pretty good idea—it won't hurt you to make an attempt to be happy." She leaned across her desk and patted Vicki's hand. "You'd be surprised. If you pretend you're having a good time, you often end up doing so. Give it a try."

IT WAS GOOD ADVICE, and Vicki tried to follow it. For the next few days she forced herself to get out and do things, even though she felt like moping around in her room. She and Portia went to the Derringham church, armed with huge sheets of black paper and gold-colored wax, and under the vicar's direction made brass rubbings. The process wasn't as easy as it looked when the vicar demonstrated. He was a fussy little man, but very good-natured, if a little pedantic. He insisted that they keep practicing until they could produce a rubbing without any smears around the edges. By the time they had produced results that satisfied him, Vicki's back was aching from the hours of kneeling on the flagstones. But her spirits felt lighter than they had for many days.

Abby was right, she decided. Pretense was good therapy. Alone, she drove several times to London, where she was stimulated by the crowds, the big red buses, the hump-backed taxicabs, the excitement. She visited wonderful shops in Knightsbridge and Mayfair, and also less frequented areas. Because of the tax position for members of the Common Market, London was full of fabric shops, and she had an enjoyable time trying to decide on new draperies for the guest rooms she'd redesigned, as well as carpeting and other accessories for the Blue Room and Wine Cellar. She haunted auctions and antique shops, talked to lighting experts and furniture designers, spent evenings working on cost estimates and generally kept herself too busy to think.

The Explorers were an immediate success. Sometimes in the evenings Vicki dropped into the Wine Cellar to see how everything was going, and she even danced a few times with some of the patrons. The only person who wasn't pleased with the innovation was George. He threatened at least once a night to quit if "that dreadful din" continued, but Vicki noticed that by the weekend he was wiping the bar with a new rhythm to his movements.

For two weeks Vicki didn't allow herself time to brood. Sometimes late at night she found herself thinking of a movie she'd seen once years ago— *Prince and the Showgirl*, an adaptation of a Terence Rattigan play, starring Laurence Olivier and Marilyn Monroe. As she remembered the story, the prince could find only a brief time in his busy schedule for sexual dalliance. Unfortunately the show girl chosen for seduction insisted that she be romanced with the proper music and words. Conscious of the passing of time, the prince supplied them, only to find to his horror that the girl had taken him seriously and fallen in love with him. The rest of the movie had dealt with his efforts to extricate himself from the "impossible" situation thus created.

Vicki certainly didn't need Freud to help her figure

out why that story kept coming to mind. The bitterness seemed to have dissipated now, she noted, but it
had left a hollow emptiness inside her that none of
her many activities eased.

She didn't see Jason at all. He called Portia daily,
however, so she was kept up-to-date on his triumphs.
His Hamlet had been an unprecedented success according to all the critics. He was rehearsing for an
upcoming television production. He'd also been
asked to do some readings of Shakespeare in Oxford,
and he'd be performing in Stratford-upon-Avon for
much of August. The queen had attended the closing
performance of *Hamlet* and had congratulated him
personally afterward.

The *closing* performance. "Will he be coming back
to the hotel to stay, then?" Vicki asked as casually as
she could, remembering suddenly that Portia's summer vacation had just begun.

"Not for a few days, thank goodness," Portia said
fervently. "The television thing is wearing him down,
he says. He's too tired to drive back at night. I was
afraid he'd turn up today."

"I thought you missed him."

"I did. I do. But if he comes back now, I won't
have a chance to see Colly, and he's leaving tonight."

Vicki looked at her, feeling a little concerned. They
were in Portia's bedroom, practicing guitar. Lately
Vicki had avoided the Meredith suite, afraid that
Jason might drop in unannounced. She was also anxious to avoid David, who had seemed a little too encouraged by her behavior toward him at the fair. But
today Portia had insisted it was her turn to entertain
Vicki.

Portia's bedroom was rather cluttered and small,

filled with her treasures: loads of record albums, a small stereo system, shelves filled with books. Vicki had already examined the impressive titles: Thackeray, Dickens, Fielding, Galsworthy. A collection of shells decorated Portia's small chintz-skirted dressing table, and theatrical posters, many featuring Jason, were Scotch taped to the walls. Portia's bedroom at Meredith Manor was much larger, she'd told Vicki, but Jason wouldn't let her put posters on the paneled walls. Abby had given her permission to do so here.

A new poster had been added, Vicki noticed. Colly Winters in a typical rock pose—guitar at an ungodly angle, curly hair flying, face contorted. She suppressed a shudder at the thought of what Jason would have to say. Yet the group was a good one, and wholesome. The boys affected the fringed buckskins of wilderness explorers, which Vicki supposed was the reason for the name of the group. Their girl singer, for some reason, dressed like a punk rocker, her spiky hair dyed vermilion and her clothing black, skin tight and studded with strange badges. But they were all healthy clean kids, with no evidence of drugs or wild behavior.

Whenever Vicki had spent any time in the Wine Cellar, she'd noticed Portia hovering around the door or peeking around the curtains at the side of the band's platform. During the intermissions she was pretty sure Colly and Portia were together. She'd seen them a couple of times down by the river, sitting together on a tree stump, talking earnestly. But Royce was always in the vicinity, and anyway, as far as she could tell, they were acting just like a couple of kids getting to know each other. Vicki was pretty sure, however, that Jason wouldn't see their friendship in quite the same light.

"You're not getting too attached to Colly, are you?" she asked Portia after a while.

Portia didn't answer for a moment. Her expression was closed, and she had bent her head down over the guitar as she fingered the strings. "I love him," she said at last.

Vicki's heart went out to the girl. There was no doubt in her mind that this was puppy love, but she knew it could hurt as much at going on sixteen as at any other time. "Does he love you?" she asked gently.

Portia shrugged, still not raising her head. "You know how men are," she said flatly. "It hasn't even occurred to him that I'm female. He thinks of me as a friend." She paused. "And that's enough for now, anyhow. I don't want to get into all that stuff until I have to."

Vicki wondered suddenly if Portia had been taught anything about sex. She couldn't quite imagine Mrs. Powell being a lot of help there.

Apparently reading her mind, Portia glanced up and grinned. "You don't have to worry about whether I know what's what," she said. "Jason sat me down years ago and told me everything. He's very practical that way." She chuckled. "The headmistress at school gave all the sixth-form girls a talk a few months ago. It's a good job I knew all about it, or I'd have been dreadfully confused. She made sex sound about as exciting as a visit to the dentist." She shrugged. "I'm not ready yet, anyway. There's plenty of time for that sort of thing, thank you very much. But I do love Colly. He's so...so different. I don't let him know I love him, though," she added. "I think it's best not to get too emotional around men, don't you?"

Vicki agreed, feeling she might well take lessons in common sense from Portia. Nobody needed to worry about this self-possessed girl. Inevitably Colly had discovered who her brother was, but though impressed, he hadn't asked for an introduction or treated Portia differently than he had before. Vicki's respect for him had increased when Portia told her that.

"You're going to miss him, aren't you?" she said sympathetically.

For some reason Portia looked suddenly and unmistakably guilty. Her startled glance flew to Vicki's face, then her expression closed again, and she bent her head over the guitar. "I expect I'll see him sometime," she said evenly. "And he's promised to write."

Vicki wasn't sure why she felt so abruptly uneasy. Portia had answered promptly, and her words were calm enough. Perhaps that was it: she seemed too calm for someone who was going to lose her closest friend in just a few hours. Of course, London wasn't far away. No doubt, Colly could drive down to see Portia quite often if Jason gave permission. That was the catch: she couldn't imagine Jason giving permission. If so much hadn't happened between them, she might have been able to influence him on Portia's behalf, but that wasn't possible now.

She studied Portia's bent head. The girl must know as well as she did that once Jason was home, she probably wouldn't have a chance to see Colly again. Yet she didn't seem concerned. She seemed almost content.

For a while they went on with their lesson. Portia had graduated to a tune called "Dueling Banjos," which had been featured in a Burt Reynolds movie. Her main problem was with the size of her hands. She was a petite girl, and her rather small fingers couldn't quite reach to the C-chord. But she had an excellent ear, and she was making good progress, spurred on by her admiration of Colly Winters. Vicki suspected that her pupil entertained ambitions of joining his group eventually. She could imagine Jason's reaction to that.

She was sitting on Portia's bed to help her with the fingering, studiously keeping her gaze from all those reproductions of Jason's face. But some part of her mind was conscious of them looking down at her. The hollow feeling that engulfed her whenever she let down her guard for a moment was beginning to return, and she was relieved when David knocked on the door and told them Mrs. Powell was serving tea.

Over tea David surprised her by inviting both her and Portia out to dinner that evening at a restaurant called Stacey's in Latham's Corners, the next town. "They serve American food—hamburgers and that sort of thing," he told Vicki hesitantly. "I thought you might enjoy a bit of home cooking, so to speak."

Vicki didn't have the heart to turn him down or tell him she didn't particularly like hamburgers. She began to regret her acquiescence, however, when she discovered that what the cook at Stacey's called a hamburger platter was a very strange dish. She couldn't ever remember eating a hamburger with bacon and eggs before.

The restaurant was nice enough, though not heavy on atmosphere. It was more of a café than a restaurant, with gingham tablecloths and whitewashed walls. The food was properly cooked and nicely presented, too.

Portia seemed delighted with the place and the meal. To Vicki's surprise she had accepted David's invitation without protest. "As long as we're back by nine," she'd added. "I do want to see Colly, and that's when he has his first break."

Since their arrival Portia had somehow managed to put away a prodigious amount of food, including two servings of French fries.

Vicki decided that her earlier uneasiness had been unjustified. Portia was still a little girl, after all, one who often seemed much younger than her American counterparts. She might think she was in love, but her emotions obviously didn't run very deep.

"You're sure you don't want more French fries?" she asked dryly as Portia pushed her plate way.

Portia shook her head, her curls bouncing. "No, thank you. I'm absolutely stuffed. We don't call them French fries here, by the way," she added teasingly. "We call them chips."

"And what, may I ask, do you call potato chips?"

"Crisps," Portia said, pleased as always to be in the role of teacher rather than student.

Vicki laughed. "I'm acquiring a whole new vocabulary," she said lightly. "Let me see now...." She checked items on her fingers as she listed them. "Two weeks make a fortnight; cookies are biscuits; candy is sweets...."

David nodded, smiling. "And what you call dessert is 'the sweet' here." He raised his light eyebrows. "Do you know the parts of the car?" He'd taught her a new word earlier when he referred to the fender

of her Mini as the wing. She had driven them all to
Latham's Corners when she'd found out David had
intended hiring a taxi because he didn't own a car.

"The bonnet, the boot and the silencer, which is
really the muffler," she said promptly and laughed
again.

She was really getting good at laughing, she decided as David signaled the waitress for the bill. Perhaps
she was beginning to heal, after all. She certainly felt
relaxed tonight, sitting here with Portia and David.
David looked almost handsome and more at ease
than usual. He was wearing dark slacks and a blue V-
necked sweater over a paler blue shirt. The color gave
more life to his pale blue eyes. He hadn't had much
to say so far, but then he never did, and he did seem
to be having a good time.

He was enjoying her company, Vicki realized.
More than once she'd felt his gaze on her. He'd told
her at the fair that he loved the way she laughed.
"Few Englishwomen have perfect teeth like yours,"
he'd said. "You light up the air around you when
you smile."

He really was rather a dear, she decided. If Kim
hadn't made her interest in him obvious, she might
even be tempted to flirt with him a little. A light flir-
tation would be good for her ego right now. But no,
she thought, looking up to find his earnest gaze on
her again. She already felt guilty about the way she'd
behaved with him at the fair, leading him on as
though she was interested in him. And all the time
she'd been using him to prevent her pain from showing.

When they returned to the hotel, David invited her
up to the Meredith suite for some of Mrs. Powell's

coffee. The coffee at Stacey's had been absolutely undrinkable—strong enough to melt the thick cup it came in, Vicki had privately decided.

Accompanied by Royce, Portia went down to the Wine Cellar to see Colly. But she came upstairs again within fifteen minutes, apparently still unconcerned about the group's departure, and disappeared into her room—to read, she said. Vicki suspected that the girl might try to sneak down to the Wine Cellar again later, but she said nothing of her suspicions to David. Tonight was Colly's last night at The Singing Tree Inn, after all. In any case, she knew that Royce, who had gone into his own room, would somehow manage to keep track of the girl. Since the day of the fair he'd kept a very watchful eye on her. Vicki wondered sometimes if Jason had really appointed him as Portia's bodyguard, or if he had just seized the excuse of the anonymous letter to use Royce as a watchdog or some kind of nursemaid.

An image presented itself in her mind as this thought, a picture of the dignified Royce in an old-fashioned nursemaid's uniform such as she'd seen in TV programs. She chuckled involuntarily, then found that David was looking at her in surprise.

"Sorry," she said. "Just a passing thought about Royce."

He smiled. "He is rather intimidating, isn't he?"

"Not as much as I first thought. I feel more relaxed around him lately. But he's terribly well-bred, isn't he?"

"Terribly. His family was connected with Cambridge University, I believe."

David's voice sounded clipped, and he'd suddenly averted his gaze, which until that moment had been

fixed on her. What nerve could she possibly have
touched on, Vicki wondered. "Where are *you* from,
David?" she asked curiously.

His mouth tightened. "The North," he said curtly.

"Oh."

An awkwardness had come between them. Vicki
had no idea what had caused it. "I didn't mean to be
too inquisitive," she said quietly.

The ever ready color stained his cheeks, and he
glanced at her apologetically. "It's a perfectly natural question, Vicki. I'm sorry if I seemed...mysteri-
ous. It's just that, well, you see, I'm not quite what I
seem."

"You're not?"

He gave a self-deprecating smile. "I'm what in
America you'd call a self-made man." His eyes
clouded, and she thought he was going to drop the
subject right there, but after a moment he smiled at
her. "I don't mind telling you, Vicki, because you're
an American. You aren't quite as conscious of class
differences in America as we are here, are you?"

"I wouldn't say that, but I suppose we aren't as
formal about such things."

He nodded. "In this country it's a person's breed-
ing that counts, in certain circles, at least." He
paused. "I was brought up in a coal-mining town.
That probably doesn't mean much to you, but I still
have nightmares about it. I can remember my father
coming home from the mine, his face and hands pit-
ted with coal dust. He had a terrible hacking cough
that I still hear sometimes in my sleep. He died when
he was fifty years old. There was a cave-in that
buried him and twenty-three others. I saw him when
they dug him out." He swallowed visibly. "My

hometown was an awful place, Vicki—you can't imagine how dirty it was. My mother would try to keep the house clean, but it was a losing battle. She'd starch lace curtains for the lounge windows, and by the next day they'd be gray."

Vicki watched him as he talked. The speech, a long one for him, had come out of him as though impelled. She felt embarrassed, not certain she wanted to be the recipient of his confidences. His face had a distant expression, as though he were looking inward and not liking what he saw. His voice had changed in some indefinable manner, too. He seemed to realize it, for he looked up and attempted a smile that didn't quite come off.

"I usually have to be careful not to let myself remember the past. My North-country accent comes back when I do. Have you ever heard a North-country accent, Vicki?"

"I don't think so, except for the Beatles. Weren't they from Liverpool?"

"My home is—was—even farther north. The accent is rough and uncouth, a different language from the one I speak now." His mouth tightened into a straight bitter line. "I used to speak that other language fluently, didn't know any better. I was meant for the mine when I was fifteen, so it didn't matter how I spoke.

"The whole idea terrified me. Having to go down under the ground every day, always being dirty, shut away from the daylight and fresh air, deep in a pitch-black hole. Confined, perhaps buried alive as my father was."

He swallowed once more, remembered horror stark on his thin face. "I ran away from home the day I finished school. My mother helped me, poor soul. She's dead now, too. I'd always been a reader, you see, and she encouraged that—over my father's objections, I might add. Because of my reading, I knew there was a better life to be had. With the little money she gave me, I took elocution lessons and found a job in a London hotel. Baggage porter. Dreadful job, but it gave me a chance to study how people should dress and move and talk. Then Mr. Meredith stayed at the hotel, and I took care of some typing for him—I had taught myself to type. His secretary had recently left to get married, and he was pleased with my work, so he engaged me on the spot."

"Does he know about your...background?" Vicki asked.

The young man looked shocked. "Oh, yes, I told him at once. Portia doesn't know—she's rather inclined to gossip, so we haven't felt it necessary to tell her—but I would never deceive a prospective employer. Mr. Meredith's attitude at the time he engaged me was that as long as I looked the part and could do the work, the rest didn't matter."

Jason had also said that Royce looked the part of a butler, Vicki remembered. Was that how he always chose the people around him? Had she looked the part of a— She cut off her thoughts before they could lead her into self-defeating avenues.

"Are you happy in your work, David?" she asked, her voice soft with sympathy. She had a feeling he'd left a lot out of the story. What must it have been like to be a fifteen-year-old alone in London with very little money and no prospects at all? Had he gone hungry? Was that why he was so thin?

David was considering her question, the bitter expression still clouding his face. "It's never easy to be at someone's beck and call," he said slowly. "But I've always appreciated Mr. Meredith's philanthropy."

He hadn't really answered her question, she realized. Was it possible that he didn't really like Jason in spite of the fine phrases he had spouted the day of the fair?

"Do you have other plans for the future?" she asked, then added hastily, "I don't mean to pry, David, I'm just interested."

He smiled more naturally this time. "I appreciate your interest, Vicki. Yes, as a matter of fact, I do have other plans. But I'd rather you didn't tell Mr. Meredith of them."

"I wouldn't dream of repeating a private conversation," Vicki declared promptly. "And anyway, I doubt I'll be seeing Ja—Mr. Meredith again."

When David darted a quick glance at her face, she hoped devoutly that her expression wasn't giving anything away. He didn't comment, however, but added vaguely that he would like to get into some kind of business for himself, and that he was saving up for it as well as he could.

Sensing that he had already said more than he'd meant to, Vicki let the matter drop and turned the conversation to her own work and the plans she and Abby had for The Singing Tree Inn.

At last she rose to go. "Thank you for a nice evening," she said. "And thank you for sharing some of your past with me."

"It doesn't make you think any less of me?" he asked anxiously as he stood up to see her to the door. "You'll still be my . . . my friend."

Dear God, she thought, what had she let herself in for? He was looking at her so very earnestly, almost pleadingly, as if it were very important that she think well of him. "Of course, it doesn't make any difference," she said carefully. "I admire anyone who has the courage to make a new life for himself. And of course, we're friends."

"Vicki. . . ." He had moved closer to her.

She had to force herself not to back up a step. She didn't want to hurt his feelings, but she couldn't prevent herself from lifting one hand in a gesture of protest. To her dismay he took it as an invitation. In a sudden clumsy movement he put his arms around her and brought his mouth down on hers, his tongue probing her mouth when it opened in surprise. Shocked into paralysis, Vicki needed a moment to recover enough to attempt to struggle free. Apparently he mistook her efforts for passion, and his grip increased, holding her closer to his slight body.

Finally Vicki managed to wrench her face away from his. "No, David," she gasped.

"We'll go to my room," he said at once. His blue eyes were blazing now, his face excited.

He really thought she was willing to go to bed with him, Vicki realized in amazement. How had she managed to give him that impression? As she stared at him, trying to collect her senses and come up with words to let him down lightly, his expression changed. Evidently he'd finally read the rejection in her face. His mouth hardened into a thin line, and his eyes narrowed. She had a swift impression of violent anger imprisoned behind the bleak sharp bones of his face, and as he dropped his arms, he assumed his usual polite studious expression. "I do apologize, Vicki," he said smoothly.

Horribly embarrassed, Vicki tried fruitlessly to search for words. Luckily, at that moment the outer door of the suite opened, and Royce appeared in the archway. He seemed startled to see them standing so close together in the middle of the room, and possibly he sensed the tension that was still hovering between them. But after a second's pause he shrugged almost imperceptibly, and his facial expression returned to the preoccupied one it had worn when he entered. "Did Miss Portia come back here?" he asked.

"Portia's been in her room for the past couple of hours." David's tight voice betrayed his annoyance at the interruption Vicki had welcomed.

Royce shook his head in a bewildered way. He looked suddenly very tired. "No, she hasn't been in her room. She was down watching the Winters lad. We both helped the boys pack up their instruments and so forth, but after their bus left, she disappeared. I thought she must surely have returned to the suite."

"She wouldn't go out this late at night, would she?" Vicki asked.

David looked at her, his mouth curling ironically. "Perhaps we just didn't see her come in."

"Maybe not," Vicki said shortly. She headed abruptly for Portia's room, the two men at her heels, but they found it empty. There was a note on the dressing table, propped on top of the shells. It was addressed to Jason. Vicki's heart sank. "You'd better open it," she said to David.

He nodded. But in spite of the urgency of the situation, he went over to Portia's desk and picked up a letter opener so that he could do the job properly. Vicki would have torn the envelope apart, and she felt a flash of irritation. However, David's precise mannerisms were a habit, she supposed.

So what on earth had possessed him to grab her as he had done? She definitely hadn't encouraged him. And why was it so impossible to be friendly toward a man without him reading friendliness as invitation, she wondered glumly. At least, he seemed to have fully recovered his poise now. For that she was very grateful.

She watched his face as he read. He looked very grim. "She's gone to London," he said at last. "She says she can't let Colly go without her, but not to worry about her. Colly will take care of her." His mouth tightened. "I'll call the police."

"No!" Vicki exclaimed at once. "If the newspapers get hold of this, Jason will be furious. She's not in any danger, I'm sure. Colly's a nice boy."

David halted in mid stride and paused to think. "You're probably right. I'll ring Mr. Meredith instead."

"No," Vicki said again.

Startled, he looked at her. "We can't just let her go," he pointed out.

"I know that. Just a minute, I'm thinking." If they called Jason, he would probably have Colly Winters clapped into jail. And it was entirely possible that all of this was Portia's own idea. She must have talked Colly into taking her along on the group's bus. No wonder she hadn't seemed concerned about him leaving! Probably she'd agreed to have dinner with David and Vicki in order to disarm them, distract them from her true purpose. She must have had this planned all along....

Abby, Vicki thought suddenly. As his employer, Abby would have Colly's address. "I'll drive to London," she told the men, still formulating plans in her head. "I'll tell Jason myself and make sure he doesn't overreact. We can both look for Portia. Abby must have Colly's address; we can start there."

"But it's after eleven," David protested. "You can't go driving up to London alone." Something flickered in his pale eyes. "I'll go with you."

Vicki swallowed. "Of course, I can go alone. I'm not a child. Besides," she added as David started to look offended again, "Portia might phone here. There's no sense waking Mrs. Powell up; she'd only worry. And Royce looks so tired, he should probably go to bed."

"Oh, no, miss," Royce protested. "I couldn't possibly—"

"It makes no sense for you to exhaust yourself," Vicki said firmly. "I'm sure David agrees with me."

David finally did agree with obvious reluctance. At least, he made no further objections. Hurriedly, but still very precisely, he wrote down directions to the Hammonds' town house in Kensington, and within minutes Vicki was flying upstairs to her aunt.

Abby sized up the situation immediately and agreed that Vicki's plan was a good one. She suggested, however, that it might be a good idea to telephone Colly's flat first.

Vicki talked her out of it. If the escapade was a conspiracy between the two young people, it would be better not to alert either of them to the fact that Jason and Vicki were going to descend upon them.

A QUARTER OF AN HOUR LATER, Vicki, armed with Colly's address and the directions David had given her, drove out of the hotel courtyard and was on her way.

It was only then that she realized she'd committed herself to seeing Jason again. Was that why this plan had occurred to her so easily, she wondered, trying to be honest with herself. Had her subconscious mind been waiting for an opportunity to be with him again?

She didn't know the answer, and after a while she stopped worrying about her own motives, concentrating instead on driving carefully in the traffic on the London Road. And yet, somewhere inside her, excitement was growing. Whatever the risk to her emotions, she was going to see Jason Meredith again—and God help her, she could hardly wait.

The feeling she had for him must be some kind of mad obsession, she decided. Surely anything so self-destructive could not really be love. And if it were an obsession, then perhaps seeing Jason again would open her eyes, make her realize that no man was worth all the suffering she was going through.

She gripped the steering wheel tighter, swallowing against the threatened onslaught of tears, not believing her rationalization for a moment. She wanted to see him because she loved him. It was really as simple as that.

CHAPTER ELEVEN

THE HAMMONDS lived in an attractive three-story town house in a row of similar houses. Christopher Hammond himself opened the door to Vicki. He seemed delighted to see her. "It's the American maiden," he called over his shoulder after inviting her in with an exaggerated Shakespearean bow.

In immediate response Jason appeared in the doorway of a side room, an expression of astonishment on his face. Vicki felt a decided thump inside her body, as though her heart had stopped beating at the sight of him. Stopped and turned over and started again, at twice its normal speed. He was casually dressed in a cream-colored shirt, dark pants and gray cashmere V-necked sweater. His hair was rumpled as usual, and he held a coffee cup in his hand. "What on earth—" he began.

"It's Portia," Vicki interrupted. "We have to pick her up in Hammersmith—I have the address. I think we should go at once."

She'd expected him to demand an immediate explanation, but after one swift all-encompassing glance at her face, he nodded briefly, set down his coffee cup and went in search of his jacket.

Within two minutes they were in Vicki's car, heading out of the Hammonds' cul-de-sac. When action was demanded, Jason Meredith did not hesitate. His only hesitation had involved the use of her car. Christopher had offered to drive them, since Jason had left his car overnight at the television studios, but Vicki had insisted she was capable of getting them to their destination. She'd thought it best not to involve the Hammonds any more than she had to, a decision Jason concurred with as soon as she explained the situation to him.

He didn't interrupt once as she told him what Portia had done, but his mouth gradually tightened until it was a straight grim line. "If that boy has harmed her in any way. . ." he began in a menacing tone that sent a shiver along Vicki's spine.

"I'm sure he hasn't," she said at once. "He's a very nice boy. Abby thinks so, too. I'm surprised he went along with such a crazy stunt, but I'm quite sure he wouldn't allow anything to happen to Portia. He's very fond of her."

"I really thought she was growing up at last," Jason said darkly, hunching forward in the passenger seat as though his posture would make the car go faster. "She deserves a larruping on the behind for this."

"Don't be ridiculous," Vicki snapped. Then as he gazed at her with utter surprise, she gave him some home truths she'd been saving up for the past few weeks.

"Portia is not a child," she said emphatically. "She's almost a woman. At least, she's *practicing* to be a woman. You seem to have the idea she'll stay a child until she's twenty-one and then suddenly blossom forth into an adult. It doesn't work that way, Jason. A girl has to try womanly things on for size for a few years. She has to grow up gradually, making mistakes sometimes, retreating back to childhood sometimes. Portia has made her share of mistakes, I know, but your treatment of her doesn't help. You've got her so regimented, so cloistered, that it would be surprising if she didn't rebel.''

"I didn't know you were a child psychologist," he said tightly. "Portia is my sister, remember; I've raised her since she was a baby. I know her better than anyone else does. And running off like this is hardly mature behavior. I can't think what possessed her. She knows how vulnerable we are to extortion."

"She loves Colly."

He made a disgusted sound in his throat. "What does a fifteen-year-old know about love?"

"Juliet was fourteen."

"Juliet was a fictional character."

"Based on truth. People can fall in love just as . . . as thoroughly at fourteen or fifteen as at forty. Portia probably knows as much about love as you do— maybe more."

She could feel his gaze on her, sense his amazement that she was continuing to argue with him. It would do him good to be amazed, she thought, and she wasn't going to back down. Somebody had to stick up for Portia. "You hold onto her too tightly," she went on. "Confining her to the hotel, not letting her have boyfriends, not letting her experiment with makeup. You're stifling her. And if you keep on this way, you are going to lose her. When you love someone, you have to hold onto them with open hands, ready to let go. If you don't, they'll wriggle free in any way they can."

Apparently he had nothing to say to that.

She darted a glance at him, then wished she hadn't.

He was staring at her with the strangest expression on his face, an expression she couldn't define. Speculative?

Probably she had said more than she should have, she thought. She'd better not say any more. In any case, she had come to one of those terrifying roundabouts and needed to concentrate on her driving. Fortunately the traffic was not too heavy at this late hour, even on this major highway.

For a while Jason contented himself with giving occasional directions, referring to the map Vicki had spread out on the console between them. But in between she could feel his quizzical gaze on her face. She had no idea what he was thinking. Was he still angry with Portia? Was he angry with her for defending the girl? She felt defenseless, forced as she was to keep her attention fixed on the road and the traffic while he studied her so intently.

At first she had been too worried about Portia to feel any awkwardness about being with him. But now she was conscious once again of his solid masculine presence, and conscious, too, of the fact that her pulses were hammering erratically in her ears. Her whole body was tense, her hands gripping the steering wheel so tightly that she could see the whiteness of her knuckles in the lights of passing cars. She was still worried about Portia, of course, but she had the uneasy feeling that her nervousness was due more to Jason's proximity. Images kept projecting themselves into her mind, images of Jason looking at her as he undressed her, memories of the way his powerful hands had felt as they caressed her body. It was only with an effort that she was able to keep herself from trembling. If he would stop looking at her, she might be able to cope.

He didn't speak again until they were almost to their destination. Then he said softly, "I appreciate your driving all the way to London to find me, Victoria."

She swallowed. There was that tender emphasis on her name again.

"Why didn't David accompany you?" he asked.

She felt color flooding her face and hoped he couldn't see it. After the hectic moments following Royce's entrance, she'd forgotten the incident with David, but now the embarrassing memory came flooding back. It was best forgotten, she told herself firmly. Probably there would be no more problem with David. He must surely have realized it would be hopeless to try such a thing again.

"I felt partly responsible for Portia's behavior," she said carefully. "I had a feeling she didn't seem distressed enough about Colly's leaving, but I didn't do anything about it. I suppose that's why I thought it better that I drive in alone. David wanted to call you, but I talked him out of it." She hesitated. "I was afraid...."

"Afraid I'd go off the deep end?"

"Something like that."

He laughed shortly. "I probably would have done. I'm still not sure I won't. I don't quite have your faith in this—whatever-his-name-is."

"Colly Winters." She exhaled sharply, exasperated. "Don't you think you should at least remember the name of your sister's only friend?"

"Her *only* friend?" He sounded astonished.

"Where is Portia going to find friends?" she demanded. "The girls at school treat her as the relative of a celebrity, as though she had no personality of her own. And you don't let her go anywhere without

Royce. What kid is going to approach Portia as long as Royce is hanging around? I realize you feel his presence is necessary for her safety, but it's hardly likely to improve her social life. That's one of the nicest things about Colly—he wasn't put off by Royce hovering over them all the time. Portia is a very lonely girl, Jason.''

"But she has Mrs. Powell and David and—"

Vicki sighed audibly and he stopped. "I suppose you're right," he said after a moment. "She needs friends of her own age."

It was a major concession, but before Vicki could comment, the road ahead turned sharply, and she had to start looking for the block of flats where Colly lived. It was Jason who spotted the address. "Good Lord, look at that," he exclaimed. "It's nothing but a tenement. I knew Portia shouldn't associate with such people."

Vicki had no retort to offer this time. The ancient building *didn't* look very salubrious. There was a lot of graffiti on the sooty gray stone walls. Many of the windows were broken and patched with tape and plastic, and the whole area looked run-down and sleazy, like something out of a Charles Dickens novel. She felt increasingly anxious. Maybe Jason was right. Perhaps Colly Winter was not someone Portia should have become involved with. Perhaps....

She couldn't let her mind ponder possibilities now. She had to find the entrance to the huge block of flats. "We might have to park in the street," she said. "I can't see—"

"The station over there," Jason said abruptly, pointing.

She thought he meant for her to park in front of the train station. But as she obediently made a U-turn in the middle of the road, she saw what he had seen—two young people standing in the shadows, looking at some kind of poster on the inner wall of an archway.

Portia and Colly.

Even at a distance there was something forlorn about the pair. Colly was still in his wilderness outfit, Portia in jeans and a padded jacket. They were holding hands. Vicki was irresistibly reminded of Hansel and Gretel. They both looked so woebegone, so lost.

The poster, she saw as she braked to a halt in front of the archway, was some kind of timetable. Both teenagers were peering at it in the dim light, concentrating so hard they didn't even hear the car's approach and didn't turn around until Jason called Portia's name.

When they did turn, the relief on both young faces was obvious. Vicki got out of the car quickly, hoping to forestall Jason's anger, but Portia ran to her brother at once, flinging herself into his open arms. "Oh, Jason, I'm so glad to see you," she cried. "I didn't know what to do, and the trains had stopped running, and we couldn't find a taxi."

Colly had hung back, biting his lower lip. One hand was worrying his mop of curly dark hair, and his face was pale in the station's uncertain light. Vicki felt immediate sympathy for him. He looked so slight, so irresolute—like a little boy playing dress-up in a game that had suddenly gone wrong.

Jason glared at him across Portia's head, looking every inch the outraged father. "I think you owe me an explanation," he said coldly. The anger in his voice was formidable.

Colly swallowed visibly, and his eyes darted from side to side as though he were desperately looking for an escape route. But his hesitation lasted only a second, and then he squared his shoulders and stepped forward, earning Vicki's admiration.

Before he could speak, Portia interrupted. "It was my fault, Jason. Colly didn't even know I was in the bus. I stowed away. I just wanted to be with him. He didn't even know I was there until after the others had gone. I sneaked out while they were unloading their stuff and hid in the doorway of the flats. I thought it was going to be an adventure, but I didn't know it was going to be so awful." Her voice ended on a wail.

Colly flinched, then drew himself up again. "I'm sorry, Mr. Meredith, sir," he said manfully. "I was going to bring her home, honest, sir. We were just looking to see if there was any kind of train, and if there wasn't, I was going to get my friends to bring the bus back. I don't have a telephone, see, and—"

Jason shook his head impatiently, halting the flow of words. Gripping Portia's shoulders, he held her away from him and looked into her face. "Are you all right?" he asked. "Did anyone try to. . . ."

"Of course, I'm all right," Portia answered in a bewildered voice. "Why wouldn't I be all right?"

There was such innocence in her voice and face that Jason was apparently convinced no harm had come to her. He let his breath out and visibly relaxed his posture. Then he looked at Colly, who had obviously fully understood Jason's implications. The boy's face had gone first white, then red.

Vicki wanted to hug him, to tell him everything was all right, but Jason evidently felt no such compulsion. The words he addressed to the lad were still clothed in ice. "As it's the middle of the night, and this is hardly the place for a discussion, I suggest you go home now," he said evenly. "I will expect you to telephone me in the morning, however, at The Singing Tree Inn. Shall we say ten o'clock?"

"Yes, sir," Colly said in a voice that reflected his misery.

"It wasn't Colly's fault," Portia insisted again, looking from her brother to Colly with a pleading expression on her elfin face.

"In the morning," Jason repeated, ignoring Portia's appeal.

Colly nodded, cast a last almost despairing glance at Portia and started across the road. His hands were in his pockets, his shoulders hunched as though he expected a blow at any moment.

For a second, Vicki was afraid Portia was going to insist on going after him. Instead she burst into tears and clung to Jason, talking incoherently. Jason looked at Vicki, his eyebrows raised. "I suppose you think I was too hard on the boy?" he said challengingly.

She bit back her heartfelt response. It seemed more politic at the moment to suggest that they go home, which she did.

He nodded agreement, extricating himself from Portia's clutches and helping the girl into the shallow back seat of the Mini before climbing in beside Vicki.

It took a while for Portia's halting explanations to make sense, but to Vicki's surprise, Jason was patient with her, not interrupting except to ask for clarification now and then.

Most of it Vicki had already figured out. The

whole escapade had obviously been Portia's idea.
Colly had been horrified to find her on his doorstep,
but he had recovered quickly and agreed that she
could spend the night. Unfortunately, though, he
had led Portia to believe he rented his own flat; such
was not the case. He actually lived with his widowed
mother. And his mother had turned out to be an
awful woman according to Portia—fat and slovenly.
She had been wearing a torn kimono and curlers in
her hair, a cigarette dangling from one corner of her
mouth.

The flat itself was incredibly small. It had only two
tiny bedrooms, one of which—the mother's—was
hung with other people's laundry. Mrs. Winters, it
seemed, took in washing for a living, and the results
of her work had been hanging from wooden racks attached by pulleys and ropes to the ceiling.

Though Colly had finally convinced his mother
that Portia should be allowed to stay, the girl had not
been able to bear the thought of sharing a room with
the woman and had insisted on leaving. Colly had
not let her leave alone, which Jason conceded was to
his credit.

The elder Meredith said very little. To Vicki's further surprise, he didn't express any anger, but really
listened to Portia as though he wanted to understand.
"I can't condone such behavior, of course," he said
to the girl. "But Victoria has explained to me why
you didn't want to let your friend go. I've been rather
blind to your feelings, I'm afraid. We'll talk about it
when you're feeling better."

"I suppose you're going to have to punish me?"
Portia sobbed.

Jason reached across the back of the seat to take

her hand. "I think you've probably suffered enough," he said kindly.

Portia promptly engulfed him in a suffocating hug, promising never to run away again and never, ever to do anything in future to upset him.

From then until Vicki drove into the hotel courtyard, Jason remained silent and thoughtful. Portia drifted off to sleep, and Vicki kept her mind fixed on her driving, feeling somehow excluded, but not wanting to add any opinions of her own. She'd done enough of that, she felt sure. Jason probably felt she'd interfered where she had no business interfering. And he was probably right.

After she stopped the car, Jason assisted Portia from the back seat, then leaned down to look at Vicki. "You must be very tired," he said gently.

She managed a smile. "A little," she admitted.

"Thank you for all you've done." He hesitated, then added, "I'd like to see you in the morning." He smiled ruefully. "It *is* morning, I suppose. About eleven? Would that be too early for you?"

"I don't really think it's necessary, Jason," she said carefully.

"I do," he said. "I have another proposition for you. I'll come for you at eleven. We can have lunch together."

Before she could guess his intention, he leaned further into the car and kissed her lightly on the mouth. "Thank you again, Victoria," he murmured. Then he smiled and was gone.

Vicki slumped over the steering wheel, letting out her breath in a long sigh. What an idiot she was. One kiss and her traitorous body was sending agitated and stupidly optimistic messages to her brain. One promise of another meeting, and her heart was soaring with hope. "I'd like to see you in the morning," he'd said, thus ensuring her of a sleepless night. Logically she knew nothing had changed. He had made his position plain enough. Why was she such a glutton for punishment? Why did she continue to do whatever he asked her to do? Had she no pride at all?

CHAPTER TWELVE

HE CALLED FOR HER promptly at eleven. Prior to his arrival Vicki had assured herself at least twelve times that she was not going to meekly fall in with whatever plans he had for her. She would simply tell him that she had work to do, and that she could not spare the time to involve herself any further with any of the Merediths.

This excuse was not at all true. Now that she and Abby had ordered the necessary items for the remodeling, there would probably be quite a long hiatus before work would commence. But lack of time would be as good an excuse as any, and she was determined to use it. Resolutely determined.

Until she opened the apartment door and saw him standing there. Immediately all her good intentions fled.

He was wearing the gray cashmere sweater he'd worn the previous night, with gray slacks and a white shirt this morning. His hair was finger combed as usual, little boy unruly, but his eyes were clear as lake water, his face cleanly shaved. He looked and smelled as though he'd just stepped out of a vigorous shower. He wasn't smiling, but as he looked at her, his gray eyes warmed.

Her whole being seemed to be disintegrating. Away from him, she could dismiss his physical at-

tractiveness as unimportant. In his presence she was
reduced to a helpless blob of jelly with no will of her
own. There was such an impact in the sheer muscular
size of him, and the energy that seemed to emanate
from him surrounded her with all the force of a mag-
netic field.

His gaze continued to hold hers, compelling in its
intensity. "Good morning, Victoria," he said gravely, his resonant voice lingering on her name in the
way that always sent shock waves up her spine. His
glance appraised her approvingly. "You look as
fresh as a spring flower."

She doubted that the compliment was deserved. As
she'd expected, she'd had very little sleep, though she
had drifted off around dawn and had not awakened
until after Abby had left. She felt definitely *un*fresh
and knew her face was drawn, her eyes shadowed. She
supposed he was referring to the pale green linen sun
dress and short-sleeved white jacket she was wearing.

"Thank you," she said tersely and prepared to
launch into her list of excuses.

And then he smiled his lighting-up-the-world
smile. "Shall we go?" he asked softly.

Somehow the words of refusal would not form
themselves properly in her mouth. Her mind had
gone completely blank. She could only stand there
like a deaf-mute, the warm brilliance of his smile en-
folding her. A second later, she had picked up her
shoulder bag and joined him in the hall, the door of
Abby's apartment closing behind her.

"I have to go over to my house for a few minutes," he told her as they descended the narrow back
stairs to the courtyard. "I thought perhaps you'd like
to see it. Afterward we can go to lunch anywhere you
wish."

She nodded dumbly. Whenever she was with this man, the force of his personality dominated hers so that she was unable to control the course of events. She was weak willed, she told herself crossly. Spineless. Stupid.

Subconsciously she had probably never intended to refuse to go with him, she admitted to herself as they crossed the little wooden bridge over the river. Why else had she dressed for an outing and applied her makeup with such care? Why else had she washed and conditioned and airbrushed her hair so that it hung in a long burnished rope down her back?

Helplessly she allowed him to take her elbow as they started across the meadow, acknowledging without protest the immediate surge of emotion that went through her as he touched her bare skin.

"A beautiful day, isn't it?" he said cheerfully.

She hadn't even noticed that the sun was shining and the sky cloudless. She had noticed that a brisk breeze was blowing, bringing a chill to the air, making her think vaguely that she should have worn a heavier jacket. She should have taken her cue from the sweater that Jason was wearing. And yet she didn't feel cold at all.

What she felt was happy, she realized with something close to despair. Just walking close beside this man across a daisy-starred meadow was enough to still all her doubts about the wisdom of seeing him again. All her senses were awake and joyful. She could feel the warm pressure of Jason's hand on her bare arm, feel the softness of his sweater brushing against her, smell the sweetness of the air, feel the sun warming her back.

Then he said, "I want to talk to you about Portia," and she came back to earth with a thud.

With an effort she made herself move away from him, freeing her arm from his hand. "I don't have anything to add to what I said last night," she said evenly.

"Lord, I should hope not." His voice was amused, and she felt herself flush.

"I suppose you think I'm a busybody," she said.

His tone of voice changed again. "I think you are a dear compassionate woman with a great deal of common sense." There was a tender note in his voice that threatened to destroy what little composure she still had.

To combat her sudden weakness, she spoke briskly. "I hope you haven't decided to punish Portia, after all."

"I have not. We had a long talk this morning, and the young man, Colly, phoned me as promised. I've agreed to let them see each other from time to time. However, I am going to arrange for Portia to go to a boarding school in September. I know of a good one not too far away. Living with other young people, she'll have more opportunity to make friends, I think, and I won't have to worry about her when I'm busy."

"What does Portia think about that?"

"She agrees. She wants me to register her under an assumed name and not make any appearance at the school. She feels that will give her a chance to make an impression of her own."

"You're quite sure this is what she wants?" Vicki asked doubtfully. The prospect sounded awfully bleak to her.

"Quite sure." His voice brooked no argument. Privately Vicki decided she'd have a few words with Portia herself.

"My problem now is what to do with Portia until then," Jason continued. "I'm going to be in Stratford-upon-Avon for much of August, and I'm not at all sure—" He broke off. "Why don't we wait to discuss this further? I'd like you to see my house without anything else on your mind. It's rather nice, isn't it?"

Distracted by their discussion of Portia and by her own still-turbulent emotions, Vicki hadn't realized that they had reached the house. Now she looked up to see it looming in front of her. She caught her breath. She had thought the house beautiful when she saw it from the hotel, but close up it was even more impressive.

She stood still for several minutes, gazing at it in delight, all else forgotten. From the hotel the view had been foreshortened, so that Vicki hadn't realized a low stone wall and gardens separated the house from the meadow. Now, standing in the open gateway, she was confronted by an enchanting expanse of flowering plants and shrubs—a riot of color that enhanced the mellow handmade bricks, which over the years had faded to a dull rose. The house consisted of three stories, with white wooden trim around the tall windows and a central pediment also painted white. The third story had dormer windows tucked into the roof.

It was a large house, but not overwhelmingly so. It looked comfortable, luxurious, but not overbearing. Vicki loved it on sight. Though she admired the Tudor style of architecture and felt a romantic response to it, she had always preferred the simplicity of classical or neoclassical lines. Meredith Manor was a fine example of pure Georgian architecture, which had originally developed from the Roman Palladian style and had made a strong impression on early-American colonial homes. From one side of the house a wide driveway zigzagged off into the distance to join a side road into Derringham.

Still entranced, she followed Jason up the graceful stone steps to the huge front door, almost breathless with anticipation of the interior.

She had forgotten about the fire and so was surprised at the total lack of furnishings in the great hall. Looking around, she could see no evidence of damage, but the smell of fresh paint was strong. Ahead of them a beautifully wrought balustrade curved gracefully at each side of marble steps that led up to the upper floors. The hall itself was floored with black and white tiles in a diamond pattern, bordered by a green key design. The walls were pale and fairly plain, the ceiling unpretentiously stuccoed in a classical design.

Impressed by the simple grandeur of the house, Vicki followed Jason in silence through a series of rooms and long galleries on the ground floor. In each room he described how it was usually furnished—with Chippendale, Queen Anne and Robert Adam chairs, tables and sofas. He seemed to know the provenance of everything he owned. Obviously his heritage meant a lot to him.

"Perhaps you'll come back again and advise me on some of the improvements," he suggested lightly. "Feel free to walk in at any time, even if I'm away. I'd appreciate your expert advice."

Unthinkingly Vicki agreed enthusiastically. No matter what her relationship with Jason was, she would love the chance to work on a house as beautiful as this.

She especially admired the library. Every wall was lined with shelves of books from the floor almost to the ceiling. In the space between was a frieze decorated with portraits of famous philosophers from Plato on. Fortunately none of the books had suffered harm. She recognized several of her own favorite classics among them and felt that she was in the company of friends.

Most of the damage had been inflicted on the upper stories, Jason told her, but practically the whole house had needed to be redone because of smoke-and-water damage.

"I don't hear anyone working," Vicki said as they started up the stairs.

He smiled briefly, and something flickered in his gray eyes. "It's Sunday, Victoria," he said.

It was a moment before she realized this meant they were alone in the great echoing house. When she did, her earlier nervousness returned.

Yet there was no real reason for nervousness. Jason had made no attempt to take her arm again, had actually stayed at a considerable distance, striding ahead of her more often than not, flinging open doors and stepping well back so that she could have an uninterrupted view.

On the second story the odor of paint was even stronger, and here Vicki could see the evidence of repair. There were bare boards here and there, new plasterwork waiting to be painted, an entire ceiling in the process of being redone. One or two of the rooms that had not been affected were crammed full of furniture covered with dust sheets, a rather eerie sight. Most of the furniture and all of the household effects had been placed in storage, Jason told her, though a couple of rooms had been kept intact so that a caretaker could stay in residence.

The caretaker didn't seem to be around at the moment, and Vicki was beginning to feel tense again—suffocatingly so, aware once more of her own erratic heartbeats. Jason, too, seemed to be affected by the echoing silence of the house. He spoke little now, almost in monosyllables, as he conducted her through the rest of the place. In the caretaker's rooms he paused and gestured toward the rear of the house. "Perhaps you'd like to see the view," he suggested.

Without waiting for a response, he led the way to the tall windows and opened one onto a long veranda that contained several cushioned wrought-metal chairs.

Vicki, following, sighed with pleasure. The back of the house was even more stunning than the front. Long formal gardens brilliant with color led to a stone-balustraded terrace with steps down to a lawn. Woods rose to the horizon beyond. Out here on the veranda she could hear birds singing, nothing else. It was as though the entire area was deserted, for not a single traffic sound penetrated the air.

She glanced up at Jason, willing her voice to sound calm. "It's beautiful—all of it," she said.

He nodded, looking at her gravely, his gray eyes studying her face. "Let me see if I can find some lemonade or something," he suggested. "Make yourself comfortable." He grinned suddenly. "Promise you won't run away?"

There had been something vaguely challenging about those last words, but he was gone before Vicki could think of a rejoinder.

Nervously she seated herself on the edge of one of the chairs and looked out at the beautiful view. The gardens displayed every tint in an artist's palette, a spectrum ranging from deepest blue through every shade of green to the most vivid of reds. Setting off the more brilliant colors were soft drifts of gray and lemon—low ground covers that she didn't recognize, but thought might be some kind of herb. On the air, mingling with the scent of sun-warmed grass, came the fragrance of roses, musky and potent. The breeze gently rustled the woodland's tall beech trees. She thought that she would like to spend hours looking at that view, if only she could do so without the disrupting influence of Jason's presence.

He returned fairly quickly, carrying two tall glasses of frosty lemon liquid. He'd taken off his sweater, she noticed. She had considered removing her own jacket, as the veranda was sheltered from the breeze, but she'd been stopped by the thought of her halter-neck dress and bare back. Not that she thought Jason intended making advances to her, but she didn't want him to think she was encouraging him to do so.

He didn't sit down right away, but stood looking out at the view, talking easily about the gardens and the ancestor who had planned them—his great-grandfather, he said. When he did sit down, he returned immediately to the subject that was evidently uppermost in his mind.

"I don't want to leave Portia at the hotel while I'm in Stratford," he said, leaning back, his long legs stretched out in front of him, his glass of lemonade in his hand. He seemed to be talking more to himself than to Vicki. She wasn't sure whether he expected her to comment or not. After a second's silence, he said slowly, "If I take her to Stratford with me, she'll be too much alone. David can't come with me—he has to work on the theater project. Royce is needed to supervise the work here at the house. And I don't think it's necessary for Portia to have a bodyguard any longer. The threat was evidently an isolated thing; it hasn't been repeated. I could ask Mrs. Powell to come along, but, well, as you pointed out, she's hardly sufficient company for Portia, is she?''

Vicki made a sound she hoped he'd interpret as agreement without encouragement. She had a feeling she knew what was coming next.

She was right. Without further hesitation he asked her straight out if she would accompany him and Portia to Stratford to act as a companion to the girl.

For a while she was too stunned by his nerve—his gall—to even reply. He was acting as though nothing had happened between them, as though she were just some kind of acquaintance who might be persuaded to do a favor for him.

On the spot she decided to remain calm. She could at least retain her dignity. Carefully she gathered words together. "I didn't come to England to be a nanny,'' she said sardonically.

He nodded. "I realize that, of course. And I shan't blame you if you turn me down, even though Portia is terribly excited to think you might come with us. Not much fun for you, I suppose. Portia is much younger than you.'' He sighed rather dramatically. "I'll have to rely on Mrs. Powell, I suppose.'' He slanted a sideways glance at her. "Of course, Portia will be terribly bored. A shame really, when it's her summer holidays.''

"I'm sure she'll be happy with you, Jason,'' she said neutrally.

"No doubt. Though I'll be busy most of the time.

Performances every night. Rehearsals. Stratford is a lovely town, Victoria."

"I'm sure it is."

"And of course, I could arrange for tickets to every performance."

She glanced over at him. "That sounds suspiciously like bribery."

He raised his eyebrows. "Not at all. I would naturally want you to enjoy the experience."

"I'm sorry, Jason," she said coldly. "I'm afraid I have too much to do. I can't possibly go haring off to Stratford."

"Hmm." He hesitated. "Actually, Victoria, I did mention my proposal to Abby this morning—we had breakfast together; what a lovely woman she is—and she seemed to think you *could* spare the time."

Astonished, she stared at him. "You spoke to Abby before consulting me?"

"It seemed the polite thing to do. She does stand in loco parentis, after all. I must admit she didn't think much of the idea at first, but when I explained it was purely a business arrangement, she—"

Normally Vicki was slow to anger, but his sheer gall ignited her to a fury that threatened to close her throat. For a second she was too angry to speak, but when she did manage to force words through, she let them pour out, making no attempt to hide her annoyance. "You had no business asking Abby's permission as though I were a child without a mind of my own," she snapped. "I make my own decisions."

He nodded, unperturbed. "So Abby told me."

"Oh." As usual he had effectively diffused her anger.

His superstar smile was suddenly very much in evi-

dence. He was purposefully turning on the charm.
She knew it was deliberate, but that didn't prevent
her from being affected by it.

"Will you accept the job, Victoria?" he asked.
"I'm sure we could negotiate a suitable remunera-
tion."

She stood up, set down her glass on the wide veranda rail and glared at him, summoning every ounce of
indignation she could find. "I don't know how you
have the nerve to ask me, after you... after we...."
She broke off, feeling foolish. He was looking at her
politely, patiently waiting for her to find words to express the inexpressible. She had the uneasy feeling he
was amused by her anger.

"Victoria," he said soothingly. "I thought we had
agreed to be friends. That day at the fair, I was
sure—"

"I made no such agreement. I'm only sorry that I
didn't realize in time that you were such a... a...."

"Cad?" he supplied when words failed her.

The word sounded silly, but she had to admit to
herself that it had crossed her mind.

He went on smoothly, " 'A rascal; an eater of
broken meats; a base, proud, shallow, beggarly,
three-suited, hundred-pound, filthy, worsted-
stocking knave'?"

"Shakespeare knew what he was talking about,"
she agreed coldly, determined not to be deflected by
his attempts at humor. "Obviously you are used to
hit-and-run affairs that have no meaning. I'm not. I
can't possibly accompany you to Stratford. I just
wish—"

"What do you wish, Victoria?" He was suddenly
on his feet, his hands lightly gripping her shoulders,
his face solemn as he gazed down at her.

"I wish I hadn't met you," she said miserably.

To her dismay her voice trembled. At once his grip tightened, and as usual her traitorous heart lurched uncontrollably.

"Do you really think you mean nothing to me, that I don't care about you?" he said softly.

"What else can I think?"

"That I care too much? That I disappeared after that night because I care too much?"

His gaze was holding hers inescapably. How clear and candid his eyes were. "Jason?" she said uncertainly.

"Don't you see that it's impossible to deny the feelings we have for each other?" he replied in a low voice. "I knew it the moment I saw you again last night. I tried to stay away from you, Victoria. I thought if I stayed away long enough, you'd get over whatever feelings you had for me. And that I could possibly forget you. But I couldn't. I kept reaching for a telephone, wanting to beg you to come to me. Several times I even started my car, determined to come down to Derringham and take you by force if necessary so that I could ease the need I felt for you. I was miserable. I thought of you so often, thought of what might have been, what almost was."

His hands were sliding down her arms to her elbows, drawing her closer. It took an enormous effort for her to resist her body's inclination to sway toward him, but she managed it, drawing herself up as straight and stiff as she possibly could. "It's no use, Jason," she said. "I'm not going to melt into your arms again."

He smiled tenderly. "Are you quite sure, Victoria, that if I were to ease your jacket off your shoulders like this and to touch the bare silken skin of your

shoulders like this with my hands and my mouth. . . ."
His voice trailed away as he suited action to words,
and she felt the shock wave of electricity that went
through her as his lips brushed against her skin.

"The caretaker," she stammered, despising herself
for such a weak excuse.

He raised his head a fraction, his eyes glinting
wickedly. "I gave him the rest of the day off," he
said softly. "Seemed a charitable thing to do on a
Sunday."

His mouth was moving downward now, tracing the
low neckline of her dress, coming perilously close to
the valley between her breasts, awakening a fierce
longing in her body, a ripple of heat along her thighs.
His hands were clasping her waist, his thumbs pressing against her hipbones, drawing her inexorably
nearer.

"Jason," she said helplessly.

He lifted his head, looked into her eyes, the grip of
his hands changing from light to rigid, forcing her
against him as though to offer proof of his desire,
pressing her tightly against his powerful masculinity.
Her hands, which had been clenched at her sides,
seemed to move involuntarily to his arms, his shoulders, moving upward to tangle in the familiar coarse-
ness of his hair. "Jason," she said again, but now
her tone had changed to one that was unmistakably
inviting.

Appalled, she moistened suddenly dry lips. For a
second more he continued to gaze at her, his eyes
darkening, and then his head lowered and his mouth
met hers. Softly at first, then demandingly, his
tongue probed the corner of her mouth until her own
mouth opened to press against his as though she

would draw his life's breath from him. She could feel his heart pounding against her breast, his hands burning their impression into the small of her back.

Uncountable minutes later, he eased her away from him, smiled. "Q.E.D.? You do find me irresistible, don't you?"

"Jason—"

His fingers touched her lips to silence. Unexpectedly his released her. "Perhaps we should finish our tour?"

Taken aback, she stared at him. "Yes, I think that would be best," she said at last.

He took her hand and led her through the caretaker's room and along the long echoing hall. The staircase caught her eyes. Probably she should leave now. Jason seemed willing not to press her too far, but it was dangerous for them to be alone—dangerous to her, anyway. His joking remark was far too close to truth. She *did* find him irresistible. Yes, she should definitely make her escape now while there was still time.

As though sensing her thoughts, he released her hand and put his arm around her waist, drawing her close to his side as he opened a door in the side of the hall.

The only furniture in the room was a four-poster bed. Everything else had evidently been removed for cleaning and repair. There was no way this massive bed could have been taken out without removing half the wall. It was obviously Jason's bed—a bed fit for a king, covered in an autumnal shade of raw silk, its pillows heaped invitingly at the head below a carved wooden canopy. In fact, Jason murmured against her hair, it *had* belonged to a king or at least was rumored to have done so. Carved and gilded, it stood in regal splendor against the wall opposite the door, its wooden canopy framed by long windows on either side. Vicki caught a glimpse of the swaying beech trees, then Jason took her in his arms again. He kissed her lingeringly, then cupped her face between his hands, his gray eyes penetrating as he gazed at her.

"Lovely Victoria," he murmured. "How could you not know that I care too much? Why else do you ¹ink I keep running away from you? Have you any idea what agony it is to hold you like this and know that I can't have you, can't make love to you?"

"Jason," she said nervously. "I'm not—"

"Let's talk about it," he said promptly, brushing her mouth with his fingertips again. Then he stepped away from her and sat down on the edge of the huge bed, patting the space next to him in obvious invitation.

Vicki swallowed. "No, I don't think...."

"Come along, Victoria, I just want you to see the design under the canopy. Honestly." He was smiling his little-boy smile, crooked and ingenuous, not to be trusted.

Nevertheless, she made no protest when he took her hand and pulled her down beside him. Putting his arm around her shoulders, he tipped her back so that she could see the underside of the canopy.

There really was a design etched into the wood. At first all she could discern were meaningless whorls and lines and blurred images that formed a surrealistic backdrop to the amused face of the man beside her. The design was probably allegorical, she decided as it began to come into focus. Vague human shapes, birds, plants and flowers covered the entire composition in a sort of dreamlike construction.

How many women had Jason Meredith lured to this bed, she wondered. How many women had gazed upward at the intricate design? It was a bed made for love, as he was a man made for love. *To love, to be loved,* her mind chanted. Deliberately she encouraged the small voice inside her that was reminding her there had still been no talk of love.

"It's called *The Garden of Earthly Delights*," Jason said.

She looked at him. His face was lighted with amusement, looking at her. "It's a copy of one of Hieronymous Bosch's paintings," he went on.

"Very...interesting," she managed.

He laughed and took both her hands in his. "Oh, Victoria, you do delight me. Do you really expect me to believe you're not feeling anything at all but interest? Is it so impossible for you to admit that you want me as much as I want you? Admit it. Admit that you want me."

His gray eyes held hers. There had been a teasing note in his voice, but there was no amusement showing in his face now. He looked almost somber, and there was an air of tension about him, as though he were holding his breath while he waited for her answer.

For a split second, time seemed suspended. The air in the room had suddenly become suffocatingly warm, as though it had solidified around her. His hands, still clasping hers, were very still. His whole body was still, waiting.

"I love you, Jason," she said softly.

He didn't quite flinch, but he came close to it.

"That scares you, doesn't it?" she said, drawing her hands free. "Why? Are you afraid I'll make demands on you, beg you to marry me?"

This time he did flinch. That was what he'd thought.

She shook her head sadly. "It's no use, Jason," she said quietly. "I can't go in for... dalliance, and that's all you want."

"I care for you, Victoria."

"But not love."

"We've already agreed I don't know anything about love. I must admit the word terrifies me—puts me into a blue funk."

He looked away from her, then back again, his gray eyes meeting hers levelly. "Will you go with me to Stratford, Victoria? Please?"

"As a business arrangement?"

"I'd rather it was a—what shall we call it—a liaison?"

The word chilled her. "Are you inviting me officially to be your mistress?" she asked, somehow managing to keep her tone light.

" 'Mother of memories, mistress of mistresses,' " he murmured, quoting Baudelaire. "Such a delightfully decadent word, isn't it? Mistress."

She wondered what he would say if she were to tell him that after Ken Marriott had spread gossip about her, one of her prospective employers had offered her a job as his mistress. She had left Los Angeles to get away from all that. And here she was again, receiving the same offer. The situation certainly had its ironic side.

"You still think you can get what you want without making a commitment, don't you?" she said wonderingly.

"I can't make a commitment, Victoria, darling. I thought you understood that. I told you about Claire."

"So because you are still in love with your wife, you think it's all right to ride roughshod over another woman's feelings?"

For a second, he seemed startled, then he stood up, turning to look down at her, plainly bewildered. "What on earth gave you the idea I was still in love with my wife?"

She stared at him. "You told me she was a wonderful woman, that you could never marry again...."

"And you interpreted that to mean undying love?"

Evidently he read her silence as agreement. "Claire and I were very young when we married," he said wearily. "She was beautiful—very beautiful—and she had the voice of an angel. People worshiped at her feet. For a long time I did the same. But I had a career, too. We were often apart. She began to imagine I was unfaithful to her. Lord knows, there were temptations. Instead of trying to reassure her, I lost my temper—repeatedly. Her own temper was anything but mild. She was an artist with the temperament that goes with the profession. We fought constantly, always over other women—women who meant nothing to me, women I hadn't touched. Her jealousy was almost psychotic."

His face was bleak, and then he sighed. "No, Victoria, at the end there was no love left...on either side."

He had averted his head to stare unseeingly at the long windows, apparently lost in the past. "One day I told her I wished she would get out of my life and leave me alone forever," he went on, his voice sounding ragged now, as though he could hardly stand to remember the scene. "I shouted at her that I wished she were dead."

He paused, swallowed visibly. "The next day she was."

Abruptly he turned his back on her, gripping the windowsill, his gaze apparently fixed on the woods beyond the garden.

Uncertainly Vicki stood up, aware of his pain, appalled at the agony that had come through in his voice, sure now that she knew the reason for it. "Her death was an accident, Jason," she said gently, touching his arm. "I realize the experience must have been traumatic for you, but you aren't God. There must have been others on that plane; were you responsible for their deaths, too?"

He swung around, took hold of her shoulders in a grip that was bruising in its intensity. "Don't spout pat psychological phrases at me, Victoria," he ordered sternly. "My friends have attempted for three years to convince me I am guilt-free. I can't accept that. Claire was a beautiful talented woman. I was a single-minded, obstinate, ambitious man who lived only for his work. By marrying her, I destroyed her and almost destroyed myself. I'll never risk that again. Of course, I know the plane crash was an accident. But the fact remains that I *told* Claire to leave, and she left—on the first airplane going to the United States. And she died. I swore then that I would never marry again. And I won't."

Abruptly he drew her close. "Forgive me, Victoria," he murmured in a voice that was suddenly free of anger. "I've hurt you, I know. I thought you understood when you talked about holding on with open hands if you loved someone. I can't make any commitment to you. I'm afraid to. But that doesn't mean I don't care about you. I do, believe me. I know I'm asking a lot of you, but can't you possibly accept me on my terms for as long as our feelings for each other last?"

Vicki clung to him for a moment, desperately wanting to hear him say the more important words: "I love you."

At last, haltingly, she lowered her arms. "Even though I love you, I would despise myself," she concluded. "I'm old-fashioned, after all, I guess."

He held her at arms' length, studying her face intently. Then the mask she had seen once before descended, closing out all expression. He nodded briskly. "I see," he said. There was no life in this voice at all. "I think the problem is, Victoria, that you don't recognize the realities of life. Love is really a very... transient emotion. I know. There was a time when I loved Claire. In spite of that, I hurt her badly, fatally, because I myself was hurt. I don't want to hurt or be hurt again. So if you cannot accept me as I am, cannot just enjoy whatever time we might have together, then I'm afraid...." His voice trailed away.

Releasing her, he opened the bedroom door, waited with chilling courtesy while she preceded him through it, then escorted her down the stairs to the front door.

For a horrible moment she was afraid he was going to simply open the door and show her out, but instead he sighed audibly and looked at her with an apologetic expression on his face. "I didn't ever *want* to hurt you, Victoria," he said wearily. "In spite of myself I admire your stand, even though it means I'm to be denied your...your company. But I'm not worth your love, believe me."

He touched his fingers to her lips as she began to protest. "Let's not argue the point, my dear. I blame myself for not listening to my own good advice. I should have stayed away from you." A ghost of a smile curved the corners of his mouth, and he stroked her hair lightly away from her forehead. "Unfortunately I'm not immune to beauty, and the chemistry between us is very strong, isn't it?" He gazed at her tenderly. "You are so incredibly lovely."

His smile became rueful. "I suppose there's no possibility that you could consider accepting my earlier proposal—a purely business arrangement? Between friends? I do still need you, for Portia's sake." He lifted his hand away from her hair. "I promise not to try to...take advantage of you again."

His face became solemn. "Of course, I shan't blame you if you think I'm a total bounder for even hoping you'll agree. Just say the word, and I'll take myself out of your life, and you can forget you ever knew me."

The loneliness of the vista his words conjured up dismayed Vicki. His voice had attempted lightness, but there was a determined note in it that told her he meant what he said. If she refused his offer of platonic friendship—refused to accompany him to Stratford—she would never see him again. Ever.

The prospect was so bleak that she had to momentarily close her eyes. When she opened them again, his face mirrored genuine concern. "Have I offended you irreparably, Victoria?" he asked. "Is it absolutely impossible for us at least to remain friends?"

She sighed. "There's no real reason for me to be

offended, is there? I was as much to blame as you for...what happened after the theater." She smiled dryly. "I could say I was under some kind of spell that night—we both were, I guess—but the truth is, I knew exactly what I was doing. And I certainly can't say I wasn't warned. You were honest with me right from the start. You told me marriage wasn't for you. I guess you were right—I just didn't want to face reality."

"You're very honest yourself," he said, the fond note in his voice unnerving her all over again. "You really are a wonderful woman and a rare one. Are you sure you can't reconsider—"

"No," she said abruptly. "But I will go with you to Stratford. For Portia's sake, trusting you to keep your promise. This can only be a business arrangement, Jason. I can't play sophisticated games. I'm not cut out for them."

He stepped back a pace, smiling wryly, raising both hands palm upward. "I promise not to touch." His expression sobered. "Thank you, Victoria. I appreciate your doing this for Portia."

For Portia, her mind echoed jeeringly. Would anyone with an ounce of insight believe she was agreeing to go with him for Portia's sake? Did he really believe it? Did she?

CHAPTER THIRTEEN

"NOT ANOTHER ANTIQUE SHOP?" Portia groaned.

Vicki smiled at her, hesitating outside the door of the tiny bay-windowed store she'd been directed to at the last place she'd visited. "This is a craft shop mostly," she told the girl. "They do have antiques, too, but the lady in the Tudor shop told me I might find what I'm looking for here." She smiled sympathetically. "I know it's boring for you. Just this one, and then we'll go down to the river and watch the houseboats for a while. Okay?"

Portia brightened and made no further objections. She loved watching the houseboats go through the locks on the River Avon. They had been in Stratford for five days, and at least once a day she'd insisted they lean on the bridge over the river, speculating on the people who rented the cumbersome craft, and weaving romantic daydreams about engaging one of them herself in the future.

The shop's small interior was crammed with all kinds of treasures. Vicki would have liked to linger over the china and pottery and copper, and especially the tapestries hanging on one wall. But for Portia's sake, she approached the small counter at once and spoke to the wizened old man who was evidently the proprietor. He looked exactly as the owner of such a shop should look, she thought—an elfin cobbler, bent and gnarled and ancient. She could imagine him working busily under a toadstool in the moonlight, tapping away at a tiny shoe. "You're Mr. Duckworth?" she asked.

He inclined his head.

"Mrs. Gardner at the Tudor shop said you would be able to help me."

The old man raised bushy eyebrows over round steel-rimmed spectacles and smiled benignly at her. "It must be so, then, if Mrs. Gardner says it is," he replied.

Vicki smiled, remembering the thin, garrulous, somewhat opinionated woman and realizing by the guarded twinkle in the man's faded blue eyes that he must have crossed paths with Mrs. Gardner before. "I'm trying to find something like this," she said, showing him the sketch of the Tudor-style lantern that she'd brought with her.

He examined it closely, holding it right under his nose. "Ar," he said and went out through a door in the back of the store.

"What a funny little man," Portia whispered. "Jason would love him."

Vicki nodded, steeling herself against the sinking sensation she experienced whenever Jason's name was mentioned unexpectedly. "Jason likes people to look the part," she agreed dryly.

Portia grinned. "Maybe that's why I aggravate him so. He's got me cast as the docile little sister, and I insist on messing up the role."

Vicki started to agree, but then stopped as the little man returned. Incredibly he was carrying a lantern that looked exactly like her sketch in every detail except size. Portia laughed. "Magic!" she exclaimed.

Vicki was inclined to agree. "That's amazing," she said. "I copied this from an old book I found on lighting through the ages."

"Ar," Mr. Duckworth said, nodding wisely, his eyes glinting. "So did I."

"You mean you made this?"

"That I did."

"It's perfect!" Vicki exclaimed, examining the lantern closely. Formed of wrought black metal, paned with glass, the lamp was beautifully crafted, true to the original in every way. "Could you make one like this but smaller?" she asked hopefully.

"I could."

"Could you make a hundred of them?"

His face creased in a shrewd grin. "If it's bargaining you're after, we'd best have some tea," he stated emphatically. Before Vicki could respond, she found herself ensconced in a comfortable chair in the old man's workshop, sipping freshly brewed tea, while he worked out a cost estimate—on a pocket calculator of all things.

Halfway through his figuring, he glanced up at Portia, who was desultorily examining some of his tools. "Most like you'd enjoy meeting my great-grandsons," he said, standing up and whisking her away through yet another door before she could have any say in the matter. "Youngsters get bored easily nowadays," he commented to Vicki when he returned. "My boys are good boys. They'll entertain the lass while we tend to business."

Vicki laughed, enjoying him immensely.

Actually, she thought as the old man returned to his calculations, she'd enjoyed herself ever since her arrival in Stratford-upon-Avon. It was impossible not to. The town itself was everything she'd expected it to be—charming and distinctly Elizabethan. Though crowded to the bursting point with tourists, the streets and historic buildings retained their old-world appeal. She and Portia had already poked around in every nook and cranny, learning all they could about the fascinating town.

Over the past few days she had learned that the area had been inhabited by Celtic tribes even before the Romans came and founded the first small settlement. Saxons had erected a monastery and a mill, and with the rise of the Guild of the Holy Cross, which fostered crafts and industries, and the markets and fairs granted by royal charters, the town had made steady progress. The community had been fortunate in its generous citizens, who had built the church, the bridge, the Guild Chapel and the Almshouses. Among those citizens, of course, was one who had brought worldwide fame to his native town: William Shakespeare.

She and Portia had explored the famous playwright's birthplace and had taken dozens of photographs of all the marvelously preserved timbered buildings in town, including their own elegantly appointed hotel, which was situated in its own quiet gardens away from the noise of traffic, yet close to the town center and the theater.

But even though she was thrilled to be in Stratford, she had found it impossible to relax completely, especially on those occasions when Jason joined them. He couldn't manage to get away from the theater very often, but he sometimes took meals with them. Vicki had managed to treat him as a mere acquaintance, but only with tremendous effort. Every time he left them to go back to the theater, she sighed with relief, glad to be free of some of the strain. Every night she sank into bed in the luxurious room she shared with Portia, exhausted by the effort of her pretense, but able to sleep only fitfully.

At the theater itself she couldn't keep up her act of not caring. Watching Jason perform, listening to his vibrant voice weaving magic night after night, she could feel herself being drawn closer and closer toward emotional disaster.

Jason himself was preoccupied most of the time, seemingly unable to relax, either. Sometimes at night she could hear him pacing the floor of his room next to hers. But she certainly couldn't fool herself into thinking she was the cause of his unrest. He was totally immersed in the parts he was playing and rehearsing, appearing oblivious to everyone around him. He surfaced only occasionally to ask her if she was having a good time, if she needed anything, if she was bored.

No, she'd told him, she couldn't possibly be bored here. Everything was marvelous—and the plays were magnificent. She felt saturated in Shakespeare, she'd added; she was almost thinking in Elizabethan blank verse.

He'd smiled at that and agreed it was difficult to escape that particular phenomenon, but his smile had been absentminded, and she'd felt he wasn't really seeing her as a person at all.....

It took three cups of tea for Vicki and Mr. Duckworth to reach agreement on a price, for he was a shrewd bargainer. But at last they were done, and he summoned Portia from the back regions of the shop. His great-grandsons came with her, two nice-looking sturdy boys dressed in cricket flannels and open-necked shirts, both with their great-grandfather's good-humored blue eyes.

Graham was sixteen, Neil fourteen, Portia told her after they'd left the shop and were walking toward the river. And she'd really liked them both. They'd recognized her name immediately, she said, but hadn't been overly impressed. "People are used to actors in this town," she added.

That may have been true of the people who lived there, Vicki thought, but it certainly wasn't the case with the press, not where Jason Meredith was concerned. A blaze of publicity had surrounded his arrival in Stratford, and even now reporters were always hanging around. Jason had been forced to adopt all kinds of devious devices to get in and out of the hotel undetected, and even Vicki and Portia had to take circuitous routes through the hotel, often leaving through the kitchens. When possible, Jason did give interviews. He often walked to the theater surrounded by people hurling questions at him. He answered them good-naturedly, often with witticisms that delighted them and were quoted verbatim in the following day's paper. But the pace at Stratford was murderous, and he did need some time to be alone.

Vicki was glad to see Portia looking so pleased with herself. Her gray eyes were positively dancing with delight over her newfound friends. They wanted to take her the following day to see Anne Hathaway's cottage at Shottery, she said, so Vicki must help her persuade Jason to give his permission.

"Well, I'll try," Vicki said doubtfully.

"You can talk him into it," Portia proclaimed, putting her hand under Vicki's arm and giving it an

affectionate squeeze. "If it hadn't been for you, I'd
have been in a lot more trouble when I ran off after
Colly." She tilted her head to look around at Vicki's
face, her expression apologetic. "I never did thank
you for going to all that bother for me, did I?" she
went on. She sighed. "Jason's always telling me I'm
an ungrateful wretch. I suppose he's right. I do thank
you, Vicki, and I'm sorry I deceived you that day."
She shuddered a little. "I learned my lesson, though.
Oh, that awful woman! How she produced someone
as nice as Colly I can't imagine. He's written to me,
you know."

"No, I didn't know." Vicki smiled at Portia fondly, delighted to see her so vivacious. She'd been
rather subdued lately, almost as subdued as Vicki
herself.

"I'm going to see him before I go toddling off to
school," Portia confided.

"I've been meaning to talk to you about that,"
Vicki said.

They had reached the river and stood on the bridge
for a while, watching one of the houseboats go
through the lock. The houseboats were mostly con-
verted barges. The living space looked terribly
cramped to Vicki, and she wondered how much fun
the woman of the family had on such trips. This particular barge had two strings of laundry flapping between its two tiny cabins, and she could imagine the
difficulties of trying to prepare meals and wash
dishes, besides caring for children. There were three
small children on board, and their mother, a woman
no older than Vicki, was holding onto two of them by
their britches as they leaned over the side of the boat.
She looked harried, Vicki thought.

But Portia was still enchanted. A good way to spend a honeymoon, she thought.

Vicki smiled. This would hardly be her idea of a good way to start a relationship. It was difficult enough for two people to get along under the best of circumstances. . . .

That was a dangerous thought, one best suppressed. "How do you really feel about going to boarding school?" she asked Portia.

Portia grinned. "I think it will be fun," she said promptly. "Nobody's going to know who I am. Did Jason tell you?"

"You might find you don't like that as much as you think you will," Vicki warned.

"Perhaps. But it's something I've always wanted to try. And anyway, I've got plans to—" She broke off and looked suddenly secretive.

Vicki felt alarmed. The girl was almost wriggling with suppressed excitement. What was she up to now? "Portia?" she said in a warning tone.

Portia looked at her sheepishly. "If I tell you something, will you keep it a secret?"

"If it's not too. . . adventurous."

The girl laughed. "Not really, but if you tell Jason, I'll kill you."

"Portia!"

"Oh, it's nothing bad. But you know I went to see the headmistress, with Mrs. Powell. I'm going to be registered under her name, you see, and my middle name: Elizabeth Powell. I'll have a whole new identity. Anyway, I talked to the headmistress and arranged to take drama classes. They have ever such a good drama department there. That's why I agreed to go in the first place."

Vicki stared at her, astonished. "But you hate anything to do with acting."

"That's what I've always said. I told Colly so, too, but he didn't believe me. He said the way I raved about Jason's acting proved that I wanted to do it myself."

Score one more point for Colly, Vicki thought.

"Why on earth didn't you say so, then?" she asked.

Portia's delicate face was solemn now. She was gazing at the sun-dappled river below them, elbows propped on the bridge rail, chin cupped in her hands. "There have been actors in the Meredith family for more than two hundred years," she said slowly. "None of them was second-rate, Vicki. My parents were top-notch. I've read the notices. People put them way up on a pedestal; they were idolized almost. When my father died, all the theaters in Shaftesbury Avenue put out their lights for an hour—Jason told me all about it. And then there's Jason himself. You've seen him act; you know how great he is."

"You were afraid to compete?" Vicki suggested softly.

Portia's glance was shy. "I expect you think that's pretty stupid."

"Not at all. It's entirely understandable that you'd worry about measuring up. I applaud your decision to do something about it now. I'm sure Jason will be delighted. Now don't worry," she added when Portia's head lifted in alarm. "I'm not going to tell him about your plans."

"I want to find out first if I'm going to fall flat on my face." Portia took a deep breath. "I'm scared to death, Vicki. Mind you, I don't want to get into Shakespearean drama—too much gore and tragedy for me. I'd like to try for comedy, perhaps musical comedy. But even so, I don't want to disgrace the Meredith name.''

"You won't," Vicki said confidently. "Success is probably programmed into your genes.''

"You really think so?'' The girl giggled suddenly. "I hope you're right.'' Her smile turned wistful. "I wish there was some easy way to find out if I'd suffer from stage fright. Jason was born knowing he was an actor, I think. I don't have that certainty. I've practiced in front of my mirror at home, but that didn't tell me much. Except that I *am* good at remembering lines.''

"Would you like to give me a solo performance?'' Vicki suggested.

Portia shook her head. "It wouldn't work. I'm really most worried about what I'd do faced with an audience.'' She sighed. "What I really need is to. . . .''

Her voice trailed away, and she lapsed into a dreamy silence that lasted through their walk home to their hotel.

Vicki was delighted that the girl had confided in her and certainly wished her well. She should have guessed Portia's secret ambitions, she chided herself. When someone seemed vehemently opposed to something, it was often because they secretly wanted to try it themselves.

In their hotel room Portia emerged from her dreamlike state long enough to hug Vicki exuberantly and thank her for being so good to her. "I think it was watching you sing that gave me the courage,'' she confided. "I thought that if you could forget yourself enough to perform in front of strangers, then maybe I could, too."

Vicki wasn't sure if that was a compliment or not, but she accepted it as such, inwardly amused. "I'm going to use you as a role model," Portia asserted. "Whenever I'm afraid, I'll just imagine I'm you—beautiful and poised and talented—and then I'll be all right."

That was a compliment indeed. Vicki returned Portia's hug. "You'll be great," she predicted and felt sure she was right. She wasn't too sure about Portia using her as a role model, though. There were some aspects of her character that wouldn't bear imitation. One of which, of course, was her inability to separate her emotions from Jason Meredith. But she could hardly tell Portia that.

As THOUGH SUMMONED by her thoughts of him, Jason joined them for tea on the hotel terrace. As soon as he asked how they had enjoyed their day, Portia gave Vicki a glance loaded with meaning. Obediently Vicki set about persuading Jason to let Portia go off with the Duckworth boys the next day.

To her surprise he agreed with alacrity and enthusiasm, seeming to emerge for once from his preoccupied state. She found out the reason as soon as Portia had danced off to telephone Graham and Neil with the good news.

"I've wanted to take you punting on the river," he informed her in a matter-of-fact tone. "I didn't think it was going to be possible because Portia has never learned to sit still in a boat. The last time we tried punting together, we ricocheted all over the river and ended up soaked to the skin." He nodded briskly. "We'll go tomorrow. I'll have a car pick us up at the side exit so we can avoid the press. We don't want cameras recording our every movement, do we?"

"But surely you have a performance tomorrow evening?" Vicki protested nervously. "I understood *Macbeth* was going to begin."

"It is," Jason agreed. "I'm dreadfully nervous about it, too. First time I've played the role, and it's a demanding one. There's a legend in the theater that it's a play of bad omen. Things always seem to go wrong when it's performed." He shrugged. "We had a final run-through this afternoon, but there's no rehearsal tomorrow. A lazy day on the river is just what I need to relax me. Do you good, too—your suntan is fading."

He *had* looked at her lately, then, Vicki thought. "The English sunshine isn't quite consistent enough to preserve it," she said casually, trying not to show her elation over the first personal remark he'd made to her in more than a week.

He nodded absently. Then to her dismay he suddenly looked directly at her and unleashed his most dazzling smile, the one that always affected her like a flash of summer lightning. "Don't be fooled by anything you've heard about punting," he said in a jocular tone. "If you have images in your mind of yourself in a drifting white gown holding a frilled parasol, while I pole us along in my striped blazer and Panama hat, forget them. Punting is a rugged occupation. You'll need to wear your sturdiest clothes."

He pushed back his chair, looking at her with a boyishly appealing smile. "We'll spend the whole day," he said cheerfully. "I'll have the chef make us up a picnic basket. I'll see to it at once."

. With that he was gone, striding through the adjoining restaurant, leaving Vicki staring dazedly after him.

A whole day, she thought with alarm. How on earth was she going to control her still-far-too-strong feelings for him for a whole day? She couldn't, of course. She couldn't even be with him for an hour without her face feeling cracked from the strain of trying to look unmoved by his presence.

Well, she would just have to manage somehow. True to his promise, he hadn't touched her once since they'd been here, not even accidentally. No doubt, he could stick to his promise even in the confines of a small boat. Obviously, in spite of all his previous talk about wanting her and needing her, his feelings for her didn't run very deep and could be easily handled.

But a whole day! The thought crossed her mind that if she'd had any sense at all, she'd have argued with him, told him she didn't *want* to go punting with him. She chose to ignore the idea. Unbidden, lines from *Hamlet*, in which she had watched Jason perform again the previous night, came to her mind:

> There's a divinity that shapes our ends,
> Rough-hew them how we will.

Fate, she thought; she'd just have to leave everything up to fate.

CHAPTER FOURTEEN

IN SPITE OF JASON'S WARNING, Vicki, remembering old movies, had expected their punting trip to carry overtones of romance—and had worried accordingly.

But there had been nothing to worry about so far, she thought, as Jason maneuvered the boat around a floating log. Many other people, probably lured by the hot midday sunshine, had had the same idea, and the river and its banks were fairly crowded.

She was seated in one squared-off end of what was a surprisingly clumsy-looking craft. It was her job, Jason had informed her, to help steer them with the aid of a small and rather ineffectual paddle. So far she hadn't needed to use the paddle very often. She'd spent most of the past two hours leaning back against a boat cushion, trailing her fingers in the cool water.

Jason stood tall in the middle of the flat-bottomed boat, looking more than ever like the original bold buccaneer. A sea king in shorts and an unbuttoned blue shirt that flapped open with every movement, he plunged the long pole he was using into the mud beneath the river, leaned on it, retrieved it as the boat shot forward, then plunged again, shooting a spray of silver drops into the air.

The whole process seemed to require a great deal of strength, which Jason had in abundance. The only

difficulty so far had been for Vicki to keep her gaze
averted from his rugged figure. It was impossible not
to marvel at the strength of his body: the sculptured
flatness of his stomach; the muscled planes of his
chest; the power of the hands gripping the pole; the
rippling strength of the thighs and long legs beneath
his cuffed khaki shorts.

He seemed to be enjoying his task—he was a man
who reveled in physical exercise—but once again he
had retreated into the taciturn mood that had characterized him during this first week in Stratford. Perhaps he really was nervous about playing Macbeth.
Portia had told Vicki that he was desperately afraid
of failure.

"He walked the streets most of the night," she'd
said cheerfully at breakfast before Jason arrived.
"He often does that before attempting a new role.
He prowls around, tearing his hair and growling at
anyone who crosses his path."

Vicki found it difficult to take his fears seriously.
With his long and successful career behind him, he
surely couldn't be worried about his acting ability.
Probably Portia had exaggerated his condition; she
had a habit of exaggerating just about everything
else.

"Are you ready for lunch?" Jason asked.

Startled, Vicki looked up at him. He was standing
still, his feet braced. He was holding the pole lightly
now, letting it trail in the water as the boat moved
lazily between suddenly narrower banks. As Vicki
pondered Portia's words, he had steered their craft
into a quiet side stream.

At first, Vicki felt relieved to be out of the glaring
sun. She was feeling very warm in spite of the sun top

and shorts she'd stripped to an hour ago. In this stretch of the river the trees arched over their heads, bringing welcome shade. But then, to her alarm, she noticed that none of the other tourists had ventured down here, probably because of those very trees. Some branches hung so low that it had become necessary for Jason to squat down in the boat. He was barely moving the pole now, waiting for her response, his strong features impassive as he looked at her.

"I expect you are hungry," she said carefully, not committing herself. Probably it would be a mistake to agree to stay in this lonely place.

He shrugged. "We should eat something, I suppose." His voice sounded gloomy. He *was* in an odd mood.

Evidently taking her evasive response for agreement, he pulled the boat to the side of the stream where the bank was fairly flat, and where there was a good-sized patch of short grass screened by a huge willow tree. Vicki scrambled out of the boat as he tied it in place, afraid that if he assisted her, she'd be affected as usual by his touch. He glanced at her sideways as though he recognized her fear, but made no comment, busying himself with the picnic basket he'd brought along.

There were tiny sandwiches and cakes in the basket, some small meat pies, fruit, a bottle of wine, a large flask of tea. Nervously Vicki requested tea, wary of the wine's possible effects. Again Jason glanced at her, but he didn't smile.

He drank tea, also. He ate very little. Vicki herself had no appetite at all, and she felt very awkward in the silence. The tension crackling in the air between them was not the sexual tension she'd dreaded. Had she offended him in some way? He seemed so withdrawn, so morose, almost melancholy.

Uneasily she leaned back on her elbows, looking up at the lacy pattern of blue sky she could see through the overhanging tassels of the willow tree. Jason was sitting next to her, but not too close. He was leaning forward, his cup gripped in one hand, a cigarette in the other, gazing at the slowly rippling water. His profile was as stern as though it had been carved from granite. His usual vibrant energy was not in evidence, though Vicki could sense it in him, hidden and held tightly in control.

"I'm probably going to end up in the blasted Tower," he said at last. His voice, usually so resonant, had a peculiarly lifeless quality, as though all emotion had left him.

"The Tower?" Vicki echoed, bewildered.

"I'm going to fail tonight, Victoria. I should never have agreed to play Macbeth. He's almost unplayable. One cannot identify with him as one can with Hamlet or Othello—his crimes are too hideous. Yet I want to elicit sympathy for him rather than revulsion. He was at heart a gentle man—a decent man, I feel, though rash and impetuous. He loved his wife, but he was the victim of that love and of his own overweening ambition, and he compromised his many fine qualities in an attempt to claim a throne he had no right to. A terribly complex individual. The role is obviously beyond me. I should have waited until I was at least sixty. I'm not sure my voice is deep enough, either, even on its lowest register." He sighed. "I'm going to be utterly dreadful."

"Oh, I'm sure you can—" Vicki broke off. Given

the utter conviction in his voice, it would be meaningless to offer platitudes. "Why do you think so?" she amended. "You've never been dreadful before."

"Yes, I have." He flipped the half-smoked cigarette into the stream and dropped his empty cup into the picnic basket. Turning toward her, he drew his mouth down at the corners in self-deprecating mockery. "What's the American expression? 'Bombed'? Yes, I've bombed before."

She had never seen his gray eyes look so empty. "When?" she asked.

"When I began. First play I was ever in."

"But that was years ago."

"Doesn't mean it can't happen again." He paused. "Lord, I've never forgotten my humiliation."

He stretched out flat on his back, hands clasped behind his head, and looked up at her face as she leaned automatically on one elbow to face him. Her own nervousness was forgotten in the face of his, though she was suddenly, disturbingly aware of the nearness of his half-naked torso now that his shirt had fallen away from it. Aware of the tanned skin her fingers longed to touch.

"Picture it, Victoria," he said grimly. "There was never any doubt in anyone's mind that I was destined to become a great actor. Not just an actor, mind you, but a *great* one. My father determined that the day I was born. There's been at least one Meredith acting for centuries, and it looked as though I would be the last of the Merediths. Devil of a lot of pressure. My entire infancy was spent in mental exercise to strengthen my ability to remember lines. My father had me reciting long passages from Shakespeare by the time I was six. If I made mistakes, I was punished. If I cried, he told me to remember how it felt to cry so I could recreate the emotion at will. Same with laughter, or anger. Later, there were vocal exercises to extend the range of my voice. Everything I did was directed toward my career as an actor...and the first night out I bombed.''

Vicki stared at him, much more horrified by the picture he'd painted of his childhood than by his early failure. There was no self-pity in his voice, but such a childhood must have marked him in some way.

''Don't misunderstand me,'' he went on, apparently noticing the quick sympathy on her face. ''My father and mother loved me. And I had physical exercise, too—tennis and cricket and football—all of that. It's necessary for an actor to be physically fit.

''All I'm saying is that I was destined from the cradle to become an actor. And I wanted to be one. It was all I ever wanted to do. It wasn't as grim as I've made it sound, either. It was like a child's game, a game of pretend. I loved it. Still do. As soon as I was old enough I was sent to the Royal Academy of Dramatic Art. Everybody raved about me. I could do no wrong. And then they put me on a public stage in front of hundreds of people, and I fell apart. I had a major role in Chekhov's *Cherry Orchard*. I came off sounding like an idiot. I stumbled, stuttered, floundered. I literally fell on my face, tripped over my own bloody feet.''

''How old were you?''

''Nineteen.''

''Come on, Jason!''

''I've failed again since then. For a long time the

critics didn't like me at all—mostly because I didn't play any part the way it had been played before. They thought I'd do everything the way my father did, so they were disappointed. So were the audiences. There was one awful time when I had nothing to play but one-night stands in darkest outer London."

"But you came through. You've played most of the truly titanic roles in Shakespeare and done them marvelously."

"I haven't played Macbeth. I feel like the Emperor in Hans Christian Andersen's story—tonight's the night everyone finds out I'm not wearing any clothes. You see, Victoria, when an actor reaches the upper heights of his profession, so much *more* is expected of him. Nowadays an actor is either practically unknown, or his name is a household word. And once it's a household word, he can't go back to being *moderately* successful. It's like being a runner, I suppose; once the four-minute mile was cracked, even a microsecond less than four minutes was unacceptable. It's the same with an author. Once he's established as a best-seller, he can't go back to the middle of the list without sinking into obscurity or foundering on the rocks of mediocrity."

Vicki sighed. He was determined to be depressed. She smiled down at him, trying to lighten the atmosphere. "You could always go back to the movies, I guess."

He looked gloomier than ever. "I hate films—can't take them seriously. Three hours in the makeup department every bloody morning. Most of the work is done in the cutting room, anyway. Bits of celluloid glued together. There's no real satisfaction in films, not for me."

Vicki sighed again. He was behaving like a small boy, she thought, determined to be miserable. And yet he really did seem uncertain. *Could* he fail? What would failure *do* to a man like Jason Meredith? A failure in Stratford—Shakespeare's own Stratford—would be disastrous.

"You won't have any problem at all," she assured him with all the conviction she could muster. "You know the part, don't you?"

"Forward and backward."

"Well, then, you'll be superb, as always."

"Do you really think so?"

The words were so obviously an appeal that Vicki didn't hesitate. "I know so."

His left hand reached to her face, touched it lightly, then moved to her hair, his fingers tangling in the long strands that had come loose from the silk scarf she'd used to tie it back. "You are always so good to me, Victoria," he said softly.

"I'm just saying what the critics will be saying," she replied briskly, trying to overcome the breathlessness that had assailed her at his touch.

"Lord, I hope you're right," he breathed.

Talking about his fears seemed to have relaxed him. The tension had gone out of his face now, leaving it smooth and unlined, young. His mouth had softened and parted. She couldn't take her gaze from his mouth.

His fingers were tightening in her hair—not hurting her, but making her aware of their pressure against her head, a pressure that was increasing as he drew her face down to his. Unexpectedly he brushed the tip of her breast with the back of his other hand.

"No, Jason," she said abruptly.

"Please, Victoria! Let me hold you. I need to hold you." There was urgency in his voice now.

How could she refuse him? How could she refuse herself? She was so tired of fighting her feelings for this man.

Sighing, she allowed him to draw her head down to his bared chest. His other arm moved around her, holding her close. Beneath them the grass was soft and springy. She could smell the warm earthy odor of it and the smell of Jason—a faint impression of tobacco and salt and good honest sweat, utterly masculine, heady to her senses.

A light breeze had sprung up while they talked, ruffling the leaves around them, teasing the edges of her hair, cooling, caressing. Nearby the stream murmured lazily, occasionally interrupted by the splash of a small fish. Somewhere a bee droned in search of a flower. She felt suspended in time and place—at ease, calm and peaceful and serene.

"I want you, Victoria," Jason said softly.

Lifting her head, she touched her fingers to his mouth, not wanting him to talk. Talking might activate the logical part of her mind, might remind her of vows made, decisions reached. Wise decisions.

Gently Jason pressed her hand to his mouth. Slowly, staring deeply into her eyes, he kissed her fingers, drawing the tip of each one into his mouth, biting it lightly, teasingly, braising it with his tongue before releasing it and going on to the next. Sending erotic impulses shooting through her body. His tenderness, his delicacy, moved her enormously. He was such a big man, such a strong man, that when he behaved with tenderness, the effect was devastating. There was a constriction in her throat that threatened tears, and her face felt loose and soft...boneless. Heat was throbbing behind her skin.

With infinite care he eased her down to her back on the sweet warm grass and leaned over her, his lips pressing lightly against each of her eyelids, his breath feathering first against her eyelashes, then across her cheek to her ear. He was barely breathing, she realized, and her own breath was held. It was as though they'd both decided that allowing breath to escape too loudly would disturb the delicate balance between them.

Continuing that same barely perceptible series of movements, his lips moved knowingly to the sensitive hollow of her throat, brushing lightly against her sun-warmed skin, tasting delicately of the skin of her bare shoulder as he eased her elastic sun top down over her breasts. Her own hands were moving, too, rising to touch the thick crispness of his hair, pressing his head closer as his lips found and caressed one soft nipple and teased it to erection. Moments later, an hour later—she didn't know—his head moved again, his mouth trailing a line of heat across her body to her other breast so that he might give to it the same loving attention. His hands had traveled to her lower body and were now gently disengaging the zipper of her white shorts.

Vicki made a small sound of protest, desperately trying to surface from the deeply relaxed, almost hypnotized state his gentle caresses had induced in her. At once his hands ceased their movements, and he held her close again, his mouth gently pressed against her shoulder. His ear was close to her lips, and she found herself lightly rimming the edge of it with her tongue, tasting again the wonderful slightly salty cleanness of his skin. She felt his body stiffen against hers, then shudder slightly as his hands increased their pressure against her hips. And now his breathing became audible, as his mouth moved across her upper body, blowing out short light breaths directly onto her skin's surface. They were moving against each other now, falling into a rhythm that seemed familiar.

Familiar. All the textures of his skin and hair and clothing were becoming familiar to her, as hers surely must be to him. This was—what—the third time he had attempted to make love to her?

He was easing himself up on to his elbows now. Slowly. His gray gaze held hers hypnotically. He was taking great care not to startle her with sudden movement, not to awaken her to a realization of what he was about to do. So careful, so gentle. So slowly he fumbled with his own clothing.

Remembering in every vivid detail the night they had returned to his suite after his performance of *Hamlet*, she could almost predict each movement he would make now, all the way to the final pressures of his body that would tell her his passion was about to culminate. And then. . . .

She was suddenly pushing him away, frantically pulling the edge of her tube top up across her breasts, desperately grasping for the logic, the sensible reasoning that had slipped away from her once more. "No, Jason," she said, somehow keeping her voice calm. "You promised—*we* promised. No more. I can't keep on doing this. I've told you I can't."

His hands reached for her, pulling her abruptly against him. "Please, Victoria," he murmured in her ear. "I need you."

Need. Need was not love. Need was a selfish thing. She could remember him telling her that day at the Tower how she banished his nervousness. "You must promise to be with me before every performance," he'd said. "I've never felt so relaxed...."

"I'm not some kind of tranquilizer, Jason," she said coldly.

Startled, he held her at arms' length, his gray eyes studying her face. "What are you talking about?" he demanded.

"You're using me, aren't you? You're nervous about tonight's performance, and you're using me to help you relax—to help you forget you're afraid."

For a long moment he stared at her, his eyes bewildered. Then very slowly his face gentled. His hand caressed the side of her face, his thumb tracing the line of her cheek, then moving lazily down to linger against her mouth. "Victoria," he said quietly, "Don't you know that I've given up the fight? Don't you know that I love you?"

She closed her eyes, slowly exhaling a long breath that seemed to have been trapped inside her forever. Without further protest she let him draw her close again—close and down to the warm softness of the grass. She was completely disarmed now, no reluctance left in her, all of her body and mind lulled by the promise in those three trite, important, wonderful words. Now she need not hold back anything. Now she was totally and completely his.

Suddenly, for no reason that she could think of, she remembered her zoologist father telling her about lemmings, the small Arctic rodents who were known for mass migrations. Having chosen their direction, her father had said, the lemmings did not once swerve from their path. They swam across lakes and rivers several miles in width, crossed over mountains and valleys, until, inevitably, their perilous journey ended in self-destruction in the sea.

What a strange thing to think of now, she thought vaguely as Jason gathered her close to him, and her senses quickened unbearably. Jason loved her. What could be self-destructive about loving him in return?

Without haste, his mouth was moving again across the heightened sensitivity of her skin, his tongue on the warm rounded flesh of her breast, lazily circling a nipple that had long since tightened in anticipation.

Drowning in wave after wave of blissful sensation, she clung to him, her mouth moving softly over him as his hands and tongue discovered the sources of her pleasure and provoked them. She in turn, overcoming her own previous timidity, brazenly explored the contours of the firm male flesh that was so strange yet so familiar to her. Nothing, she thought hazily, could be more achingly arousing than this—to be touched and to touch, without fear, without embarrassment. It was almost as though each move they made had been rehearsed over and over until it came naturally, without conscious volition.

Time had ceased. She had no awareness of the outside world. Screened by the lazily moving fronds of the low-hanging willow, they were in a world of their own, where no one could see them or intrude. Only sensation existed, building to a peak, subsiding, climbing unbearably again. And all the time his voice whispered to her, telling her how lovely she was, how much he desired her, how difficult it had been for him to stay away from her.

Above her the willow green canopy blurred as he

bent over her, lifting her to him, arching her hips to fit against his own. The lacy sky-willow designs advanced and retreated, whirled and shimmered and finally disappeared as his head moved closer to hers. There was nothing gentle about him now. His kisses were driving and intrusive, his hands forceful and impatient, the contours of his body hard and ungiving against hers. And she wanted no gentleness now.

Determinedly she closed off her mind to thought and surrendered herself to her own burning all-consuming need.

She was falling, falling free, falling through air grown heavy and thick, but still unable to support her. She was falling into space, her mouth making little incoherent whimpering sounds against his as he responded triumphantly with words, "Yes, my darling, yes."

CHAPTER FIFTEEN

GLOWING, VICKI DECIDED. That was the word to describe the way she looked tonight.

She stood in front of the antique dressing table in the room she shared with Portia, gazing at herself in the mirror with an almost narcissistic pleasure. Surely her eyes had never shone so green. Never had her hair gleamed with such golden fire, the lighter streaks making it look as though it were touched with moonlight as it floated down behind her shoulders. Even her skin glowed, her tan refurbished by the sun she'd exposed it to today. And her mouth seemed fuller, redder. It had the bee-stung look of a mouth that has been repeatedly and most lovingly kissed.

Gently, sensuously, she smoothed the fabric of her camisole-top dress over her hips, enjoying the way the color of the shot silk changed from green to blue according to the light. Her whole body felt as though it glowed, too—with an inner fire that not all of the lovemaking beside the river had quenched.

"You look absolutely super," Portia announced as she emerged from the bathroom.

Embarrassed to be caught admiring herself—an activity that was usually foreign to her—Vicki laughed nervously and turned away from the mirror. "You look pretty spiffy yourself," she joked.

Portia acknowledged the compliment with modestly downcast eyes, a modesty that was belied by her gamin grin as she twirled around to show Vicki the fullness of her blue-and-white cotton skirt. With it she was wearing a sleeveless white blouse trimmed with *broderie anglaise*. Her freshly shampooed curls caught the light and shone with a vitality that matched her smile. "It's smashing to be a girl, isn't it?"

Smiling, Vicki agreed, delighted to see Portia so happy. Evidently the day in Shottery with Neil and Graham had been a success. Portia hadn't stopped talking since she'd come home.

Which was just as well, Vicki thought as she slipped her feet into bone-colored sandals and picked up her matching clutch purse. If Portia had been her usual observant self, she would definitely have noticed Vicki's own tremulous excitement—and the tender note in her voice as she'd bade Jason goodbye and good luck an hour or so before.

She had never in her life felt so happy, nor so sure that this time her happiness would continue. No negative statements or denials of commitment had marred the wonderful afternoon.

Jason had held her afterward for a long time, talking to her softly about herself and the effect she had on him—how she chased the bitterness from his soul and made it possible for him to laugh at himself and his fears.

About four o'clock they had reluctantly returned to the boat, punted lazily back to the dock and walked hand in hand to the hotel, heedless of the passing tourists who had stared at them—at him—unabashedly. It was incredible, Vicki thought, that even in an old shirt and grass-stained shorts, he *radiated* presence—that superstar quality that made him stand out in any crowd.

Later Jason had joined her and Portia for afternoon tea on the terrace, though, as was his habit, he'd eaten very little, promising another meal later, after the play.

Mention of the play had reminded him of his nervousness, but he'd made an obvious effort not to withdraw into his earlier taciturn mood.

When he left, it hadn't been possible for her to say any intimate words to wish him well. She had seen his sidelong glance at Portia and realized he wanted her to be discreet, at least for now. But she hadn't minded that. She knew she would be seeing him later, after the play. There was time, all the time in the world.

THE ROYAL SHAKESPEARE THEATRE overlooked the River Avon. It was a huge brick building that had disappointingly reminded Vicki of a factory. The interior, though, had proved to be comfortable and well equipped. It was crowded, as it was every night. Tickets had been sold out for weeks.

She sat with Portia in the middle of the stalls. As she looked around at the throngs of people, she wondered mischievously what they would think if they knew she had, this very afternoon, made love with the man they had come to see.

Even the glimpse she'd had in the foyer of Sig and Sabrina Lindstrom had not dampened her spirits. Probably they'd come down only for the performance of *Macbeth*. They hadn't seen her, fortunately; they'd been surrounded by a group of friends. Sabrina, of course, had looked as stunning as ever in an ivory silk suit, her black hair gleaming like ebony against her dramatically pale face. For a second a chill had touched Vicki in spite of the evening's muggy heat, but it had passed quickly. And as soon as the Three

Witches appeared on stage to the accompaniment of thunder and lightning, she forgot Sabrina, forgot herself.

Jason, as always, was magnificent. Perhaps, Vicki thought, it was necessary for an actor to be overstrung and nervous before a play in order to give of his best. There had certainly been no reason for Jason to be fearful. His Macbeth was heartstopping, played at white heat with an intensity and fervor that transfixed the audience as surely as though his words were swords, hurtling outward to pierce them to the heart. Every line issued forth with grace and clarity as the gallant and fearless soldier of the opening act deteriorated to the evil but terrified villain who, his hands dyed with blood, fought wildly and brutally for his life.

Jason's portrayal was breathtaking, yet restrained enough that it did not dwarf the other players. Susan Carmody played a delicate tormented Lady Macbeth, and her husband, Christopher Hammond, was sensational as Malcolm. Another actor whom Vicki had not seen before—named Trevor Lassiter, according to her program—played a vigorous Macduff.

Yet there was no mistaking who was the star. Jason's performance went far beyond his physical power and electrifying voice. It was a tour de force of intuitive intelligence, timing and delivery. Vicki especially thrilled to the words that were her favorites in all of Shakespeare's works:

> Life's but a walking shadow, a poor player,
> That struts and frets his hour upon the stage,
> And then is heard no more; it is a tale
> Told by an idiot, full of sound and fury,
> Signifying nothing.

She had thought that perhaps tonight, because of the intimacy between them, she would be conscious of the man behind the role. But her experience was as before. Tonight Jason Meredith *was* Macbeth, and the transformation was not due solely to the aging makeup and beard and elaborate costuming. Every gesture, every bit of body language, every beautifully articulated word, served to convince the senses of the watcher that here indeed was Macbeth, just as Shakespeare had conceived him. As though, she thought, remembering their conversation on the drive home from London, Macbeth had taken over the body of Jason Meredith for a while, so that he could reveal himself to all.

The final dueling scene was the most dramatic she had ever seen on a stage. She was totally caught up in the exciting realism of the sword fight. So much so that she was actually rooting silently for Macduff until Portia leaned against her and whispered in a worried-sounding voice, "Do you suppose Jason remembers he's supposed to *lose*?"

Vicki could see the reason for Portia's concern. Jason gave no quarter to his opponent. He fought as though his life depended on it, which, of course, as Macbeth, it did. His energy and skill were amazing, his agility and instinctive grace astounding. It was difficult for Vicki to believe, now that Portia had brought her down to earth, that this was the gloomy man who had predicted disaster and a sentence to the Bloody Tower, the same man who had loved her with such passionate tenderness a few short hours ago.

Could such a man as this, such a giant in so many ways, really love her?

At the final curtain a tumultuous ovation confirmed Jason's triumph. There were fourteen curtain calls, and during most of them the audience was calling for him alone.

"How on earth can he doubt himself?" she murmured to Portia when the theater finally quieted.

Portia grinned. "He'll be the same way next time he has a first. Absolutely convulsed with anxiety. Most great actors go through the same thing, I understand. Jason's all right if he finds something to distract him, otherwise he sinks into despair. You seem to help him a lot," she added with a somewhat knowing grin.

Vicki managed to answer casually, but she was suddenly feeling a little less happy, a little less confident. *Had* she just served as a distraction for Jason? Was there no more to their love than that?

A few minutes later, pressed in among the crowd in Jason's dressing room, she was almost convinced that she had indeed been used only as a tranquilizer. She understood, of course, that Jason, now buoyant and smiling among his friends, gratefully accepting their rapturous praise, could hardly make a point of singling her out for attention. But surely he could have caught her eye, smiled, at least noticed her.

Portia was at his side, hanging on his arm, gazing up at her brother with pride and adoration. Sig was there, too, talking in a jocular way to the people around him. Sabrina was nowhere in sight, not at first. It was about five minutes after the crowd formed that she came in. To Vicki's surprise she made a beeline toward her rather than toward Jason. Vicki soon found out the reason for that.

"I'm surprised to see you here," Sabrina drawled.

"Why wouldn't I be here?" Vicki countered.

Sabrina's black eyes shone with malicious amusement. "You aren't going to trot out that silly story about you and Jason being engaged, are you? I've known that that was a farce right from the start."

"Really?" Vicki managed.

"But of course. Jason and I concocted that story between us in order to lay poor Sig's worries to rest. Surely Jason admitted that to you?"

Though shaken, Vicki was determined not to give way to this imperious woman. "I had a pretty good idea," she said casually.

"Naturally he wouldn't try to pull wool over my eyes, my dear. He knows I'm not given to jealousy, but an engagement would have been a bit much for me to swallow." She glanced archly at Vicki's face, which was by now, Vicki was sure, glowing with furious heat. "I expect you know that Jason and I are lovers," Sabrina continued. "We have been for a long time. Unfortunately our romance has had elements of a Shakespearean farce—I married Sig just a year before Claire died and left Jason free at last. But we are about to write our own happy ending. Jason has had long enough to get over his guilt complex, don't you think?"

Vicki managed a stiff smile, but by now words were beyond her.

Sabrina's smile was triumphant. "I'm going to be here for a week, did Jason tell you? He absolutely insisted I come down to amuse him between performances. So boring for him, poor pet, so far from London. Sig will stay on a day or so, but then he has to return home. I'm afraid you'll feel rather left out, won't you? But then you have Portia to look after. Jason told me you'd kindly offered to help with her."

Her smile became a little thin. "You've really been terribly helpful, my dear, and very convincing. Sig is quite taken with you. He believed your entire performance." She paused, then gave a brittle laugh. "I do hope that Jason's attentions haven't gone to your head?"

Before Vicki could respond to that gibe, Sabrina turned her head and laughed again, a merry tinkling sound that jarred Vicki's already overstretched nerves. "Look at him," she said fondly, indicating Jason across the room. He was listening to something Susan Carmody was telling him, his gray eyes intent on her flowerlike face, bringing all his attention to bear on her. Probably, Vicki thought bitterly, making her feel that she was the only person in the room he wanted to talk to.

"He does so *crave* admiration," Sabrina went on in her precise British voice. "Perhaps that explains his need to go from woman to woman the way he does. It's fortunate that I understand him so well." She patted Vicki's arm lightly. "Watch that he doesn't make an attempt on your virtue, my dear. Jason can never resist a conquest." Her smile faded abruptly, her facial muscles tightening into a cold mask that reminded Vicki of David Brent's expression when she had rebuffed his pass.

"Do remember this, my dear," Sabrina added very softly in a voice that cut through Vicki with the deliberate hardness of a diamond drill cutting through stone. "Jason is mine. Whatever game he is playing with you, it's just a game. He always returns to me."

With that she was gone, leaving Vicki standing motionless in the suddenly airless room. It was at that moment that Jason finally looked in her direction. She saw one eyebrow raise in a comical gesture that seemed to signify he would be with her very soon. Some of the people here, she knew, were planning to go on to dinner at an old inn overlooking the river, not far from the theater. Jason expected her to go, too! But she knew suddenly that she couldn't go through with it. She couldn't act as though nothing had happened. The things Sabrina had said made too much sense, especially when Vicki coupled them with Portia's remarks about her helping him to relax. He had used her. Probably the only reason he'd said he loved her was that she'd had enough sense for a moment to call a halt to his advances. He must have realized she wouldn't ever submit to him unless he said the magic words. And magic words came so easily to him.

What a fool she had been.

No, her mind immediately countered. She had not been a fool. She loved him. She had given him herself out of love. He was the one to be pitied, not her. Any man who simply used people for his own ends would never know happiness.

But neither would she, she added to herself, still standing frozen where Sabrina had left her. As long as she tortured herself by staying close to Jason, she would never be happy again.

Hurriedly she pushed her way through the crowd to Portia, who had been elbowed aside by the crush of people still congratulating Jason. "Brilliant phrasing," she heard one woman say. "Marvelous performance," another added. "The definitive Macbeth at last."

Jason's voice answered. "No performance of the

great Shakespearean roles can be definitive," he said
sternly. "Every actor takes a different view of every
character. That's what gives Shakespearean drama
such lasting appeal."

The woman smiled, evidently delighted to be lec-
tured by the great man.

"I've got a headache," Vicki whispered to Portia.
"I'm going back to the hotel. Make my excuses for
me, will you?"

Portia looked at her sympathetically. "What a
shame. You do look a bit peaked. D'you want me to
come with you?"

Vicki shook her head. "Stay and enjoy yourself."
Somehow she managed one more smile. "Maybe you
can pick up pointers from the cast."

"I already did," Portia said eagerly. "Weren't
those witches fab? And did you notice the number of
walk-on parts? All those servants and soldiers and at-
tendants? I'm going to talk to one of them, see how
he got a part like that."

"You do that," Vicki said wearily, unable to pretend any interest in Portia's enthusiasm right now.

Jason's prediction had been right, after all, she
thought as she hurried out into the night. Except that
the disaster he'd predicted was all hers instead of his.

CHAPTER SIXTEEN

JASON KNOCKED on her bedroom door at nine o'clock the next morning. Still in her white terry robe, her hair tied loosely in its nightly braid, and her face innocent of makeup, Vicki opened the door to him. He was dressed in a smart gray suit, white shirt, dark tie. He looked refreshed, invigorated—glowing, she thought with irony. His dazzling smile indicated that he expected a welcome.

"I'm in the most awful hurry," he said as soon as she appeared. "I overslept a bit, and I have an appointment with Sabrina for breakfast."

Hardly an auspicious start to her day, Vicki thought.

"Have fun," she said evenly, stepping back as he seemed about to reach for her.

A quick frown drew his dark brows together. "Are you still unwell?"

"I'll survive."

"Portia told me you had a headache, but she assured me you would be all right. I couldn't get away from everyone, I'm afraid, and by the time I did, I thought you were probably asleep, so I didn't disturb you. And of course, Portia was hovering around...." He hesitated, frowning again when she didn't respond. "Is your headache still bothering you?"

"Not at all. There never was a headache. It was simply the best excuse I could think of. I'm not as inventive as you."

"Now look here, Victoria, what on earth. . . ." His frown deepening, he looked over his shoulder to where Portia lay sleeping, wrapped in a cocoon of blankets, only the tips of her curls showing on the pillow. With an abrupt gesture he grasped Vicki's arm and pulled her into the living room of the suite, closing the door behind her. "Are you cross about something?" he asked, sounding genuinely bewildered.

"Why should I be?" she asked in a voice loaded with sarcasm to cover the pain that was threatening to tear her apart. "Your number-one mistress has turned up and staked a claim on you, so *naturally* I can't expect you to spare time for me."

"My mistress?"

"You and Sabrina planned our supposed engagement between you, didn't you? She knew the truth about us all the time."

His face cleared. "Oh, that. Well, no, not exactly. It was all my own idea. But I did have to own up to Sabrina almost immediately." He laughed. "She's much too sharp to accept anything at face value. She knows me too well."

"Obviously."

His gray eyes studied her face intently for a long moment. "You're jealous of Sabrina," he said wonderingly.

"No, I'm not jealous," she lied. "I'm angry. I don't like to be used. Or ignored afterward."

"That's what you think, that I *used* you? We *are* talking about yesterday, aren't we? You said that word then, I remember."

She nodded.

"I see." His gaze had become remote, withdrawn. Then the old bitter expression settled on his face. "Lord, I can't believe it. Though I should know better by now. I never found a woman who doesn't become threatened by my career sooner or later. No woman seems able to accept the fact that I *have* to see other women, or understand that my time is not always my own." His mouth twisted. "You might have copied those words from Claire—she threw them at me often enough. 'Used.' 'Ignored.' " He glanced at his wristwatch, then sighed. "I'm really very late, Victoria. Sabrina and I have some problems with the Derringham theater project, and then I have a rehearsal. Perhaps we can continue this . . . this discussion later." His voice was extremely polite now, as though he were talking to a stranger.

"Perhaps," she said stiffly, matching his tone even though she wanted more than anything in the world to fling herself into his arms and beg him to forgive her.

Forgive her for what? She was in the right, wasn't she? She hadn't said anything about being threatened by his career. His career wasn't the issue here, only Sabrina. Did he really expect her to go on as before in spite of Sabrina?

"I don't suppose you'll have time for me today," she said in that same cool voice. "Perhaps I can make an appointment with you for tomorrow morning before I leave."

The muscles of his face tightened. "Please don't threaten me, Victoria."

"That was not intended to be a threat. It's a decision I reached during the night." Such a long sleepless night.

"I see." His gaze searched her face with such intensity that she had to avert her eyes. "I certainly can't hold you here if you've made up your mind to go," he said wearily. "Do you really plan to leave only because Sabrina's arrived? You'd leave me in the lurch? And Portia?"

"I'm sure you'll both survive without me. I've already decided to wait until tomorrow morning so you'll have time to make some other arrangements for Portia."

"How very thoughtful." If he would just smile at her. If he would just banish that coldness from his voice, tell her she'd made a mistake. That he hadn't used her; he loved her....

He started toward the door. She couldn't let him leave like this. "Jason," she said uncertainly.

He didn't turn. "I don't think you understand how very destructive my marriage was," he said slowly. "Destructive not only to Claire, but to me. I can't go through anything like that again...ever."

The door closed behind him. While she was still staring at it, feeling as though her world had disintegrated around her, she heard from the hall outside Sabrina's clear imperious voice. "There you are, darling. I was about to break down your door and drag you out by your hair."

"Sorry, love," Jason said easily. "Domestic problems. You know how it is."

"Indeed I do." Sabrina's tinkling little laugh struck through Vicki like knives thrown by a magician.

Domestic problems.

THE DAY SEEMED ENDLESS. Stratford had lost its charm. Vicki wandered around for a while after checking with Mr. Duckworth on the progress of the

lanterns he was making for her and arranging for
their shipment. But she couldn't recapture her
former delight in her picturesque surroundings. For a
long time she stood on the little bridge watching the
houseboats and admiring the swans, but not really
seeing either. She'd always despised jealous women
when they were jealous without cause. But Sabrina
had *told* her she and Jason were lovers. Surely Jason
couldn't expect her to accept that? It had been hard
enough for her to accept the role of mistress; how
could she possibly rationalize being *one* of his
mistresses?

She couldn't, of course.

She felt totally alone, even though there were
tourists all around her. Portia had stayed on at Mr.
Duckworth's shop as soon as she'd found that Neil
and Graham were leaving in the afternoon for Scotland. Poor Portia. She had finally begun to make
friends, only to lose them. First Colly, now the Duckworth boys. Sad. Everything was so sad.

Walking slowly, Vicki returned to the hotel, trying
to decide if she should go to tonight's performance,
but knowing all the time that she would. This might
be her last chance to see Jason on the stage. Besides,
Portia wanted to go, insisted that they should both
go.

Portia was in an odd mood when she returned.
There was a simmering excitement about her, and an
evasiveness when questioned that reminded Vicki of
the disastrous attempt she'd made to follow Colly to
London. "You aren't planning on stowing away on
the train to Scotland, are you?" Vicki asked her, not
very seriously.

"Gosh, no," Portia said, her pale gray eyes as
innocent as a baby's. "Apart from anything else, I

can't miss the play tonight." She giggled. "Research, you know."

There was something about that nervous giggle that bothered Vicki, but she didn't press Portia for an explanation. She was conscious of an apathy that seemed all-embracing. It was all she could do to dress for the theater, in a white sun dress this time. The weather was still very hot, around ninety degrees; the air still and humid as though there was a storm brewing.

At the theater Portia had barely settled in her seat before she was off again, muttering something about obtaining a program although they each already had one. She hadn't returned by the time the play commenced, and Vicki, to her annoyance, knew she wouldn't be allowed back in until the end of the first act. She supposed she should have followed Portia out, but it was too late now. She couldn't interrupt the others in the audience now that the play had begun.

Determinedly Vicki tried to put Portia out of her mind so that she could lose herself in the play. But tonight she couldn't surrender herself to the magic. She had already noticed that Sabrina was again in the audience a few rows ahead, and she was very conscious of Jason up there on the stage. And of the distance that had opened up between them. She was also worried about Portia. *Something* had been going on in the girl's mischievous mind. Yet surely Portia had enough sense to wait nearby until she was allowed in. She couldn't have planned another disappearance, not after the disastrous failure of the last one. No doubt, she'd turn up in time for the second act, full of remorse and apologies.

So clear in Vicki's mind was the image of a re-
morseful Portia that she did manage to relax a little,
after all, until the beginning of act 1, scene 6.

Duncan, the king of Scotland, had arrived at Macbeth's castle in Inverness and had received a cordial
welcome from Lady Macbeth, unaware of the sudden
death his hostess had planned for him.

Macbeth was about to struggle with his conscience,
greatly concerned about the consequences of killing
Duncan. But Lady Macbeth would have none of his
procrastination and excuses. Bolstering his courage,
she would persuade him to carry on with the proposed assassination.

It was a pivotal scene in the play. Everything that
was at stake was about to come together dramatically. The scene was set in a room in the castle. Several
servants stood about the stage, while others bearing
dishes passed out of the dining hall.

Vicki, bracing herself for Jason's next entrance,
paid no particular attention to the slightly built ser-
vant who seemed uncertain of the placement of the
exit. It wasn't until Jason, soliloquizing his first line:

"If it were done when 'tis done, then 'twere well
It were done quickly,"

paused for a heartbeat's length, staring at the boy,
that Vicki realized the "boy" was Portia.

Visibly trembling, Portia dropped her dish—a
metal tureen. The lid fell off and clattered against the
wooden boards, turning over twice before coming to
rest. Collectively the audience gasped. Someone
laughed nervously.

The incident was over in less time than it took to

notice it. Portia retrieved her dish and its lid, bobbed an apologetic bow and raced off the way she had come. Jason, turning to face the audience, continued smoothly:

> ". . . if the assassination
> Could trammel up the consequence, and catch
> With his surcease success; that but this blow
> Might be the be-all and the end-all here. . . ."

Vicki's heart was thudding like a drum. Her mouth was dry with a metallic taste in it. How could Portia have done such a thing? Why?

She almost groaned aloud, remembering the answer to the last question. She could hear Portia's voice saying, "I wish there was some easy way to find out if I'd suffer from stage fright." Dear God, Jason was going to be furious.

THAT, SHE FOUND OUT LATER, was something of an understatement. Jason's rage knew no bounds. Soon after the play ended, and Vicki had finally tracked down a white-faced Portia—cowering in a doorway at the back of the theater—Jason appeared. He'd obviously changed his clothes in a hurry. His shirt was barely buttoned, bunched into the top of his pants. His jacket was flung over his shoulder, and there were smears of makeup around his jawline where he'd swiped at it in his haste. Grim-faced, he reached around Vicki to grab Portia's arm. Hauling her out to the street, he flagged a taxi and bundled her in, pausing only to coldly inform a couple of hovering reporters that he had absolutely nothing to say, and that if they valued their skins they would do likewise.

Vicki barely managed to get into the cab herself before it took off down the street, the driver galvanized by Jason's crisp-voiced order to hurry.

At the hotel Portia tried to run ahead through the door, but Jason caught her arm again and escorted her in that same grim silence to their suite. Vicki thought she'd rather be anywhere else but with these two right now, but she also felt that Portia needed someone on her side. She had done a terrible thing, of course, and she deserved Jason's anger, but still, she *was* very young. She hadn't thought. . . .

"You never think," Jason roared at his sister as soon as the suite door closed behind them. "You go blindly ahead doing these stupid, idiotic things, and you never think of the consequences."

"I wouldn't have dropped the dish if you hadn't glared at me," Portia stammered. There was no blood left in her face now. Her eyes looked enormous. She was trembling from head to toe.

"I think Portia's suffered enough," Vicki put in. "She knows now—"

"That isn't good enough," Jason shouted. "Of all the mad things to do. I almost had a heart attack right on stage. Are you trying to ruin me?"

"Of course, she's not," Vicki protested, but was immediately quelled by a forbidding glance from Jason.

"Why?" he yelled at Portia. "Can you possibly tell me why?"

Portia hesitated. Vicki could almost see her debating whether to tell her brother of her own stage ambitions, and then deciding not to.

"I thought it would be fun," she said lamely.

Vicki could understand that the girl had said the

first thing that came into her head, unwilling as she was to reveal her future plans. But she could not have said anything more likely to enrage her brother further.

Feeling sure she could only add fuel to the fire, Vicki made no more attempts to interrupt. Portia had set her mouth stubbornly and refused to speak in her own defense. Head bowed, she stood silently, defiantly, while Jason raged on about the respect due the theater, the respect due *him*, the tenuous grip an actor had on his audience at the best of times. About how quickly their attention, their suspension of disbelief, could be lost.

Only when his anger finally began to cool, did Portia offer any other explanation. "I wanted to be on stage with you just once," she said plaintively.

If she'd expected that statement to disarm him, she was mistaken. "I hope you enjoyed it," he said flatly. "It will be the last time."

When Portia looked at him as though he'd struck her in the stomach, Vicki stepped forward. "Portia didn't mean any harm, Jason," she said carefully.

He turned to look at her, his gaze raking over her as though she were something unclean. "Women," he said bitterly. "How the devil am I supposed to get on with my work when you both conspire against me?"

"Vicki hasn't done anything," Portia said. "She didn't know I talked to that boy and bribed him to give me his place. It wasn't her fault." The last word ended on a wail, and she burst into tears, burying her face in her hands.

"Oh, God!" Jason exclaimed. "Was ever mortal man so put upon?"

The words sounded so melodramatic, so Shakespearean, that Vicki, her nerves strained to the breaking point, giggled convulsively.

"You find this amusing?" he asked, fixing her with a steely eye. Again her traitorous mind flashed an image of a bold buccaneer. Any second now he'd be ordering her to walk the plank.

"Of course, I'm not amused," she offered lamely. "It was just that you...well, you...." Vicki let her voice trail away, suddenly feeling very weary—and hopeless in the face of Jason's unforgiving anger. "Perhaps Portia should come home with me tomorrow," she said evenly.

Portia raised her head and looked at Vicki, saucer eyed, her tears drying on her cheeks. "You're leaving Stratford?"

"Tomorrow, yes."

"But why?" The girl looked from Vicki to her brother, then back again, her eyes alert, curious, her own escapade apparently forgotten.

"It's very boring for Victoria here," Jason said tersely before Vicki could reply. "I don't have the time to squire you both around. You can't expect her to enjoy hanging around with nothing to do."

Vicki felt her face flame. He was speaking of her as though she were a spoiled child. Of course, he could hardly tell Portia the real reason for her departure, but all the same....

"I have to get back to the hotel," she explained to Portia. "Now that Mr. Duckworth is doing the lanterns, there's really no reason for me to stay. I'm not bored," she added with a sidelong glance at Jason's averted profile. "But I've begun to feel guilty about deserting Abby. She did invite me to England, after all."

Portia nodded. "I suppose you're right. We'll both go back, then."

"If you want to."

"She doesn't have any bloody choice," Jason said angrily.

Vicki ignored him, speaking only to Portia. "Do you want to go back?"

"Yes, please. I can't face *anybody* after tonight." She shuddered, and Vicki's heart went out to her. She must be sure to reassure Portia later, she thought; make her understand that just because she'd made a mistake it did 't mean she should give up her ambitions. She would tell her the story Jason had told her yesterday about his own unfortunate beginning, she decided with a sudden dart of malice. Probably he hadn't told his sister that particular tale.

Vicki forced herself to look at Jason, schooling herself to ignore the tremor that went through her at the sight of his tautly held body, the rigidly controlled expressionless mask that was his face. "Should we take a train?" she asked him stiffly.

"Of course not," he said at once. "The train stops at every bloody village on the way. I'll arrange a limousine and chauffeur for you, naturally." He hesitated, his stiff posture easing, his face softening. "Portia, perhaps you should go to bed," he said with his gaze fixed on Vicki. "I'd like to talk to Victoria."

Vicki shook her head. The last thing she wanted right now was to be alone with Jason Meredith. Only God knew what he had in mind, but she wanted no part of it. "We have nothing to talk about," she said coldly. "Go ahead and join your friends. I expect Sabrina is waiting for you."

"As a matter of fact, she is." His glance was challenging.

Vicki turned away from him abruptly, afraid she was about to follow Portia's example and burst into tears. "I'll see you in the morning, then, before we leave," she managed.

"You're determined to go?"

"Yes."

"Very well." The ice was back in his voice.

Keeping her back turned toward him, she waited for him to say something more. After a moment of almost tangible silence she heard his footsteps cross the floor, followed by the quiet closing of the door.

Aware of Portia's curious glances, she managed somehow to straighten her shoulders and proceed through the door into their shared bedroom.

To her relief, Portia didn't pester her with questions as they prepared for bed. The girl didn't speak until Vicki was about to turn out the light, and then she merely muttered, "Good night."

"You aren't going to let this change your mind about acting lessons, are you?" Vicki asked into the darkness a moment later.

Portia's bedsprings creaked. "No," she said after a short silence. "I don't think so."

"Good," Vicki said firmly. Then, closing her eyes, she willed herself to sleep.

IN THE MORNING she discovered she was not to see Jason again, after all. Portia greeted her with the news that Jason had already left for another meeting with Sabrina. Some kind of emergency, he'd said.

"Sure," Vicki said dully, too exhausted after another dream-disturbed night to even dispute the "emergency." She *had* slept, determined to do so, but she had not been able to anesthetize her subconscious mind. All night it had hurled up images of Jason lying beside her on the riverbank, looking at her with love, touching her, caressing her.

The dreams would fade with time, she told herself. She'd had nightmares about Ken Marriott after his unsuccessful attempt to force his attentions on her. The nightmares had passed. These dreams would, as well.

She wished she could believe that.

An hour later she and Portia were on their way back to Derringham, sitting together in the back of a luxurious air-conditioned limousine, both of them engrossed in their own thoughts. The threatened storm had not yet materialized, Vicki realized, welcoming the comfort of the air conditioning after the muggy air outside. But looking listlessly out at the passing countryside, she saw that there was a heavy cloud bank rising over the horizon, moving toward the town. She hoped there would be a storm—a cloudburst. At least, then, she wouldn't have to torture herself with images of Sabrina and Jason together by the river.

CHAPTER SEVENTEEN

THE FIRST PERSON Vicki and Portia saw when they arrived at The Singing Tree Inn was David Brent. He was behind the reception counter, leaning against the bank of pigeonholes, talking in a low voice with Kim. The receptionist was resplendent in a black satin dress, her bright red hair tortured into a knot on one side of her head.

Vicki had managed to file away in some forgotten corner of her mind the last disastrous meeting she'd had with David. But as Kim greeted her with her usual good-natured enthusiasm, the memory came flooding back. David meanwhile turned to face her, straightening his shoulders and fussing nervously with his tie and the lapels of his suit jacket. He looked very embarrassed, but whether that was because of his own recollection of their last meeting or because she'd seen him being friendly toward Kim, Vicki couldn't decide.

"Back so soon?" he queried. "Is anything wrong?"

"I'm in disgrace again," Portia told him with a wry grimace, saving Vicki the need for an immediate explanation of her own.

David lifted his gaze to the lobby ceiling and heaved an exaggerated sigh. "What did you do this time?" he asked.

Portia grinned, her usual high spirits evidently restored completely. Vicki wished she was as resilient. "Vicki will tell you," the girl said airily. Commandeering a hovering porter to carry the luggage, she set off toward the elevator.

Briefly Vicki explained Portia's latest escapade to Kim and David. Kim thought the whole thing was "just a bit of a lark; why did Mr. Meredith 'ave to get so grotty about it?" David himself took the incident more seriously, but conceded with his old shy smile that at least it had brought Vicki back sooner than expected, and that was all to the good, wasn't it?

He must have noticed Vicki's nervous reaction, for he blushed furiously and said at once that he hadn't meant to offend her. To her dismay, he then insisted on escorting her up to Abby's apartment, incurring a disappointed, "Oh, David," from Kim, which he ignored.

As they walked across the lobby, he muttered a rather shamefaced apology for his previous behavior and begged Vicki to forgive him. It certainly wouldn't happen again. "I don't usually act so precipitately," he assured her gravely outside Abby's door.

He looked so abject that she didn't have the heart to stay angry with him. "Just be sure it *doesn't* happen again," she said crisply, relieved that she was to be spared further emotional turmoil. "I said I'd be your friend, but that's all I promised."

At that he gave her a boyish smile that was positively sunny, a smile so appealing that she found herself agreeing to have afternoon tea with him the following day. There was an interesting place nearby, he said—a Quaker settlement called Jordans that he wanted to show her.

At least, an outing would help to distract her from thoughts of Jason Meredith, she thought, as David shook hands with her formally and went off to get Portia settled in.

Abby was not in the apartment. Vicki hesitated, wondering if she should go in search of her right away. No, she decided, first she'd unpack and change her clothes.

In Vicki's bright yellow bedroom, a couple of letters were propped up on the dressing table, one from her mother and one from Josh Hendrickson. Vicki opened her mother's letter eagerly, knowing Ellen Dennison's good-natured gossip would cheer her up and provide yet another distraction.

"Good news!" Ellen had written in her bold clear hand. "Ken Marriott has received his *just deserts*! It seems he tried to seduce Alice Tremaine, your replacement, during a work-session weekend in Sacramento. You *do* remember what a militant feminist Alice is? She *marched* into Josh's office and *demanded* action against Ken. Ken was questioned, and ALL was revealed! Josh is mortified, the partnership dissolved, and *your* reputation cleared! Josh is writing to you today."

Smiling at her mother's exclamatory writing style, Vicki set the rest of her letter aside for the moment and picked up the heavy cream-colored envelope from Josh Hendrickson.

Josh was indeed mortified. His investigation of his partner had revealed other indiscretions...with clients. He wanted personally to assure Vicki that every designer in town had been informed of the real facts behind the termination of her employment with Hendrickson and Marriott. In partial restitution he had reinstated her on the payroll from the date of her dismissal. She would, of course, be paid all monies due from that date. He hoped she would return to her former position as soon as her "vacation" was over.

Vicki carefully folded the letter back into its heavy envelope, wondering why she didn't feel more elated. She was relieved, of course, that her name had been cleared. But she felt only sadness for the dissolution of the long partnership between Ken and Josh.

Now she could go home as soon as the renovation of The Singing Tree Inn was complete. She could return to the job she'd loved. Shouldn't she feel more excited at the prospect?

Sighing, she lifted her suitcase onto the chintz-draped bed. If she hadn't met Jason Meredith, she thought, the good news from home would have delighted her. But she *had* met him, she *had* fallen in love with him. And after she left England, she would probably never see him again. How could she not feel sad?

AN HOUR LATER, after she'd refreshed herself with a cool shower and changed into her comfortable "uniform" of cotton shirt and linen slacks, Vicki went in search of Abby, suddenly dreading her aunt's predictably curious reaction to her early return.

To her relief, however, Abby was engaged in conference with a man in her office. She was unable to do more than greet Vicki warmly, saying she was delighted to see her looking so tanned and well. Then, after a moment's hesitation that seemed surprisingly uncomfortable on Abby's part, she introduced Vicki to the man she'd been talking to. He was of average height, a sturdy craggy-featured man with graying brown hair, attractively bushy eyebrows and a sandy mustache. Probably in his mid-fifties, Vicki thought. He was wearing baggy gray slacks and a tweed jacket with leather patches on the elbows. He transferred an unlighted pipe to his left hand so that he could shake hands.

"This is Inspector McAdam," Abby explained. "He's retired now, but he used to be with Scotland Yard."

"There haven't been more thefts, have there?" Vicki asked in alarm.

"No, dear. But Ian's a...a friend, and he's offered to help in the investigation."

There was an oddly hesitant note in Abby's voice that alerted Vicki's interest. She looked at the man more closely. He was very good-looking in a comfortably rumpled pipe-smoking sort of way. Not as dazzling as Jason, of course, but still attractive. His handshake had been firm and businesslike, but there was nothing businesslike in the glance he gave Abby. Definitely fond, Vicki thought. And Abby was looking a little flustered and extremely pretty, the severity of her usual dark suit relieved by a very feminine canary yellow blouse with a ruffled lace jabot.

"Abigail and I can continue our discussion later if you've business with her," Inspector McAdam said with a pure Scots accent that enchanted Vicki. His eyes were almost the same shade of gray as Jason's, she noticed, and they held a similar amused glint.

"My business can wait," she assured him. Turning to Abby, she raised her eyebrows in a teasing gesture that was rewarded by a quick stain of pink in Abby's cheeks. "I'll go take a look at the Blue Room," she said. "Did you hear anything about the new carpeting?"

"It arrived yesterday," Abby said, regaining her usual aplomb. She grinned at her niece. "You must have charmed everyone out of their minds. I thought it would take at least a month. And the painter brought over some paint chips for you to look at. I've put everything in the little conference room on the second floor."

"Good, I'll get started, then," Vicki said, briskly heading for the door.

"It was a great pleasure to meet you, Victoria," the inspector called after her with a glorious rolling of *r*'s.

Vicki turned to smile at him. "The pleasure was mine," she said, barely avoiding the temptation to mimic his contagious accent.

Her smile faded as she closed the door behind her. Somehow, seeing Abby and her friend so comfortable together had increased her depression. Why on earth had she felt it necessary to compare the man's looks with Jason's?

Despair gripped her so sharply for a moment that her feet faltered, and she had to stand still, gathering herself physically as though she'd been struck by an acute illness. As perhaps she had, she thought morosely when she finally managed to make her way to the stairs. Her illness might not be fatal, but she had the feeling it was terminal. How could she ever look at another man after Jason Meredith? Stupidly she had given herself to a man who made all other men pale by comparison. She couldn't even excuse herself on the grounds of blindness. She had gone into the...the situation with her eyes wide open, fully aware of the possible consequences that she now had to face. What price all her good resolutions now?

Squaring her shoulders as she entered the little conference room, she vowed that she would not let herself dwell on the immediate past. She would lose herself in activity and forget Jason Meredith—simply erase him from her mind.

SHE HAD CAUSE TO REMEMBER her resolution the next day when David took her to tea and insisted on talking about his employer. Every word he uttered conjured up an image of Jason in her mind. Well, she thought, taking refuge in a saying her father had told her was a slogan for the United States Army Air Force: "The difficult we do immediately; the impossible takes a little longer." Obviously it was going to take a long time for her to forget Jason Meredith.

"Did you say something, Vicki?" David asked, glancing uncertainly at her.

"No, nothing." God, was she talking aloud to herself now? She forced herself to pay attention to her companion. He had been talking about Jason's fiery temper, telling her she mustn't worry about Portia, that Mr. Meredith always forgave her indiscretions in time. "I expect he was concerned about the theater emergency," he was saying. "That would make him a bit edgy."

Startled, Vicki stared at him over the plain oak table in the restaurant he'd selected. "There really *was* an emergency?" she asked sharply, her teacup stopped halfway to her mouth.

David looked puzzled. "There was some doubt?"

"No, of course not." She took a deep breath. "I

was thinking of something else. What emergency did you mean?''

He still looked rather blank. ''Didn't Mrs. Lindstrom meet with Mr. Meredith?''

''Oh, that. Yes, she did. I didn't really pay attention with Portia and all—'' She broke off before she sounded any more idiotic. ''What exactly was it all about?''

He sighed. ''These things always happen whenever Mr. Meredith is out of town. The contractor had a soils engineer make some tests on the proposed theater site. Soil bearing pressure tests, I believe they are called. It appears there's a possibility that the site's proximity to the river could cause a high water table in the ground. The tests showed that a building of the size planned cannot be erected without first driving in supportive pilings. Which naturally would increase the costs. The alternative would be to procure another site on higher ground.

''Mr. Meredith has his heart set on duplicating the setting of the Royal Shakespeare Theatre in Stratford, so I expect he will decide on the pilings. But of course, others had to be consulted. Mrs. Lindstrom thought they might be able to persuade the man who donated the land to underwrite the extra expense, but she had to meet with Mr. Meredith to determine his reaction. . . naturally.''

''Naturally,'' Vicki echoed.

There really had been an emergency. Why hadn't Sabrina told her about it?

Silly question. Sabrina had obviously wanted Vicki out of the way or at least rendered harmless. And Vicki had immediately believed the woman's assertion that Jason wanted her with him in Stratford.

Which, of course, he probably had, but not for the reason Sabrina had given. But surely Sabrina wouldn't have lied about Jason being her lover. Would she?

"Vicki?" David prompted.

"I'm sorry, David, I'm a bit distracted today, I guess. So much to do at the hotel. I keep thinking I should be back there getting on with—" She broke off as he began to look offended. Good God, she really must concentrate. Nothing had changed, anyway. Jason was convinced that she'd left Stratford out of mere pique over Sabrina's appearance. And he had certainly seemed delighted to be having breakfast with his "old friend."

Sorry, love. Domestic problems.

No, nothing had changed.

"This is an interesting place," Vicki said brightly to David, determined to banish thoughts of Jason altogether.

David immediately looked mollified. Had he thought she was bored in his company? She must be more careful. She already knew he was sensitive to hurts, real or imagined.

"A Quaker settlement, you said?" she prompted and made herself pay attention as David launched into a monologue about the old farmhouse in which they were dining.

It was here, he told her in his precise, somewhat didactic manner, that William Penn, the founder of Pennsylvania, was buried. Nearby was the May-flower Barn, supposedly built with the timbers of the Pilgrim Fathers' *Mayflower*. Under the direction of a committee of the Society of Friends, Jordans, with its guest house, refectory annex and dining room, was now a center for guests and conferences.

The place certainly had a friendly atmosphere, Vicki agreed. She and David had already explored the peaceful charm of the gardens, and she had genuinely admired the unspoiled beech woods that surrounded the farmstead. Their tea had been a simple one, but ample, consisting of feather-light scones and jam, and a selection of sturdy slices of iced cake.

After tea David suggested she drive them both to another neighboring village so that they could visit Milton's cottage. By now Vicki was feeling restive, but she agreed with his proposal, knowing that if she returned to the hotel, she would start brooding again about Jason and wondering if she'd misjudged him. *Could* Sabrina have lied? Did it make any difference now, anyway? Considering that she'd accepted the older woman's statement with such alacrity and had treated Jason to a display of jealousy that he'd implied had rivaled Claire's?

"We're here," David warned. Vicki brought herself out of her reverie again, barely in time to step on the brake in front of their intended destination.

"I'm sorry, David," she said with a sigh. "You must think I'm a terrible woolgatherer."

"You don't have to apologize to me," he said sharply, surprising her with his tone of voice.

Taken aback, she stared at him. "I quite understand," he said in a voice that made no attempt to hide bitterness. "I've already realized that your mind is occupied with thoughts of your absent lover."

Appalled, she continued to stare at him, unable to think of anything to say. "Portia told me Mr. Meredith 'absolutely adores you,'" he said harshly, imitating Portia's effusive tones in a way that wasn't at all amusing. "I can hardly blame you for preferring his company to mine. The great Jason Meredith has much more to offer than a humble secretary. I'm surprised you even consented to waste your time with me today."

"Now look here, David," Vicki said, finally recovering her voice and with it an exhilarating shot of temper. "I came with you today because you asked me to come. So far I've enjoyed myself. And I certainly don't think of you as a *humble* secretary, any more than I think of myself as a *humble* interior designer. I thought we were going to be friends. If that's not good enough for you, say so, and we'll call it quits. But don't think you can make personal remarks about Jason Meredith and me, because I won't put up with them. And besides, they just aren't true."

To her dismay, her voice trembled on the last statement, belying her indignation.

At once David was apologetic, his high cheekbones flaring with one of his bashful blushes. "I'm sorry, Vicki," he stammered. "Please forgive me."

She swallowed. "All right," she said ungraciously.

His pale blue eyes were studying her face alertly. "He's hurt you, hasn't he?" It was his turn to sound indignant. "No, Vicki, don't be cross. I don't mean to pry. But I hate to see you falling for Jason Meredith's highly publicized charm. He's been advertised as devastating to women so many times that he believes it himself. And I hate to see someone as sensible as you, as *vulnerable* as you, getting hurt by him. I'm really astonished at your naiveté.

"You must know, I'm sure, that if he ever does marry again, he will marry Sabrina Lindstrom. I understand she's divorcing her husband as soon as the theater is completed. That's why she went rushing off to Stratford. She was quite distraught at the thought of a delay in plans. Divorce is not as simple in England as it is in America, and any delay at all now is unacceptable to her. Naturally she and Mr. Meredith don't want to upset Mr. Lindstrom until he's chipped in his share of the funds, and the transaction is irrevocable. Personally I think she's terrified that Mr. Meredith will find someone else in the meantime. She quizzed me quite thoroughly about your relationship with him, I must tell you. She even told me some absurd story about a pretended engagement between the two of you. I told her nothing, of course. Not out of loyalty to him, I might add, but because, well, I do have a certain fondness for you.''

How had she failed to notice what a prim little mouth this man had, Vicki wondered. What on earth was she doing in his company, anyway? Why was she subjecting herself to these painful revelations?

But she must face the facts. David's diatribe might be very unpleasant and a bit on the spiteful side, but it did confirm Sabrina's statement.

She felt a squirming sensation, picturing Jason and Sabrina gleefully setting her up as Jason's fiancée in order to keep Sig from learning the truth about their plans. Had it really been necessary for Jason to make love to her? Couldn't she have served just as well as a...a *decoy*, without him going quite so far?

At the edge of her consciousness she was aware that David was now regarding her with a pity in which an underlying satisfaction showed. Probably, she decided, Jason had not intended going so far, but had been first bemused by the roles they were playing. Then, later, he had been unable to resist taking as his due the gift that she had so willingly, so naively, offered.

"You are quite mistaken, David," she managed to say finally with a surprising degree of conviction. "You've allowed Portia's overactive imagination to color your thinking. Jason—Mr. Meredith—and I are barely acquainted. I admire his acting ability, of course, and I've grown very fond of Portia, but that's all."

Without waiting to see if he believed her lies, she opened the car door and emerged into the sunshine, managing with a strength she hadn't known she possessed to overcome the slight dizziness she felt as she stood up. She even managed to smile brilliantly—at least, she hoped her smile was brilliant rather than sick—as David took her arm and steered her toward the attractive historic old house they had come to see.

Afterward Vicki had only vague memories of Milton's cottage. She remembered a huge country fireplace with pots hanging from hooks, a carved thronelike chair. A small library that included copies of *Paradise Lost* and *Paradise Regained*—titles that awakened echoes in her own bruised soul—and a charming elderly woman guide who must have thought this latest American visitor was deaf and dumb. She certainly couldn't remember having said a word. But somehow she managed to get through the rest of the afternoon and to say a reasonably cheery thank-you to David outside Abby's apartment door.

A SECOND LATER she collapsed facedown on her bed, determined not to weep, but weeping, anyway. Abby found her there when she came up to prepare for din-

ner. In her weakened state Vicki was unable to make
any pretense of normalcy, and Abby soon elicited the
entire story of Vicki's affair with Jason—between
sobs and exclamations about her own stupidity.

Her aunt's first remedy was a stiff shot of brandy,
which at least had the effect of stopping Vicki's tears.
She'd begun to fear that they were unstoppable.
Then, to her surprise, Abby sat on the edge of her
bed and announced that she'd guessed a lot of what
was going on, but that she didn't believe for a moment there was anything between Sabrina and Jason.
"I haven't met the woman, but Simon knew her and
told me what she was like. Jason has far too much
sense to fall for a man-eating barracuda like Sabrina
Lindstrom," she added staunchly.

"But David said—"

Abby snorted. "That young man is not as smart as
I thought. He's obviously jealous of Jason. Not sur-
prising, I suppose. But you can't go on hearsay,
Vicki. I'm surprised at you. You must at least *ask*
Jason for the truth. As far as I can tell, all you've
done so far is to accuse him."

"I couldn't possibly—"

"Nonsense. You've earned the right to ask him.
And he deserves to know what Sabrina said."

"He didn't deny she was his mistress."

"He wouldn't. That's typical Meredith. There are
several centuries of arrogance behind that young man,
Vicki. And he *is* a man, remember. Underneath that
superstar exterior he has all the usual defenses men are
cursed with, not the least of which is his pride.

"I've never believed all those stories about Jason
and women," she added, completely reversing her
former stand. "Those stories are all part of the

superstar image. Jason's a hardworking man, dedicated to his craft, or calling, or profession, or whatever you want to call it. And he's a good man. My Simon wouldn't have bothered with him if he wasn't. You should at least give him the chance to explain himself."

"I doubt that he wants to now."

Abby stood up. "We'll just have to wait and see, won't we?" she said briskly. Then she smiled at Vicki. "Come on, darling. Let's have some dinner, and I'll tell you all about Ian McAdam. I know that you were wondering about him." She paused, grinning. "Not bad, is he?"

"Not bad at all," Vicki managed with what felt like a watery smile.

Evidently encouraged by her attempt at humor, Abby led the way into the living room, chattering blithely about Ian McAdam and his helpfulness, and what a blessing it was to have good friends.

This last was certainly true, Vicki thought as she forced herself to respond to Abby's cheerful mood. She was feeling a lot less desperate now that she'd poured out the whole sorry story to her aunt, even though she was not convinced by Abby's sudden championship of Jason's honor. *Sorry, love. Domestic problems,* she heard again in her mind.

It was all very well for Abby to suggest she ask Jason for the truth about Sabrina, but as far as Vicki knew, she wasn't likely to be given a chance to speak to him or even to see him again.

But one thing she *was* determined upon. Whatever happened in the days ahead, she was going to avoid David Brent. *That* kind of emotional abrasiveness she didn't need.

CHAPTER EIGHTEEN

SHE MIGHT AS WELL STOP making decisions, Vicki decided the next day. It wouldn't do any good to make up her mind she would avoid David Brent unless she could persuade him to avoid her.

He sought her out at noon. She was in the Blue Room with the contractor Abby had engaged—a denim-clad, slightly built, surprisingly sinewy young man with curly blond hair and eyes as green as her own; a nervously energetic type who smoked incessantly and shot out orders to his men with the rapidity of machine-gun fire. He had arrived at seven A.M. on an enormous motorcycle and had immediately taken charge. Looking Vicki over, he had told her to call him Ned, and that he would call her Vicki. But she was not to worry that he'd get too familiar; he didn't believe in "fraternizing" on the job.

Amused to be set so firmly in her place, Vicki was enjoying her work with the efficient fellow. Because the carpeting had arrived so early, followed so auspiciously by Vicki herself, Abby had decided to close the Blue Room for a while. Breakfast, lunch and buffet dinner would be served in the Wine Cellar and afternoon tea in the lobby. But she didn't want the restaurant out of action for long, naturally, so as Ned put it, "Haste was the watchword."

Workmen were already on the job. The tables and

other furnishings had been removed, and the men were now taking down the ugly chandeliers, which Abby had shrewdly managed to sell to a hotelier in Latham's Corners. Others were taking down the draperies and ripping up the worn carpeting. Vicki and Ned were sitting at a card table in the corner, ignoring the noise and dust as they examined sketches and discussed materials. It was there that David Brent found her.

"I'm really very busy," she told him as politely as she could when he asked for a word with her in private.

"It's important," he said tersely.

Vicki sighed and got to her feet, not pleased at being interrupted. But David's thin face was tense, his mouth a grim line.

"There's been another theft," he told her as soon as she'd accompanied him out to the hall.

"Oh, no. Poor Abby. What is it this time?"

"An attaché case full of money—two thousand pounds. It was taken last evening or during the night from a guest's room, number 302. I was in the foyer just now, and Kim told me about it."

Vicki frowned at him. "Why are you telling me?"

He looked surprised. "I thought you'd want to know."

"I realize it's bad for Abby, of course, but I really don't think I can do much about it, David. I'm sure Abby and her inspector friend can handle it. Now if you'll excuse me...."

His hand gripped her arm with surprising strength as she turned to go. "You don't understand, Vicki. I...." He took a deep breath. He was looking very agitated, she realized.

"Was Portia with you yesterday evening?" he asked abruptly.

"Portia? No, I haven't seen her since we returned from Stratford. I was very tired last night, and I had to check the work that had been done while you and I—" She broke off. "Why are you asking me about Portia? She hasn't disappeared again?"

His prim mouth was pursed tightly, his brow furrowed in a worried frown. "No, she's here today. But I'm just not sure... I *can't* be sure...."

He hesitated, and for a moment she was tempted to shake him, but then he went on with an air of candor, "I haven't wanted to say anything, Vicki, but these thefts have always occurred during times that Portia has felt deserted by Mr. Meredith."

"So?"

"She was gone last evening for over an hour."

"Did you ask her where she was?"

"Of course. She told me she was just rummaging around the hotel. She was restless, she said."

"That doesn't mean she was stealing, David. Don't you think you're jumping to some rather far-fetched conclusions?"

"Mrs. Carstairs didn't have any problems until we moved in here."

Vicki suddenly remembered that Abby herself had wondered if Portia was involved in the thefts. She'd said as much on Vicki's first night at The Singing Tree Inn. But now that Vicki knew Portia.... "No," she said firmly. "I don't believe it."

"Portia bought a guitar this morning, Vicki."

She stared at him. How self-righteous he looked, she thought disdainfully. How had she ever thought him to be an attractive man? But still.... "Jason doesn't give her much pocket money,'' she murmured almost to herself.

''She said he gave her extra while she was in Stratford. Do you know if that's true?''

''No, I don't know. How would I know?'' She let out her breath, suddenly exasperated. ''Really, David, this has nothing to do with me. I suggest you talk with Jason.''

''I can't do that! He'd be furious with me if I suggested—''

''Well, I'm not going to talk to him about it. Maybe I'll talk to Portia later, but I'm certainly not going to accuse her of anything.''

His face was clearing. ''Thank you, Vicki. I knew you'd help. I'm a bit worried, you see, because there were several letters waiting for her from that boy.''

''Colly?''

''I have the feeling she's planning something again. I do feel responsible for her, but I don't want to get her in trouble unnecessarily.''

''I'm sure you don't,'' Vicki said vaguely, though she wasn't sure at all. There was definitely a suggestion of self-satisfaction in David's expression, as though he'd be pleased if Portia turned out to be the thief. Which wasn't possible. She could agree with him that Portia, feeling neglected, might try to get attention, but she'd stake her life on the girl's honesty.

''I'll see what I can do,'' she said at last, wanting mostly to get rid of David so that she could get back to work. Through the open door of the Blue Room she could see Ned leaping around like a ballet dancer, directing operations. She wanted to be in there with him, dealing with uncomplicated things like carpeting and lighting and paint. "I'll talk to her later," she repeated, and David finally seemed satisfied with that.

BUT AS IT HAPPENED, it was not until the next day that Vicki had time for Portia. By then, she'd heard the story of the theft from Abby, who was up in arms about the whole thing. For a moment Vicki had pondered passing on David's suspicions, but had decided to keep her own counsel for a while.

When she did manage to talk to Portia, the conversation wasn't too satisfactory. Portia was delighted to be the owner of a guitar and wanted her help with the tuning. Vicki did ask her casually where she managed to get the money to pay for the instrument, which was a good one, and Portia answered just as candidly that Jason had given it to her. Colly was coming to see her in a day or two, she added. She'd "rung" his friend's house to let him know she was back. "I have to practice a lot so I can dazzle him with my prowess," she said happily.

Vicki nodded, promising to help. She was unable to think of any other way to question Portia without coming out with an accusation, something she certainly wasn't going to do on the basis of such slim evidence. Nonetheless, the acquisition of the guitar bothered her. There had been a stubborn quality to Portia's mouth when she'd insisted Jason gave her money, and she'd changed the subject rapidly. It *was* something of a coincidence that the girl had bought an expensive guitar the day after the money disappeared, but Vicki was quite sure there must be an explanation—even if she wasn't sure Portia was telling the whole truth.

But it was really none of her business, she decided after a couple of days of fruitless worrying. The guest who had lost the attaché case had been questioned, and it turned out that he'd taken the money with him to a meeting, hoping to make a deal of some kind. When the deal fell through, he'd brought the money back—he thought. The whole thing sounded pretty shaky to Vicki, as it did to Abby and Inspector McAdam.

So PROBABLY, Vicki comforted herself, there was nothing to worry about at all. She was standing in her bedroom one afternoon, looking out at a drizzly gray sky and trying to decide what to do with herself. The Blue Room had been stripped, and the walls had been painted. Tomorrow the carpeting would be laid; then she could supervise the painting of the heraldic symbols and the arrangement of the furnishings. But for the moment there was nothing for her to do.

The river reflected the sky like a sheet of slate, punctured at intervals by sporadic drops of rain. Not a good day to go out, and yet she felt like moving around, like getting out of the hotel.

Beyond the meadow Meredith Manor loomed against the low cloud layer. Such beautiful proportions. Such a solid unpretentious house—a place that spoke of harmony and grace and quiet living.

She laughed a little wryly. Quiet living had not been a feature of her acquaintanceship with the Merediths so far.

But it was a lovely house. She felt drawn to it. And Jason had told her she could walk in anytime, she remembered. He'd wanted her advice.

No. It would be the height of masochism to return to Meredith Manor.

And yet. . . .

She found herself searching out a hooded rain-proof jacket from the huge old wardrobe in her bedroom, fully aware that she was being foolish.

But Jason was still in Stratford-upon-Avon. Only the caretaker would be at the house, and perhaps a few workmen. Portia had told her the renovations were still under way. She could at least see the house one more time.

Picking up her sketchbook, just in case she happened to have some ideas, she let herself out of the bedroom and headed for the back stairs. Masochistic or not, she was going to Jason's house.

The caretaker, a spry Cornishman with twinkling brown eyes, didn't seem at all surprised by her request to see the house. She found him in the front garden with a very elderly gardener, helping to replace some shrubs that had been trampled by careless workmen. As soon as she introduced herself, he waved her on into the house, saying that Mr. Meredith had told him some time ago that she might "coom by."

Avoiding the back regions, where she could hear the sound of hammering, Vicki wandered happily through the rooms on the ground floor. Ornately framed oil paintings had been hung in one of the long galleries, evidently returned after cleaning. Ancestral portraits, obviously; rows of them. Here and there she saw strong features that reminded her of Jason's, and there was an occasional hint of Portia's mischief in some of the younger women's eyes. Many of the subjects were in Shakespearean costume. Not because they had lived at that time, she guessed; probably they were the actors in the crowd.

Entering a small breakfast nook overlooking the front flower gardens, a room Jason had shown her on her earlier tour, she discovered that the window frames were in place now, but the sills had yet to be added. Wide sills, she hoped. It would be a shame not to take advantage of the morning light that would be sure to shine through all those windows.

Pulling a drawing pen from her raincoat pocket, she idly sketched the way this room would look if she were doing it: plants on wide windowsills; flowered wallpaper; the parquet floor left uncarpeted and gleaming; white wood furniture; a glass-topped table....

Upstairs she found more use for her pen. Remembering the location of Portia's bedroom, she entered it, smiling as she recalled the girl's desire for modern furnishings. Not plastic and bean bags, though, Vicki thought, looking around the long, wide, airy room. But the area would lend itself to a bed-sitting-room, a casual place where Portia could entertain friends. Visualizing the way it might be, she sketched an upholstered divan, some low armless chairs—covered in honey-toned leather, she thought; she'd seen some nice ones on her search for materials in London. There would be a low table over here, with four round chairs on castors for easy moving. And Portia could mount her beloved posters on screens to avoid marring the paneled walls.

She looked at the finished drawing. Not bad. Young, but not childish—a far cry from Portia's chintz-skirted dressing table and ruffled bed. She could at least give the drawing to Portia, let her take it from there.

Back in the hall, she hesitated, knowing that she wanted to go into Jason's room. Definitely masochistic, she scolded herself. Yet she couldn't resist the urge. And perhaps, she told herself with little conviction, by seeing the room again she could exorcise the ghost of Jason that constantly haunted her.

Taking a deep breath, she opened the door.

"Hello, Victoria," Jason said.

The earth tilted, and she couldn't find her footing. Paralyzed with shock, she stood frozen in the doorway, staring at him as though he were indeed a ghost. He was sitting on the edge of his massive canopied bed, half-turned toward her, looking as though he were prepared to pose for a portrait in oils of *Man in a Shadowed Room*. She could almost see the title, written in Gothic script on a three-by-five card, set in a metal frame attached to a gallery wall.

He was wearing a beautifully tailored oatmeal-colored sport coat, brown shirt and pants. His hair was tousled as though he'd run his hand through it several times. His eyes looked definitely sad.

Vicki's heart turned over. "What are you doing here?" she asked stiffly. "The caretaker didn't tell me—"

"I don't suppose he knew. I arrived while he was helping the gardener unload shrubs from a lorry. I wanted to be alone for a while." His mouth twitched, but didn't quite form a smile. "It's a rare luxury, being alone."

"Then I'll go," Vicki said at once, starting to pull the door closed.

Immediately he was on his feet, exclaiming, "I wasn't talking about you! Please stay. I *want* to see you."

She barely noticed his protestation. As soon as he had moved, she had noticed a flash of white. And now, as she stared at him, she saw that his right hand was swathed in bandages. "What happened?" she demanded.

He lifted his hand and looked at it, then grinned ruefully. "I'm afraid Trevor Lassiter—Macduff, remember—and I got rather carried away in the final dueling scene last night. I was pressing him to the wall, and I stumbled. This was the result. It seems the theatrical superstition about *Macbeth* is based on truth."

"How bad is it?"

"Not nearly as bad as it looked at the time. Blood was streaming all over the place. The audience loved it. Took quite a few sutures. The doctor has forbidden me to use it for a week. Damn nuisance, but good for Trevor; poor blighter's been dying for a chance to play Macbeth."

With a shrug he dismissed his injury and looked at her directly. "I was trying to decide if I should come to see you, Victoria," he said evenly.

Vicki swallowed, waited.

"I'm afraid I behaved rather irrationally in Stratford," he continued, then he suddenly thrust his left hand through his hair, and his voice took on an irritated edge. "Why the devil are you dithering in the doorway? I'm not going to attack you." He sat down on the bed and gestured to a spot beside him. "Come and sit down. We can't possibly have a proper conversation across a room."

Vicki didn't move. "Perhaps we could talk somewhere else?"

"For heaven's sake, Victoria, there *isn't* anywhere

else. It's too damp to sit on the veranda, and I don't want to intrude in Trelawney's room. The caretaker,'' he explained as the name left her blank.

Hesitantly Vicki allowed herself to be persuaded to sit beside him, but not too close. Even so, she was immediately aware of the powerful body next to hers as he shifted fitfully, lifting his right hand and cradling it in his left. Obviously the wound pained him more than he had admitted. She wanted desperately to touch him, to soothe him. *Typical woman,* she jeered silently at herself. *We're all Florence Nightingale at heart.*

With a sigh Jason turned his head to look at her, his gray eyes quizzical. "You could take your jacket off," he said.

"It's not necessary."

He didn't insist. "What have you been drawing?" he asked, indicating her sketchbook.

"Just a few ideas I had for Portia's room and the little breakfast room downstairs."

"May I see?" Without waiting for permission, he lifted the sketchbook off her lap and began turning pages awkwardly with his left hand. She clasped her own hands in her lap, restraining herself from helping him.

"Very nice," he murmured. Having examined the two latest sketches, he started flipping through the pages, remarking on the changes she'd worked out for the hotel. "Abby must be very pleased with you," he said, still turning pages. Then his hand stilled, and his mouth twitched into a brief smile. "You *are* talented, Victoria," he said.

Glancing at the sketchbook, she drew in a sharp breath. She'd completely forgotten the attempts she'd made to sketch him. But there they were.

When he looked up, amusement glinted in his eyes. "I'm very flattered," he said.

She thought it best to say nothing, and after a second his expression sobered. "I'm sorry you had to witness that scene with Portia," he said softly. "I hate scenes like that."

"Then why do you start them?" she asked him. "You were the one doing all the shouting."

"You thought my anger uncalled-for?"

"No. Under the circumstances you had every right to be angry. But you could have asked for an explanation first."

"I seem to remember that I did."

"Well, you could have—there *were* extenuating circumstances."

"Such as?"

Vicki floundered. She'd painted herself into a corner now; she couldn't explain Portia's action without revealing the girl's plans. "That's between you and Portia," she said evasively.

"All right. Then what about you and me?"

"There is no you and me," she said ungrammatically.

"Isn't there, Victoria?" His left hand lifted to touch her face, his fingers tracing the line of her cheekbone.

She sat immobile, determined not to flinch away or to respond to his touch. "I want to ask you a question," she said firmly.

"Very well." His fingers were stroking her hair now, tucking it behind her ear, following the line of it down to her shoulder. "You always smell so marvelous," he murmured.

She forced herself to look at him coldly, waiting

until he dropped his hand. "I'm sorry, Victoria," he said, but there wasn't a note of apology in his voice.

"I've realized that I had no right to throw accusations at you," she said levelly. "So I've decided to ask you straight out. Are you having an affair with Sabrina?"

He stiffened, and for a second she thought he would refuse to answer. But then he said, "No."

She waited, but evidently he wasn't going to say more. "She told me you were lovers," she said bluntly.

His eyes showed shock. After a moment he sighed. "I see. I'm sorry, Victoria, I thought you were jumping to conclusions. I didn't know you had concrete evidence." He shrugged, looking away from her. "Sabrina lied."

"Why would she do that?"

"The ways of women are beyond me."

There was a brief flash of his white teeth. The room had suddenly become more gloomy, the sky outside more overcast. Vicki could hear the muffled sound of rain on the veranda outside. As she looked beyond Jason, she saw raindrops splash on the window, splatter and run down the rectangular panes. Jason seemed to be turning something over in his mind. Abruptly he fished in his jacket pocket, pulled out a cigarette and lighted it. Standing up, he went to the window and opened it slightly, evidently intending to use it in lieu of an ashtray. With his back turned to her, he finally spoke again. "I've come to admire your forthrightness, Victoria. I want to be as forthright with you. I did make love to Sabrina—once—during my marriage to Claire. It was something I regretted immediately." He turned to face her, his gray gaze fixing on her face. "As I told you before, Claire constantly accused me of having affairs. Her accusations were unfounded. I'd be foolish to expect you to believe I've lived the life of a monk since Claire's death, for I haven't. But while we were married, I was faithful to her. I can be old-fashioned, too, I suppose. I've never approved of cheating. However, during a low spot in my life I allowed myself to think that if I were to be judged guilty, I might as well *be* guilty. Sabrina was close to hand. She wasn't married to Sig then, though we all knew him—he was one of Claire's closest friends. Actually Sabrina married Sig right afterward, after I told her it could never happen again."

He sighed. "It wasn't fair to Sabrina or to Claire, but it happened. I didn't ever feel tempted to start it again."

"Sig thought differently."

"Yes, he did. It's possible he was *led* to think differently."

"By Sabrina?"

"It's not very honorable of me to say so, but yes, I think Sabrina *wanted* Sig to believe we were still involved. Evidently she wanted you to think the same thing. I don't know why."

"Perhaps she hopes it will happen again."

"It won't."

Could she believe him?

She looked up at him, drawing in her breath. "I owe you an apology, Jason. I shouldn't have believed Sabrina without checking with you first. I thought... she told me you'd insisted she come to Stratford."

"I did. I had to. There was some business over the theater...."

"Yes. David explained it to me. Is it settled now?"

He nodded. "We're going to use pilings." Without thinking, he raised his right hand to rub his forehead, then winced. Throwing his cigarette out of the window, he came back to the bed and sat down. "You must think I'm a very selfish person. And I suppose I am. I've put up with Sabrina's nonsense and tried to keep Sig happy for one reason only: the future of my theater. It's very important to me. I've had this dream all my adult life of founding a new company, watching it flourish and grow. It's not easy to attract young actors and actresses to the theater when television and films hold out such glittering promises of fame and fortune. Yet what would it be like to have no live theater?"

He answered his own question without pausing. "It doesn't bear thinking of. It's going to be an Elizabethan theater—part of it open to the skies—with a thrust stage. There's no such thing in England, can you imagine that? I want it to be a place where the young can get a start, encouragement, instruction. And I want to do other things besides Shakespeare, keep in touch with contemporary drama. Sabrina is a brilliant woman in spite of her faults. She knows theater. She knows what works and what doesn't, and why. I need her expertise, and Sig's money would certainly be a help. I'm hardly destitute, but I can't fund the whole thing myself. It shouldn't be one man's theater, anyway. It should belong to everyone."

He broke off and glanced at her rather sheepishly, apparently aware that his voice had taken on a crusading quality. "I sound as though I'm giving one of my fund-raising speeches, don't I?"

Moved by the way his strong features had radiated enthusiasm, Vicki was unable to answer for a moment. Then she managed a smile. "You've got me convinced, anyway. I'll grant you it's a worthwhile cause."

His eyes met hers, conveying a challenge. "So. Is Sabrina disposed of?"

"I guess so. I...you're *not* planning to marry her?"

"She told you that, too?"

"No...." She hesitated, not wanting to involve David.

"I'm not going to marry anyone," Jason said flatly. "I've told her that before. Now, what of you and me, Victoria?"

Her breath caught miserably in her throat. "I don't know, Jason. Things are still the same, aren't they?"

"You mean as far as promises of forever are concerned?"

"I...yes."

"Why do we need promises? We have tenderness, caring, intimacy, love. Anyway," he added soberly, "do you really think we are suited for anything long-term? We've already given a demonstration of what can happen. I'm always going to be an actor. I'm probably always going to go off the deep end every time I have a new part. I never think I'm going to be any good. It's not fair to any woman to expect her to put up with such idiotic behavior. And I really cannot abide scenes, Victoria, even when I'm the cause of them. The only real solution is for me to be responsible to no one. Selfish attitude, I know, but permanently exposing a woman to my tantrums would be even more selfish."

Vicki stared down at her hands, which were clasped tightly in her lap. No marriage is all smooth sailing, she wanted to tell him. Her own parents had quarreled often and loudly. And she remembered Abby and her first husband, Don, fighting over the most trivial matters. Yet their marriages had held. And they had seemed stronger after each argument was over, as though a breeze had swept through, cleaning out debris. Allowing each partner to breathe easier, with the knowledge that it would take more than arguments to separate them.... And twice she had helped Jason overcome his nervousness before a performance. He had told her so himself.

But she could say none of this without appearing to be begging him to marry her. She still had a shred of pride left.

The alternative would be to do as he wished. To seize the moment, to take what they could while their indisputable passion for each other lasted.

And where would that end? Most likely with Jason tiring of her, turning away. She'd already experienced rejection from him, imagined and real. Apart from any moral considerations, could she bear a final rejection? Wouldn't it be better to end their relationship now while they still had some respect for one another?

"I'm sorry, Jason," she said quietly, aware that the next words would be the most difficult she'd ever have to say. "I think it would be best if we didn't see each other again."

"I see," he said heavily.

Evidently he wasn't going to argue with her. Had she wanted him to?

"You know," he said in a conversational tone that

startled her with its evenness, "I truly don't think you can just get up from this bed and walk away from me."

She stared at him. He was looking at her very soberly, very directly.

"Of course, I can," she said, immediately annoyed that her voice sounded so uncertain.

"Can you, Victoria? Can you really?" He was deliberately holding her gaze, his left hand moving slowly up her arm to her shoulder, gripping it, easing her closer to him. "Don't you remember the riverbank?"

She swallowed. "I remember."

"Do you remember this?" The back of his hand brushed against her breast, bringing every nerve ending to life. It was as though she wasn't wearing a coat, a shirt, as though she were naked to his touch. She felt her breast's immediate response, the stiffening of the nipple, the automatic distension of the breast itself. In intimate association the muscles of her thighs tightened and tensed. He knew how to touch a woman, this man. There was never any sudden movement, no grabbing or pawing. None of the uncouth tactics David Brent or Ken Marriott had employed. His touch was feather light, seeming to draw heat to her skin's surface as he gently, so gently, traced the rounded contours of her breast through the layers of fabric under his hand.

"Jason," she whispered helplessly, but he cut off her tentative protest with his lips, soft and pliant against her own. Somewhere in her mind she realized that his fingers were manipulating buttons. She could even marvel that he was so skilled when he had the use of only one hand. But the part of her mind that

was functioning seemed cut off from the rest of her.
His hand was brushing aside fabric now, skimming
delicately over her breasts. His own shirt was open,
but whether he had unfastened it, or she had, she
didn't know. She only knew that she was suddenly
pressed against the hardness of his chest, feeling the
silkiness of hair against the heightened sensitivity of
her breasts, feeling the warmth of him, the solid male
familiarity of him.

Her arms were around him now, her hands
clenched in the bunched fabric of his shirt. When had
he taken off his jacket? She neither knew nor cared.
She was lifting the shirt away from his back, her
hands sliding across warm muscle, tantalizingly
smooth flesh, feeling the responsive groan in his
throat vibrating against her lips as his mouth drew
breath from hers and returned it to her. Mindlessly
she gave kiss for kiss, her lips demanding and receiving more pressure, more strength, for the time for
tenderness was past. She might object to grabbing,
but there came a time when gentleness was not
enough, when the rough bruising of hands made
urgent by passion, the deliberate abrasiveness of
tongue against eager flesh, was desired, even necessary.

Somewhere, she knew, still simmering in that small
functioning part of her brain, was the certainty that
she was heading for disaster again. How coolly she
had assessed her choices a few moments before, how
easily he had disposed of her rational conclusions.

She didn't care. She wanted only to feel his body
against hers once again, all of him pressed tightly
against all of her. His mouth making patterns against
her neck, he began to move, to roll himself onto the

bed, pulling her with him, her long hair trailing sensuously across his naked chest. She was falling again, she thought vaguely. No, not falling; she was sinking down into a kind of voluptuous forgetfulness from which she might never return.

His exclamation of pain aroused her. Face creased, he lifted himself away from her, easing his injured hand out from under her body where she'd crushed it unwittingly. "Sorry, love," he murmured as his head bent to hers again.

But the interruption had awakened her to full recognition of her stupidity, her weakness. Pulling away from him, she rolled to the edge of the bed and sat up, snatching her shirt around her and knotting it firmly at her waist.

"Victoria?"

She didn't turn around. "I didn't intend this to happen, Jason," she said breathlessly.

"No more did I." Ruefulness was clear in his voice. "It seems to be inescapable, doesn't it?"

"We aren't animals, Jason. We can control the. . . the things we do."

"You may not be an animal, but are you quite sure about me?" he countered. He was kneeling on the bed beside her now, and as he spoke, he lifted her hair, gave a mock growl and pressed his lips to the nape of her neck, sending a shudder of response along her nervous system.

Determinedly she straightened her spine. "No, Jason. Please, you're not being fair. I don't want to—" she breathed deeply as her voice faltered, started again "—I don't want to make love to you. I can't stand to be some kind of plaything. Every time we make love, I end up feeling cheap and shoddy and upset."

There was a silence, then she felt his weight shift as he eased himself around her and stood up. He looked down at her after he'd tucked his shirt back into the waistband of his pants. He was smiling, she was amazed to see—smiling easily, confidently, his gray eyes those of a conqueror. "You'll change your mind," he said. "It's absolute rubbish for you to feel shoddy. You're not a promiscuous woman. We love each other. It's not as if—"

Peremptorily she cut him off. "No, I won't change my mind." The sudden anger his easy assumption had caused gave her voice a ring of determination.

His gaze flickered for a second, then fixed on her face. "I do love you, Victoria."

"You don't know anything about love. Love isn't something you offer for the time being, until things change. Love means taking risks, making a commitment...."

"Marriage?" he queried, turning down the corners of his mouth.

Obviously he wasn't going to take her seriously. He thought he could simply charm her into acquiescence as he had before, as he had probably charmed dozens of women. She sat up straight and glared at him. "Yes, marriage," she said firmly. "But you don't need to worry, I'm not demanding marriage from you. I'll wait for somebody who doesn't have your hang-ups about killing his wife."

It was a terrible thing to say. She knew that before he flinched, but it had to be said if she was going to persuade him to leave her in peace so that she might have a chance to heal.

For a moment more he contemplated her, hesitating as though he had something more he wanted to say. Then he sighed deeply, bent down to kiss her very lightly on the lips in an almost sexless way. "I have hurt you, haven't I?" he murmured. "You're not a person to whom cruelty comes easily."

Straightening, he nodded briskly. "You're quite right. I have nothing to offer you." His eyes were remote now. She saw him swallow as though his mouth was as dry as her own. "You've brought a great deal of brightness into my life," he said suddenly, unexpectedly. "I thank you for that. I won't bother you again, of course." He hesitated. "I've said that before, I know, but I mean it this time. Obviously I'm not...not good for you. Forgive me, Victoria, you were right to stop me. It was very unfair of me to—"

He broke off.

She looked down at the carpet, dreadfully afraid she was going to cry. The silence seemed to stretch indefinitely. It seemed an age before he moved, reaching around her for his jacket, pulling it on. She heard the scrape of his lighter as he lighted another cigarette. Why didn't he just go?

Abruptly she remembered that they were in his bedroom, in his house. She was the one who had to leave. But at the moment she wasn't sure her legs would hold her.

Portia, she thought suddenly, grasping at straws. She would talk to him about Portia. That would get her back to normal, and then she could find the strength to leave.

"I have another question, Jason," she said, glancing up at him.

He inclined his head.

"I...it's about Portia. Did you give her money to buy a guitar?"

An expression of astonishment appeared on his face. "A guitar? Lord, no, this is the first I've heard about a guitar. I haven't been to the hotel yet. Portia has a guitar?"

Vicki nodded. "She told me you'd given her money before we left Stratford."

"Why the devil would she tell you that?" he asked wonderingly.

"More to the point, if you didn't give her the money, where did she get it?"

"From David, perhaps?"

"No. David thinks...well, he feels there's a possibility...."

When she hesitated, Jason strode again to the window and flung his cigarette out, his voice cutting across her hesitation. "Spit it out, Victoria."

Still she hesitated, wishing devoutly that she hadn't brought the subject up. "There was another theft at the hotel," she blurted out. "Money this time."

He reached down for her so swiftly that she was on her feet before she knew it, his good hand gripping her arm like a vise. "What the devil are you talking about? Are you accusing Portia of stealing?"

"No, I'm not. I just thought you should be aware of what David thinks. There is some doubt about where Portia got the money and—"

He released her so abruptly that she almost fell back on the bed. She had to save herself by catching hold of his arm, barely missing his bandaged hand. "Jason, I didn't mean to imply that Portia was a thief—" she protested.

"Didn't you?" His voice was harsh. "You seem to have a very suspicious nature, Victoria. First you accuse me of philandering, and now my sister is the target." He looked at her coldly, chilling her with the intensity of his gaze. "Understand me now. A Meredith could not possibly be involved in anything criminal. *Anything*. Portia has been guilty of mischief in the past, yes, but this! Such an accusation is inexcusable."

"I didn't make an accusation," she interrupted, but he was beyond hearing her. He was striding from the room, throwing back over his shoulder the statement that he would deal with David at once.

And then he was gone, his footsteps echoing down the marble staircase, the outer door slamming in his wake.

Feeling desperately that she had handled everything badly, yet knowing there was no way to make things better, Vicki sank down on the bed. Clasping her hands tightly between her legs, she stared at them, willing them to stop shaking.

CHAPTER NINETEEN

SHE HEARD NOTHING. All the following day, as she supervised the laying of the carpeting in the Blue Room, she expected to hear something from someone about Portia. But there were no repercussions at all.

At last she couldn't stand the suspense any longer, and she called the Meredith suite from the lobby, promising herself she'd hang up if Jason answered.

David picked up the phone, and hesitantly Vicki asked if Portia was all right. "Yes," he said curtly. "She denied everything, of course. And Jason believed her."

"That's a relief. She explained the money?"

"I suppose she must have done."

"Then everything is okay?"

"Hardly." He paused. "You'd better come up here, Vicki. There's something I have to show you. Neither Portia nor Mr. Meredith is here. Now would be a good time."

"Oh, I don't think—"

"I want you to help me decide whether or not I should go to the police."

"The police? Good God! What is it David, what happened?"

"Come up and I'll show you." His voice was implacable.

"But David—" Vicki stared at the receiver in her hand, realizing belatedly that he had hung up.

No, she wasn't going to risk another confrontation with David Brent. And yet, what had he meant about going to the police? Would he actually pass on his suspicions about Portia?

She would have to go, she supposed. At least, she wouldn't be alone with him. Mrs. Powell and Royce would surely be there.

She had guessed incorrectly. She discovered after he let her in that no one was in the suite but David. Mrs. Powell had gone to London with Portia to shop for school clothing, and Royce was at the house.

"What is it you wanted to show me?" Vicki asked briskly, wanting only to get it over with so that she could escape.

"In here," he said and led the way to Portia's bedroom. Picking up the largest conch shell on Portia's dressing table, he handed it to Vicki. It was stuffed with five-pound notes.

"The missing money was all in fivers, I understand," he said with a grim note of satisfaction in his voice.

Vicki put the shell back down on the dresser as though it had burned her. "Portia might have saved it," she pointed out. "She must get gifts of money sometimes from relatives or friends."

"You don't really believe that's where it came from?"

No, she didn't. But she felt a strong reluctance to agree with David that the money might have been stolen by Portia. For one thing, she didn't believe it. For another, he seemed so pleased by his find.

"Portia must have satisfied Jason about the guitar," she pointed out.

"Not necessarily. Don't you think he'd protect her, whatever she did? She is a Meredith, after all." He paused, his pale eyes narrowing as he looked at her. "Incidentally my esteemed employer was furious that I'd divulged my suspicions to you."

Vicki felt heat rise to her face. "It was probably wrong of me to tell him, David," she apologized. "It just. . . came out."

"Well, I'm not one to hold a grudge," he said evenly, but again there was something in his voice that made her think he wasn't telling the truth.

Carefully she edged out of Portia's bedroom into the hallway of the suite, trying to appear casual about her retreat. "Perhaps I should talk to Portia again," she said. "Now that we know Jason didn't give her the money, I can maybe persuade her to tell me—"

"Do you really think she'll admit the truth?"

"I don't know. But you see, David, I don't agree with you on what is the truth here. I don't believe Portia stole that money or any of the other things."

"I suppose *he* convinced you that a Meredith couldn't be a thief?"

"As a matter of fact, he. . . Jason has the impression I *do* agree with you. I didn't have a chance to explain. . . ."

David was suddenly looking tremendously pleased, his blue eyes shining like glass under water, his high cheekbones flushed pink. "That's why he was so angry, then," he said softly. "You've done it now, Vicki. Nobody insults a Meredith and gets away with it. I had to scramble a bit myself, make him think it was more your idea than mine, that you'd influenced me. I'm terribly sorry, but my job was at stake, you realize.''

"I really don't care, David," Vicki said wearily. "Now if you'll excuse me...."

"Can't you have a cup of tea with me? I really want to discuss this some more. I have to decide where my moral obligations lie."

"You'll have to decide without my help. As far as I'm concerned, Portia came by that money in some way that is perfectly explainable."

His mouth twisted. "He's got you brainwashed, hasn't he? You can't see past him." His face suddenly softening, he took a step forward. "If you'd just give me a chance, Vicki, I know I could make you like me instead of him. I'm not such a bad sort of chap, honestly. He's not worth your time. You're too special, a golden girl." He smiled shyly. "I call you the golden girl to myself—your hair, your golden skin...."

Thoroughly alarmed, Vicki backed up a step and almost tripped over the foot of a coatrack that she'd forgotten was behind her. As she put out a hand to steady herself, David reached for her, catching her off balance. Pulling her into his arms, he pressed his mouth against her own. Wrenching her mouth away, pushing against his shoulders, Vicki tried to break free, cursing her own stupidity in coming to the suite. "Don't touch me," she hissed at him, making no attempt to hide her anger. But his only response was to pull her closer as he attempted again to capture her mouth with his own.

And then the outer door opened, and Jason Meredith walked in.

David released her at once, turning smoothly to his employer with an apologetic smile. "Excuse me, Mr. Meredith," he said.

Jason didn't reply. He was staring at Vicki, his gray eyes showing shock and the beginnings of something else. Contempt?

How clean he looked, his short-sleeved white shirt immaculate against his tanned throat, his dark trousers crisply pressed. She could guess how she appeared to him, flushed and distraught, her clothing disarranged.

He was not going to speak, she realized. He was obviously waiting for an explanation. He would believe her, she knew, if she told him David had made a pass at her, an unwelcome pass. And David would lose his job. How could she take the responsibility for that?

David was looking at her anxiously, she saw out of the corner of her eye. Well, she wasn't going to let him off altogether. She would just not give any explanation at all. It didn't make any difference now what Jason thought of her, anyway.

"I was just leaving," she said evenly.

He still said nothing. He stood aside, holding the door open for her with his left hand. His right hand was still heavily bandaged, she saw. She wanted so badly to touch him. She couldn't bear to see him looking at her so blankly.

As she hesitated, David said from behind her, "I'll see you later, Vicki."

"No," she said and saw Jason's eyes narrow as though he was suddenly not quite so sure of what he had seen.

But he didn't stop her from leaving. And probably, she thought as she made her way up the stairs to Abby's apartment, David would give his own version of the incident. What she really needed to do, she decided wearily, was to get away from all Merediths and anyone connected with them.

BUT THAT WAS NOT TO BE. Standing at her bedroom window later that same day, dully watching the flush of evening sunset that was reflected in the calm river, and trying to keep her gaze from wandering toward the house that loomed in the distance, Vicki caught a flutter of movement among the willow trees. Without real curiosity she tried to make out what she had seen, and realized finally that she was looking at a woman's blue and white skirt. No, not a woman's—a girl's. Portia was out there by the river, and she was not alone. Was Jason with her?

Unable to stop herself, Vicki opened her window and leaned out, narrowing her eyes in an attempt to discern the features of the man sitting with Portia on the wide stump of a tree.

Colly. It was Colly Winters. He was dressed in denim pants and a short jacket. That was why she hadn't noticed him at first. With his black hair he blended into the shadows.

She remembered now that Portia had mentioned he planned to come down. Jason must know about his visit, then, she supposed. And it was none of her concern.

But she *was* concerned. She'd talked to Portia for only a few minutes since their return from Stratford. And she had felt increasingly that Portia should know the depth of David's suspicions of her before he carried them any further.

She could go down to the river with the sketch she'd made of Portia's proposed bedroom, and at the same time she could make sure Portia wasn't planning anything drastic, like running away again. In spite of all that had happened, she felt a responsibility for the girl. No, that wasn't quite right. She cared about Portia; Portia was her friend.

Portia was not pleased to see her. That was evident in the way she turned at the sound of Vicki's footsteps, then looked abruptly away. Colly smiled at her, though. "'Ow are you, Miss Dennison?" he asked politely.

Vicki smiled back at him, then looked at Portia. "Are you mad at me?" she asked.

"Whatever for?" Portia's clear young voice was unnaturally heavy with sarcasm. "Just because you told Jason I was a thief?"

"I didn't say anything of the sort," Vicki said firmly.

"You implied it, then."

"I didn't do that, either. I did tell him you'd bought a guitar with money you said he'd given you. He assumed from that that I was accusing you of taking money from the hotel. I was trying to tell him that *David* suspected you, but he got the idea—"

"David!" Portia was standing up now, her piquant face flushed with anger. "David's known me for years! He'd never say—"

"Nevertheless, he did." She held Portia's indignant gaze.

Faltering, Portia suddenly looked very young. "You *didn't* accuse me?"

"No. I didn't believe David was justified, even though you had lied about the money. You did lie about it, didn't you?"

Shamefaced, Portia looked at the ground, scuffing the packed soil with the toe of her sneaker. "Well, that was a fib, yes." She looked at Colly. "I suppose I might as well tell her?"

"Might as well," Colly agreed.

Portia took a deep breath. "I've already told Jason and got an awful tongue-lashing for it. Colly loaned me the money for the guitar. He sent it while we were in Stratford. Jason's already paid him back." She looked defiantly at Vicki. "I suppose you think I shouldn't have borrowed from Colly, either."

"I see nothing wrong with a loan between friends."

"Oh. Well, anyway, Jason didn't think much of it." She grinned suddenly. "He did increase my pocket money, though, so something good came out of it."

Vicki hesitated, wanting to ask Portia about the money David had shown her, but afraid the question might alienate the girl again. Instead, she handed her the sketch and explained it to her while Portia excitedly commented on each feature and finally pronounced the design to be "super."

"Have you told Colly the legend of the singing trees?" Vicki asked after a while, wanting to prolong the ease that was between them again.

Portia smiled. "Of course. We even went over there earlier to see if we could hear them." She made a face. "Not a peep out of them."

"I 'spect they think we're too young," Colly said cheerfully. He glanced up at Vicki. "I suppose *you* think we're too young, don't you, miss?"

Vicki sat down on the stump beside him. "For what?" she asked teasingly.

Portia leaned over and hugged her. Evidently she

was forgiven. "You know what for," she said. "Colly and I love each other." She screwed up her face in mock anger, glaring at Colly. "He finally said so, anyway."

Vicki looked at Colly as Portia seated herself on his other side. He was regarding her very solemnly, waiting for her answer. She would have to proceed with care. "No, Colly, I don't think you're too young," she said finally. "Love isn't a respecter of age."

"See," Portia exclaimed, wrinkling her nose. "I told you Vicki would be on our side."

"Now wait a minute," Vicki said with alarm. "That doesn't mean I can countenance—"

"You don't have to worry, miss," Colly interrupted gently. "I'm only here for a couple of hours, and then I'm going off to Cardiff with my group. I probably won't see Portia for six months or more." He hesitated. "Portia and me...we aren't going to run off with each other or anything daft like that."

"I've grown up now," Portia added gravely. "I don't do silly things like that anymore."

How long ago was it that Portia had chased after Colly to London, Vicki wondered. Two weeks? Three? "I'm glad to hear it," she said. "You've got a lot of schooling ahead of you."

Portia's head bobbed in agreement. "Colly has to get established, too. It's going to take years and years. We might even fall in love with other people by then. But it's nice to have someone to love now."

Colly beamed at her. "It sure is," he agreed. "And who knows, maybe we will still love each other when Portia's a famous actress—"

"And musician," Portia put in.

"And musician. And I've made it into the big time. I think I can, you know," he added solemnly, turning to Vicki.

"I'm sure you will," Vicki said, meaning it.

She rose to go. No need to worry about these kids, she thought. They had more sense than she had ever shown. But she still hadn't warned Portia properly about David. She should probably say something more.

No. They were both looking up at her so trustingly, Portia's brown curls close to Colly's black ringlets, both young faces radiating happiness. She couldn't cast a blight on this evening for them. She'd wait until she could talk to Portia privately before saying anything more about David Brent, she decided.

It was a decision she would soon regret.

CHAPTER TWENTY

VICKI WAS IN THE BLUE ROOM the next morning, working with Ned, when she heard her name being paged. Now what, she wondered wearily. She had slept little the previous night, suffering from too great a mixture of emotions, none of them happy ones. At least, here in the Blue Room, soon to be renamed, she could feel she was accomplishing something as her designs came to life in front of her eyes.

The new moss green carpeting was installed, the new lighting completed, the furniture replaced. Today painters were beginning on the heraldic designs on the window wall, and so far they were looking very good indeed. In the next day or so Hugh Lester's nephew, whose ideas and drawings had passed both Abby's and Vicki's delighted inspection, would begin on the Singing Tree mural. Vicki had some ideas about it and was just beginning to disclose them to Ned when Kim's voice came through the PA system.

"I suppose I'll have to go see what's up," she said apologetically.

"Right you are," Ned replied. "I'll keep an eye on things here."

In the lobby Kim handed her a telephone. "It's Portia Meredith," she whispered. "She sounds awful upset."

Vicki almost groaned aloud, but managed to speak

calmly. "What can I do for you, Portia?" she asked into the receiver.

A tear-laden voice came back to her. "Could you please come up here, Vicki? I need you on my side."

"What's wrong?"

"Please?" Portia repeated, and Vicki, sighing, agreed to come up right away.

Affected by the pleading note in Portia's voice, she took the elevator to save time and bumped her way to the third floor. Mrs. Powell opened the door of the suite to her. Her plump face was set in lugubrious lines. "They're all in there," she said, gesturing toward Portia's door. Then she shook her head sadly. "I just don't know what to think," she said and wandered back to her kitchen, leaving Vicki alone in the little hall, feeling very alarmed.

When she opened the bedroom door, Portia flung herself at her, tears running down her face. "They don't believe me," she sobbed. "I know they don't. I made them let me ring you, Vicki. They'll believe you."

Vicki held the girl close for a moment, feeling the sobs shaking her slight frame. She looked over the top of Portia's head at Jason, who was sitting on the edge of his sister's bed, his face grim. "What happened, Jason?" Vicki asked.

Before he could answer, David spoke. "Mrs. Powell found this when she cleaned this morning," he said, pointing to a gray attaché case that lay on the bed next to Jason. "It was concealed under the skirts of Portia's dressing table." With an air of understated drama, he stepped forward, flipped the catches on the case and displayed the contents to Vicki. Five-pound notes, dozens of them. "There's almost two thousand pounds in here," he added, stressing the word, "almost."

Vicki held Portia at arms' length and looked directly at her. "Do you know anything at all about this?" she asked.

Portia was hiccuping now, still crying, but she held Vicki's gaze, her gray eyes bewildered. "No," she said.

Vicki nodded. "I believe you."

Portia collapsed against her with yet another sob, and Vicki held her tightly, staring defiantly at the two men.

Jason was looking up at her with a bewildered expression on his face. "You were the one who wanted me to doubt Portia in the first place," he said harshly.

"If you had let me finish, you would have learned that I didn't suspect Portia at all," she said crisply. "I had the feeling she'd lied about the guitar, and that bothered me. And I'll admit I was troubled when David seemed to think she might have stolen things in an attempt to get attention. It seemed possible—for a few minutes. But I've never seriously entertained doubts about Portia. And I have none now."

"Then how did the bloody thing get here?" Jason asked, gesturing with his uninjured hand toward the case.

"Portia?" Vicki asked.

The girl shook her head.

"Colly wasn't up here, was he?" Jason asked abruptly.

Portia pulled free of Vicki and whirled to face him. "Oh, Jason," she wailed. "Even if he was, he wouldn't—"

"He had enough money to lend you for a guitar," David said softly. "And he first came to see you the day the money disappeared, didn't he? You told me you were rummaging around the hotel, but Royce told me he saw you with Colly."

To Vicki's surprise, his voice was quite kind, as though he regretted having to point out these facts. It was at that point that she began to wonder....

"He got that money for playing here," Portia said firmly. "And he wouldn't steal, not Colly. He was with me the whole time, anyway." Her tears had given way to anger now that her beloved Colly was under suspicion.

"Well, however the bloody thing got here, it has to be returned," Jason said, standing up. He ran his fingers through his already rumpled hair and looked rather sheepishly at Vicki. "I'm sorry you got hauled into this, Victoria. And I'm sorry I misunderstood you the other day. I should have known you're not the kind of person to accuse unjustly."

"It's all right, Jason."

He was looking at her with more than a ghost of his old tenderness, his gray eyes clear, his mouth curving at one corner in an attempt at a smile.

Poor Jason, she thought suddenly. He'd had a hell of a few days. Fights with jealous women, lacerations in his hand, his beloved sister accused of theft.

"Yes, well...." He was clearing his throat now, looking away, snapping the locks on the case. He picked it up, then put his bandaged hand on Portia's shoulder. "We'll have to take this down to Abigail," he said heavily. "I think you'd better come with me, love, as it *was* in your room."

Portia nodded. "Mrs. Carstairs will believe me," she said.

Vicki hoped she was right. "Inspector McAdam might want to talk to you," she warned Portia. "But don't worry, he's a nice man."

Portia nodded again, but her attention was fixed on Jason. "Do *you* believe me?" she asked, and the fear in her voice made Vicki's heart ache.

Jason leaned down, kissed his sister tenderly on the cheek. "I do," he said. "I'm sorry I doubted you, love. It won't happen again."

He glanced at Vicki. "Would you mind waiting here till I've talked to Abby?"

Conscious of David behind her, Vicki hesitated. But Mrs. Powell was in the suite, she remembered, and possibly Royce was around, too. She could hardly come to any harm. If Jason wanted her to wait, she would wait. "I'll be here," she promised.

As soon as Jason and Portia had left the suite, she hurried into the living room and sat down on one of the overstuffed chairs, preparing herself to ward off any sexual attack.

But she needn't have worried. David followed her slowly, leaned his shoulders against the mantelshelf and looked down at the thick cream-colored carpeting with a distracted air. It was a while before he spoke. Then he said, "Do you really believe Portia is innocent?"

Vicki nodded. "I do."

"But the evidence—"

"When an honest person looks you in the eye and says she didn't do something, evidence doesn't matter."

He laughed shortly. "I hardly think that would count in a court of law."

"We're not talking about law courts; we're talking about how I *feel*. And I feel she's innocent." She hesitated. "Which makes me wonder, David. . . ."

His head came up, his eyes narrowing. "Yes?"

"What happened to the money in the conch shell? I didn't hear it mentioned."

"I didn't say anything about it," he said with a virtuous air that struck her as false. "You convinced me she must have obtained the money elsewhere. It wasn't until Mrs. Powell found the attaché case that I decided my first suspicions were correct."

"And now?"

"I haven't changed my mind. Of course, it might have been Colly who put the attaché case there. I didn't think of him until Mr. Meredith mentioned him. He was up here last night looking at Portia's posters. I haven't quite figured out how he could have done it, but—"

"There were thefts long before Colly came on the scene," Vicki reminded him.

"Quite, but all the same. . . ."

"In fact, they started right after all of you moved into the hotel. You told me that yourself, when you were trying to fool me into thinking Portia was the culprit."

"Fool you? Vicki, what are you saying?"

"Just how fond of Kim are you, David?" she asked.

He did a good job of looking astonished. He might have been an actor himself. "Kim?" he repeated blankly.

"It occurred to me while we were all in Portia's room that no one was wondering how Portia could have got the money out of the guest's room in the first place. I know guests are often careless with keys—Abby told me that—but I began to wonder. And when you jumped at the chance to put the blame on Colly, I suddenly for no reason at all remembered your friendship with Kim."

He was looking at her almost pityingly now, his thin mouth pursed in sardonic amusement. "You sound like someone out of Agatha Christie."

"Perhaps. Someone who wrote detective fiction once said that to solve a crime one must look for the little oddities in people's behavior. I've always thought it odd that you would be so. . . friendly with someone like Kim. Not quite your type, is she?"

She could almost see his brain racing, trying to decide if she really knew anything or was just trying to draw him out. "Kim's a good sort," he said uneasily at last.

"I agree." Vicki was amazed at how calm her voice sounded, considering the fact that her heart was hammering in her chest like a wild thing, and her hands were becoming clammy with fear. She was so afraid she would say the wrong thing, give him some excuse to evade her inquisition. It was necessary to strike the proper balance, to carry him along until somehow she could make him give himself away.

"Kim's a *very* good sort," she said soothingly. "I've noticed that you often go down to the front desk to chat with her."

"No law against that."

She must be getting close; his voice was getting rough around the edges, losing its painfully acquired cultured accent.

"I suppose not. I noticed, though, that when Portia and I came back from Stratford, you were behind the counter within easy reach of the room keys. I didn't attach much significance to that at the time, of course. Why should I? But when I put it together with your friendship with Kim, I wondered if possibly you were *using* her, making her think you liked her, so you could get to the keys easily. Then there was the fact that you, as well as Portia, have been in the hotel every time something disappeared. The fact that you could easily have put the five-pound notes in that shell yourself *and* hidden the attaché case under Portia's dresser. Well, it seems to me that a good case could be made—" She broke off. There was no need to go on. The man was crumbling before her eyes. Funny, she thought, she hadn't expected him to give way so easily. Obviously she had overestimated his strength and underestimated his mental instability.

He was suddenly leaning forward over her chair, his hot breath fanning her face as he hissed at her. "Why shouldn't I take their money, their valuables? You've seen them—the women dripping with furs and jewelry, the men driving fancy foreign cars. I've never had a car, not even a bloody bicycle. I've had to save every penny I ever made, hoping someday to have enough to do something for myself." His eyes were inches from her own. Horrified, she stared into them and glimpsed madness in their depths.

He backed away just as she was beginning to wonder if she had gone too far, exposed herself to danger. She couldn't hear a sound from the kitchen. Surely Mrs. Powell hadn't gone out? Was Royce there? Or was he over at Meredith Manor as usual, supervising the work? What had she been thinking of, to accuse David outright when she was alone, unprotected?

And yet, she didn't think she had anything to fear.

He was leaning against the side of the fireplace now, gazing morosely into its empty depths. "It's tough to watch people who have so much when you're one of the 'have-nots,' isn't it?" she said, making her voice sympathetic.

"It bloody well is," he agreed. "Bloody Jason Meredith and his Jaguar and his great house. What did he ever do to deserve any of it? Struts across a stage shouting out words some other bloke wrote. Why the bloody hell should he be so well-off?"

His voice had relapsed almost completely into his original Northern brogue. But why was he suddenly raving about Jason? What did Jason have to do with thefts from hotel guests?

Suddenly, with a chill that turned every vein in her body to ice, Vicki understood. David Brent's rage against the wealthy had naturally included Jason. And he must have *acted* out of that rage.

"You set fire to Jason's house, didn't you?" she asked softly.

He nodded, smiling. *Smiling!* "Would have got the whole lot if Portia hadn't interfered," he said proudly. "Cost him a few quid that mess did, insurance notwithstanding. Served him right. I'd warned him. Wrote him a letter, I did, just before that. Told him he should share some of his money with them that had not, or else he and his precious sister wouldn't wake up one morning. Not ever, they wouldn't. Had it all planned. I was right by the French windows in Meredith's study; all I had to do was walk away as soon as I was sure the fire had taken hold."

Stunned by the depth of the man's hatred, Vicki searched her mind for some idea of what to do.

David had turned all the way around now, with his back to her, his forehead resting on the mantel. His shoulders were shaking, but she couldn't decide if he was laughing or crying. It didn't make much difference. Somehow she had to get herself out of here and find help.

The corner of her vision caught a movement. Mrs. Powell was peeking around the corner of the archway. Evidently she'd been listening, for her plump face showed shock. As Vicki caught her eye, the stout woman jerked her head in the direction of the outer door and raised her eyebrows. Vicki nodded, then held her breath as she tiptoed across the open space.

"You were never angry with *me*, were you, David?" she asked loudly, hoping to cover the sound of the door's opening.

"No," he said in a quiet tone, turning to face her. He had been crying, after all, she saw. His eyes were moist. But they showed none of the madness she had seen earlier. On the contrary, he seemed quite calm—which under the circumstances was an even surer indication of his disturbed state. "No," he repeated. "You're an American. I never felt you looked down on me."

"I don't," she stated. She had to keep him talking, keep him calm. He hadn't heard Mrs. Powell leave the suite. "I always liked you, David."

He looked at her sadly. "That sounds like the past tense."

"No, it just came out that way."

"But you don't care for me, do you, not really?"

"I—" God, what could she say? "You haven't given me a chance," she stammered. "I hardly know you, after all."

"It didn't take you long to get to know *him*."

"That's your imagination, David. I hardly know Jason, either."

His face brightened. "Is that true? I thought you were in love with him. You looked at him as though you were."

"Oh, I might have been a bit star struck," she managed to say.

"Isn't everybody?" he said gloomily. "Looking at him like he was the sun-god or something. Nothing but a bloody actor. Actors used to be considered rogues and vagabonds in this country. Still should be." His smile was a parody of his former shy grin. "You should have told me that was all you felt for him. I wouldn't have put the blame on Portia if I'd known that. I was only trying to make a rift, make him mad at you."

"Well, you succeeded," Vicki said. "He'll probably never speak to me again."

"Do you mind that, Vicki? If I thought you didn't mind, I'd. . . ."

He was coming toward her again, and his expression was changing, becoming suspicious. "You're being awfully nice to me all of a sudden. Why?"

Once more he was bending over her, his hands gripping the arms of her chair. Heart thudding, Vicki shrank back as far as she could. "What did I say? What did you make me say?" he demanded, and there was a note of hysteria in his voice.

She swallowed, desperately trying to think of words that would reassure him, calm him. But her mind was blank, terrified. David's face, suddenly contorted beyond recognition, loomed close to hers, and she saw out of the edges of her vision that his hands were rising, moving toward her.

And then suddenly David seemed to leap into the air and jump sideways. While Vicki was still staring, astonished by this phenomenon, she saw that he had not moved of his own free will, after all. Jason had lifted him away from her. Now he was drawing back his right hand, his bandaged right hand. There was a flash of white as the hand connected with David's jaw. The young man arched backward, hit the wall and slowly subsided, his legs crumpling until he sat slumped in a heap, his eyes closed.

Jason turned toward Inspector McAdam, who was just entering the room. "Take care of him, will you?" he said in a polite conversational tone. Then he bent down over Vicki. "Are you all right?" His face was deathly pale.

"I'm fine," she managed. Then, to her horror she saw that blood was seeping through the bandages on his hand. "Your hand, Jason," she gasped.

He looked at it without much interest. "Looks as though I've broken a few sutures," he said carelessly. "I didn't stop to think when I saw David bending over you like that. I thought he was going to attack you."

"He was," Vicki said faintly. "I'm not sure if he was aiming for my throat or my—" She broke off. "It was my own stupid fault. It wasn't the first time he lost control of himself, but...."

Jason straightened up, looking aghast. "D'you mean that when I came upon you yesterday, he was—" He broke off, evidently unable to put into words the horror that was showing on his face.

"That was my own fault, too," Vicki said in as soothing a voice as she could manage. "I knew it wasn't safe to be alone with him; he'd already tried something once before. But I was worried about

Portia, and he insisted I come up here...."

"Why the devil didn't you tell me?"

Vicki winced. She didn't need to be told how stupid she had been. "I didn't want him to lose his job," she said in a small voice.

"Lord, girl, I've admired your compassion, but you carry it too far. *You didn't want him to lose his job*," he repeated wonderingly. "I wouldn't have sacked him; I'd have *killed* him."

Behind Jason, Inspector McAdam cleared his throat. Vicki had completely forgotten there were others in the room. So apparently had Jason. He was obviously startled. He glanced apologetically at the older man, then looked beyond him. "What have you done with him?" he asked grimly.

The inspector smiled. "I asked Abigail to ring the local station. A constable came and took him away. I'm afraid, lassie," he went on, looking sympathetically at Vicki, "there are going to be a lot of questions. We're going to need to find out exactly what's been going on here."

Vicki nodded. Accepting his hand, she let him pull her to her feet, not surprised to find that her knees were distinctly weak.

"You can't question her now," Jason protested. "Look at her, she's obviously all in. After what she's been through—"

"Don't you worry yourself, Mr. Meredith," the inspector interrupted, rolling every *r*. "We'll give the lassie a fair chance to recover from her ordeal. And you, too, sir," he added, glancing at Jason's bandaged hand, which was now ominously scarlet. "You'd best get yourself to a doctor. I'll arrange to get all the necessary statements later."

"Are you okay, Vicki?" Abby asked breathlessly from behind him.

Vicki looked up and laughed, on the edge of hysteria. Her aunt's chignon had come loose, and her hair was hanging fetchingly over one shoulder, making her look like Dorothy Lamour in *The Road to Bali*. She was gazing fixedly at Vicki, her face bright pink with exertion, her hazel eyes wide and brilliant.

Evidently deciding Vicki had come to no harm, she sank abruptly down on the crimson sofa, took a deep breath and let it out in a series of little puffs.

"You sound as though you ran all the way up the stairs," Vicki said, still trying to keep her voice calm.

"I did," Abby admitted with a rueful grin. "Mrs. Powell rushed in and told us what was happening. Very concisely, by the way," she added with a smile over her shoulder that brought a flush of pride to the housekeeper's plump face. "Everyone dashed out to the elevator, Portia in the rear. I didn't think this was any place for her, so I grabbed her and held on while I called the police station. Then I made her wait with Kim, which took a lot of persuasion. By the time I'd convinced her to stay, the elevator was gone. I rang for it, but it seems to be stuck between floors. No one in it, thank God. I'll have to get it replaced, I guess. There's always something going wrong around here."

"You'll cope as always, Abigail," Inspector McAdam said with an admiring smile.

"Yes. I expect I will." Abby and the sturdy Scotsman exchanged a glance that seemed to Vicki to have more than a trace of satisfaction in it. Well, well, she thought, but there was no time to dwell on the relationship now. It was important that Jason get to a doctor right away. She offered to drive him, but her offer was politely turned down.

She was to rest, Jason told her. After all the questioning was done, and this whole chaotic business was over, he would come to her and see if they couldn't get "other business" taken care of at that time.

She mulled this over after he'd gone. She knew precisely what "business" he was talking about, of course. But still nothing had changed as far as he and she were concerned. There wasn't much point in talking about it anymore.

She knew, of course, that if Jason wanted to see her, he would see her. He was not one to take no for an answer.

Eventually, of course, he would have to. But at least, she would see him alone one more time.

CHAPTER TWENTY-ONE

THE NEXT FORTY-EIGHT HOURS were a nightmare. Vicki went over and over her statement to the police until she could have recited it backward. The first night she didn't sleep at all, for as soon as she closed her eyes, she saw David's contorted face glaring at her, his hands reaching for her. For hours she lay staring at the ceiling, reliving the incident, hoping that by doing so she could exorcise it from her mind. The things David had stolen previously had not yet been recovered. He'd sold them all to a pawnbroker in London, apparently, and the police there were questioning the owner. It was to be hoped the valuables could be traced.

She did sleep on the second night, for Abby insisted on giving her a sleeping pill. Normally Vicki avoided any kind of medication, but she recognized that for a few hours she needed oblivion.

She woke the next morning feeling rested but woolly-headed, a fact that confirmed her distrust of drugs. "I suppose I'll have to appear in court?" she said to Inspector McAdam when he turned up to have lunch in Abby's apartment.

To her surprise, he hesitated. "You will, aye, if Brent comes to trial."

"You mean he might not?"

He glanced at Abby, who nodded. Then he turned

back to Vicki, his gray eyes apologetic. "It seems our young friend had some kind of breakdown last night. He started sobbing uncontrollably, then...well, screaming and trying, literally, to climb the walls."

Somehow the nice Scottish burr in his voice made the scene more vivid than it might have been.

Vicki shuddered. "Poor David."

"Aye. It's sad to see a man with such intelligence misuse it. The mind is a strange thing. It can go along for years plotting deviousness and revenge, and when it succeeds or fails, something gives way." He sighed heavily. "Anyhow, Mr. Brent has been taken to a mental institution for psychiatric evaluation. I mind it will be a while before he comes out."

Remembering David's horror of confined spaces, Vicki shuddered again. "He won't be locked up, will he? I mean...."

The inspector reached across the table to pat her arm with his large freckled hand. "Don't you worry yourself, lassie. This is the twentieth century; we've no Bedlam nowadays. The hospital is a nice place in the country. He'll do just fine there. Mr. Meredith intends to make sure he's properly cared for." He paused. "Yon's a good man, Mr. Meredith."

"Yes," Vicki agreed.

JASON TELEPHONED HER an hour after Abby and the inspector had left. There hadn't been a moment in which she and Jason could talk alone since David had been taken away. At the sound of his voice, her heart began its usual erratic beating, but it slowed as she realized what he was telling her.

"I have to go back to Stratford at once," he said. "The *Macbeth* curse had struck again. Trevor's developed laryngitis, of all things. I *told* him he smoked too much.''

"But your hand," she protested.

He chuckled. "I'm going to fight the duel left-handed. Quite a challenge, actually. I've never attempted that."

"Who will play Macduff if Trevor's out of action?"

"Christopher Hammond's been playing that part. There was a general reshuffle when I had to bow out."

"Christopher Hammond!" she exclaimed, remembering the furious duel the two had staged in *Hamlet*. "For goodness, sake, be careful."

"Are you worried about me, Victoria?"

Until then his voice had been light, deliberately so, she thought. She understood his forced levity. So much had happened that it was impossible to chat in a normal way, especially on the telephone. But with his question, he had lowered his voice to a more serious note.

"Yes, I *am* worried," she said just as seriously.

"Don't be. I'll be careful. And I'll be back on Saturday."

"Good. You'll be in time for Abby's opening of the Blue Room—I mean the Tudor Room. We're planning quite a show."

"I wouldn't miss it." He paused. "And afterward we'll talk."

"Yes."

There was another awkward pause. Then Vicki said hesitantly, "I'm sorry for what I said to you. . . . about Claire. That was unforgivable."

"I suspect I deserved it." Another silence. "I really must go now."

"Yes."

In a way, Vicki decided after Jason had hung up, it was just as well Jason had been called back to Stratford. She was pretty sure that their next confrontation was going to be the final one, and she was certainly not in shape for any more emotional stress. It would be good to have a few placid days in which to gather her resources.

THE NEXT FEW DAYS, however, were far from placid. Abby had determined that she would open the newly christened Tudor Room on Saturday, and she was not about to put up with any delays. So naturally everything went wrong. The tablecloths and napkins Vicki had ordered were the wrong size and shape. Somehow bundles had been mixed in a warehouse, and another hotel had received their order. It took Vicki a dozen phone calls to get that problem ironed out.

A second panic was caused when three of the new concealed fixtures refused to light up, and it was found that the wiring had passed them by. Then, of course, there was the fact that Arthur Lester, Hugh's nephew, could not possibly complete the mural in the limited time available, and he certainly couldn't be rushed. It was Vicki's idea to partition off that side of the long room with thick gold ropes attached to stanchions, lay a dropcloth over the carpeting, and let Arthur proceed at his own slow pace as a sort of extra feature of attraction. It was a solution that pleased everybody. Arthur was not the type of artist who required solitude. A gregarious young man, he enjoyed talking to people as he worked and was actually looking forward to drawing a crowd of observers every day.

Finally the night of the opening arrived. Vicki dressed carefully in a newly acquired gown, a floor-length dress of soft white lawn with a square-cut neck and long bunched sleeves banded with green silk ribbons. The high waistline, edged with more green ribbon, emphasized her small waist and high firm breasts. Her hair, which she had braided overnight, cascaded in soft waves down her back.

Abby had presented her with a pair of beautiful satin slippers in the same shade of green. Vicki lifted one foot and turned her ankle this way and that, admiring the slipper in the wardrobe's full-length mirror. Then she stood up straight and checked the full effect.

Anne Boleyn waiting to be presented to Henry VIII, she decided. Would Henry VIII, also known as Jason Meredith, put in an appearance? And would she lose her head? Again?

Portia joined her on the staircase as she went past the Merediths' floor. The girl looked pert, sprightly and totally feminine—extraordinarily grown-up in a long blue dress of a similar style to Vicki's. She was carrying her guitar, as Vicki was. Abby had hired a string ensemble to play Elizabethan music throughout the first dinner in the newly decorated restaurant, and Vicki, with much foreboding, had consented to sing. Portia had learned a simple tune that she was going to play as a sort of counterpoint to Vicki's guitar during her rendition of "Greensleeves."

After they had admired each other's appearance, Vicki and Portia headed for their places on the platform at the end of the Tudor Room. Sitting decorously on her little gilt chair, her guitar alongside, Vicki had a good view through the long diamond-paned windows of the courtyard, the river and trees. For the time being, strings of fairy lights were hung in the bushes on each side of the courtyard. Later, old-style lamp posts would be installed.

She let her gaze return to the room and decided that she had done well. It was always gratifying when a design turned out the way she'd envisioned it. The room looked gracious and elegant. Mr. Duckworth's lanterns, which had arrived only the day before, were a perfect additional touch.

Arthur had made a good start on the mural. At one end the pregnant Amanda, wearing her long white gown, was gazing out of a window, pensively waiting for news of her absent husband. During the next few weeks the design would be completed, the final panel depicting Amanda again, this time her face transformed with joy. She would be listening to the trees singing, hearing their promise of happiness, while behind her in the distance the horse bearing her wounded husband approached.

The musicians were already tuning their instruments. The restaurant was crowded with well-dressed patrons who seemed to be set on enjoying themselves immensely. Waiters in green velvet tabards over white shirts and Tudor-style breeches and hose bustled in and out, balancing great silver trays on their upraised hands. The air seemed electric with anticipation. So far, Jason had not appeared.

"Isn't it great to see everyone so dressed up?" Abby whispered when she came to check that everything was in readiness. "Such a nice change from the scruffy blue jeans everybody seems to wear these days. It's like old times."

Vicki grinned at her. "I suppose Inspector McAdam is among those present?"

Abby blushed. "He is, as a matter of fact. It seemed only polite to ask him after all the help he's given us."

"Oh, yes. One must be polite, mustn't one?"

Abby wrinkled her nose at Vicki. "Show some respect for your elders."

"How can I when my elders look so young?"

She was thanked for the compliment with a kiss on the cheek. Abby did look young tonight, she thought, as her aunt picked her way down the stairs at the side of the little stage, moving carefully in her usual absurdly high heels. She was wearing a lovely close-fitting jacket and a full-length skirt of heavy rose-colored silk that contrasted beautifully with her glossy brown hair. Vicki watched as she made her way between tables, stopping every once in a while to greet friends or hotel guests, before she joined Ian McAdam at a table set for two.

The inspector looked very distinguished in a tuxedo, Vicki thought. He and Abby seemed to have something going, that was for sure. His head was bent very close to Abby's now, and Abby was smiling as brightly as a young girl. Yesterday Vicki had questioned her aunt quite closely about her relationship with Ian McAdam, but Abby had seemed reluctant to say too much. "We're good friends," she'd said firmly. "That's enough for now."

The conductor was raising his baton. The orchestra was about to begin its first selection. Vicki reached down for her guitar so that she would be ready when her time came. As she straightened, she saw Jason.

He was sitting several tables away, facing her, and was dressed magnificently in black evening clothes, a white formal shirt and bow tie. His hair was smoothly brushed. As he caught her glance, he raised his wineglass in a silent toast, his gray eyes holding her gaze across the heads of the people in between.

Here was no bold buccaneer. This was an urbane, handsome, sophisticated man-about-town. Yet not a superstar, either. There was a glint of humor in those gray eyes that seemed to invite her to share his amusement at them both—so dressed up in fancy clothes, looking as though they'd never sprawled naked together on a riverbank.

Yes, this was the real Jason Meredith, smiling engagingly at her alone as he sipped his wine. She noticed that he was holding the glass in his right hand. Only a thin strip of gauze covered the wound.

For the space of several seconds he continued to hold her gaze, and her pulse, which had quickened when she first saw him, slowed and steadied.

A moment later, as he set down his glass, and the connection between them was broken, she saw that he was sitting between the Lindstroms. Sig was elegant in a dinner jacket, Sabrina stunning in a low-cut dress of burgundy satin that made the pastel dresses of the other women in the room look pallid. Her bare shoulders gleamed white as marble.

Vicki let out her breath on a long sigh. *Sabrina.* There would be no opportunity to speak to Jason alone tonight.

She saved "Greensleeves" until her last number, her fifth song of the evening. The first four songs were well received, especially the one Vicki had hurriedly written for the occasion, "The Ballad of the Singing Trees." Sig, Jason and Abby led the applause each time, with Sabrina clapping politely.

Vicki stole a glance at Portia from time to time,

hoping the girl was not becoming restless sitting still
for such a long time. But Portia seemed content, even
serene. She sat very straight, a small smile playing
around her lips, a dreamy expression on her elfin face.
Probably, Vicki thought with affectionate amusement, she was dreaming of the day when she would be
on stage, in the spotlight, her name in lights.

Vicki's performance of "Greensleeves" was intended to be the high point of the musical evening,
timed to coincide with the ending of the meal. After
the song a flaming dessert would be served dramatically by Jean-Paul. The orchestra would play again
while the guests relaxed over their demitasses of coffee, but Vicki and Portia would then be free to eat
their own meal.

During the brief intermission Abby came up to the
platform and made a short and gracious speech of
welcome to the assembled guests. She introduced her
niece, adding that she was also the designer of the
Tudor Room, an announcement Vicki had not been
prepared for.

Then the lights dimmed, Vicki noting thankfully
that the dimmers worked without a hitch. A small
spotlight illuminated her as she stood up and moved
to center stage, and she began to play.

It seemed to her as she sang the ancient words that
they summed up completely the tangle of emotions
she had experienced during the past several weeks.

>   "Alas, my love, you do me wrong,
>   To cast me off discourteously,"

she sang, deliberately not looking in Jason's direction, though she was conscious of him gazing at her.

"And I have loved you so long,
Delighting in your company."

She sang, noting with some watchful part of her
mind that her voice sounded more mellow than it had
ever sounded. Each note seemed liquid and golden,
throaty on the low notes, clear and true on the high.
Portia's accompaniment was faultless. Her hours of
practice had paid off.

There was a second's silence as the last note died
away, Vicki holding it as long as she could. Then the
lights brightened, and the room echoed to enthusiastic applause. Smiling, relieved she hadn't let Abby
down, Vicki bowed and indicated Portia, who stood
and accepted her own share of applause with remark-
able aplomb. A born performer, Vicki thought. She
felt a sudden conviction that Portia was destined to
go far.

A waiter had set two additional places at Abby's
table, and the performers were served as soon as the
desserts had been attended to. Vicki toyed with the
food on her plate, telling herself she'd lost her appetite because of the stress of performing. It had
nothing to do with the fact that Jason had risen to his
feet as she and Portia left the stage, looking as
though he intended to follow them, only to be persuaded to sit down again by Sabrina's hand on his
arm. From where Vicki sat now, she could see only
Jason's profile. He was listening to something Sig
was saying, frowning in concentration. No, not in
concentration—anger.

As Vicki watched in curiosity, unable to tear her
gaze from the scene, Sabrina stood up. In a low voice
she said something very rapid to both men and hur-

ried out of the room, brushing against several tables as she went. A minute later, Jason stood up also, his face grim and tight, and followed her out. Sig raised a hand to a passing waiter and gesticulated at the champagne container Abby had ordered for each table. Evidently he was asking for a refill.

Somehow Vicki managed to move enough food around on her plate to pass for eating. She also managed to respond to Abby and to Ian's comments on her singing, which were very favorable indeed.

But her mind was buzzing with questions and doubts, and she had difficulty concentrating. Evidently after a while her inattention showed. "Is something wrong, dear?" Abby asked.

The sympathy on her face and the glance she gave toward the Tudor Room's exit indicated she had seen Jason leave.

"I...no," Vicki managed. Then she pushed back her chair. "If you'll excuse me, there's someone I'd like to talk to, do you mind?"

"Go ahead, darling," Abby said softly.

"Aren't you going to have any pudding?" Portia asked. She'd already finished her own, scraping the dish with all the avidness of a small child.

"I'll take some up to the apartment for Vicki later," Abby told her, wincing over the word "pudding" used to describe Jean-Paul's magnificent dessert.

Vicki smiled down at the girl. "You can have mine," she said and was rewarded by a beaming smile.

Sig had already drunk half of the bottle of champagne. He didn't seem to be enjoying it much, Vicki thought as she slid into the seat next to him. His lined face was set in a very somber expression that didn't lighten even though he tried to summon a smile for her.

"What happened, Sig?" she asked quietly.

"What happened?" he echoed, enunciating each word with a care that showed he was not unaffected by the champagne. "What happened is that my beautiful wife showed too much attention to our mutual friend, and I told them both to. . . to go away."

His Scandinavian accent was more apparent than usual, an indication of his distress.

"There's nothing between Jason and Sabrina, Sig," she said gently.

"That is what Jason has told me."

"He's telling you the truth."

"Then answer me this: why did Sabrina leave Stratford the same day as Jason, the day he cut his hand?"

"I suppose their business must have been completed. There was some problem about the theater."

"I heard much talk about that. Soil bearing or boring, or some such thing. Very boring." He laughed at his own joke and poured himself another glass of champagne. "The trouble is, you see, Vicki," he continued, leaning confidentially close to her, "My wife is in search of revenge."

"Revenge for what?"

"For Claire. I made the mistake of confessing to her that I had been in love with Claire for many years, and that Claire was coming to the United States to be with me when she was killed."

"But I thought. . . surely Claire left England because of the quarrel she had with Jason?"

He laughed, rather painfully, Vicki thought. "But

of course, she did. What Jason does not know is that she—what is the word—engineered, that's it, engineered that quarrel so she would have an excuse to leave him and make him think it was his own fault.'' His head wagged from side to side, and he smiled at Vicki, his eyes dilated and owlish. ''She was a devious woman, Claire.''

Vicki swallowed.

''I loved Claire for so long,'' Sig continued. ''Since she was seventeen.''

''Then why did you marry Sabrina?''

He laughed shortly. ''Good question. Claire seemed...out of reach. I needed someone. And Sabrina was willing. I suppose we both settled for second best. But then, Claire seemed more approachable once I was married. Strange creatures, women. She was fed up with Jason. He'd stopped indulging her the way she wanted to be indulged, the way she *should* have been indulged. I...I would have given her everything. At last she agreed to go away with me, to meet me in the States, make a fresh start. And then, when she was almost in my grasp, *bang*! Airplane gone. Fate.'' He laughed again, then made a face. ''Not funny. Made Sabrina angry. Not because I loved Claire, no. Thing was, I didn't confess until long after Claire died. Too late for Sabrina to pass information on to Jason and take him for herself while he was too weak to defend himself. And she was already married to me. Honorable man, Jason. Would have nothing to do with a friend's wife.''

''Well, if you know that, why do you keep insisting they are having an affair?''

He looked suddenly tired, more sober. ''Because,

my dear, my very dear Vicki, it is less of an insult to my aging manhood to pretend that Jason is luring Sabrina away than to face the fact that she did not really want me in the first place. I think she only wanted to show Jason she could get a husband. And now, what use am I to her now? She plans to leave me, I think, if she can convince Jason to take her."

"And you don't want to lose her?"

He looked at her quizzically. "Men are also strange creatures, are they not, Vicki?" He shook his head. "No, I do not want to lose her. She adds a certain. . .something to my life. Excitement? I do not want to be alone, Vicki."

There was a silence, then Vicki asked gently. "Jason doesn't know about you and Claire?"

"He does not."

"But surely you know that Jason feels guilty because he thinks he was responsible for Claire's death."

He nodded. "Better him than me."

Vicki looked at him. She should feel sorry for him, she supposed, but she didn't. Uppermost was a feeling of distaste.

And also, she conceded, a desire to go to Jason and tell him about Claire and Sig, so that he could finally realize he had wasted all of that guilt.

Excusing herself from Sig, who didn't seem to notice that she was leaving, Vicki hurried out of the restaurant and headed for the back stairs. She had no idea where Jason had gone, but it seemed logical to start with his suite.

As it happened, she never did reach the suite. As she emerged through the fire door into the shadows of the upper hall, she saw the door of the Meredith suite open and stopped in her tracks. Sabrina came out, followed by Jason. As she watched, Sabrina turned and said something in a very low voice to Jason. He replied, smiling, and she suddenly flung herself into his arms.

Without waiting to see what happened next, Vicki turned tail and bolted down the steps. On the bottom landing she hesitated. She couldn't go back to the restaurant, not now. She should have gone up to Abby's apartment.

She could still do that, she supposed. But what if she ran into Sabrina and Jason on the stairs? He considered this staircase his own.... The river, she decided. She would walk by the river for a little while. She was certainly in need of air.

Skirting the bushes in order to avoid being seen in the illumination of the fairy lights, she crossed the little wooden bridge and walked along the bank on the other side of the river. When she reached the plane trees, she hesitated again. She didn't want to cause a repeat of Portia's ill-advised prank, and she *was* wearing a long white dress. Finding a stone ledge where another bridge had once stood, she sat down on it, drawing her feet up under her skirt to keep her satin slippers out of the damp grass.

SHE WAS STILL SITTING THERE half an hour later, gazing at the smoothly flowing river in which a few stars flickered, and the pale reflection of the night's full moon floated gently, when Jason came along the riverbank and found her.

Portia, he said, had seen her go. Drawn to the windows to look at the river, she had watched Vicki cross the bridge. A moment later, when Jason reentered the restaurant, she'd informed him of the fact.

"May I join you?" he asked. His voice was without inflection.

Vicki nodded and moved a little so that he could sit down.

"You saw me with Sabrina," he said after a moment's silence. "I heard the fire door bang. I realized it must have been you when Portia told me where you'd gone."

"Yes. I saw you."

"And?"

"And nothing. I've been trying not to jump to any conclusions."

"Well, that's a relief."

There was another silence. Vicki looked up at the trees above her head. The edges of some of the leaves were turning brown, she noticed. The summer was almost over. Fall would soon be here. Faintly, from across the river, she could hear the strains of the string ensemble in the Tudor Room, borne on the late-evening breeze.

"Sabrina told me an interesting story," Jason said, still without inflection.

Vicki turned her head to look at him. In the shadows cast by the moonlight she couldn't make out his expression. He seemed like a stranger sitting there. "She told you about Sig and Claire?" she asked.

"Yes. It seems she'd wanted to tell me for months, but was afraid of Sig's anger."

"She's not afraid now?"

He hesitated. "I think she doesn't care anymore whether Sig is angry or not."

"I see."

He laughed shortly. "I don't think you see at all, Vicki, any more than Sabrina did. Evidently she expected the news to catapult me into her arms. Filled with relief, finally guilt-free, I would beg her to leave Sig and run off with me."

"And did you?"

"Does it look as though I did?" She saw the flash of his smile in the shadows. "The scene you witnessed was a sort of last gasp, Victoria. I had already informed Sabrina that, grateful as I was to be told the truth, I had no intention of marrying her or resurrecting our short-lived affair. I can be very direct when I want to be."

"I know."

He smiled again. "I thought she handled herself very well. Admirably, actually. She was quite icily polite and told me she wouldn't trouble me with her presence again. But then, outside the door, she must have decided to give it one last try." He sighed. "Poor Sabrina. She doesn't really love me, you know. I think Sabrina loves only Sabrina. But she's thought for so long that I'd make a good prince consort to her queen that it's become sort of a habit. I sound callous, I know, but she's deviled me for so long. I suspect she'll stay with Sig and live happily ever after with all his lovely money."

He paused for a moment before going on. "Before coming after you, I spoke to Sig. I told him once and for all that I had no designs on Sabrina, that I knew about him and Claire and bore him no ill will. I also told him that the engagement between you and me was not true at the time I announced it. I apologized for deceiving him and said it was up to him if he wanted to withdraw from the theater board." He laughed shortly. "I don't know if he understood me or not." He was a little...under the weather. I'll probably have to tell him again. Did I do the right thing, Victoria?"

"That's not for me to say." Then she relented. "Yes, you did the right thing. I've not felt comfortable about deceiving Sig."

"Are you still angry with me?"

"Not at all. After the way you saved me from David, I don't see how I could ever be angry with you again."

He lapsed into silence, probably, she thought, thinking of David—as she was. Her guess proved correct a minute later, when he commented on the time he'd found her in David's arms.

"That was the first time in my life I was ever struck with jealousy," he said.

"I thought you despised jealousy?"

"It's easy to despise what you don't understand." He mused a while in silence again, then said, "Jealousy is a primitive sort of emotion, isn't it? I thought I'd suddenly become a deaf-mute; I couldn't speak, couldn't hear." His voice was harsh. "I began to realize some of what Claire had gone through. Mind you, she made it all up in her imagination, but it must have been painful. I should have understood, should have reassured her, instead of going off my rocker all the time. It's a shame I didn't understand her better or know about her and Sig. Lord, I'd have wished them well. I can't imagine why she didn't tell me. All that agony for nothing."

Vicki wasn't sure if he was referring to Claire's agony or his own. She was feeling very strange, sitting there, listening to him muse aloud. Disoriented.

She had no idea what the result of this conversation, if it could be called a conversation, would be. Not being sure, she didn't know what emotion to feel, and so she felt none, except for a kind of empty anticipation. Sooner or later, Jason was going to tell her what, if anything, he wanted of her, and then she would have to decide what to do. Until then, all she could do was sit here in suspended animation, waiting.

The breeze had become stronger in the past few minutes, chilling the skin exposed by the low-necked bodice of her dress. She shivered involuntarily, and at once Jason took off his dinner jacket and placed it around her shoulders. She could feel the warmth from his body clinging to the satin lining, comforting her.

She felt his hand move suddenly at her side, and was afraid he was going to touch her. *Not yet,* she pleaded silently with him. *First I have to know where I stand, where we stand in relation to each other. Don't ask me to respond physically until my mind knows how to feel.*

But he was only searching for a pack of cigarettes. Removing it from his jacket pocket, he lighted a cigarette and blew out a thoughtful cloud of smoke. "Guilt is a funny thing," he said slowly. "Sabrina told me my wife was deserting me when she died, and I immediately felt as if I'd been reincarnated with a whole new conscience. The power of a few words is amazing, when they happen to be the truth. They alter one's perspective in any number of ways... about marriage, for example."

Vicki stiffened in automatic protest. "Jason, you don't have to—"

"Yes, I do." Firmly he quelled her interruption. He had still not touched her in any way, but he was looking directly at her face now. Even in the semi-darkness under the trees she could see the penetrating intensity of his gray eyes. "I've told you how I felt when I saw you in David's arms," he said. "That was a murderous feeling. I hope never to have it again, but I probably will. One can't love someone as much as I love you without occasionally feeling twinges. I expect you'll have some more, too. It stands to reason. Two beautiful people like us are bound to attract attention from members of both sexes."

The warmth stealing through her body now was not solely due to the weight of his jacket around her shoulders. The teasing note in his voice, the old familiar teasing, had dissolved his strangeness. Hope was beginning to hover at the edges of her consciousness, begging to be allowed to enter, but hesitating, still not certain. "Jason," she said tentatively, "I'm still not prepared to—"

His lips extinguished her words, brushing softly against her own. "I'm not finished yet," he said sternly. "Don't interrupt."

"Sorry," she whispered happily, certain now.

Another shining glance. "As I was saying," he continued. "When I saw you with David, in his arms, I realized how very much I loved you and was suddenly terrified that I'd lose you. I think I would have killed for a chance to talk to you before going back to Stratford, but there wasn't an opportunity. And in any case, it seemed a good idea to let things simmer for a while."

"Yes," Vicki agreed. There was tension in her voice.

He was smiling wickedly now, fully aware of the strain she was under. "So while I was in Stratford, I did some thinking." He stopped and drew deeply on his cigarette, causing her so much frustration she could have shaken him. "Oh, by the way," he said abruptly in a completely different tone of voice, frustrating her even more, "I forgot to congratulate you on your performance tonight. Very professional. I love the way you sing. It sends the most terrifying shivers up and down my spine."

"I take it that's supposed to be a compliment?" Vicki asked dryly.

He laughed and put his arm around her shoulders, drawing her close. "It certainly is. You were absolutely marvelous, you know. And you looked exactly as Lady Greensleeves should look. Glorious. Golden."

She felt a small chill, remembering that David had used that word to describe her. But she dismissed the thought at once. There was no room for David Brent in her memory just now.

Abruptly Jason threw his cigarette into the river. She saw the arc it described in the air, heard the hiss as it hit the water.

And then he said, "Do you remember the first time I took you out—to The Black Swan? And you told me I looked like Rex Harrison in *My Fair Lady*?"

She nodded, not trusting herself to speak. By the tone of his voice she knew that he was finally getting to the point.

"Well, that's what I thought about in Stratford. You remember toward the end of the movie when Rex sings, 'I've grown accustomed to your face'?"

She nodded again, waiting.

"I realized that *I* had grown accustomed to *your* face. That I wanted to see it every day for the rest of my life."

His other arm was around her suddenly, his bandaged hand under his jacket pressing gently but insistently against her spine, pulling her to him.

Her own hands lifted to touch his face, holding it gently between her palms. "I've grown accustomed to your face, too," she said softly.

He kissed her gently. "Will you marry me, Victoria?" he asked.

For a moment she studied his face, wishing that there was more light so she could be sure there was no doubt showing in his eyes.

"I decided in Stratford that I wanted to marry you," he said as though he'd heard her thoughts. "That was before I knew about Claire and Sig. The guilt I felt about Claire's death didn't seem as important suddenly. And I wasn't afraid of hurting and being hurt. I'd recovered from my blue funk, I suppose. Took me long enough. I knew suddenly that together we could make a success of marriage."

"You told me once that your only priority was your work," she reminded him gently. "You said you couldn't share your life with any woman."

He laughed shortly. "I did, didn't I? What a prig I can be. I suppose I thought that was true...at the time." He paused. "*Will* you marry me?" There was a suddenly worried note in his voice, as though he were afraid after all that she might refuse him. And he was sitting very still, that vital energy held in check for once.

She smiled at him, wanting to tease him by making him wait for an answer, but knowing she couldn't

when the answer was waiting so eagerly on her lips. Life with Jason Meredith would not be easy, she knew, but life without him was unimaginable. "Of course, I'll marry you," she whispered and surrendered herself to his kiss.

A long time later—how long, Vicki was never quite sure—he raised his head and looked at her. The fingers of his right hand traced her lips, the strip of bandage rough against her chin. "I want to take you to my house tonight," he murmured.

She nodded.

"Tomorrow I have to call a board meeting. Terribly stuffy affairs, board meetings, but we need to find a new literary adviser, I'm afraid. I'm not going to want to leave you. But I shall have to."

She took a deep breath. She might as well set the tone of their relationship right now. "You have your work to do," she said firmly. "Just as I have mine. I'll be needed at the hotel. There's still a lot to do."

He smiled, the dazzling smile that had sealed her fate the first time he bestowed it on her. Then he inclined his head, his eyes glinting mischievously. "I suppose when the hotel is finished that you'll be unemployed? We can't have that, can we? May I tell the board, Miss Dennison, that I've found an interior designer for our theater?"

"You certainly may, Mr. Meredith," she said formally, thrilled at the prospect.

And then she stood up with him and looked toward the gray outline of Meredith Manor looming across the moonlit meadow. Her home now. Hers and Jason's. And Portia's. And Mrs. Powell's and Royce's and Trelawney's, and heaven only knew how many others.

Jason sighed. "You realize, of course, that as soon as I mention you to the board, I'm also going to have to tell everyone we're engaged. Which means the news hounds will be upon us, not to mention the fan magazines. We'll be inundated."

Vicki laughed at the resigned note in his voice. "Your female fans are going to hate me," she teased. "Do you suppose they'll ever forgive me?"

He appeared to consider the question for a moment, his face solemn. "Eventually," he said at last. "But in the meantime, they will want to know everything about you, including what you eat for breakfast, how you take care of your hair and your marvelous skin, and where you buy your clothes, what kind of lingerie you wear, and how often you clean your teeth...." He took her in his arms, looking down at her, his smile crooked. "You won't have a lot of privacy at first. Do you think you can endure it?"

"We'll manage to find *some* time alone, won't we?"

"Oh, yes." His voice was determined.

She put up a hand to smooth his hair, which was tumbled as usual, and felt a sense of wonder that she now had the right to make such a proprietary gesture. "I guess I'll survive," she said softly, letting her hand slide down the side of his face.

He smiled, turning his head to kiss her palm, awakening her senses to familiar and welcome disorder. "I do love you, Victoria," he said. His voice was gentle.

But Victoria wasn't listening to him. She had suddenly become distracted by a new sound above the faint strains of music, the murmur of the river, the lapping of water against the bank. Finger to her lips, she looked up at Jason, then beyond to the trees that arched above their heads. Stirred by the breeze, the brittle-edged leaves were rustling, clinging together to form funnels for the wind to blow through. They were humming a melody as old as the trees they had grown from, a melody as ancient as time itself.

"Listen," she whispered. "The trees are singing!"

"Naturally," he said, and there was as much confidence in his voice as though he had personally arranged the whole thing.

Legacy of
PASSION
BY CATHERINE KAY

A love story begun long ago comes full circle...

Venice, 1819: Contessa Allegra di Rienzi, young, innocent, unhappily married. She gave her love to Lord Byron—scandalous, irresistible English poet. Their brief, tempestuous affair left her with a shattered heart, a few poignant mementos—and a daughter he never knew about.

Boston, today: Allegra Brent, modern, independent, restless. She learned the secret of her great-great-great-grandmother and journeyed to Venice to find the di Rienzi heirs. There she met the handsome, cynical, blood-stirring Conte Renaldo di Rienzi, and like her ancestor before her, recklessly, hopelessly lost her heart.